Praise for *The Ordinary Truth*

"[Richman's] to-the-horizon sentences cast a spell, her cactus-prickly characters get under your skin, and her barbed-wire plot makes a mark. With tough women and sensitive men, desert-dry humor, hot-springs sensuality, heartbreaking secrets, escalating suspense, and a 360-degree perspective on the battle over water, Richman's twenty-first-century western is riveting, wise, and compassionate." —*Booklist* (starred review)

"Jana Richman writes us into the lives of three generations of Baxters with the sure hand of a formidable storyteller. With warmth and compassion, she moves each character toward an inevitable, harrowing moment when every one of them must deal with the consequences of their secrets and lies. *The Ordinary Truth* tells a page-turner of a story about love and loy-alty, loss and regret—and, ultimately, the stunning absolution of the simple truth." —*Stephen Trimble*, author of *Bargaining for Eden: The Fight for the Last Open Spaces in America*

"Jana Richman's novel of the contemporary west carries deep currents. Four women affected by water and time and a ranch-ing lifestyle of Nevada bring to life present-day issues of change. Even more, with a unique voice, Richman crystallizes how secrets and silences flow through the generations promis-ing both river teeth of memory and open floodgates of passion. Writer and theologian Frederick Buechner wrote that a great story must seek, treasure, and tell secrets. Jana Richman's *The Ordinary Truth* does all three with depth of characters, beauty of language and a haunting understanding of the landscapes that define us." —*Jane Kirkpatrick*, bestselling author of *Where Lilacs Still Bloom*

ALSO BY JANA RICHMAN

The Last Cowgirl

"Richman's mastery of the emotional geography is illuminating and calls to mind the work of Pat Conroy." –*Kirkus Reviews*

"A warm story of good folks who make bad decisions and then have to live with them." –*Publishers Weekly*

"Readers will be irrevocably drawn into this top-notch fictional debut from an amazing new talent." –*Booklist*

"*The Last Cowgirl* is an engaging and good-humored read that shows how profoundly a person can be shaped by the landscape in which they grow up, whether they want to be or not."
–*New West Magazine*

Riding in the Shadows of Saints: A Woman's Story of Motorcycling the Mormon Trail

"Openhearted and uncommonly balanced."
–*Entertainment Weekly*

"Tartly funny." –*Chicago Tribune*

"Surprising and refreshing." –*Philadelphia Inquirer*

"Much to admire in [this] moving memoir … [Richman] can write lyrically and unsentimentally about the most intimate experiences." –*Newsday* (New York)

THE ORDINARY TRUTH

Jana Richman

Torrey House Press, LLC
Utah

11/18

First Torrey House Press Edition, November 2012
Copyright © 2012 by Jana Richman

This book is a work of fiction. Reference to real people, events, establishments, organizations, or locales are intended only to provide a sense of authenticity and are used fictitiously. All other characters, and all incidents and dialogue, are drawn from the author's imagination and are not to be construed as real.

The poetry that appears on page 46 was written by Steve Defa and used with permission.

Published by Torrey House Press, LLC
P.O. Box 750196
Torrey, Utah 84775 U.S.A.
http://torreyhouse.com

International Standard Book Number: 978-1-937226-06-0
Library of Congress Control Number: 2012938794

Cover and book design by Jeff Fuller
http://shelfish.weebly.com

for Steve

THE ORDINARY TRUTH

KATE

I'll be sitting in my corner office—like I'm doing now—
tinted glass from floor to ceiling, watching the sun drop
behind the boxy horizon of Las Vegas skyscrapers and antici-
pating the neon dawn of evening, when for no good reason an
image of my father will appear. A cloud, a shadow, a reflection,
and there he is relaxed forward in the saddle atop Moots, his
palomino gelding, arms crossed over the horn, looking amused
to find himself surrounded by glass and steel. Moots stands
lazily, his long-lashed lids drooping over soft brown eyes, one
back leg bent so my father tilts slightly to the right. Dad holds
an easy smile and seems as if he has something to tell me. On
a good day, I'll lean back with a cup of tea gone cold, kick my
heels off to prop my feet on the garbage can, and exhort him
to speak. And he does. Soft and soothing, like he's speaking
to a ten-year-old. "How you doing, Katydid?" he says to me. I
smile and tell him I'm doing fine, and for a moment we both
believe it.

Chiseled and carved. That's how I remember my father.
Tall, lean, and muscular. Hair colored by the midday Nevada
sun and styled by a strong Spring Valley wind. Skin like sand-
stone washed repeatedly by rain leaving behind the delicate
traces of its travels. Beautifully nicked-up working hands. A

fine piece of art. I don't share this description with anyone because I hate the indulgent smiles, as if I'm too stupid to know that my mind has done the work of the sculptor over the last thirty-six years.

Three years ago, a hundred and fifty dollar-an-hour therapist told me I was in love with my father, that I had deified him, brushed away his imperfections, and no other man in my life had a chance of measuring up. Jesus. What a waste of a good hundred and fifty bucks. The origins of my phantom heroes have been clear to me since I was old enough to masturbate. Every fantasy man I've conjured up has wind-blown hair, a straight-teeth smile, and starbursts around brown, puppy-dog eyes. A person doesn't need a wall full of degrees and certificates to figure that out.

I still see that therapist, though, for numerous reasons. One, I make more money than my lifestyle can adequately disperse, and I'm a patriotic American—I believe in spending more than I earn, but I can't find the time. Two, when I said, "I sure as hell hope that's not the depth of your insight," he smiled and nodded in a way that made me think it probably wasn't. Three, there weren't any therapists around Omer Springs in 1975 when I really needed one, and four, who the hell knows? It might help.

On days when things don't feel so good, like today and like most days, Dad doesn't speak to me at all. So I ask him, "If you have nothing useful to say, why are you here?" and he gently touches the reins to the left side of Moots' long neck, turning him off to the right, gives me one last knowing smile and a nod, and fades into the sinking sun. My imagination is pathetic. That's the best I can conjure up—a man riding off into the sunset. I feel flat, like the spot on the tinted glass where Dad just faded away.

My life is permanently and unevenly split, like a pine log too green for the ax that found it. October 10, 1975, Dad's alive, the last day of the first part of my life—the short but solid piece that remains upright on the chopping block. October 11, 1975, Dad's dead, the first day of the rest of my life—the fragmented piece that flies through the air and lands awkwardly on the ground. A messy gash. Everything is now measured by the event—*two years before . . . five years after . . .*

My first ten years were like a poorly made molten chocolate cake. I lived in the rich, gooey center in irrepressible bliss and extravagant happiness. I had no reason to go toward the edges, but deep in my gut I knew they were burnt and crispy, and it was me who caused the brittleness. What other conclusion might a young girl reach upon observance of the painfully cheerful faces coming toward the blessed center and the strained, resigned faces moving back toward the edges? With the exception of Dad, that's where the adults in my life—Mom, Aunt Ona, Uncle Nate, Grandpa and Grandma Bax—resided, there on the sad, hard edges. And when Dad was gone . . . hi-ho, the derry-o, the cheese stands alone.

Yes, I mix my metaphors. Chocolate, cheese. What difference does it make? It all melts in the end.

LEONA

Sometimes, when a spring day turns unexpectedly warm and the house feels like an unrinsed plastic milk jug lying in the sun, I set a lawn chair in the fine dirt under the budding cottonwoods on the west side a the working pens and ponder the perplexities a life. From here, I can watch the goings on a Nate, Nell, and Skinny. Today they're preg testing cows. I don't spend much a my time this way, mind you, I have work a my own to get done. But every so often I sit here just to chew on things awhile.

People used to say me and my sister Charlotte was like twins. We was only a year apart in high school, eleven months apart in age. Char and Ona—that's how everybody referred to us. But we ain't twins, and I can tell you that's a good thing. Char's the only one what warned me about marrying into a set a twins. She said, "Ona, you ain't just marrying Nate, you're marrying Nell too. You gotta understand that. It's like trying to separate egg whites from their yolks—it can get real messy." Course Char'd just rotated into her third decade a life when she said that, which gave her some wisdom I'd yet to come by. She shoulda known I wasn't yet possessed a the capacity to hear her. Now, all these years later, I'm clear on what Char was saying, and I maybe shoulda listened to her. Course, I'm not sorry I married Nate. I loved him when I was a freshman in high school and love him just the same only different fifty years later. But that don't make living with him and Nell any easier. Not that we live in the same house as Nell, God forbid, but we do live on the same piece a land.

No one much says "Char and Ona" no more, living as we do on either side of a twelve thousand-foot mountain. Nowadays, I'm more likely to hear "Nell and Ona" as if we was sisters—twins even. Seems marrying Nate somehow inserted me into the middle a all that. Folks round here sometimes call me Nell and vice versa her Ona. That tends to rankle me cause we ain't one iota alike, and I imagine it don't sit well with her neither for the same reason.

I'm just no good with secrets and half-truths—that's what it is. And Nell, God save her, can't seem to operate any other way. Darn near every story that comes outta her mouth has some sorta bend to it that don't belong there. And Nate, bless his heart, backs her up at every turn. Cause if he didn't, who would? That's what he asks me, and that's a darn good question. The answer is nobody. That's what I tell him. And he says, "exactly," which apparently he thinks proves his point.

It mighta been different if Nell hadn't stuck her head out into the world a good two and a half minutes before Nate did. I believe Nell musta turned and claimed her birthright at that very moment, establishing Nate's position in life a covering her backside. And I'll be darned if he ain't continued to do it for more'n seventy years now—as if he don't have no choice in the matter. Nell says jump, and Nate don't even take the time to ask how high—he just starts a hopping like a jackrabbit.

Take today for instance. Nell's sitting on the top pole a the four-pole fence as if on a throne a some sort, clipboard resting on one knee, while Nate and Skinny scurry around below her.

Nell's minions. Folks round here might say I'm exaggerating, but fact is whenever one a them needs something from the Baxter Ranch, they drive up the lane looking for Nell, not Nate, cause there ain't no doubt about who's in charge around here.

Skinny, our hired hand, has got the dirty job today, buried up past his elbow in a cow's rear end, but he doesn't seem to mind. And he's fast. If he has a few boys to keep the cows moving between the Powder River fence panels wired together to form a narrow lane, he can preg test thirty cows an hour. At least he could if Nate and Nell didn't slow him down with their bickering.

"A925 open," Skinny calls out. Nell checks her clipboard.

"Goddammit, Nate, that's that replacement heifer was open six months ago," Nell says. "I knew we shoulda culled her then."

Nate takes his hat off and runs a hand through what hair he has left. "I know it," he says. "She's just so pretty to look at, I can't believe she won't produce."

"She ain't pretty enough to keep feeding."

"I hate to cull a cow like that. Think a the calves she'd have."

"I'm thinking a the calves she ain't having, you old fool. We ain't giving her another chance. Culling pen!" Nell calls out to the young boy working the front end a the squeeze chute.

Nell sits ten feet away with her back to me. Nate climbs up and sits next to her. Their feet are covered with work boots and their heads with navy blue ball caps, the words "Baxter Ranch" and the profile of a steer embroidered in gold on the front. A tuft of gray hair spits out the little hole between the cap and the plastic sizing band from both a their heads, and more hair spills out underneath the band bubbling in sweat on their necks. Nate tucks his matching blue Baxter Ranch

T-shirt into his jeans, cinched with a team-roping belt buckle that tips below his belly. Nell wears her blue T-shirt out over the top a her jeans.

The T-shirts and ball caps were my idea and maybe the only idea a mine that Nell has ever embraced, though she'd never admit it. Every year Baxter Ranch holds an annual bull sale, and about ten years ago I suggested we give away a cap and T-shirt to everyone who purchased a bull. They were such a hit we've done it every year since. Now Nate and Nell don't dress in nothing else. I didn't intend to dress the twins like a mother would do for ten-year-olds—I didn't know it would turn out that way, although I guess I shoulda—but it's fine by me cause it makes my job a doing the laundry an easier one.

"My butt's getting sore sitting here," Nell says, climbing off the fence and handing her clipboard to Nate. "Let's finish up this bunch here and stop for the day. I'm gonna take a walk down to the crick." Jasper, Nell's yellow lab and constant companion, scrambles outta the dirt next to my chair to follow her. "Skinny, I'm leaving you in charge," Nell says. "Not one lame or open cow gets out that gate into that pasture. I don't give a shit how pretty she is."

Skinny nods and grins. He's a quiet man, as many Navajos are.

"Skinny's a man can appreciate a good-looking cow himself," Nate says. "You're in dangerous territory leaving him in charge."

Skinny giggles with his arm buried four inches past his elbow.

We live on the Baxter Ranch in Omer Springs, Nevada, partway up Spring Valley. This here ranch has been in Nate and Nell's family since 1885 when their great grandmother proclaimed she was tuckered out and decided to stay right here, although that's not the full story. It never is with this family. The truth—or as close as I can get to it—is that Sarah Jane Atkinson married Ed Baxter against her family's wishes. Ed wasn't a bad sort, but he was drunk on mineral dreams ever since some fool left his newspaper on the counter of Ruby's Diner in St. Louis where seventeen-year-old Ed bused dishes. Ed folded up the page where the headline screamed "Motherlode Discovered in Pony Canyon, Nevada" and tucked it into his left shirt pocket. By the time he found the wherewithal to head west with Sarah Jane by his side, Pony Canyon was well on its way to being one a the most over-rated and under-producing booms in Nevada history.

It took five hard years and a stillborn child to entice Ed to lay down his pride in a letter to his father-in-law requesting two train tickets back to St. Louis and admittance into the family's mercantile business. Ed and Sarah Jane had traveled many days by wagon in blistering heat before Ed let slip that old man Atkinson had sent word that a job would be waiting upon arrival, but the train tickets would not be forthcoming— they'd gotten themselves into a territory where no refined man would tread, and they could, by God, get themselves back home.

Upon that news, Sarah Jane yanked the reins from Ed's hands and pulled the horses and wagon to a stop. She took a look around and said, "that way" pointing directly north up Spring Valley, stopping by a crick at nightfall, never to move again.

That sounds like something Nell would do, if you ask me. Nell musta inherited that woman's stubbornness. She didn't get it from Flora, her own mother. Flora was just as nice and sweet a lady as ever walked God's earth. Tended to her husband and family; wasn't no mulishness in her. Maybe that sorta thing skips a generation or two. Seems to be a little in Cassie so that would verify my theorizing.

Katie's different though. Some folks might see pighead-edness in her, but they'd be mistaken. What you're seeing there is a girl damaged and confused—that's all. She got that way a lotta years ago cause this family let her down, which leads us back to Nell's willfulness. What goes around comes around, they say. I don't know if that's what was meant by that saying, but it fits nonetheless.

Nell

A deeply rutted lane leads to the crick that flows between the alfalfa fields and the foot a the Snake Mountains. I caused the ruts by bringing the tractor up from the lower field in a rainstorm. I make a mental note to come out and grade the lane, but I'll probably never get it done. I'm low on follow-through these days.

If an old woman pushing up against the far end a life has any sense at all, she won't spend too many a her few remaining days trying to figure out how things ended up the way they did. Apparently I ain't got that kinda sense. Course it don't help that all the folks in Omer Springs are asking me, "What's going on with Katie?" as if that's a question can be answered with some degree a certainty like the current price a hay. When I shrug in response, folks get downright snippety. "She's your daughter, Nell!" they proclaim as if that's something mighta slipped my mind.

I've stopped going to the post office in direct avoidance a that question—the post office being one a only two places in town where a person'd run into another. Ona picks up my catalogs and bills for me these days and hands em to me personally. Course she could just leave em on the kitchen table, but that would deprive her a giving me a disapproving click a her tongue as she hands them over.

I've stopped frequenting Frank's Place also, but I miss his chili. It ain't that good, but I don't like cooking for myself. Staying away from Frank's has also put quite a crimp in my social life—fact, wiped it clean away less you count Nate's hovering and Ona's clucking. I don't. I used to take my evening meal with Nate and Ona, but the tension that runs through a place gets pulled tight enough to choke a person in the company a others. I'd just as soon spend my evenings alone.

I miss Cassie, miss her like crazy. If she was here to sit under the cottonwoods and play a game a gin rummy with me, sharing the irregular meanderings a her mind while I beat her at cards, I wouldn't be feeling so old and lonely. If Cassie ever focused solely on her cards, she'd beat me every time. That girl's mind can count up numbers and work em out in all sorts a combinations, but every time she starts out saying, "Grandma Nell, did you know . . ." she tends to set her cards down on the picnic table face up while she wanders into some alcove a useless trivia. Can't help but look and see what she's holding in her hand. Take some sorta saint to turn away and I ain't no saint. I don't consider that cheating. Cheatin'd be looking at the reflection a her cards in the pickup truck window behind her. I do that too. So like I say, I usually beat her, but she don't seem to mind all that much. Believe that girl got shorted the gene that calls for competition.

But Cassie ain't here, and I'm not sure why. Don't feel right. Nothing feels right around here no more. Used to be I could make everything okay just by walking down to this spot on the crick and hanging my old, tired feet off the bank. Now the crick's so damn low—even after a good winter—my feet hang four inches above the water. Cassie's excuse for not being here this summer is some job she couldn't pass up in Las Vegas. I'm not buying that. I know when I'm being lied to.

CASSIE

There's something about a Nevada whorehouse can make a girl weepy around the edges. Near the third pass of Waylon Jennings' *Honky Tonk Heroes*, I can barely talk myself into sticking with the plan. I do have a plan—a long-range plan. My short-term plan is to get old Maggie—she owns the place—to play something other than Waylon or Merle before I rip my own ears off. Mick, the bartender, has assisted me in slipping some White Stripes into the rotation, and sometimes if Maggie's real busy with other stuff—such as bawling out the kitchen staff, most of whom smile and nod and politely say *no problema, mi mamacita llenita* while Maggie smiles and nods back and lets them go on believing she doesn't know what that means—we can get away with that for a while. But usually as soon as the first few notes of *Blue Orchid* seep blessedly through the speakers, Maggie bellows at Mick that unless he has some job offers from NASA lined up he best *get that shit off there*. Mick winks at me, indicating we'll try again later. On a slow day, I split my time between refining my long-range plan and fantasizing that Jack White steps out of a limo, spots me on the last barstool where I spend the majority of my time, and falls in love—at that point, screw the plan.

To be honest, and I almost always am, my long-range plan is short on details. It basically consists of sitting on a barstool in a Carson City brothel until Mama and Grandma Nell start speaking to each other. How long that might take is anyone's guess. But this idea that they can use me as a conduit to communicate—if you want to call it that—instead of speaking directly is beginning to piss me off. In fact, both of them as good as drove me here themselves. And if I've inherited anything from them at all, it's their obstinacy. I don't know what happens when three stubborn women each take up ground waiting for the others to move, but I aim to find out.

Everybody pretends this is all about water rights and Mama's job with the Nevada Water Authority, but I know damn well there's more to it. Not that water isn't enough to tear families apart in this state. I've seen grown men beat each other bloody over a diverted irrigation ditch. But I've been watching Mama and Grandma Nell all my life, and over the span of those twenty-one years, their conversations have been steadily dwindling like a spring creek at the end of a long, hot summer. It seems the two of them have simply exhausted themselves, run underground. So I have to ask myself: what is it between them that takes so much effort? I don't know the answer to that yet, but I intend to find out. Hence, my radical—and possibly impulsive—plan. I know of only one thing that will undoubtedly force them to the surface. Me. More specifically, my safekeeping. What better threat to an innocent girl's welfare, I figure, than a Carson City whorehouse?

If, per chance, Mama and Grandma Nell don't cooperate with my plan, this could be a long summer. Jack White can fill only so many hours of a girl's mind before he becomes tedious enough I could be sick of him before he gets here. The next best thing to Jack White is Big Joe. Well, that's not actually true.

There are a significantly large number of measures between Jack White and Big Joe, but Joe's the only one likely to walk through the door of the Wild Filly Stables. That's why whenever I hear the clanking ladders on top of his roofing truck as it drops off the pavement into the gravel parking lot, I sit up and straighten my spine. Big Joe has a deep laugh and a warm touch and he's not stingy with either one. Joe's not exactly a regular here—more like an irregular—so it's tough to predict when he might show up. But when he does, sometimes he just wants to sit at the bar and talk. Simple as that. And that's my specialty. He doesn't even have to pay for my time, just buy me a Coke. And he doesn't even have to do that because Mick gives me those for free.

Normally when a customer spends all his time at the bar it's because he's a first-timer and hasn't yet worked up the courage to step beyond that point. That's where I come in. I can't help smiling at anyone who walks through the door—it's just my nature—and Maggie says I have the look of a girl who couldn't scare a fly off a horse's ass.

Maggie has fixed me up some. She took inventory of me the day she decided to let me stay. I was wearing what I thought to be "hip" jeans—realizing once I left the ranch that Wranglers caused people to draw conclusions that were accurate but annoying—and a trendy pink T-shirt with the word "pink" written on the front in rhinestones.

"What size are those jeans?" Maggie had asked.

"Eight," I said.

She nodded. The next day she gave me three pairs of size six low-ride, skinny-leg jeans that cut off my ability to breathe if I don't sit directly upright.

"That's good," Maggie said when I complained. "You slouch too much anyway. You have nice little breasts—you should lead with those stead a acting like you wanna tuck them away somewhere."

To force the issue, she gave me a dozen low-cut tank tops and three lacy bras that squeeze and push what little I have up and out the top of the tanks. Then she painted my toenails orange and put sandals on my feet with heels so high I have to kick them off just to walk behind the bar. She also let loose my hair so it hangs down my back to my waist, whereas I'm used to a single braid, and she cut me some shaggy bangs. She planned to "update" my hair from ordinary brown, but when she placed the L'Oréal box of "red hot cinnamon" hair color in front of me, my stuttering must have persuaded her otherwise. Instead, she detracts from the drabness of my hair color by arriving at the bar each morning with a makeup kit that looks like it came out of the clown's dressing room at a circus and sets to work on my face. *Not too much, though,* she says, *don't want you looking like a common whore,* which cracks her up every time, causing her ample breasts to heave forth and tap my right arm.

Sometimes I catch a glimpse of myself in the mirror behind the bar and then imagine Grandma Nell, Uncle Nate, and Aunt Ona seeing me like this. I don't know whether to laugh or cry. Mick says I don't look any different than any other UNLV co-ed, and I guess that's true. But I look different than Cassie from Omer Springs. I can hear Grandma Nell's voice saying, "You ain't gonna get much work done in a getup like that."

It's my job to make a guy feel like stopping off at the whorehouse to purchase an orgasm is no different than stopping at the 7-Eleven to purchase a six-pack of beer. Maggie has figured the optimal amount of time a guy should spend talking to me is seven minutes. Any more than that, she says, and he begins to feel like he's sitting at a soda fountain with his kid sister. If that happens, he'll get teary-eyed and leave with his money in his pocket.

With Big Joe it's different though. As I said, sometimes he never gets any further than the bar just because talking is all he feels like doing. If anybody else tried that, Maggie would grumble about it for two days straight, blaming both me and Mick for pushing her to the poorhouse. But she's sweet on Big Joe. Everybody here is sweet on Big Joe. Even Mick seems to enjoy his company. I have attempted to monopolize Joe's time when he's here, but he says, "Cassie, it just don't work that way with me so don't build no ideas around that."

That's my real name—Cassie Lee Jorgensen. Actually it's Cassie Lee Caswell, but I feel more like a Jorgensen because I was raised mostly by my Grandma Nell, who was a Baxter until she married Henry Jorgensen. Besides, Cassie Caswell is a little too catchy. I tried using Lola—lots of girls here use a stage name—but even with my new push-up bras, I cannot pull off a name like Lola. Before I could think of something more appropriate, Cassie got circulated and, in fact, put on the Wild Filly Stables website. In addition to being the reassuring decoy, I am currently the resident webmaster for the Wild Filly Stables, so I'd be hard-pressed to deny putting it there myself. Most girls here would rather their families not know where they are, but I don't share that concern. It's not that my family won't be upset to find out I'm working at a Carson City brothel—that is the plan after all—but they sure as hell shouldn't be surprised. Mama says I've been feral as a barn cat since the day I was born.

There might be some truth to that. I do get what I have identified as surges of discontent from time to time. I blame those surges for getting me kicked out of two kindergarten classes when I was six years old—once for pummeling a boy who broke my pencil and once for mouthing off to the teacher, although I wasn't really mouthing off. I was simply trying to explain to her that I hadn't taken a nap since I came kicking and screaming (so they tell me) from my mother's womb, and I had no intention of doing so now, particularly not on a hard tile floor with nothing but a towel for cushion. I have heard that kindergarten napping has since been done away with, and I like to believe that I, and feral children everywhere, played a pivotal role in that decision.

My eviction from two schools before the age of seven basically got me kicked out of the city of Las Vegas where Mama and Father (I wasn't allowed to call him "Dad"; these days I just call him "Dipshit") lived and landed me in Omer Springs with Grandma Nell where it was thought my wildness could be tamed through hard work and open space. Didn't work quite that way but I can't blame Mama or Dipshit for that. They had no way of knowing all that open space tends to nurture the wild, not tame it. Well, Mama maybe should have known that, but she seems to have assimilated into her city surroundings quicker than snowmelt into a south-facing slope.

That's why she hates it that I call her "Mama." I didn't start out that way, but after so many years of hearing Grandma Nell refer to "your mama," I picked up the language and can't seem to set it back down. In fact, I've been told I picked up a whole bunch of things from Grandma Nell, not the least of which is her manner of speaking. Whenever I answer the phone at the ranch one of Omer's old men will say, "Nell, that goddamn bull a yers has broken through that fence again and is in with my heifers" before I can make him understand I'm not Nell. "Well, my hell," they all say, "you sound just like your grandmother." How can that be true when there's an entire generation between us? But even I sometimes hear Grandma

Nell's voice and words coming straight out of my own mouth, and I don't like it one bit, which sounds exactly like something Grandma Nell would say.

Grandma Nell and I even share the same birthday—May twenty-fourth—and there's something spooky weird about that, like all people who share that birthday also share pieces of one another. But Bob Dylan was born on May twenty-fourth also, and I have no song-writing abilities that I'm aware of and Grandma Nell is nothing like Bob Dylan, except they might be about the same age. She would tell me the Dylan thing is just one of those irrelevant paths my brain insists upon strolling down until it reaches a dead end, which it seldom does. Still, it seems a piece of Grandma Nell got implanted directly inside me and it takes up an awfully big space. Nevertheless, I have made a conscious effort to stop using Grandma Nell's chosen words, but the use of "mama" annoys my mother enough that I hate to give it up.

Mama—known as Katie to her family, Katherine to her boss, and Kate to her boyfriend—is the deputy water resource manager at the Nevada Water Authority. She doesn't talk much about it—in fact she refuses to speak to me about it at all—but from what I've witnessed it's her job to gather up all the water in the state—of which there is precious little—and sell it to the highest bidders. The high bidders invariably reside in Las Vegas, and the low bidders reside in places no one has ever heard of—places like Omer Springs, which is in the Great Basin. Of course, that doesn't really give a person much to go on since most of the entire state of Nevada is in the Great Basin.

Before I found my way to the Wild Filly Stables for the summer, I was a freshman in UNLV's department of environmental studies. The area of study was Grandma Nell's idea and a strange one at that. She said the burden was on me to balance out the evil perpetrated against this earth by my mother. Grandma Nell can be a bit melodramatic at times, and her rhetoric had reached a crescendo ever since the evening toward the end of my senior year in high school when we caught Mama's appearance on the ten o'clock news. Grandma and I always watched the news before retiring for the night—one of those things that made me feel as if I were living the life of an old woman—when suddenly Mama's face loomed in front of us in full living color. At first we were so surprised and excited by it, we almost missed what she was saying.

"By God, that's Katie!" Grandma yelled, spilling her evening coffee and startling Jasper, who jumped off the rug with a yelp. "Don't she look smart in those suits?" I started to respond, but Grandma shushed me saying, "Listen, listen!"

It probably would have been a good thing had we missed hearing the words that came with the appearance because Mama was announcing the Nevada Water Authority's new project to accommodate the exciting and unprecedented growth of the city of Las Vegas over the last few decades—a trend city leaders hoped would continue unabated. Mama went on to explain that the two billion dollar project, which was only in the planning stages, entailed sinking 285 miles of pipeline into the desert to suck water from the spring and aquifer that runs right under our ranch and, in fact, every aquifer under every ranch in the neighboring Nevada and Utah basins, and deliver it to the thirsty citizens of Las Vegas. That's not exactly the way Mama said it, but that's the way Grandma Nell heard it, as did everyone else outside of Las Vegas.

Up until that TV appearance of Mama's, the evil perpetrators in Grandma Nell's life were, in fact, the graduates from environmental studies programs. Who would have guessed

Mama had the power to align ranchers and environmentalists on the same side of the barbed wire in one fell swoop? At the same time, Mama managed—and she must have known this—to abruptly tweak her relationship with her own mother. Up until that point, Grandma Nell and Mama coexisted as if they were living in a perpetual elevator, where the proximity won't let you entirely ignore those there with you, but the doors will open soon enough that there's no reason to engage at a meaningful level. After Mama's appearance on the news, Grandma Nell stepped out of the elevator for good, letting the doors close on Mama.

Ever been out working on a bright winter day without taking much notice of your own dependence on the sun's heat? The smallest cloud can drift in front of the sun—not taking more than ten seconds to pass—and chill you to the bone. That's what happened the night Mama appeared on TV. A bone-cold chill entered the room and hung there. I sat stock-still waiting for Grandma Nell's heretofore impenetrable exterior to reestablish itself around her body.

"Cassie," Grandma finally said, "there's only two things really matter in this world." And then she paused for a good long time before continuing. "The place you belong and the family you belong to."

I had heard this before. I guess you could call it Grandma Nell's philosophy of life. Grandma usually finished up this way: *Your mama's a little confused about both a those things, but she'll come around.* So I waited for her to continue in that vein, but she never did. She snapped the faded gold La-Z-Boy closed with her lower legs and pulled herself up out of it. We had never before gone to bed without watching the weather forecast.

"A person ought never to have to choose between those two things," she said.

Then Grandma Nell shut off the light, puttered out of the room with Jasper at her heels, and left me tipped back in my blue La-Z-Boy in the dark. I have since determined that seeing vulnerability in the one adult you depend upon can permanently damage a kid.

⸻

Omer Springs is in Spring Valley, not too far east of Ely, although, to get from one place to the other a person would have to go over or around the twelve thousand-foot-tall obstacle known as the Schell Creek Mountains. Because of this, I spent the better part of my teen years—when I should have been hanging out on street corners sucking in nicotine—on a bus seat bouncing between Omer Springs and Ely, where I attended high school. Omer Springs isn't much of a town—not on any map I've ever seen—still, if you added up all the people who have called Omer Springs home over the years, you might break one thousand. Or you might not. I've never tried adding everybody up, although I might some day. I do like numbers. At any given time, there's between fifty and a hundred people in Omer Springs depending on who's visiting and where a person chooses to draw the boundary lines. Basically it's just a cluster of cattle and sheep ranches, and they're not even all that clustered—more scattered throughout the basin.

Somewhere near the center of the scatter sits a small, white, freshly painted building. A new coat of paint is applied every five years, which serves a dual purpose of making the only public building in Omer Springs presentable and keeping it glued together. The building houses both the post office and one of the last remaining one-room schoolhouses in Nevada. Across the street and around the corner from the school sits Frank's Place. Beer and beans—that's all he sells. And that's pretty much the extent of downtown Omer Springs.

I always found it a little weird that Mama and I both had the same elementary school teacher—Marietta Foster—but I'm over it now. Mrs. Foster—even though she's as old as Grandma and not nearly as sharp—still serves as both postmaster and teacher of Omer Springs, the reason being that Marietta's house is part of the same building. Marietta's daughter, Georgia, who deals cards at the Hotel Nevada in Ely, delivers groceries to her mother every other week, and folks figure Marietta hasn't been more than three miles in any direction from the schoolhouse since she attended Georgia's wedding in Ely thirty years ago. The building itself is owned by the White Pine School District, but Marietta has lived in it longer than most in town can remember and has taken up ownership. So moving Marietta out of her jobs means moving her out of her house, and that's not something the folks of Omer Springs would ever do. Doesn't much matter anyway. There are no kids left to teach in Omer Springs except Hank Mortensen's grandkids, and they get home-schooled. And although the post office has official post office boxes, most people pick up their mail before Marietta ever gets it into the box.

I attended school there from first through eighth grade, technically speaking. Since all grade levels were taught together and because I got futzed around in Vegas for a year or so, I was never quite sure what grade I was in—and no one seemed to care—but I do know I was there for at least eight years, maybe more. That factor became painfully clear when I got to high school and found myself older than everyone else in my class. I questioned Grandma Nell about that and got the usual response: a shrug and a suggestion that I take a fishing lesson—learn how to catch and release instead of reeling in and hanging onto the small matters of life. Grandma Nell likes to repeat that often—I guess you could say that's another of her philosophies of life. But I think one must first determine the size of the fish before one can decide whether to release it. My gut feeling is that Grandma Nell may have released a few things over the years she should have reeled in or vice versa.

The "springs" part of Omer Springs comes from the fact that in various places in the valley, spread out in a nice sort of equitable way, underground springs bubble up above the ground. In one place in particular, a few miles southeast of the post office, the spring comes up enough to form a decent swimming hole and a migratory birdbath. Officially it sits on the north end of the O'Riley ranch, but after Mavis O'Riley put a picnic table under an old cottonwood there, the town named it Omer City Park and ran an electric line to make it official. I don't know if the humor was intentional, but it cracks me up any time the words "Omer" and "city" get used in close proximity. The park is used for the annual Fourth of July potluck and an occasional milestone birthday celebration. The park's claim to fame, however, in a whispered but almost proud sort of way, is the swimming hole's capability to pull unwary folks down to its reedy bottom and hold them there until their lungs fill with water and their eyes pop wide. That's what happened to Grandma Nell's brother, Leroy. That might be one of the most excitedly recited stories in Omer Springs, running neck and neck with the hunting accident death of my grandfather, Henry Jorgensen.

No one really knows where the "Omer" part of Omer Springs came from, but a few theories have been floated. Some attribute the name to an old miner, others to the Goshute Indians, and some to the Mormons—we're not that far from the Utah state border. Grandma Nell buys into the old miner theory but says it won't much matter if Katherine Ann—that's what Grandma calls my mother when she's feeling a little

23

bristly—gets her way. There won't be an Omer Springs left to worry about. Grandma Nell thinks that would make Mama happy, but I'm not so sure. Though I don't know what would make Mama happy—I don't believe I've ever seen her in such a state—so could be Grandma Nell's right.

What Grandma Nell's right about and what she isn't, I haven't yet determined. I do know that old people latch onto certain "bits of wisdom" as they call them and repeat them over and over. I know this for two reasons: one, because a good number of politicians running for office in this state get on TV and say, "My daddy used to always say . . ." followed by a "bit of wisdom," and two, because Grandma Nell and Uncle Nate—who is actually Mama's uncle, not mine—have a few of their own. Grandma Nell's favorite, of course, is the one about the place you belong and the family you belong to being the only things that matter in the world. I suspect Grandma Nell got that one right.

Our ranch, known as the Baxter Ranch, sits several miles down the valley from the post office at the convergence of Cleve Creek, Indian Creek, and Stevens Creek—pronounced "crick" if you want to sound like you're from Omer Springs. I don't necessarily. That means at the compound, where three houses sit at angles meant to balance privacy and proximity, we're shaded all summer by big, old cottonwoods. That also means it's the prettiest ranch in Spring Valley, and I would say that even if I weren't a part of it.

The cottonwoods gnarly roots bump up under dirt sparsely dotted by tufts of grass, and an old swing hangs on long, thick ropes from a high branch suggesting nothing but happiness and contentment could ever reside on the Baxter Ranch. Sitting in that swing looking east, a person's eyes would wander pleasantly over working pens and green squares of irrigated farmland until they rest upon the willows lining the creek that runs along the base of the Snake Range. If you were to turn around in the swing and look west, your eyes would jump the gravel road that runs straight up the valley to a flatland of greasewood, sagebrush, winterfat, and shadscale until the climb into the Schell Creeks gives over to juniper and pinyon. Looking south, your eyes land on a large metal garage and workshop that Uncle Nate put up to house the tractor and other equipment about the time I arrived at the ranch. Just beyond that, Skinny's place—a small shed turned into a cabin—is partially blocked from view, which he no doubt appreciates. North of the yard is a big, old, falling-down barn with deep summer shadows and the musty smell of bygone crops of hay wafting from the loft.

If I let a picture of the ranch settle in my mind it seeps down through my body and puffs out in four directions from my bellybutton, roiling like trapped water. Before long the picture starts to fill itself out. You got Uncle Nate standing with one leg propped on the lowest fence pole, slapping hay leaves out of his gloves, talking to Grandma Nell as she saddles her mare, Queenie. You got Jasper chasing Ol' Yeller, one of about eight barn cats, under the pallets holding stacks of firewood. Cottonwood leaves rustle and shimmer in the breeze and irrigation sprinklers chug in the distance. Birdsong is so constant, one has to focus to hear it. Aunt Ona pulls weeds in the vegetable garden, fenced to keep out skunks, deer, and Jasper, and in another minute Skinny will show up and sit silently on his horse until someone acknowledges his presence. That would have been me, which makes my absence from the picture all the more noticeable. And when that happens, I have to grip my barstool with both hands to keep myself from walking out the door and driving 375 miles to complete the picture.

The town of Omer Springs—and every person in it—changed the night Mama appeared on television. The bitterness that crept through the house that night spread swiftly over the ranch before saturating the entire town. Less than a minute after Grandma Nell left me sitting in the dark, Uncle Nate and Aunt Ona stomped in through the back door.

"Nell?" Uncle Nate called. "Nell!"

"I'm right here, Nate," a bodiless voice said in the darkness. Grandma Nell had only made it from the living room to the dining room before sitting down again.

"Did you see—"

"I saw it."

I pulled myself up from the La-Z-Boy and flipped on the dining room light.

"Turn that thing off," Grandma Nell instructed, without pulling her head up out of her hands. I did as told and instead turned on a dim corner lamp. Uncle Nate dropped into a chair next to Grandma Nell, and Aunt Ona, her hair in rollers and her housecoat buttoned to the top, took up the chair next to him. I followed suit, sitting in the only empty chair remaining in the half-darkness.

I would never have described our small family as joyful before that moment. Those three always had a making-the-best-of-things way about them. But in the next sixty seconds I saw—to use one of Grandma Nell's words—their gumption die, and I understood immediately that this thing my mother had unleashed was something no one could make the best of.

"What do you make of it?" Uncle Nate asked.

"How should I know?" Grandma Nell answered.

"Could be they're just blustering," he said.

"Who's they?" I asked.

"That outfit your mama works for," Uncle Nate said. "Could be this is a tactic they're throwing out to get more water from the Colorado River—alarm everybody then agree to back off in exchange for taking more from the river."

"Could be," Grandma Nell said, "and could be they're serious about this."

"I don't see how they could be," Uncle Nate said. "They'd put every rancher north a Vegas outta business."

"And you think they care about that?" Grandma Nell said.

"Hell, this is our land, Nell! They can't take our water out from under us!"

"I'm sure there's some law against it," Aunt Ona said.

"You think those fancy Las Vegas lawyers ain't already looked into the legality before they announced such a thing, Ona?" Grandma Nell said. "I think we can be damn sure they've done their homework on this."

The phone rang. I rose to answer it.

"Leave it," Grandma Nell said. I sat back down. "Apparently we ain't the only ones watched the news tonight."

"Well, we oughta see what people think about this," Aunt Ona said.

"As if that's some sorta mystery, Ona," Grandma Nell answered. "I'm going to bed."

"Nell, let's call Katie and talk to her about this," Uncle Nate said.

Grandma Nell looked at Uncle Nate as if having trouble interpreting the meaning of his words. Then she turned and shuffled out of the room with Jasper on her heels as the phone started ringing again. I had never before seen my grandmother shuffle.

Five pickup trucks pulled into the yard the next morning before Grandma Nell and I had finished breakfast. I answered the knock on the door. It was Red O'Riley.

"Where's your grandmother, Cass?"

"She's eating breakfast."

"I'm right here, Red. Come on in."

"Wonder if you might come on out here, Nell. A few of us would like to have a word with you."

I looked out the door to see a small group gathering around the picnic tables under the cottonwoods. Uncle Nate and Aunt Ona had just emerged from their house and were walking toward the group.

"Let me get my boots on," Grandma Nell said. Red O'Riley nodded and walked away.

"Grandma?"

"How'd ya sleep last night, Cass?"

"I didn't."

"Me neither."

The group became silent as Grandma and I walked toward them.

"How y'all doing?" Grandma Nell asked.

"Not very good, Nell," Hank Mortensen replied. "I suppose you saw the news last night?"

Grandma Nell nodded.

"What we gonna do, Nell?"

"Damned if I know, Morty."

"Have you talked to Katie?"

Grandma Nell shook her head.

"You gotta talk to Katie, Nell," Fitz Walters said.

Grandma Nell didn't respond.

"Nell, what they're proposing is illogical," Red said. "They can't pump water outta this valley without ending agriculture here. We've been in a drought for thirty years. We barely have enough water to keep going ourselves."

"I agree with you, Red," Grandma Nell said.

"My family's been in this valley pert near long as yours, Nell," Morty said. "I was born and raised here just like my parents and just like my kids and my grandkids. And I plan on dying here. We gotta fight this thing."

"I ain't arguing with you, Morty," Grandma Nell said.

"You gotta talk to Katie, Nell," Fitz said again.

"But I ain't calling Katie," Grandma Nell said.

"You gotta, Nell!"

"I'll stand with you boys and fight this thing till my dying breath," Grandma Nell said. "But I ain't calling Katie." Aunt Ona stepped forward.

"Nell, I think—"

"Did Washington chat with Cornwallis before the battle of Yorktown?" Grandma Nell asked.

"Oh for heaven's sake, Nell. She's your daughter!" Mavis O'Riley said.

"I ain't forgot that, Mavis."

"Nell," Red said, "if we're gonna fight this thing, we need information. We gotta figure out what they're thinking, how fast they're moving, and what sorta studies they've already lined up. I don't want to sound the alarm before it needs to be sounded, but every one a us knows what kind a devastation we'd be facing if that harebrained plan goes through and that pipeline gets laid. Last night Katie said they planned to take fifty thousand acre-feet a water per year outta this valley. We'll be living in a dust bowl if they do that and you know it. Good God, Katie should know it! She grew up here. Where the hell you gonna put your heifers when they come off the mountain,

Nell, if that spring in your meadow dries up?"

"I'm aware a what's at stake here, Red. But it ain't gonna do no good to call Katie about this."

"That city pulls in billions a year," Morty said. "Money equals power, and we ain't got a damn thing to compete with that."

"That ain't true, Morty," Uncle Nate said. "The Baxter Ranch alone produced over a million pounds a beef last year and two thousand tons a hay. A good portion a that went to feed the people a Las Vegas and the cows that provide milk to the people a Las Vegas. And that was just this ranch alone. You add in all your ranches and that's not nothing."

"Well, that's the kinda information we're gonna have to get out to people to make our case," Red said. "I say we get organized. I'm gonna make some phone calls and suggest you all do the same. Let's get a meeting set up with ranchers from the other valleys hit by this news."

"Nell, Nate," Morty said, "if you can talk to Katie and get us some information on this it sure would help." Uncle Nate nodded and looked at Grandma Nell, who stared at the Snake Mountains as if she were standing there all alone.

When the pickups had driven back down the lane and the dust had settled, Uncle Nate reached out for Grandma Nell's elbow.

"Nell, let's go in the house and call Katie."

"Nate, the time for talking to that girl has come and gone. I ain't calling her and neither are you. That's final."

"But, Nell—"

"Final." She turned to me. "Cass, I always hoped me and your mama would find a way to circle back around to each other and figure things out. I'm clear now that ain't gonna happen. But I don't mean to ever tell you what sorta relationship you can or can't have with your mother. That's between the two a you. The plan's always been that you'll go back to Vegas when you finish high school so you can go to college. You'll be leaving in a few months. That ain't changed."

"But Grandma, what's—"

"That ain't changed. Now we got work to do."

The three of us watched until Grandma Nell disappeared into the darkness of the equipment garage.

From that morning forward until I left for college at the end of summer, I remember the ranch in extremes—sunny days were oppressively hot and if a breeze blew at all, it blew like a blast furnace; flies, always plentiful around the corrals, were bitingly aggressive in sheer numbers; stinging ants infiltrated the house to be found in the pantry, the sheets, the La-Z-Boy recliners. My trips to the post office that used to take up to a half hour by the time I got stopped by our BLM herder to "tell Nell she's got a lame cow I just put into the south allotment" and by Bea Walters to "give this gardening catalog to your Aunt Ona" took less than thirty seconds as folks I'd been talking to since I was six barely nodded in my direction. They'd be gathered in groups of two or three talking in the most animated way when my appearance would silence them. They were never rude, just seemed suddenly uncomfortable with me, as if I had shown up in town a complete stranger. When I heard the words, "Katie's daughter" slip into the air surrounding them, I momentarily pondered who they might be referring to. In the company of Omer Springs folks, I held a perception of myself only as Nell's granddaughter.

The more everyone pushed Grandma Nell to seek information from the primary source—my mother—the deeper Grandma Nell dug in against it. The annual July Fourth picnic, which took place a month or so after Mama's TV appearance, was more rabble than celebration and got worse after Grandma Nell stood on a picnic table and planted her feet between a bowl of potato salad and a crock of baked beans to warn that if one more person hinted at the possibility that this mess could be resolved by a simple phone call from her to Katherine Ann there'd be hell to pay.

I decided not to leave for college. One, because it meant going to live with the enemy, and two, because it made my heart hurt to leave the ranch in that condition. If I couldn't leave with that place intact, if I couldn't leave with the image of that old swing hanging sweetly from the cottonwood, then I couldn't leave. At dinner one night I announced my plans to stay.

"The hell you will," Grandma Nell said. "You're leaving next week as planned."

"Grandma, I'm staying. I can't go like this."

"Ain't no use your staying here. Nothing you can do."

"Nell's right," Uncle Nate said. "We're gonna be fine here, Cassie. You have a whole life ahead a you. You need to stick with the plan to go to college."

"But—"

"But nothing," Grandma Nell said. "This ain't negotiable. As of August eighteenth, your lease here ends. I got plans for that room you're using."

"Cassie, you'll always have a home here," Aunt Ona said, reaching out for my arm.

"Ona, stay outta this," Grandma Nell said. "She has a home until August eighteenth is what she has."

Aunt Ona blushed red and pursed her lips. Uncle Nate looked at his plate.

I knew she was half bluffing and half serious. If I left, my room would stay intact. But if I stayed, she'd have the bed and my belongings cleaned out before noon on departure day.

"Sides, your mother's expecting you," Grandma Nell said.

"How do you know that if you haven't spoken to her?" I asked.

"I left her a message," she said. And indeed she had. Several months after I got to Las Vegas, I was cleaning the old messages off Mama's home phone voice mail and ran across my grandmother's. *Katherine Ann, Cassie will be delivered to your address before 4 p.m. on Saturday, August eighteenth.* End of message. And that's exactly what happened. Skinny drove me and a few boxes to Las Vegas and delivered me to my mother's doorstep like a UPS package.

By the time I left, Grandma Nell had stopped talking to almost everyone in town and had started calling Uncle Nate the "Baxter Ranch spokesman." I had never thought of my mother as a powerful woman, but in that single television appearance she managed to suck every bit of humor and life from this valley as if to symbolize the sucking power of the future pipeline.

KATE

"Talked to Nell recently?" Derek asks. He's lying naked, flat on his back ("in *savasana*," he tells me, "which will return blood circulation to normal") on top of two down comforters spread across the hardwood floor of our living room. I'm doing the same per his instructions. I never follow his instructions unless they suit me. He knows this and it makes him smile. Almost every damn thing makes Derek smile.

"If you plan to make love to me again—and I assume you do—best not bring up my mother," I say, pulling an edge of a comforter over myself—just enough to cover one leg, one hip, and one breast.

"Are you cold?"

"Yes," I lie. Derek thinks we should all be comfortable with our bodies *because they serve us well.* Personally, I'm comfortable with my discomfort. I'd like to cover his naked body also. I don't believe men are supposed to look like Derek— white and smooth. No scuff marks. He reminds me of the white patent leather Easter shoes Aunt Ona once bought me. No one could figure out why she bought them—we never went to church—but she insisted every girl should have some. Every once in a while, even long after I had grown out of them, I retrieved them from their tissue nest inside their cardboard bed to stroke their shiny surface. My fingers reach to stroke Derek's jutting hipbone.

"You're saying we cannot make love again if we talk about your mother now?" Derek asks.

"You got it."

"Try letting go of the compartments in your life, Kate."

"Not a chance."

"You might find they're not necessary."

"I'm sure they are."

"You might find that you can love both me and your mother at the same time."

"You're creeping me out."

"How long has it been since you talked to Nell?"

"Choose right now. Sex or my mother. It's up to you."

"How long has it been?"

"Since we fucked?"

"Since you talked to your mother."

"Okay, my mother it is. Not the choice I would have made given those options." I turn toward him and prop myself on one elbow. "I have no idea."

"You can't remember the last time you talked to your mother?"

"No, I can't. I suppose it was before the pipeline announcement."

"Kate, that was almost a year ago."

"Actually a little more than a year. You make it sound like we have no communication at all, but we do. I know exactly what's going on with her. She talks to Cassie; Cassie talks to me. I talk to Cassie; Cassie talks to her. It's a beautiful system. You're a systems designer, Derek. You should know the rule. Don't mess with something that's working smoothly."

"Why don't you and your mother talk to each other directly?"

"Why? Why does everyone think that mothers and daughters are supposed to have lovely, close relationships?"

"Don't you want that with Cassie?"

"I have that with Cassie." As expected, that makes him pause, but he quickly determines I have purposely baited him to shift the conversation.

"Don't you want it with your own mother?"

"We have what we have. Aren't you the one preaching that we need to make peace with what is?"

"That's why I bring it up, Kate. You haven't made peace with it."

I flop on my back and pull as much of the comforter over me as possible. He props himself on an elbow and moves closer, pressing the front of his body along the left side of mine. I fight the urge to edge away and he knows it. His straight, waist-length gray hair—usually pulled back but now loose—falls to one side of my head like a curtain. With slender fingertips, he gently traces the scar that runs from the corner of my mouth to the jawbone below my earlobe.

"Let's go out there, Kate. Let's go for a drive."

"Are you nuts?" I say, turning my face away from him so he can't reach the scar.

"You don't even have to acknowledge you're going to see your mother—even to yourself," he says dropping back into *savasana*. "You can pretend you're going only to see Cassie."

"Again, are you nuts? Don't you know I'm the most wanted woman in Omer Springs? Don't you know we'll never make it out alive?"

"Come on, let's take a few days and go out there. Those are your people, Kate. They won't turn their back on you just because you're doing your job."

"Derek, you're a city boy. A very sweet and very naive city boy. Let me fill you in. You can mess with the rancher's daughter and get away with it. You might even be able to mess with the rancher's wife and still come out okay. But you mess with the rancher's water, you can't expect to just waltz into town one day, unarmed and unprotected. That you're damn sure not going to get away with."

"Then why are you doing it?"

"Like you said, I'm just doing my job."

"And that's all there is to it?"

"Yes, sweet Derek. Sometimes things are absolutely as simple as they seem—no deep dark recesses to explore, nothing lurking in the corners."

"That's seldom true, you know."

"But utterly possible."

"But unlikely."

"Okay, I'm done here," I say throwing the comforter off and standing up. "I'm going out for sushi. You coming?"

"Must have hit a nerve, Kate," he calls after me as I round the corner on the stairs up to the bedroom. "When you're more comfortable standing and walking naked in front of me than you are staying to talk, that's a sure sign of something!"

I shut the door to the bathroom, turn on the hot water, and sigh deeply as it washes over me. I work a fifty-hour week in a much-despised position. In a state like Nevada—the most arid state in the nation—the job of deputy water resource manager creates more loathing than that of a mafia hit man, which until recently, here in Las Vegas, was a position of some stature. At least as a hit man, if you did your job well, someone would buy you a drink at the end of the day. Not so as a water resource manager. The loathing is widespread, and even folks who might agree with you don't want to say so in public. To make matters worse, my boss has decided to make me the public spokesperson. He believes that a "soft woman" elicits less animosity—no matter the message—than a fat, white man. Sexist, yes, but probably true—not that I consider myself soft.

So I look forward to weekends—quiet, uneventful weekends. But first I have to get through Friday evening—designated date night. Derek's idea. And he doesn't mean dinner and a movie. He means candles, wine, low-playing jazz, and lovemaking. And I'm not talking "you get off, I get off, and we're done" sort of lovemaking. I'm talking hours of excruciatingly slow exploration of every arc, every breach, every tuck of a naked body. And after sex—talking. Then more lovemaking. Then more talking. Ad nauseum. Until daybreak. He's every woman's dream. Except mine. I tell him we are not right for each other. I'm a cold, hard businesswoman who can't possibly waste an entire evening every week on such pursuits. He tells me this particular pursuit is not a luxury—it is essential for a human soul, especially the soul of a cold, hard businesswoman. That's how he speaks. Words like "soul" and "spirit" flow from him without even a hiccup.

I'm fine with the midweek sex. It's goal-oriented. The objectives are clear. It's practical and efficient. That makes Derek smile. He likes the midweek sex also, he says, but the Friday night date must stay. I remind him that I'm six years older than he is, and that at forty-six, I'm possibly too old to appreciate the Friday night dates. He says, "On the contrary; you might be too young. You fuck like a teenager, like you have someplace to go later. But I'll teach you how to make love like a fully-realized adult." Those are the kinds of things he says: *fully-realized adult*. What the fuck does that mean?

I will admit Derek has taught me a thing or two about

the physical body. I never knew, for example, that a person could ride the edge of an orgasm for two or three full hours. And when you finally take it to the other side, no cliché you can think of—mind-blowing, earth-shattering—can possibly touch the reality of it. Derek calls it a spiritual transcendence. Although I would never use such language, I can't argue with that. So on the one hand, Friday evenings are spectacular. My body starts to quiver getting ready for work Friday morning just thinking about it. I try not to schedule any meetings on Friday because my mind tends to wander and conjure up images all day. But here's the problem: after one lovemaking session and before the next, comes the talking. Derek claims it's all part of the same intimacy, that the words matter, that two people can't reach the physical/spiritual eclipse without a full understanding of each other's interior design. But he doesn't want to talk about anything so simple as the weather or politics or current events. He wants to talk about what makes a person wake up in the middle of the night feeling as if someone has a two-handed grip on her heart and an elbow chokehold on her throat. That's when I want to scream, "Please, just shut up and fuck me."

NELL

It reminds me a my honeymoon, that's what it is—standing in the boiling sun looking at this irrigation pivot shooting water straight up to the sky. Reminds me a that Ol' Faithful we saw up in Yellowstone—1954 that woulda been. What a trip that was. Dad had a brand new Chevy pickup that Nate and Henry had bought him with their army wages. We loaded it with camping gear and the four a us kids—me and Henry and Nate and Ona—crammed ourselves into it before Dad had a chance to get it dirty. Course Dad didn't mind. At that moment life was headed down a freshly graded road with all the rocks picked out. Didn't occur to any a us—cept maybe Ona—that a few boulders pushed up at the smooth surface from underneath.

Pickup trucks weren't big back then like they are now, so we weren't sprawled out to say the least. I didn't mind at all—the closer I could get to Henry's body, the happier I was. I don't even think Ona was suffering, though she would never let on she liked riding all those miles tucked in under Nate's arm, halfway on his lap. She didn't like people being public about their feelings for one another. Henry and I didn't mean to embarrass her, but Lord help us, we couldn't keep our hands offa each other.

"That's how I feel every time I look at you, babe," Henry had said as we stood watching Ol' Faithful spouting upward. "Feel just like a geyser."

Ona had blushed the color of bougainvillea bracts and a few strangers standing around us chuckled. Henry didn't care. That man was shameless in love. If he was standing here now, he'd strip off his clothes under this gushing water and invite me to do the same. Henry never missed an opportunity to turn a chore into a moment a life. About everything on this ranch reminds me a Henry. You'd think thirty-six years would wipe away the traces of a man, but I can tell you it don't. Fact, the opposite. Henry's buried in the family plot a few hundred yards off the lane that leads to the crick, but that's the least a him. I don't find no need to go sit down there staring at the stone that marks his grave. He's like those old cottonwoods hanging over the yard—every storm just sends his roots deeper into the earth and shoots his presence out over the top of us.

I get a wrench outta the truck before ducking under the water toward the shutoff valve. The water splashes cold directly on top a my head. Jasper, a ridiculously happy yellow lab, follows.

"For God's sake, dog, no use both of us getting soaked."

After the initial shock, though, the water feels good on this old body, and I suppose Jasper's thinking the same. I lean against the pipe, the fine spray from the joints hitting me just below the chin, and take my time shutting off the water. How long had it been since I stood under an irrigation sprinkler or took a dip in the crick on a hot day? Seems only a child can recognize the sense a that. And Henry.

At the end a each summer day, Henry would swing into the yard, unhook whatever he might be dragging behind the tractor, then whistle for me. Man, that man could whistle.

As soon as Henry'd start whistling, Ona'd start clucking. *He sounds just like he's whistling for a dog, and you go running with your tongue hanging out,* she'd say. Poor Ona. She never could shake loose whatever had her tightened up. Still hasn't. It's the Baptist in her, I suppose. Damn right I'd go running. I'd climb up behind Henry on the tractor and nudge him forward in the seat, wrap my legs around his waist, and bury my nose into the collar a his work shirt where that sweet-smelling, salty-tasting sweat glistened on his neck just below his fine, straggly hair. Henry used to sweat clean. He'd pick up the smell of whatever he was doing at the time. If he was breaking a colt, he'd smell like a hardworking horse. If he was cleaning out the barns, he smelled like cow manure. If he was mowing hay, he'd smell like fresh cut grass.

"Hang on, babe," he'd say, reaching back to grab my thigh just below my butt. Every time the same, "Hang on, babe," as if one day I'd forget to do just that and he'd lose me off the back a the tractor. We bounced out to the far end a the south pasture where during the first summer Henry arrived at the ranch, he and I had built ourselves a little swimming hole by damming up a wide place in the stream with boulders and sticks. Just like a couple a beavers.

Henry would jump off the tractor then swing around to lift me off. He'd grab me with sureness, doing a half-turn before setting me on the ground using the same move he used to pull a sack a grain outta the truck and swirl around to set it on top of a barrel. My mind would make that connection every time I felt his biceps taut under my palms. Henry moved over the earth with certainty and ease. It's impossible to think of him as a child learning to walk. I only met Henry's mother one time—at his funeral—and I asked her about that. She nodded as if she knew exactly why I'd asked but offered no information.

"Ain't you coming in, babe?" Henry would ask every time as he dropped his pants on the grass-lined bank and tiptoed on tender feet toward the cold, clear water. He never waited for an answer cause he already knew the answer. Sure, I was coming in. But not until I gave myself the gift of leaning up against a tree in the shade to watch him strip naked and unabashedly cross in front a me on long, muscular legs. That man was proud a that body—no doubt about it—and it was his God-given right to carry that sorta pride. There wasn't an inch a him—and I mean not one damn inch—that wasn't beautiful.

But Henry wasn't no pretty boy like that dandy Katherine Ann married and divorced. That man actually got manicures! And that ain't the only thing about that man that causes a bit a queasiness. I'm still not convinced he's really Cassie's father. Seems sex would be too messy for a man that fussy. No, Henry was drop-dead gorgeous but he was made from pure testosterone. He was a laboratory-perfect male specimen. It stirred something primal in me to lean my back against the craggy bark of a cottonwood and watch my man walk naked across the land. Henry knew it, too. He'd often dawdle for just that purpose, getting almost to the water then going back to get a pack a cigarettes outta his shirt pocket or some such thing. Then he'd stand right close to where I was sitting, look off into the distance and light himself a smoke. He'd take a deep drag and exhale slowly as if he was in deep contemplation. Then he'd sorta look at me outta the corner a his eye as if to say, "what the hell you looking at?" pretending it was pure happenstance that he was standing naked in front a me having a smoke by the stream.

When Henry finally made his way to midstream—where the water came to just above his knees—he'd take a deep breath, start swearing like a crazy man before his privates ever hit water, and in one fell swoop plunge straight down to a seated position on the rocks lining the bottom.

"Goddamn sonofabitch this water's cold! Nell, get your sweet ass in here!"

That's what he'd say every time. That was my cue to stop giggling and shed my own clothes while he watched me, elbows resting on knees, cigarette completely dry between the fingers of his right hand, water streaming gently around him. I was like Henry in that way—for whatever reason neither of us had ever picked up any shame about our bodies, which I found out along the way a life is a rare thing.

"Get out in the sunshine where I can get a good look at you, woman," Henry'd say. "It's been many long merciless hours since I've had something worthwhile to rest my eyes upon."

"Really? What do you rest your eyes upon when you're cutting hay?"

"Don't. Keep em closed the entire time. Ralphie barks like crazy when I reach the end a the field. That's the only way I know to turn around and go the other way. Ralphie's a trained seeing-eye dog." Ralphie was a yellow lab I'd given Henry for our first anniversary. They'd been inseparable ever since. There were actually two Ralphies during Henry's lifetime at the ranch, but they are indistinguishable in my mind. Ralphie tested the water the moment we got there and was then content to lie in the sun a few feet downstream and give us our privacy, barely raising his head when his name was mentioned.

"Well, you can open them now," I said, stepping gingerly into the water and creeping closer to Henry. Unlike him, I liked to edge my way in—letting the icy water settle into my skin inch by inch.

"My eyes haven't blinked since you stepped outta those jeans, babe. You just take your time inching over here. I'm plenty confident you'll reach me before dark, and I'll be waiting."

And that's how Henry and me ended every summer day for the first ten years a our marriage. I'd sink down in front a him in the water, and he'd unbraid my hair to run his hands through it, and I'd groan with pleasure.

"Don't ever cut your hair, babe," he said. "Would you make that one promise for me?"

"I'm liable to get this thing caught in the baler and lose my scalp in the process," I said. "Should cut it off right now."

"I'd still love you with or without a scalp," he said. "But having this hair spread over my naked body when we make love does something to me."

"And what would that be?"

"It sets me free, Nellie, calls out the unfettered man in me. I look down and see your auburn hair flung out over my belly, and I think *that's her, that's my woman.* And when we're old and still loving each other, I want to look down and see your long gray hair spread over my skin. So would you promise me that please?"

"On one condition."

"Anything."

"You'll braid it for me every day."

"It's a deal."

"If you stop braiding, it's coming off."

"I'll never stop. I wrote you a poem," he said one day the summer before Katie was born, pulling himself outta the water to the bank. He reached into the back pocket of his jeans, pulled out a folded piece a paper, waded back in and handed it to me. I took it with wet hands and unfolded it carefully while he settled back into the water behind me. It was written in pencil in Henry's left-handed scribble.

give me my animal body
and you give me god
whether I am riding the
crest trail on moots
or making love to my
woman it is the holy
abandon that unleashes
my soul upward

I carefully folded the paper into my palm and leaned heavy against him. There was something in that moment when I read the poem—Henry's legs around my hips in the cold stream, my back against his warm chest, the sun cutting sharply through the cottonwoods, the water circling gently around us—a brief moment when I knew Henry would one day stop braiding my hair.

The first hot day a summer when Katie was two years old, I climbed onto the back a the tractor, draped my arms around Henry's neck and felt a small pat on the top a my hand. I peeked over Henry's shoulder to see Katie settled on the tractor seat in front a Henry, the hand that normally grabbed my upper thigh wrapped instead around her tiny waist.

"No, Mama," Katie said tapping my hand. "Just two."

Henry tipped his head back and laughed. "Sorry, babe," he said with a sheepish grin, "looks like I'm taken."

I slid off the back a the tractor.

Once we get the water turned off, Jasper stretches in the sun. I strip off T-shirt and jeans, lay them on the hood a the truck to dry, drop the tailgate and pull myself up on it, shivering some from the breeze in the air.

"I know you're laughing at me now, Henry," I say. "I know exactly what you'd say . . . 'woulda made more sense, Nellie, to strip off them clothes before you went into the water.' Sure it woulda, but I guess I couldn't allow myself the image a this old woman working in her underwear."

My thighs are the color a milk straight from the cow. Loose skin falls over bone and muscle and gathers on the sides like gauzy fabric unrolled from a bolt. If I stick my legs straight out, my flexed thigh muscles rise slightly under the gauze. *Well, okay*, I think. *At least there's that.* I make a quick inspection a body parts in the harsh sun. All there, all in relatively good working order—at least the ones that need to be.

"If you'd stuck around, Henry, I mighta never lost touch with this body a mine. A woman thinks differently of herself when there ain't no man looking. I couldn't hold onto it—can't bear to cast more'n a passing glance into a mirror—too much pain skipping under the skin once you were gone."

I lean back against a sack a grain Nate was supposed to unload and never did. Guess we're both low on follow-through these days. The sun infuses heat back into my body, and for a moment I allow myself an indulgence—Henry's hand moving slowly from ankle upward, lingering, brushing, stroking. I got nineteen years a Henry's touch—not near enough.

———

Henry, a birthday present from Nate, was the most beautiful man ever to walk the face a the earth—at least the parts I had been traveling, which I admit amounted to a miniscule percentage a the total acreage. May twenty-fourth, mine and Nate's nineteenth birthday. I was sitting on the front steps a the farm house—where Nate and Ona live now—my head swirling with excitement and envy waiting for Dad to come from the Las Vegas airport where he'd gone to gather Nate. Nate had been gone a year—joined up with the army as soon as he turned eighteen and got sent posthaste to Korea. I'd only ever been in two states in my life—Nevada and Utah, which I could hit with a stone if I got a good wind-up—and I was eaten up with the unfairness a that. Dad tried to quiet me down so as not to upset my mother, who was only too aware a the absurdity in my reasoning—being jealous a Nate because he got to see a foreign country when the odds a him never returning to Omer Springs were high enough that Mama would drop to her knees in earnest prayer in front a the stove one minute and the washing machine the next, as if God were housed in modern appliances. And maybe, since Nate's war wages had purchased that brand new washing machine, that made a certain amount a sense.

I don't know how they did it, but up until the time Nate joined the army, my parents had succeeded in raising us up like the balanced scales a justice. When Nate got a horse, I got a horse; when Nate got a hunting rifle, I got a hunting rifle. I don't know that things would have evened out in quite the same way if Leroy, our older brother, hadn't drowned in the swimming hole when he was eight and we were four, but he did, and our lives were thus lived accordingly.

For the first few months after Leroy died, my mother tried to suffocate me. Not on purpose, but she got so's that she figured I was as good as dead the minute I stepped outside, so she set about making sure that never happened. Nate had it easier'n me cause he was a boy and expected to help out on the ranch from the time he could walk. There wasn't that sorta expectation built in for me, but I apparently set it for myself two months in advance a Nate getting there. That's when I started to walk—two months sooner'n Nate. Mama said once I did start to walk, I walked straight out the back door onto the mud porch, learned to hit the screen door with my full body weight, tumbled off the single step into the dirt, picked myself up and headed for the old barn. She said Nate would sit on the kitchen floor and howl in rage at my absence until he finally figured it out himself. Back then, Mama would just holler out the door to Leroy to keep an eye on me and go about her business. But after Leroy died, Mama took on a strain that life would blindside her the moment she let down her guard. That's how she came to the decision that I would be her kitchen helper where she could keep an eye on me. She might just as well a locked me in a cage. My child's mind misinterpreted her desire to protect me as punishment for Leroy's death, and my reaction was to pit myself against that poor, grieving woman until she gave in. I broke as many things as I could find as fast as I could find them. Still, it took my mother a good three months to reach the point of exaspera-tion required to send me out the door. Once she did, I never looked back.

When Nate signed up for the army at the end a high school I aimed to do the same, and my father readily agreed that would do me good. But my mother, in an unusual show of authority, told my father that she intended to be outlived by at least one child to whom she had given birth, and I would be staying home. It was not discussed further. I had spent the year since Nate left plotting my escape from Omer Springs. Dad shot down one plan after another—including becoming a dancing girl at The Flamingo—but said as soon as I came up with a plan that sounded a tiny bit plausible, he'd get behind it. I believe he was sincere about that, but before I could come up with anything, Nate came home on furlough and gave me Henry.

From my perch on the front porch, I could see the dust

cloud swirling from the pickup truck that carried him a good ways in the distance.

"They're coming!" I called to Mama. She came outta the house smoothing down everything in sight—her hair, my hair, the porch railing, her dress, my face—until I started swatting at her hands. "Good lord, Mama, calm down." But for whatever reason, my own heart was thumping like a jackrabbit crossing the road in front of a speeding car. As the white a the pickup came into focus, Mama was the first to make out three heads stead a two.

"Who on earth do they have with them?" she said. "Nell, go change the sheets on your bed."

"What in God's name for?" I demanded. "I ain't giving up my bedroom to some dog Nate's dragged home with him."

Before Mama could respond, the truck swung into the lane and slid to a stop. The passenger door opened and out dropped Henry, looking every bit like a freshly rescued yellow Labrador, that sheepish how-could-you-not-love-me look those dogs carry spreading across his face over a prominent nose and set-tling into deep brown eyes. Nate might as well have tied a red bow around Henry's neck and handed him to me on a leash. Although Henry still had another year to finish up in the army before he'd make it back to Omer Springs again, I knew from that first moment when he crushed my bare toe in the dust trying to make a good impression on my mama by stepping up to shake her hand, he was mine and I was his and there was nothing and nobody in the world could change that.

Until Katie was born.

Jasper jumps into the pickup beside me, and I rush to wipe away tears as if the dog might get ideas.

"I'm a crazy old woman, Jasper. Could be I spend more

time talking to a stinky, old dog and a dead man than some might consider healthy."

A vulture makes several passes overhead, low enough that I can see the red beak and the white etching on the underside of its wings. It catches a thermal like a surfer catching a wave, rising with each pass. The pivot gurgles and spits, clearing its pipes, sounding like an old man first thing in the morning. Birds chatter. Sprinklers chug in the next field over. The Schell Creek Mountains on the west and the Snake Range on the east enfold me and Jasper into the scene. My literal slice of life. I have taken this place for granted, there's no doubt about that. But when a woman gets to be my age, by damn, she ought to be able to take a few things for granted. Now all I can take for granted is a goddamn gusher every time I turn the water on.

"Jasper," I say, sliding off the tailgate, "if Katie's gonna steal all the water outta this valley and deliver it to Vegas, I wish she'd hurry up and do it—resolve my most pressing problem right now."

I pull on jeans and T-shirt hot from the sun, ignoring an urge to strip them off again and find another gusher to stand under.

"Let's go to town, old dog. I need a beer and a bowl a chili and some company doesn't smell like it's been rubbing on a dead cowhide. We can't avoid folks forever, you know?"

Leastways that's what Ona keeps telling me. "You can't avoid folks forever, Nell," she says in that way she has a saying things, like she's scolding a five-year-old. But truth is, a person can avoid folks almost indefinitely out here. That's the beauty a the place. Ona shoulda been a schoolmarm rather than a rancher's wife. She's not worth a damn at ranch work—too soft—but she can set a nice table and feed a crew, I'll give her that. She reminds me a my mother that way. In other ways too.

Not in looks. My mother was a tiny thing and Ona's got some heft to her, but my mother ran a tight house and Ona does the same. A day for laundry, a day for baking bread and cakes, a day for taking the rugs out to the fence for a good beating—fact, Ona sorta reminds me of a generation past. Most days—unless she's going over to Ely, in which case she puts on her Ely pant-suit—Ona still wears those button-up-the-front cotton dresses just like my mother used to wear. Don't see that much anymore. Not even sure where a person'd buy those things. Course, Ona doesn't buy hers—she sews em. Just like my mother did. Ona did trade out the sensible black shoes of my mother's era for a pair of Nike light hikers with special-made supports.

I first hear and then see Ona's car coming down the road. I duck behind the truck, slinking down into the weeds by the front wheel, pulling Jasper down with me. Foolish and immature—like I'm hiding from the mean girl in school. Cept the mean girl was always me. Ona's not mean, but there's something about her can make a woman flash through every moment a disgrace she's ever experienced in her life, and I'm not in the mood for that right now.

"I'm tired," I say, pulling Jasper in close. "At some point life started pushing me back stead a pulling me forward, and I'm just dog-tired, dog. Time for somebody else to figure things out; I ain't got the energy anymore." I rest my cheek on top a Jasper's wet head and look toward the corrals. My stomach flutters with the exquisite beauty of it. "That's just as pretty a scene as any person could ever imagine, Jasper. How could anybody do to this place what Katie's proposing to do? It don't matter that only a few people ever drive up this valley to see it—that ain't the point. The point is it's here and ought to be left alone. Period."

I push Jasper away to begin the unattractive task of pulling myself off the ground, planting my hands flat in the wheat grass. "That's odd, Jasper," I say, pausing on all fours. "Why would you suppose this grass here is flattened down?" I lean closer to the ground to get a good angle on the sun. The trail of flattened grass disappears behind the truck. "Those ain't my tire tracks. Too narrow for one a our trucks." I struggle to pull myself off the ground, then squat again next to the now-silent irrigation pivot. I been blaming that good-for-nothing kid Nate hired to do the maintenance on these pipes this season—we've never had so much trouble with leaky joints before—but something don't feel right here. Then again, seems I've had that feeling a lot lately.

LEONA

On my way home from Ely, I spot Nell's truck parked deep in the north pasture. Wonder what she's up to? She's been acting peculiar since this thing with Katie come up, and she wasn't the most predictable woman in the world to begin with. She's been awful short with people lately, and I ain't fond a being the target for her agitation, so I'm not inclined to be checking on her.

Char and me had a good visit today like sisters ought to do. In the early days, I figured me and Nell would become close, but it ain't never happened. The only time I hear "Char and Ona" in the same sentence anymore is when I take Char with me to Anderson's Foodtown in Ely. That's where Char lives. She married herself a copper miner just like Dad. Her husband died in 1978, three days after Kennecott announced their plans to close the Ruth mines and lay off every miner in Ely—all fifteen hundred of em. Char said he sat down on the couch with a cup a coffee and asked her did she think it was cold in there. She got up to check the furnace and when she came back, he was dead as a man could be, coffee cup balanced on his knee, not a drop of it spilled. Char never remarried, and I don't think she's any the worse for it.

Now that Char's kids are grown with lives a their own, I've tried to talk her into moving on over to this side a the mountain and live here on the Baxter Ranch. Plenty a room. But she says she'd miss going to church on Sundays. Not much opportunity for that over here, but I find a way to worship on my own. Nobody round here has much interest in joining me in that pursuit, though it wouldn't hurt em none. In the first year a our marriage, Nate and me would take thirty minutes or so on a Sunday morning to share the scriptures and join hands in prayer. Then one icy winter day, Nell barged into the kitchen just as we were closing up the Bible. She came in as she always does—halfway through a sentence before she even gets the door shut behind her—took one look at the Bible on the table, snorted through her nose, and said to Nate, "Let us know when you're ready to get to work, Jehovah. Henry's having trouble getting the old Case started, and we could use some help feeding this morning." That sorta irreverence is just typical a her. After that, Nate always found pressing work that needed to be done on a Sunday morning till I finally gave up on any sorta communing with God other than a quick blessing on the food, and even that gets set aside if Nell's sitting at the table.

Sure, Char's right about staying put in Ely. It's my own selfish need for some good female company keeps me nudging her to move closer. She's the only one I can talk to bout certain things. Not that I have secrets I'm working to keep—that's Nell's territory—but some things don't never come up in natural conversation round here.

Nate says Nell's secretive ways started when their older brother Leroy drowned in the swimming hole. Not that Nell had anything to do with that—just one a those freak accidents. Leroy was a good little swimmer, they say. Just got himself tangled up in some reeds while he was paddling around on the bottom, which he liked to do. Nathaniel—that's Nate's daddy—knew exactly where he was gonna find Leroy when he didn't show up for dinner that night. Nate said when his daddy carried Leroy's waterlogged body into the house, his mother's face contorted up into a silent scream, but all you could hear was pond water dripping onto the wood floor.

So you can see why Flora—that was Nate's mama—would set a rule that Nate and Nell could never go near the swimming hole. But setting a rule for Nell is paramount to delivering an engraved invitation to do the opposite. Every time Flora would remind that girl to stay away from the swimming hole, Nell'd pack herself a lunch and go straight there. And every time Flora would ask where they'd been, Nell would say they'd been playing hide-n-seek behind the haystack, and Nate would have to confirm that. And even though Nell's braids'd be barely dried from the sun on their walk home from the swimming hole, she'd stand her ground, and apparently Nate couldn't see fit to do anything other than stand there next to her lying to his own mother.

Nate says those white lies flowed out of Nell perennially, just like Cleve Crick flows from the mountains. And though we've had some years of drought, that crick is still flowing. And so is Nell. And it seems to me Nell's prevarications grew at the same rate she did—from kid-sized fibs into the kinds of adult-sized untruths that can do some real damage. So when people ask me why Katie's doing what she's doing, I want to say the answer ain't all that puzzling as you might think. Instead, I do what I've always done. I mind my own business. Problem is, Nate is my business, and that makes Nell my business and right on down the line—Katie and Cassie too. That seems to be the lifelong conundrum the good Lord seen fit to hand me.

I haul in several bags a groceries before I notice Nate sitting at the dining room table staring at the picture on the wall. I argue with myself about whether to stop or keep moving with my chores.

"What're you looking at?" I ask him.

"Nothing," he says.

What he's looking at is a large rectangular picture ("painting" according to Cassie, who seems to think that being born in a fancy Las Vegas hospital gives her responsibility for fixing up our speech patterns) a the Baxter Ranch, looking in at the corrals and cottonwood trees from the east. It was painted by a young fella Henry picked up hitchhiking one day on the gravel road that goes straight up the gut a Spring Valley. When Henry asked where he was headed the boy said "nowhere," and that'd been the truth cause this road don't go nowhere but here. So Henry asked if he wanted to stay at the ranch and work for a while. Turned out the kid wasn't worth his supper at ranch work and had a knack for twiddling with machinery until some part snapped off in his hands—but he kept trying. Got so after a while, every time Nate and Henry'd see him coming, they'd give him a horse and send him out to some remote location to count cows. Knowing the boy's tendency for wandering aimlessly, they knew it'd take him most a the day to return. When the boy'd report the count, Henry'd take a pencil outta his shirt pocket and thoughtfully write the number down on any old fence post he happened to be standing by. Then they'd send him out in another direction. That boy musta left Nevada thinking we live in fear a misplacing our cows. If you look real close, you can still see some a those numbers Henry wrote all over the place.

Nathaniel and Flora fed the boy regardless a his abilities—they was that kinda people. Then one day he was gone. We went out to the bunkhouse and found that freshly painted picture propped up against the table—no note or nothing. At the time, none a us could figure why anybody'd want a picture of something they could just walk out the door and see for their selves. Nathaniel wrapped the thing in an old tarp and stuck it in the tack shed behind the grain bin where he stored oats for the horses. Some years later we saw that fella's picture in the *Review-Journal* next to another picture a our ranch that he'd just sold at some fancy New York gallery for eight thousand dollars. In them days, that was a god-awful lotta money—still is around these parts—so Nathaniel unwrapped the picture, no worse for wear, and hung it there on the wall.

Seems like lately, Nate's as much a part a the picture as the picture itself, and I don't believe it's good for a man to wallow in a place like where Nate goes when he looks at that picture.

"That's the prettiest picture I've ever laid eyes on," he says to me, and for a minute I think he might start bawling.

"Well, you ain't really laid your old eyes on that many pictures." I'm not so sure it's worth bawling over, but I knew what he meant. He wasn't bawling over the picture; he was bawling over this place. More specifically, he was feeling the heavy weight a the life he didn't live. That's what us old people do when we inch closer to the underside a the earth.

Just like a dying mother worrying about her kids, Nate worries about who's gonna take care a this place after he's gone. He has assigned emotions to this land—he loves it, and he thinks it loves him back. It don't do no good to explain to him that land is land—it don't have no capacity for feeling good when he's walking over it and feeling bad when he's buried in the depths of it. It will just go on being land with or without him.

Nate says he knows, a course, that land is just land, but then he stops short from saying what else he's thinking, which is that I can't possibly understand: I don't know how dirt gets into a person's blood cells and becomes part of his DNA cause I wasn't born and raised on the same piece a ground that's been walked over by six generations a the same family. That's true enough I guess, but that don't change the current situation.

With Katie's announcement, Nate has switched from worrying about who's gonna take care a the place to worrying about whether there'll be a place worth taking care of. This has been a year a nasty words and television appearances and meetings with officials and conflicting reports about how much water flows under our feet and who has a right to it. It's a wonder any of us have accomplished any work at all. Good heavens, the announcement itself might be enough to put us outta business before the pipeline ever gets here.

After the initial shock though, the whole mess put a little birr into Nate that I haven't seen in years. He's riled up, and that's a good thing. At least he is until Katie comes on television, which she does now with regularity, announcing a new report that confirms there's plenty a water to share and they are moving ahead with plans for taking it. Then Nate gets real quiet. Until one a the environmental groups comes on TV and announces a conflicting report about dwindling water aquifers and calling the pipeline a crazy idea. Then Nate gets riled up again. But not nearly enough. Otherwise he'd call Katie up on the phone and ask her about this flat out. Stead he's doing what he's always done, which is to follow Nell's orders even when they don't make a bit a sense whatsoever. Everyone in these parts has seen Nell's stubbornness, so they ain't expecting that will shift anytime soon. Instead, they're looking for Nate to grow a backbone and get on the phone to Katie. Well, they can take it from me—Nate and Nell share a lot more'n this land. They share a brain, and unfortunately it resides in Nell's head.

Something's gotta give with Nell. Last few months, she's moving like she ain't got a thing in the world to do, and I only seen her like that one other time in my life—right after Henry died. Once something starts vexing her it's like she forgets how to go through her days. And, a course, when Nell's outta sorts, Nate's outta sorts right along with her. They also share a central nervous system. Then I start feeling anxious, and pretty soon Skinny's the only one getting any work done around here.

Still, it's a good thing stuff is bubbling up to the surface, but that don't necessarily mean this family will pay it no mind. I've seen it before—in fact, I've lived in the middle of it. It's sorta like burying a dead cow too shallow—the buzzards dig and pull the hide to the surface, but the Baxters can go a staggering number a years riding circles around the old hide, all the while it stinking to high heaven. One a those reeking hides was pulled up between me and Nate a lotta years ago, and we been stepping over it longer than I thought possible. By that, I mean that me and Nate have never once had a serious talk about our childless condition. Imagine that. More'n fifty years we been married, and we ain't once talked about it. Char says folks call that the elephant in the room. According to her, it's unhealthy to allow elephants to stomp around a room forever. Elephant or rotting hide, don't much matter what you call it, but there ain't much use in approaching the old thing at this stage in the game.

In the early years, Nate'd joke about getting me pregnant all the time. Embarrass me to pieces with his comments about how we needed to step up our practice, throw in a few more plays. Nine full years passed from the time me and Nate and

Nell and Henry was married till Katie was born. During that time, Nate's jokes progressed from friendly to anxious, and that anxiety'd blow around the ranch a bit. He'd set Flora to hand wringing and Nathaniel to brooding, but Henry'd just slap him on the back and tell him he had nothing to worry about. *All in good time, brother,* Henry'd say. *All in good time. In the meanwhile, you might just as well have yourself some fun,* Henry'd say with a wink and a wicked smile. That was Henry. Always acting inappropriate if you ask me. Course nobody ever does.

The four of us—me and Nate and Henry and Nell—was married at a double wedding. I shoulda put my foot down right then and there—a girl deserves her own gosh darn wedding for heaven's sake—but I didn't. I remember Char trying to tell me that, but she wasn't near direct enough—she was just dancing around the edges. I believe that's cause she didn't want me to feel bad about wearing her wedding dress, so if she'd started in on insisting I have my own wedding it mighta occurred to me that I also oughta have my own dress. But Mama and Papa couldn't afford that—they still had six more kids at home and Papa only worked sporadically since an accident at the mine left him with half a brain. But deep down I knew I shoulda insisted on a wedding a my own. This ain't gonna come out sounding right, but it was sorta like Nell was marrying both of em—like both Henry and Nate belonged to her, and that double ceremony was hers alone.

The first few years after we was married we lived high on hope and expectation. Seems like the fields were flush with thick grasses, the cattle were fat, and the machinery never broke down. But when a few years passed without neither me nor Nell coming up pregnant, well it was like when you walk out to the middle a your field and notice alkali leeching to the surface in places you never saw it before. An unsettling feeling starts to percolate. And every month, the borders of that little patch a alkali seem to etch out further into the green parts until all you can do is stiffen up your lip and turn away. You don't really notice things are changing, but one day you feel a dryness to life that didn't used to be there. Then before you know it, things are turning brittle and breaking apart.

At first, though, it was sorta a running joke between Henry and Nate—who might turn out to be the *best* man so to speak. I didn't like that sorta talk one bit, but Nell'd whoop and holler with the two a them and rub up against Henry like some floozy from Carson City. Honestly. But Henry and Nell was always acting like that—they couldn't keep their hands offa each other for more'n five minutes. They'd be in the middle a saddling a couple a horses and next thing you know, the two a them'd disappear into the tack shed and come out again five minutes later flushed and laughing and buttoning up clothing. Good Lord. Like the rest a us should just set down a spell and wait for them to finish up whatever it was got started. Whenever Henry used to drag a field, Nell would ride behind him on the tractor, both legs wrapped around his middle and chewing on his neck for God and all to see. I couldn't believe Flora and Nathaniel put up with that sorta behavior, but they just went about their business as if it didn't concern them. Maybe they were just used to that from Nell, being's she done what she darn well pleased her whole life anyhow. I told Nate he should say something to Nell and Henry and he said, "What for, Ona? They're just doing what comes naturally." To dogs, maybe. Where I come from, humans act a little more civilized in polite society. Apparently not on the Baxter Ranch.

Nell never let on she was pregnant with Katie until she was past the point a denial. Ain't it a little strange for a woman not to announce she's with child? Not Nell. She went right on driving the tractor, bouncing over irrigation furrows—which is what we had back then—like nobody's business. I ain't saying nothing about it, but that ain't the way I woulda handled things had it a been me. That's all I'm saying. Specially since every person on this ranch—cept maybe Nell herself—had been obsessing going on nine years about that very issue: when the first a the next generation might come along.

I guess you could suffice to say that no one was surprised when Nell came up pregnant and I didn't. Including Nate, I suppose, though he shoulda known better. Just cause I don't peacock around in public don't mean I don't know how to take care a my husband.

After Katie was born, Nate never once mentioned us having kids again. Clamped up tight and never said another word about it, as if he'd lost some big race. I tried to get him to talk about it a few times—asked him once if he'd ever thought we might adopt a child of our own.

"Char's friend Naomi adopted a kid last year through the Mormon Church," I told him. "Maybe we could try that."

"First of all, Ona, we ain't Mormon," he said. "And second, this here's Baxter land, always has been, always will be. You can't take a kid born in the middle a Philadelphia or China and turn him into a Baxter. Ain't gonna work that way."

That was the end a that conversation. I tried one more time to ask Nate did he think any less a me cause I couldn't get myself pregnant.

"It takes two to make a baby, Ona," he said. "I ain't laying all the blame on you."

I wanted to keep talking till some truth dribbled out, so from time to time I would bring it up again. Then one day he said he didn't want to have this conversation ever again. That was forty years ago. So we never did.

NELL

The screen door to Frank's Place sticks and screeches across the concrete floor, so it's common for all eyes to lift briefly and take note a who's entering. The sound and the movement go together instinctively, like tapping to a beat, no conscious intent to make the person entering uncomfortable, but I am nevertheless. There's only three people in the place besides Frank—Fitz Walters sitting at the bar and a couple I've never seen before taking up space at one a four tables, which explains the RV parked out front. They'd be the adventurous type a RVer—like to get off the beaten path and now lost as hell after following their GPS without the common sense to question the dirt road laid out plain as day in front a them. I elbow Fitz Walters in the ribs.

"You're on my stool. Show an old woman some courtesy."

"Well, hell, Nell," Fitz drawls. "You ain't been here for a while." He tumbles off the stool in the opposite direction. "I figured this stool was up for grabs."

"Well you figured wrong, Fitzy. Frank, could an old woman get a bowl a chili and a cold Bud?"

"Sure thing, Nell," says the stout man behind the counter, placing a full bowl, ladled out of a crockpot the moment I walked in, in front a me. He sticks a spoon in the bowl, then fills another bowl with chili and a saucepan with water and puts them on the floor by my feet. Jasper devours the chili before Frank gets back around the bar. Fitzy has taken up the stool next to mine and is looking at me like I have three eyes.

"What you staring at, Fitzy?"

"Just wondering if you're planning on coming back into the fold, Nell."

"I'm here, ain't I? Now drink your beer and don't ask me any stupid questions."

"Wouldn't dream of it, Nell."

"Nice to see you and Jasper back," Frank says. "My business dropped off about twenty percent when you stopped coming in."

"It's a damn good thing you never had a foolish notion a making a living off this place, Frank."

"You speak the truth there, Nell. Glad to have your company, nevertheless."

"You might be the only one feels that way."

"Not sure about that. I limit myself to my own business."

"That must make you a lonely man around these parts."

"Keeps my blood pressure down."

"It also casts a shadow a suspicion on your head."

"Could be."

"You should hear some a the rumors been spread about you in the twenty years since you showed up here."

"Don't care to."

"Some say your name ain't even Frank."

"That's what it says on the sign out front."

"Pretty damn handy since that sign's been here a helluva lot longer than you have." He smiles, uncaps a bottle a Budweiser and sets it down next to my chili. "How'd you come by this place, Frank? Wasn't more'n a week after Melvin, the old Frank, died before you showed up. That's fine timing on your part."

"What's up, Nell?" Frank says, leaning back against the counter, his arms folded. "Not like you to swim in water's already gone under the bridge."

"I live in fear, Frank, that one a these days your picture is gonna pop up on my television on America's Most Wanted, and I'll be expected to choose between justice and chili."

"Hell of a predicament, Nell."

"But a damn sight better than the one I'm in."

The screen door screeches again. Nate and Ona take up the first and second stool on my right.

"Nice to see you out and about, Sis," Nate says. "Ona saw your truck out to the north pasture, but by the time we got there you were gone. Hoping we might find you here." Frank has their chili ladled and their beer opened before they get settled on their stools—there being a need for a person's butt cheeks to find a good fit on the old stools if a person hopes to stay longer than ten minutes.

"I'm hoping I picked a slow night for my re-entrance," I say.

"Should be," Nate says. "Big meeting was last night."

"Exactly why I picked tonight."

Frank's business may have dropped off initially when I stopped coming, but it's since picked up. In fact, I'd say it's tripled—from about five folks a night to near fifteen—thanks to Katie. Lordy, how one little girl—one woman—can stir things up. I can't hardly call her Katie no more. Seems like that little girl—the one that used to howl at Henry's ridiculous gyrating imitation of Elvis—is long gone. I'm not sure Katherine Ann has laughed out loud in more'n thirty years. If she has, she hasn't done it in my company.

Frank's is now the weekly meeting place for everybody in Spring Valley, and the monthly meeting place for five surrounding valleys, the sole purpose a which is to figure out a way to stop Katherine Ann from stealing our water and bankrupting every one a us. I haven't been attending those meetings, but Nate keeps me informed. He said at first some just couldn't wrap their heads around that notion of a three hundred-mile pipeline—it was just the most absurd thing they'd ever heard—and they shrugged it off. But some knew, as I did, that it wasn't no joke. Katie and that company she works for are dead serious about this. When that idea started to settle into folks, well, that's a stone-cold dread that enters a person and takes hold. That's when the real constitution of a person emerges. Some get angry, some depressed, some resigned, all of which are pretty quickly followed by despair.

Nate and Ona been going to all the meetings. Nate says I should too, and he's right, a course. One a these nights I might get up the courage to do just that, but for now I'd like to sit on my stool at Frank's and have a bowl a chili. Ain't an easy thing for a mother to contemplate—plotting against her own daughter.

KATE

I step out of the elevator on the twenty-fourth floor at exactly 7:40 a.m. and look in both directions to an empty hallway. Thank God—7:40 it is. For the last several weeks, I've been arriving earlier and earlier on Monday mornings in an effort to avoid Matt Shilton, who for the last ten years of Mondays has been greeting me at the elevator, coffee and muffins in hand. We used to be good friends; he believes we still are. We met in grad school twenty years ago and became friends under circumstances I'd just as soon forget but Matt loves to remember. After a year of knowing the other only from the perspective of heated graduate seminar discussions, we spoke our first direct words to each other because there's something about dark pools of water steaming in the middle of a desert under a moonlit sky that inspires a belief in ridiculous clichés such as "opposites attract."

At the end of every school year, UNLV geology department grad students scattered tents on a barren knoll fifteen miles southeast of Austin, Nevada—ostensibly for a week of "geothermal study," more aptly described as an experiment in human behavior. At this spot in the desert, natural mineral water flows from several springs at 128 degrees, through a channel down the slope of the knoll and into several hand-dug soaking pools located at varying distances from the source to control the temperature of the pools. It was in the closest and hottest pool that Matt found me at 2 a.m. the first night we arrived.

Matt and I represented two divergent factions of geology grad students. He was brilliant but never serious; I was serious but not brilliant. He was idealistic; I was pragmatic. Both factions aimed to save the human species from itself, but our approaches differed vastly. To Matt, my pragmatic approach represented a deadly compromise of the human spirit. To me, his idealistic approach represented a romantic impasse. What Matt and I did apparently share was insomnia.

Had I arrived to find the pool already occupied, however, I certainly would have opted to walk thirty feet farther to the next pool. That would have been the courteous thing to do. When Matt arrived to find me there, he grinned, pulled off sweatpants and sweatshirt as if I were one of his buddies and eased himself into the pool directly opposite me. It was—and still is—true that people who frequent natural hot springs are supposedly comfortable with public nudity, which is why I haven't been to one in twenty years. I averted my eyes until I felt Matt's feet bump against mine on the bottom, at which point I figured he was settled into the water and it was safe to look up. When I did, he was still grinning.

"Alone at last," he said. "The moment we've all been waiting for."

"Funny," I said sinking deeper into the water.

"So, what's your real story, Katie Jorgensen?" he asked.

"Huh?"

"Why are you here?"

"Couldn't sleep," I said.

"No, not that. Why are you here? On this trip, in this

program, at this college? Where did you come from? How did you get here?"

I shrugged, remembering why I didn't like Matt. Too close for comfort. He had an uncanny ability to bore into the epicenter of a person using only a few casually tossed-off questions. I had watched him do it to others in seminar—shut them down completely with a comment or question that perfectly skirted the edges of their subconscious motivations—the ones they didn't even know they had until Matt coaxed them into the room. No way I was going to have this conversation with him.

"How did *you* get here?" I asked.

"Oh mine's easy. My father was a geologist—worked for the U.S. Geological Survey. Took me and my mother with him all over the west. Including Nevada. I loved the state from the moment I saw it. The last bastion of unpopulated space. That's my story. Straight line from birth to sitting naked in this hot spring. The burning question is, how did you get in here with me in all your glorious, naked splendor?'"

I shrugged again and sank deeper into the water. I don't remember what I told Matt that night. I only know what I didn't tell him. I had gone so many years on the ranch never speaking about my father that I had begun to think of his memory as sacred. I believed then—and still do—that speaking about him would somehow cheapen his life. So I never told Matt of my father's innate curiosity and romance with the ingredients of the earth. I never told him of my father's fascination with human insignificance in the grand cycles of the universe. And I never mentioned how the romance had died with my father, and how the study of geology was my sterile attempt to woo back stirrings my father had planted in me. I didn't tell Matt that we had it backwards—that he should have been the pragmatist and I should have been the idealist, that my birthright had been interrupted, and I resented Matt's untroubled passion for the subject we shared.

In response to his endless questions, I likely mumbled something brilliant such as "I like rocks." Whatever story I came up with wasn't enough to encourage Matt to vacate the pool and leave me in peace. We spent a dangerous amount of time in the pool that night—both of us trying to outlast the other. Matt's intention was to see me crawl out of the water naked; my intention was to prevent that. Matt won.

Besides insomnia and the study of geology, we discovered that we also shared a love for beer, which is how we justified waking up in the same tent at 7 a.m. the next morning. By the end of the week, we knew we could either continue our intellectual debates or be lovers, but not both. Since the former seemed more satisfying—in fact, more exciting—than the latter, we chose the former and have never questioned that decision in the twenty years since.

After college, Matt went to work for a conservation group, and I went to work for the enemy—the Nevada Water Authority—both intent on proving the virtues of our distinctive approaches. Still, we met every Tuesday night over our maturing love for beer to discuss what we both referred to as "the pending western water wars." Ten years after we graduated, the conservation group's chairman of the board was arrested for embezzling, and Matt was out of a job. By then he had a wife, two kids, two dogs, and less idealism. Still, it took some talking to get him to switch sides. My boss jumped on the idea—what better way to quiet his enemies than hire one of their own. In exchange, Matt agreed on the basis that he would not do anything to compromise his principles—although the older he gets, the more muddied his principles are—so he's basically in charge of making a city that was built on excess understand why it should care about conservation of any sort. The answer is pretty simple: the growth of greed and gluttony skids to a halt when the water stops flowing. But because most people hold tight to the belief that the origin of water is the faucet, Matt's job is not easy. When he came to the NWA, Matt also had to agree never to speak with the press and to sign a confidentiality agreement, which he signed with his usual air of disregard. Matt ended up with a title and salary equal to mine, which only bothers me when I let it. He keeps me sharp, makes me laugh, and every once in a while convinces me that I should quit taking things so seriously. I like having him around—or at least I used to.

For the last ten years, Monday morning sessions have slowly replaced our Tuesday night beer ritual. We meet in my office because it has a better view than his and because I was wise enough to hire an assistant named Heather who has little or no curiosity about the real world. She can, however, report on anything a person would want to know about the virtual world of television, internet blogs, and Facebook, which, I suppose, is her real world. Shortly after I hired her, when I couldn't muster up a veneer of interest in her reportage of Britney Spears' fall from grace, she quickly dismissed me as out of touch with reality, and we have blessedly never since attempted a conversation beyond that required to get a little work done. She doesn't ask about my weekend, she doesn't ask how Cassie's doing in school, who Derek is, where I'm from, how often I go home, or if my mother's still alive. She never wants to discuss NWA business. When Matt and I close the door to commiserate about working for a pompous ass, she doesn't come in searching for missing files just as we get going. Matt's assistant—also named Heather—does. My Heather doesn't care. She cares about leaving at five o'clock, having her parking paid for, and using every last scrap of vacation and sick leave she has coming, usually as quickly as it accumulates.

On the down side, my Heather has certain resolute principles steeped in her own reality that manifest in some quirky ways. For example, she deems it her responsibility to vote. Not in a democratic election of any sort—that she wouldn't be aware of—but she is still carrying a grudge against me for the one time we had a report deadline that kept her late at work in the evening—although she was paid double time—and caused her to miss an American Idol vote. She still blames me for not saving the contestant wrongly—according to Heather—voted off that particular week. She also—and I'm sure this principle is rooted in some reality show—will not lie to cover for her boss the way Matt's Heather does when he goes to the gym in the middle of the workday. So this morning when I arrive early enough to avoid Matt and sneak into my office, asking Heather to tell him I'm in a meeting, she says, "Yeah, sure." When Matt shows up, she says, "She's in her office, go on in."

"I like your Heather," Matt says, kicking the door closed behind him and dumping muffins and coffee onto the table. "I wouldn't want her working for me, but I like that you have her." He slouches on the couch and slurps his coffee.

"I'm really busy this morning, Matt."

"I'll bet you are—got the water grab on your plate."

"Dammit, Matt, use that term one more time, and I'm never speaking to you again."

"Katie, Katie, Katie—a little touchy on the issue."

"Don't call me Katie."

"You used to let me call you Katie. I remember a certain spring night—"

"Give it a break, will you? You're getting tiresome."

"Have you noticed that all the people in your life are getting tiresome, Katie?"

"Yes, I have, now that you mention it."

"Note a common denominator?"

"What's your point?"

"You're on edge, Katie."

"I don't need you to tell me that. I have an expensive therapist and a boyfriend to tell me that."

"But do they know the source of your edginess like I do?"

"That's what I always hated about you in school, Matt. So damn smug."

"You're stealing from the poor to give to the rich. That would make anyone edgy."

"And so damn simplistic."

"No reason to make it any more complicated than it is. The blueprint was drawn up in Owens Valley a century ago."

"First of all, the realities of the Owens Valley water trade—"

"You mean water theft—"

"—are wildly distorted and misinterpreted. Furthermore, with current environmental safeguards in place, something like Owens Valley could never happen again. Things are different now. We can protect both the environment and the ranching and still bring water to the citizens of Las Vegas."

Matt uncrosses his legs and leans forward, elbows on knees, looking at me with a goofy smile. "Keep going, Katie, because I love the next part."

"Get out, Matt. I'm tired of having this conversation with you."

"Come on. I want to hear the part where you say that after we spend two billion dollars to bury three hundred miles of pipeline in the desert and flip the switch to pump two hundred thousand acre feet of water a year from six basins into Las Vegas, we'll monitor the impact carefully. I love the part where you say if we see any negative impact to either environment or agriculture we'll shut those pumps down immediately. That's my favorite TV speech of yours, Katie. I've recorded it, and when I get bored in the evenings I sometimes play it back for entertainment purposes."

"Get the hell out of my office."

"I especially love envisioning you telling the fine, rich folks of Vegas 'tough noogies—you can't water your sixty golf courses because we're killing a little fishy known as the Bonneville Cutthroat up in the Deep Creeks so we're shutting down the pumps.'"

"We just negotiated an agreement with the U.S. Fish and Wildlife Service promising exactly that—that we'd stop pumping if there's a negative impact."

"Oh, an agreement between the federal government and the Nevada Water Authority! Boy, do I ever feel relieved now."

"I have no reason to believe those agreements won't be honored."

"You have every reason to believe it; you just don't want to."

"What happened to all that idealism you used to have, Matt?"

"Idealism and self-deception are not synonymous. The problem is, Katie my dear, you don't believe a word coming out of your own mouth right now. And that, my lovely friend, is why you're so edgy these days. Not to mention the fact that it's your own people you're fucking over."

"Get out of my office."

"Talk to me, Kate. I'm all you have. It's a sure bet you aren't sharing these feelings of guilt and betrayal with young Derek."

"You have no idea what Derek and I talk about."

"Guilt and betrayal?"

"There's none to talk about."

"Liar, liar, pants on fire."

"Very mature, Matt. Get out of my office now."

Matt pulls himself up off the couch and walks forward with his arms out as he if plans to hug me. I turn away. "We've been friends a lot of years, Katie."

"And your point is?"

"I think I just made it." He shrugs and leaves the office. I close the door behind him and lean my forehead against the cold, thick glass of my office windows—windows designed to never open, to never allow outside air to interfere with my comfort. From my twenty-fourth floor corner office, I can barely see the edges of the city as they spill into the desert. I pull my head back and notice several forehead smudges on the windows—apparently I do this a lot. A stack of papers on the desk waits for my attention—environmental studies, Colorado River studies, geological studies, hydrology studies, reports, newspaper articles, interviews. Put a spin on them, Kate. Do your thing.

I push them aside, pull up my email and open a message from Cassie. *Nothing much to report from the beautiful metropolis of Omer Springs*, she says. *Grandma Nell as grouchy as ever. Aunt Ona about the same. Town on edge over the water thing. Uncle Nate looking really old.*

Odd for Cassie to bring up the water thing. When she came to live with me last year, for the sake of household peace, I put a moratorium on discussing the intricacies of my job, although I have no doubt that she and Derek discussed that and more in my absence. Also odd for Cassie to send emails every few days. Come to think of it, odd for her to be sending any email at all. The only place with internet access in Omer Springs is the school. Why would Cassie drive into town every other day just to report what I already know—nothing ever changes in Omer Springs.

Nothing ever changes in Omer Springs. I carry the thought with me like an adolescent carries her own pillow on a long plane ride. A familiar smell, a touch of softness against one cheek, a place to rest a tired head. I've tucked the notion away just in case. In my own private Idaho, when my tightly stitched life begins to pop its seams, I'll find my way back to the Omer Springs where the world spun at just the right speed and angle. I'll sit on the wooden plank seat of the swing Dad hung from a high cottonwood branch, wrap my hands around the thick rope, twist around and around until the ropes won't twist anymore, then lean back into a horizontal position, pop my legs out straight, and let it go—a swirling upside down world of dappled sunshine, blue skies, green earth, and laughter. The song of western meadowlarks will rise in the air, and Dad will say, *Listen, Katie, do you hear that? The meadowlarks are saying, 'Katie's a pretty little girl. Katie's a pretty little girl.'* I'll be home; I'll be safe.

Of course the notion—or delusion, if you want to be more precise—is significantly more comforting than the reality and as useless as the dollar bill an old woman has sewn into the pocket of her favorite sweater, just in case. Something already changed in Omer Springs. The place now soaks up pain and misery like fine sand pulls in a summer rain, so that when you take a step, it oozes out from under your feet.

CASSIE

Mick, a curlyheaded, burley man in his late fifties who has a way of looking at you like he knows what's good for you, fills a glass with ice and shoots it full of Coke from the fountain. He sets it on top of a cocktail napkin in front of me.

"Thanks," I say without looking up from my computer screen, subconsciously waiting to hear *that shit'll kill you,* which is his usual response. When I don't hear it, I look up to find him standing in front of me, leaning straight-armed, both hands propped against the bar. Once he has my attention, he pulls a piece of folded paper from his shirt pocket and slides it across the bar.

"What's this?" I ask.

"I drew you a map to some hiking trails close by—up in the Mount Rose Wilderness. Under that mask Maggie puts on your face every morning, you're beginning to look pasty as hell."

I close my computer and pull the napkin out from under the Coke to dab my eyes. Lately I've been spilling tears with such little provocation everyone stopped asking me "what's wrong?" a week ago.

"I've never spent a summer indoors before, Mick. I think I'm gonna suffocate."

"Yeah, no shit," he says. "Some people can spend their whole lives indoors. They like the idea of climate control—makes them feel powerful as hell. You ain't one of those people, and you been sitting on that stool for a month now. Get outta here, Cassie. If you're not gonna go back to Spring Valley where you belong, at least get out into the sunlight for a few hours. You look like hell."

Over the last month, Mick had coaxed from me with little effort every detail of my life, but I know little about him. Closely cropped, curly gray hair hugs his perfectly round head. He doesn't drink. He doesn't smoke. He's respectful to the women who work here, and he never touches one. He's kind. He makes me feel safe the way Uncle Nate makes me feel safe. And that's all I know. I never pegged him as the hiking type. In fact, I never considered him in any setting other than standing behind this bar. Never wondered where he might go, what he might do on his days off. Does he have a family? A wife? It's a standard rule here that you don't dig too deeply into anyone's life or reasons for being here. I'm the exception to the rule. Everyone seems to know exactly why I'm here, and I'm pretty sure they're all waiting for me to come to my senses and leave. Since Mick knows so much about me, I think it fair to ask about his life, but he knows what's coming before it gets here and quickly turns the conversation back to me.

"The Fourth of July'll be coming up soon," he says. "What do you usually do on the Fourth?"

"The whole town gets together for a picnic," I say, choking up again thinking about Skinny and Frank working under the awning without me. "I usually help make Indian fry bread. Then Uncle Nate, Skinny, and I saddle the horses and ride into the Snakes to check gates left open by picnickers."

"Well, you're gonna have to go on your own two feet here,

but it'll do you good," he says, unfolding the map he's drawn to go over it.

"Sometimes I can't quite figure out why I'm here, Mick, spending my summer in a whorehouse."

"Hell, we've all been wondering that since you got here, Cassie, but best not let Maggie hear you talking like that."

I'd already been lectured twice by Maggie for using direct language. I don't like euphemisms, but Maggie calls her business a brothel, not a whorehouse, and the employees here are called ladies, not whores or prostitutes, and no one has sex; they have parties. I got my aversion to euphemisms from Grandma Nell—she likes to be direct. At one time I equated directness with truthfulness, but I am beginning to rethink that. Mama, on the other hand, I've learned since moving in with her, can drive a person to extremes with unspoken words unless there's a camera pointed at her or a microphone stuck in her face. Then she can be rather eloquent and convincing, downright impressive in fact. Grandma Nell claims people want to be lied to—makes it easier for them to do the unconscionable things they do—and that's why Mama gets paid so well. Personally, I've never known my mother to lie, but that could be because we never talk about anything of significance. In the last year, the number of conversations my mother and I have *not* had must number in the hundreds, and the top two topics on the "no conversation" list are water and family.

Anyway, Grandma Nell made that comment about my mother and lying at dinner one night when I was still living at the ranch, and Aunt Ona shot a whole kernel of corn straight out through the space between her front teeth. We sat silently waiting for Aunt Ona to comment on Grandma Nell's theory, but she just reached across Uncle Nate's plate to retrieve the corn kernel from where it had landed next to the butter dish, placed it on the edge of her own plate, and shook her head. Satisfied she had nothing to say on the issue, Grandma Nell transitioned smoothly into a discussion of repairs needed on the manure spreader.

It was my loathing of mealymouthed types that attracted me to Bets, my best friend at UNLV, the smartest student in my program, and the source of my whorehouse idea. When I got to UNLV, the ranch hung on me like the smell of dog on Jasper, and it didn't take more than a week to find out I represented enemy number one to most environmental studies students. At first that bothered me, because I saw a certain camaraderie between ranchers and environmentalists; we share a powerful love for the land. Within my romantic expectations of college, having no experience to inform me otherwise, I assumed that I and my fellow students would share pints of beer and mugs of coffee while we listened to one another's points of view and realized that we weren't so far apart in our views after all. Once that expectation got obliterated all to hell and I let go of seeking understanding from my fellow students, I settled into the program just fine. Given no other choice, I kept to myself, nurtured my own views, and after my first year of study, I'm more convinced than ever that a person can be both a rancher and an environmentalist. I aim to be exactly that when I leave UNLV.

Bets was the opposite sort of outcast. She constructed a jungly exterior around herself made up of body piercings, jet-black hair, and wickedly brilliant and cynical responses to the quixotic earth-savers who surrounded her. When, at the end of the second week, we were told to partner up for a semester-long eco-project of our choice, I was surprised, utterly relieved, and a little bit scared to find Bets tapping me on the shoulder. After we became friends, I asked her why she'd picked me that day. She said I was the only student in the class who hadn't yet put her ignorance on display, and she thought that to be a worthy trait in a person.

One day toward the end of the school year, Bets let on that her parents didn't have the money to send her to college, and other than a tuition scholarship, she was paying her own way—and her own way happened to include a very cool off-campus apartment. I pointed out to Bets that I had never seen her go to work, and she said she only worked during semester breaks and summer, which would explain her sudden and secretive disappearance during those times. I said that must be some good job if that's all she had to work, and she said her job literally sucked (her words, not mine) but the pay was excellent. Bets didn't immediately buy into my plan. In fact, she finds my plan absurd, and I appreciate her telling me that, but thus far it's the only one I've come up with.

"I'm having trouble picturing you as a prostitute," Bets had said when I offered to join her this summer. "But maybe I'll learn something new about you." Then she shrugged. "Sure, pack a bag. You won't need much. I can't imagine you have the requisite brothel wardrobe tucked into a drawer somewhere. We can buy you some things when we get there unless you change your mind beforehand—and you will."

And I almost did.

"It's only sex," Bets had explained to me on our drive from Vegas to Carson City—via a detour to Omer Springs—when I sat up from where I was slumped in the passenger seat of the Honda Element Dipshit had given me for my twenty-first birthday and began to express misgivings about my plan. At the time—about midnight—we were on a very lonely stretch of the Loneliest Highway in America.

"Only sex?" I said.

"That's the way I think about it," she said. "Not a big deal."

"How do you figure sex is not a big deal?" I had only had sex twice in my life, and both times it seemed like a very big deal before, during, and after the act.

"The key is keeping your head and your heart out of the equation. That's the first thing I learned."

"Oh."

"Once you let either one of those things in there—start thinking too much about what you're doing or do something stupid like fall in love with one of the guys—you're fucked. No pun intended."

"Sounds like one of those things they teach you in school—theoretically sound, practically impossible."

"I promise you it is not."

"How do you not think about what you're doing?" I asked her.

"It's a job like any other job. It's no more demeaning than flipping burgers and putting up with some condescending jerk-off waving a fucking pickle he didn't want in front of your face like it would kill him to push the goddamn thing off to the side and keep his mouth shut."

"I take it you worked at McDonald's once."

"Girlfriend, I'm only twenty-four and I've worked a good portion of all the low-paying, demoralizing jobs this world has to offer. I've scrubbed the urine and shit of the most arrogant assholes—again, no pun intended—off toilets at the Las Vegas Country Club. Don't get me wrong. I'm not saying I want a career on my back—that's why I'm in school—but it's not the worst job I've ever worked, and it pays a hell of a lot better than most. This is one long fucking highway."

"Where are we?" I asked, peering into the darkness at the moonlit desert outside the window.

"Somewhere between Ely and Carson City—how the hell would I know? My usual route is Highway 95. I'd already have next month's rent paid if I hadn't let you talk me into the Omer Springs detour—not that it wasn't enlightening."

"Okay," I said. "Got it. Whorehouse Rule Number One: No heart. No head."

"No pun intended?"

"I actually planned that one," I said.

"Funny," she replied, without a smile. "Whorehouse joke. I love whorehouse jokes."

I reached over and cranked the radio up; Bets turned it back down.

"Cassie, I'm serious about this. Not everyone is cut out for this kind of work."

"I can handle it."

"What makes you think so?"

"If you can do it, I can do it."

"Brilliant reasoning process."

I reached over and cranked the radio up; Bets turned it down again.

"I sure as hell wouldn't do it if I didn't have to," she said. "I wouldn't do it if I had a mother with a high-paying job writing out checks for my college fund. And I damn sure wouldn't do it just to prove some sort of point to my family or whatever the hell this little plan of yours involves."

I focused on the edge of the road where the headlight met the darkness near the front bumper, trying to momentarily snag with my eye a swatch of sagebrush as it slid by. Driving away from Omer Springs on a warm summer night made me feel like a calf corralled away from its mother for weaning. I felt like opening my mouth and filling the night with one long, sad bawl after another.

"There's something wrong in my family, Bets," I said, pulling myself out of Omer Springs and back to the dark highway, steeling myself to stick with my plan.

"Hell, Cassie, there's something wrong in every family."

"No, I mean really wrong. I mean eat-you-from-the-inside-out-like-maggots-in-a-dead-cow sort of wrong."

"I don't know, Cassie. Your dad's kind of a dickhead and your mom's a little cold, but—"

"My dad doesn't matter—he's a harmless sort of dickhead—and this doesn't have anything to do with him."

"Maybe your grandma didn't like your mom's choice when she married your dad."

"She didn't. Hated it. But Grandma Nell would not only forgive Mama for that, she'd embrace it as an opportunity for incessant needling. Whatever's gnawing away at the Jorgensen family predates my father. This is between Mama and Grandma Nell."

"What was your Grandpa like?"

"I never knew him. He was killed in a hunting accident when Mama was ten. But from what I've heard, he was quite charming."

"What happened?"

"That, my friend, is an excellent question."

"What does your mother say about it?"

"Nothing at all."

"What does your grandma say?"

"Somehow, and I don't know how, I was born with the knowledge that I was not allowed to ask that question."

"Maybe it's time you ask it anyway."

"I plan to. But not until I get Mama, Grandma Nell, Uncle Nate, and Aunt Ona all in the same room so they can't pass me off to the next one. And that's not as easy as it might sound. In fact, I don't know that I've ever actually witnessed that sort of family gathering since I was seven years old."

"That's fucked up."

"That's what I'm trying to tell you. That's why I'm sticking to my plan."

I reached over and turned the radio back up. Cat Power. Bets started singing. I joined her. Singing along to Cat Power on the way to the cathouse. Those are the kinds of things I appreciate about Bets.

In spite of Grandma Nell's intentions to neutralize my mother's malevolence by sending me off to an environmental studies program, Mama also thought the plan a solid one and offered to pay my tuition if I agreed to live with her. At the end of the summer after the pipeline was announced, at both my mother's and grandmother's insistence, as if each were outdoing the other with their show of magnanimity, I moved to Las Vegas and into my mother's condo, which she shares with Derek, her nerdy, cool boyfriend.

That started off a big to-do between Mama and Dipshit because he doesn't approve of her living with a man "outside the sanctity of marriage" and didn't like the idea of me being exposed to that sort of lifestyle. Meanwhile, Dipshit is married to a woman eight years my senior, eighteen years his junior, with big fake boobs, the cost of which prevents him from contributing to my college education. I have two currently adorable—soon to be insufferable—toddling stepsiblings who call him Father.

The living situation with Mama and Derek turned out to be okay. I like Derek. In fact, I currently like him better than Mama or Grandma Nell or Dipshit. He's a computer systems designer by day and an amateur jazz musician by night. He's totally zen. I have not yet figured out what he sees in Mama, and I don't think she's quite sure either. It's not that she's unattractive, actually the opposite. She has base beauty—the kind you don't get from makeup or hairstyles or clothing or jewelry—just a simple coming together of all physical structures from head to toe in a near-perfect way, with the exception of a scar that runs from the right corner of her mouth to the outer edge of her jawbone. But she wears the scar well—never attempts to shift away from it—so it barely distracts from the fineness of the overall picture. In fact, it seems to tie the whole package together with pretty pink string.

Mama does her damndest to hide her attractiveness under severe business suits and practical, short haircuts—she seems embarrassed by it—but it emerges in spite of her efforts. Every time she catches Derek staring at her—which he does with amazing consistency—her body subconsciously slouches and her face contorts. She seems to be encouraging him to leave, but he appears to be in love with her.

Living with my mother and Derek had a politeness-of-strangers way about it. I remember a few visits from her shortly after she took me to Omer Springs to live, but the more years that went by, the less frequent the visits became. Uncle Nate often said, "We should take you to visit your mother," Aunt Ona would nod enthusiastically, and Grandma Nell would grunt, but I understood the words held more apology than intent.

Before I left the ranch for college, I had assumed family dinner took the same form in all households—an evening meal around which family members reviewed the day past, previewed the next, argued a little, and discussed their own variation of what came in the mail and who said what at the post office. That never materialized at Mama's condo, though not for lack of trying on Derek's part. My mother and I seemed to naturally set up patterns that allowed us minimal interaction on any given day. If my classes didn't start until 10 a.m., she went to the office early. If I had no evening classes, she worked late. Other than the first night I moved in, we managed to avoid dinner together for nearly a month before Derek wrangled us in to celebrate his own birthday.

Several times after I moved in with them, I tried to force my mother into a discussion about the water issue, but I kept coming at it in a non-direct way, giving her too much time to deflect. The last time I tried was the evening of Derek's birthday. What I found out is that my mother is a fierce adversary—the folks in Omer Springs have good reason to worry.

I still feel bad about ruining Derek's birthday, but the pipeline had been the topic of a heated discussion in my seminar that morning, which may have been a good opportunity for me to point out that ranchers and environmentalists are sharing the same side of this issue, but I chose instead to perpetuate my ignorant country bumpkin image, which allows me to be blessedly dismissed and ignored most of the time. Nevertheless, the discussion had stirred up my worry for Grandma Nell and Uncle Nate. So I simply asked Mama, "What's up with that pipeline?"

Well, flustered is the only way I can describe her reaction, as if she never expected the topic to come up, though she certainly must spend the majority of her waking hours thinking and speaking about said topic. Her face flushed red, then purplish, as she cast around the table for help from Derek before regaining her composure and settling into a furious glare directed at me.

"I will not be explaining myself to you," she said with control, as if speaking across a large conference table. Then she pushed against the table, disturbing the birthday wine, and left

Derek and me gazing into our bucatini carbonara.

"Are you okay?" Derek asked.

"I'm sorry, Derek. I didn't mean to mess up dinner."

"You've nothing to apologize for, Cassie."

"Apparently I've managed to uncover yet another unmentionable topic in my family."

"You've run across a few others, have you?"

"Yes, haven't you?"

"Yes."

"What is wrong with this family?"

"I'm not sure, Cassie. I'm not sure."

After that we went back to our formal ways and separate schedules, which worked out fine for the remainder of the school year.

I left for Carson City three days after my twenty-first birthday, which, because of my totally screwed up pre-college education, fell at the end of my freshman year. Mama assumed I would be spending my summer at the ranch; I didn't correct her. Bets and I did drive out to the ranch on our way here, but we only stayed overnight. I told Grandma Nell I had a summer job in Vegas. Step one of my plan—both of them believing I was with the other would be a good way to demonstrate the pitfalls of them not speaking to each other.

——◆——

When I emerge from my room, Maggie is sitting on her usual stool at the far end of the bar.

"Who the hell gave you the day off?" she asks, taking note of my non brothel-like attire and hiking boots.

"Mick drew me some maps to some hiking trails. I'm going to go check them out."

"Does Mick pay your salary?"

"Nobody pays her salary," Mick says. "You'd think doing

your bidding for nothing would be enough to send her back home where she belongs, but she's too damn stubborn."

"Since when is room and board nothing?" Maggie asks.

"Since your boarder here don't eat more'n a bird," Mick replies.

"Hell, she drinks her salary in Coke every day," Maggie says.

Mick goes into the kitchen and comes out carrying a paper bag. "Here," he says handing it to me. "I had the kitchen pack you a lunch."

"Let me see that," Maggie says, grabbing the bag from Mick's hands and peering inside. She grunts her approval before folding the top back down and handing it to me. "You got water? Mick, give her a couple of bottles of water. Let me see that map you're talking about."

I pull Mick's maps out of my back pocket and hand them to Maggie as Mick pushes three bottles of water across the bar and winks at me. Maggie unfolds the papers, pulling her glasses from their storage place—her cleavage—and spreads the maps on the bar in front of her. "Which one of these you doing?" she asks.

"I thought I'd do the Ophir Creek trail."

Maggie looks at Mick, and he nods.

"Pay attention to where you are out there," Mick says. "There are a couple of sections of trail that aren't marked very well." Maggie keeps looking at Mick. "She'll be fine," he says to her. "She grew up on a ranch, Maggie. She knows how to read the land."

"Well I ain't about to send out a search and rescue party, so like Mick says, pay attention to what you're doing out there." She refolds the papers and hands them back to me. "You got sunscreen?"

"I'll stop at the Top Spot and get some on my way out of town."

"Here," she says to me, while she signals to Mick with her right hand. "Pick me up some butterscotch Lifesavers while you're there." Mick opens the cash drawer and hands Maggie a five-dollar bill. She shakes her head. Mick puts the five back and gives her a twenty, which she gives to me. "Make sure you buy decent sun block—at least a thirty. You got that? And that water ain't for carrying; it's for drinking."

"Okay," I say. "Anything else you need at the Top Spot?" Maggie releases me with a nonchalant wave of her hand, and Mick winks again.

It had been a little over a month since Bets and I had exited the doctor's office in Carson City after getting blood drawn and what can only be described as a McDonald's drive-thru gynecological exam in preparation for my new employment as a Carson City prostitute, although, technically speaking, the brothels are outside the city limits. Bets had taken one look at me when we stepped into the hot, midmorning sun and proclaimed that I was not yet ready to face Maggie at the Wild Filly Stables.

"It's the combination of blood loss and heat," I had told her.

"Well, you're going to want all your wits about you the first time you meet Maggie. She sets out to intimidate new girls, and she's pretty good at it."

Bets drove us into the desert at the edge of town, and we settled into the shade of a boulder. She lit a joint and passed it to me.

"Don't know how pot and more heat are going to help," I said.

"Cassie, I'm not sure you're cut out for this," she said.

"How much money could I make for the summer?" I asked her.

"Well, I make a good chunk of cash, I can't deny that, but I work twelve hours a day, seven days a week for three months. And I have a steady clientele I've built up over the last three years. I'm already booked solid a month out."

"You mean twelve hours a day doing—"

"That's exactly what I mean."

"My God, I don't think I can do that, Bets."

"That's what I've been trying to tell you for the last three hundred miles."

"How can you do that?"

"I already told you—it's better than a lot of shit jobs I've had, and I don't think about it much beyond that, which is why we are going to stop talking about it now."

"But what about my plan?"

"Your plan? Let me see if I have this right. Your plan is to do something that will get your mother and grandmother riled up enough about you that they will forget they aren't speaking to each other and come running to save you?"

"That's the plan."

"Then what?"

"That's as far as I have it worked out."

"Shit, Cassie, that's a lame plan."

"Tell me something I don't know."

"Well, Maggie acts tougher than she really is. I can probably talk her into giving up a room for a night or two before you start back to Omer Springs."

"But I can't go back to Omer Springs! What am I going to do there all summer?"

"Hell if I know. I have no idea what people do in places

like that. What did you do every summer before this one?"

"Hauled hay, fenced, worked cattle, irrigated."

"Sounds awful."

"Actually, I like all that stuff."

"Then what's the problem?"

"The problem is that I cannot be in the middle of my family anymore. Grandma Nell's been getting crazier by the minute ever since Mama went on television and announced that pipeline. The whole town's gone schizo. If Katherine Ann Jorgensen, deputy water resource manager of Nevada Water Authority wasn't also Katie Jorgensen, Henry and Nell's baby girl, I think they'd have a bounty out on her. I'm staying here for the summer, Bets. I'll just do it."

"Come on. Next stop is the sheriff's office, where they fingerprint you and treat you like a common criminal instead of a common whore. Then I'll let you flip through the two-inch thick three-ring binder outlining the rules at the Wild Filly Stables. That might persuade you otherwise."

"Do you really think it was wise to get stoned before we go to the sheriff's office?" I asked.

"I most certainly do," Bets replied.

⁂

"I ain't running no homeless shelter for confused, wayward girls, Ilsa," Maggie had bellowed that first day I met her. She poured herself a club soda, the flowing sleeves of what appeared to be a floor-length, low-cut shimmering nightgown skimming the surface of the bar as she moved. I found out later that Maggie had her "gowns" (*don't call it a damn nightgown!*) special made, and she had a closet full of them, similar in style and fabric but varying in color and design. "She wants to work, she can work, though she don't really look up for the job. Otherwise, she can get her skinny ass out the door."

Bets and I were sitting on two swiveling, red velour-covered barstools drinking Coke through those skinny, stirring kind of straws. My eyes were just barely beginning to adjust to the low-lit interior of the Wild Filly Stables bar, and I was marveling at the luster of the place. Everything gleamed—the glasses, the mirrors behind the bar, the brass around the bar, the dark wood bar itself. Mick was shining glasses with a bar towel, just like every bartender in every movie I'd ever seen, and stacking them against the mirror. Still grousing about my appearance in her establishment, Maggie grabbed mine and Bets' glasses and turned to refill them, shooting the Coke into the glass full force and stopping precisely at the rim.

"Who's Ilsa?" I whispered to Bets after seeing that Maggie was going to continue her tirade for a bit.

"That's me," Bets whispered back. "Men love exotic foreigners. When I'm not too tired, I have a decent accent to accommodate the name."

"Very *Casablanca*," I said.

"Exactly," Bets said. "Maggie, it's only for one or two nights while Cassie gets a bit of sleep and figures out what she wants to do. We've been driving two straight days, for hell sakes."

"And you wanna tell me why it took you two days to get here from Las Vegas?" Maggie said. She put the refilled glasses down in front of us with a definitive thud, jiggling the ample bosom, lined with the years, spilling out of her gown.

"We took a few detours."

"And now it's my problem, that it? How do you figure? Mick, you think it's my problem Ilsa's friend here's been driving two straight days and is now looking for a free room?"

"She's sitting on your barstool, Maggie," Mick said, winking at me. "That makes her your problem."

"How does everything become my problem?" Maggie continued. "How do the problems of this world find their way through my door, I ask you?"

"Must be your charisma," Mick said.

"It's bullshit is what it is," Maggie said. "You get that damn computer figured out for me, Mick?"

"I told you, Maggie, I can make any drink any person can name—you can challenge me on that any day of the week. But you ain't gonna get a computer designer for bartender wages. You're gonna have to unclench that tight ass of yours and hire somebody."

"Oh, I miss the old days," Maggie said, pulling herself onto the stool next to Bets, "when you could hire a guy actually knew how to do a few things."

"I can fix your computer," I said.

Maggie pulled herself up with elbows and breasts on the bar to look past Bets at me. "I ain't even told you what's wrong with the damn thing," she said. "What makes you think you can fix it?"

"What's wrong with it?" I asked.

"Probably nothing," she said, settling back onto her stool. "Everybody here's just too damn stupid to work it."

"I can work it," I said.

Maggie looked at Bets, and Bets nodded.

"I'll give you room and board for as long as it takes you to get it working right," Maggie said. "Anything beyond that, you'll have to work alongside your friend here."

Bets started to protest.

"Deal," I said, cutting her off. I figured if nobody there knew anything about computers I could stretch it out for the summer, but in the end, I didn't have to. It took Maggie less than a week to realize she'd found just what she'd always wanted in me—a girl she didn't have to pay to run all the menial errands of her life. And that's how I ended up occupying the end barstool at the Wild Filly Stables.

———

I know that my concocted plan is extreme in nature, but if you twist your mind in just the right way, which I am adept at doing, it can make a certain amount of sense. I set out to be a prostitute for the summer, and if I'm to believe Grandma Nell, prostitution runs in my family. She says Mama prostitutes herself every time she walks out the door to go to work. I was a sophomore in high school the first time Grandma Nell said this to me. We were sitting at the kitchen table with Uncle Nate and Aunt Ona, finishing off a beef stew we'd been working on more than a week. On the rare occasions when she cooks, Grandma Nell has an unexplained tendency to cook for twenty people at a time, and it's almost always beef stew. I reminded Grandma Nell that my mother worked at the Nevada Water Authority in broad daylight—I wasn't sure where Grandma Nell might be thinking she worked—but in response, Grandma Nell pulled the M to Z volume of *Funk and Wagnalls New Standard Dictionary of the English Language* out of the junk cupboard, spilling a cache of old Christmas cards across the floor in the process, and dropped it on the kitchen table with a thud, causing my milk to slop over the edges of my glass. She pushed the book toward me and instructed me to look up "prostitute."

"Nell, you shouldn't be speaking that way to this child. What the hell's wrong with you?" Uncle Nate had asked.

"She ain't a child anymore, Nate," Grandma said, looking me up and down.

"Still, Nell."

"What's it say? Read it out loud," Grandma said to me.

"Prostitute: A person who performs or offers to perform an evil service for gain. A base or unprincipled hireling."

"Evil service? Hireling?" Aunt Ona said. "Nell, I believe you may need to invest in an updated dictionary."

"There you go," Grandma said, ignoring Aunt Ona. She leaned over and slammed the book shut, sending a flurry of dust into the air and almost catching my fingers in the process. "If that ain't a perfect description of Katherine Ann, then I don't know what is."

"Nell, for hell sakes," Uncle Nate said.

"Ever wonder why dictionaries all name themselves 'new'?" I asked, tracing the title of the old *Funk and Wagnalls* with my fingertips. I flipped the first few pages. "This dictionary was published in 1938. I think that shows staggering optimism on their part."

"Cassie, your mind does catch some strange snags," Grandma Nell said. She said that a lot. "What're our numbers for today?"

"Fifty-eight for the men; sixty-one for the women."

Uncle Nate waited patiently for an explanation, which Grandma Nell provided.

"It's Cassie's theory, based on her daily reading of death calls—"

"Obituaries," I corrected.

"—in the *Review-Journal*, that the experts who claim to know the average life span of men and women in this country—and in Nevada in particular—are a little off."

"According to my calculations, you and Grandma should be dead now," I explained to Uncle Nate. "Aunt Ona should be dead before her next birthday."

"Well, I hope to live long enough to get some hay baled tomorrow morning," Uncle Nate said.

"I don't want you guys writing my obituary when I'm dead," I said.

"Well, I sorta figure it will be the other way around," said Grandma Nell, "but for the hell of it, I'm gonna ask anyway. Why not?"

"Have you ever noticed how the obituary writer tries so hard to make the dead one sound special and how utterly ordinary they all end up?" I asked.

"No, Cassie," Grandma Nell said, "because most of us have better things to do with our time."

"Everyone fights courageous and valiant battles with cancer and lives life to the fullest and loves the outdoors and lights up rooms with their smiles. It's tedious stuff."

"Exactly why we don't read it," Grandma Nell said.

"But it's written with such wretched desperation. *Please, please, please* they all beg, *please understand how extraordinary this ordinary person really was.* One of the reasons I keep reading these things is in the hopes that I'll one time see someone write the honest-to-god truth. *He was a miserable coward who hated the outdoors and wasted his life in front of the television. We're glad he's gone.*"

"If it makes you feel any better, Cassie, feel free to write that about me when I die," Uncle Nate said.

"But it isn't true about you, Uncle Nate."

"Well, just to even things out. I'm fine with that. Come on, Ona, let's get outta here. Appreciate the stew and the cheerful conversation."

"If you all are leaving the writing of your obituaries up to me," I told them, "I'm going to write the ordinary truth."

Aunt Ona paused as if she were about to say something. I held my breath. Aunt Ona had been pausing as if she had something to say for as long as I'd known her. Uncle Nate and Grandma Nell pretty much just ignored it, but I figured if the world paused just long enough with her, Aunt Ona might finally say what's on her mind. I wasn't sure how long that might take, but I wanted to find out. I mentioned this to Grandma Nell once, and she pointed out once again that I have a mind made of fine silk—snags easily. But I figured Aunt Ona was hoarding some information pertinent to my life, some little tidbits that could fill in a few blanks—like why Mama and Grandma Nell had always spoken to each other with such polite formality that unless you'd noticed the same deep-set, narrow, gray eyes dominating the faces of both, you'd think they'd just met that very moment.

"The ordinary truth," Aunt Ona repeated. "Ain't nothing wrong with that." I believe she might have continued, but Grandma Nell was already up clearing dishes, Jasper was yawning, and Uncle Nate was headed for the door. Aunt Ona pushed her breath out through the space between her front teeth, signifying her decision to say nothing more.

NELL

Nate and Skinny move around me with nails and hammers, making repairs on the picnic tables under the cottonwoods in preparation for hauling them down to the city park. Skinny, a course, is not skinny less you look at him from only the butt down. He's a wedge-shaped Navajo, mid fifties, arrived here twenty years ago in an old pickup looked like it'd been used as a bowling ball. Skinny's only way outta the truck was to crawl out the window or take the time to twist open the baling wire holding the door shut. At that time, he chose the window, but he's since removed the baling wire for easy entrance and exit. Now whenever he makes the turn at the end a our lane, that door flies open, and when he takes the next turn in the opposite direction, it closes.

Skinny told us he was looking for work and didn't seem inclined to share much more'n that. He was a good bit older'n most looking for ranch work, but Nate took him on and gave him the standard speech: *The work is hard and the pay is fair, but it ain't gonna make you rich. If we ain't satisfied with the work you do, we'll ask you to move along and 'spect you'll do so without causing no problems.* Skinny gave one nod in lieu of a handshake, and he's been here since.

Most a the boys who stop here disappear a their own volition when the work starts interfering with their romantic notions a being a cowboy. Cept for Skinny, seems we don't keep a hand longer than a season these days. I showed Skinny to the bunkhouse that day and told him to take his pick a the available bunks—we had two no-goods working for us at the time who had less than stellar housekeeping skills. Skinny had his belongings in an army duffel slung over one shoulder, but stead a setting it down he walked to the back window and looked out at a falling-down shed surrounded by dilapidated corrals at the south end a our property, where my grandmother used to keep her milking goats.

"It's a mess, but you're welcome to it," I told him. "You'll find tools and materials for fixing it up in the barn. Take what you need outta here to give yourself a place to lay your head."

Ona thought Nate and I had lost our minds. Said there wasn't no reason for a Navajo man like that to leave his people and his place less he was running from something. I figure she was probably right. I don't know much more about Skinny now than I did twenty years ago, cept that his last name is Joe and his people come from the Four Corners area of New Mexico, and when he thinks about them he gets a look a sadness across his brown face that could pry open your heart and bleed it dry.

Skinny worked out a deal with Nate to run his own small sheep operation on part a the Baxter Ranch, which made the entire town a Omer Springs shake their heads at us. Everybody knows that sheepherders and cattle ranchers don't mix. Even now, the sheepherders gather at one end a Frank's bar and the cattle ranchers at the other. Still, Skinny managed over the years to get himself some public grazing permits, not an easy thing to acquire in these parts. That alone says a lot about Skinny. In exchange for the broken-down corrals a ours he uses, he supplies us with lamb and mutton, usually in the form of a fully cooked dutch-oven meal left wordlessly on the bench in the mud room.

Skinny had arrived at the Baxter Ranch about this same time a year—just before the Omer Springs July Fourth potluck—and during that time Frank's place was full a talk about the outlaw Indian we'd taken in. Nate and me didn't pay that sorta talk much mind cause folks round here just need something to gnaw on from time to time, and it don't take much to get them chewing their cuds. Then Skinny showed up at the potluck with all the makings for Indian fry bread, which everybody accepted with such enthusiasm they were forced to accept the Indian making it, which put an end to the talk.

"Nell, old girl, could you move yourself to one a the other tables so Skinny and I can repair the one you're setting at?" Nate asks me.

Skinny grins at me. We have exchanged few words over the years, but I believe we connect somewhere around the gut—hold a sorrow. That might be an old, white woman's delusion, but since Skinny ain't ever gonna speak up and refute it, it's mine to keep.

"I'm skipping the potluck this year," I tell Nate. "Spending my Fourth a July right here."

"Like hell you will," Nate says. "You're gonna get yourself a lawn chair and plop your old butt in it down at the park."

"I'm not feeling social these days."

"Then you'll fit right in. Nobody sees much cause for celebration this year."

"Then what we all gathering for?"

"Cause that's what we do on the Fourth."

"Things change, Nate. Haven't you noticed?"

"This ain't the time for breaking tradition. Right now,

that's all anyone round here has to hang onto."

"I don't think I'll be missed much if I sit this one out."

"You're wrong about that, sis. You been sitting out the entire year, and you've been missed like hell. I miss you. Everybody misses you. They depend on you—they always have. You own the largest ranch out here."

"*We* own the largest ranch out here."

"Just the same, Nell, you know what I'm talking about. There ain't been a decision made in Omer Springs during your lifetime that you ain't been the lead horse on. You were the one who stood up and fought the expansion a the Moriah Wilderness."

"If you remember right, I lost that fight."

"Don't matter. Folks are scared and confused, and the one person they depend on to gather em up and calm em down and put a plan in place ain't nowhere to be seen."

"Clan mother," Skinny says, waving a hammer in my direction.

"Skinny's right, Nell."

"I don't wanna be anybody's goddamn clan mother."

"Not a choice," Skinny says.

"Skinny, you pick the damndest times to join the conversation." He hammers another nail into the table, refusing comment on my observation. "In case everybody hasn't noticed, I'm not all that well-suited for motherhood." Neither of them responds. I look toward Nate's house. "What's Ona up to?"

"Nell, you've lived among these people your entire life," Nate says. "That's a damn long time. You're going to the park tomorrow if I have to hogtie you and haul you down there myself."

"You've become a little bossy lately, Nate."

"Somebody had to fill the void you left."

"What the hell am I gonna say when everyone starts bugging me about talking to Katie?"

"I think folks have pretty much given up on that idea, Nell, but just in case, you can do what Skinny and Frank do whenever anyone probes them beyond the polite into the personal—nod and smile and hand them a plate a food. Seems to work for them," Nate says.

Skinny smiles and nods as if to show how it's done.

"Those two were smart enough to set the precedent a keeping their business to themselves from the git-go. None a the rest of us had that kinda foresight," I say, watching Skinny's fat, nimble fingers wind baling wire around the end of a table to pull the splitting wood down to the frame. He grins and chuckles without ever looking up.

"Whatdaya say, Skinny? Will you put me to work making fry bread this year so's I can avoid the usual Omer Springs chitchat? You're gonna need an extra person anyway, with Cassie gone."

"Cassie was in charge of oil," he says. "You can do that. Make sure it stays hot."

"Good enough."

"Apparently you ain't never seen what Nell can do in the kitchen, Skinny," Nate says. "Things you never thought a putting in the weapon category can become instruments a death once Nell gets hold a them. And this year's picnic will sure as hell be an emotionally charged one. That ain't no time to be putting something like hot oil in Nell's hands. You better take her off oil detail and put her in charge a dough—something with less potential to cause injury to herself and others."

"Can't," Skinny says. "Dough takes a real Indian." He looks at the ground thoughtfully. "Paper products," he says, nodding in my direction as if he's solved the world's biggest problem. "Napkins, plates, and forks."

His eyes catch mine briefly before we both shift our gaze to the ground.

———

I remember the first Fourth a July after Henry died, another one I didn't feel like showing up for. But in a town this size, absences are notable—especially after something like that happens—and the July Fourth picnic is the annual summing up. Always has been. Folks can go on about their business the rest a the year—visit family elsewhere, pass kidney stones and so forth, but come the Fourth, you show up at the park with a dish in your hands. Period. In the hospital or in the ground would be the only two legitimate excuses for not being there— and the hospital is questionable. The year after Henry died, everybody in town was looking forward to the Fourth a July picnic as the measuring stick to see if I was doing all right or gone plum crazy.

The reality was the latter. I knew it, but thought I was hiding it pretty well. We had gone through the winter after Henry's death in silence. The entire family. Nobody knew what to say, so they didn't say anything. We don't get a lotta snow in this valley, but that winter seems like it never quit snowing. It took till the next May before it all melted.

Katie and I shared the same house, but I'm not sure we spoke a hundred words to each other during those months. She didn't go back to school until the following January, and nobody seemed to mind or even notice. Henry had driven her to school every morning and picked her up again every after-noon. No one dared step into that role, as if to do so would confirm his death, so she simply stopped going. In those months, Katie would get up before daylight, fix herself toast and jam, and leave the house before I got outta bed. On the rare occasion she might hear me stirring before she got herself out the door, she'd stay in her bedroom with the door closed until I went outside. Then she'd make her escape.

When the weather allowed it, Katie saddled a horse and headed straight for the Snakes. I never knew until years later where she went. If it was cold outside, Katie would slip into Mom and Dad's kitchen or into Nate and Ona's. They'd get up to find her asleep by the wood stove, feed her breakfast, and then invariably they would send her back home to me. *You and your mama need each other right now*, they'd say. Damn fools, all a them. A flagrant and raw tension festered between us. She woulda been better off almost anywhere but with me. I tried. I really tried because I promised Henry I would. But the only thing that had ever tethered me and Katie together was buried in the family plot. That's a horrible thing for a mother to say, but that's the truth of it.

I awoke before dawn the morning a the picnic. It had been nine miserable months without Henry. I stood before the open closet looking at his shirts, which I often did, talking to him as if the clothing still held the man. There were empty hangers among the shirts that I'd never noticed before.

"Henry," I said that morning. "I don't know how to live with Katie. I look at her and all I feel is the loss a you, and she feels the same when she looks at me. I'm gonna try to set that aside and be a mother to her like I promised. Starting today. We'll go down to the picnic—mother and daughter—and make you proud a us. And who knows—maybe little by little we can help each other."

With that, I closed the closet doors and went to Katie's room. I didn't intend to wake her—it was still early—but wanted to look upon her and see if I could feel something that a mother might feel when she gazes upon the sleeping face a her daughter. When I opened the door, the light from the hallway hit her directly. She had her back to the door and the covers flung off. I recognized Henry's denim work shirt covering her back. I moved closer. Her pillow was on the floor, and her head rested on one a Henry's white T-shirts. I felt something rise in me, but I couldn't at the time identify the emotion. Grief? Sadness? Maybe even a rush a compassion for that suffering child? Any one a those woulda been appropriate. But it was none a those—not purely, anyway. It was jealousy. Henry was mine from the day I met him. And he was supposed to be mine forever. But I'd lost him ten years prior—the day Katie was born. Up until nine months before, I made it through my days holding onto dreams a having him back, dreams a putting things back to the way they'd been before she came along. That was never gonna happen now. So what right did she have to him? What right did she have to sleep with the scent a him next to her body when I no longer could?

I shoulda picked that child up and held her in my arms. I shoulda buried my nose into Henry's shirt covering her small, bony shoulders and told her that I too love the feel a him next to me, that I too often sleep in one a his unwashed shirts where an identifiable scent still lingers by which I can tell what he was doing on the day he wore it. At the very least I shoulda turned right around and closed the door behind me. But I didn't do either a those things. I didn't mean to hurt her; I just wanted Henry's things back. They belonged to me. But by the time I reached the bed and pulled the T-shirt out from under her head, she was already awake. By the time I ripped the front snaps of his shirt open to expose her frail chest, she was sobbing. When I left her sitting on the bed in only her underpants, she was wailing. I closed the door to block the sound.

KATE

My therapist has horrible taste in carpet—some sort of black and brown squiggling pattern designed to hide dirt and spills, something you would put in a pediatrician's waiting room. The carpet, however, is likely not the only reason I feel like an anxious child waiting to see the principal every time I arrive at this office five minutes early, which I try to never do. Today I'm a full ten minutes early after a news conference—strategically staged on the hour in front of the Bellagio dancing fountains and ten-acre lake of reclaimed water—ended with too little time to return to the office. I like to time my appointments so I'm walking in just as my therapist appears in the waiting room to retrieve me. That way, I avoid both the carpet and the perpetually serene look on the face of the woman who holds the time slot before mine. She invariably gives me one of those no-teeth-showing smiles, as if she's discovered some secret to life I've yet to understand. I hate her. So I keep my head down and swipe at the tiny screen of my iPhone in an attempt to ignore the sound of the water chimes on the table next to me until my therapist's face bops cheerfully and calmly around the corner and says "Kate" as if the face and head are only loosely attached to the lanky body that follows. All this tranquility unnerves me.

When I'm finally settled in the worn, brown chair in his small office clutching the pillow that, I suppose, is meant to offer back support, he begins as usual.

"So, last week we were talking about your father," he says.

"No we weren't," I say. "You always think we're talking about my father. You think everything I say, do and think is about my father."

"Let's talk about your life with your father—before the accident."

"Let's not."

"What are you afraid of?"

Christ almighty. I don't know why I keep coming to this guy. Those lines are straight out of a manual, aren't they?

"Why can't we talk about crappy sex or bad marriages, like you do with your other clients?" I ask him. "Why do you always want to talk about my past?"

"We can talk about anything you want. Would you like to talk about your relationship with Derek?"

"Not really."

"Why not?"

I swear to God. What does this guy want from me?

"No reason. I just don't have anything to say about Derek."

"Things going all right with the two of you?"

"Fine. Except he digs too much. You two have that in common."

"Isn't that what you pay me for?"

"Well, that's a damn good question—probably the best one you've come up with in months."

"What's Derek digging for?"

"Another excellent question."

"Does it bother you that he digs?"

"Yes. And it bothers me that you do, yet I write you checks

for it. I should have my head examined."

"That's funny."

"I wasn't trying to be."

A silent pause. This guy loves those. I suppose all therapists have that silent pause down to an art, especially with us so-called high-strung types who don't have the patience to out-pause them.

"Derek wants to drive to Omer Springs and meet my mother."

"How do you feel about that?"

"Which part?"

"All of it."

"I don't see any reason for it."

"Do you need a reason to visit your mother?"

"Yes, I do."

"Why is that?"

"Because if I show up in Omer Springs without a good reason, everybody's going to assume something's wrong."

"Who's everybody?"

"Nell. Uncle Nate. Aunt Ona. Cassie. The entire population of Omer Springs."

"And why would they assume that?"

"Because if I show up in Omer Springs without a good reason, something would be wrong."

"And why is that?"

"I don't know what you mean."

"Couldn't you explain to your mother that you came to visit because you miss her?"

"No, I could not."

"Why not?"

"Because that would be a bald-faced lie. Do you lie to your mother like that?"

"So you don't miss your mother?"

"No."

"Do you miss anything about Omer Springs?"

"Yes."

"What?"

"My father."

"Let's talk about him."

"Do you ever get the feeling we're talking in circles here? I've been coming to you for three years, and I feel like I'm trapped in a game of fox and geese."

"You often refer to children's games to describe your life, Kate. Are you aware of that?"

"Are you suggesting that I'm stuck in adolescence, that my development got retarded somewhere around the time of my father's death? Because, again, that would not be one of your most profound insights. That's sort of a no-brainer, isn't it?"

He smiles—a calm, serene smile. I notice my jaw is clenched.

"Tell me a memory of your father."

"Why?"

"Why not?"

I shrug. "I don't like to talk about him."

"Why not?"

I shrug again.

"Do you feel like he betrayed you by dying?" he asks.

"No. I'm not ten. I understand that shit happens and people die."

"Did you understand that at the time?"

"I have no idea what I did or did not understand at the time."

"Did you blame your mother for your father's death?"

"No one blamed her. Like I said, shit happens. It was an accident."

"But you missed your father after the accident?"

"Of course."

"What did you miss most about him?"

"There is no single one thing—I missed all of him. Everybody did."

"Of course."

"No, not 'of course.' You don't get it. Any other person on the ranch could have died, and we would have been fine. We'd have mourned like people do and then gone on with life. After Dad died, there was no going on. People say 'life goes on' as if that's a given, but it's not."

"Tell me about him, Kate. Tell me what made him so special."

"I can't. You just had to know him."

"Let's try this. Close your eyes and picture one particular moment with him."

I look at him, and he nods reassuringly. What the hell. I'm paying him a ridiculous amount of money, might as well play along. I lean back in the chair and close my eyes. Immediately, Dad comes into focus, which is not all that unusual, although I don't tell my therapist that. My mind begins to fill in details of the picture, and I'm jarred by my therapist's voice.

"Tell me what you're seeing, Kate."

"Dad at our summer camp on the mountain."

"Who else is there?"

"Nobody else. Just me and Dad. Every summer we hired a cowboy to camp on the mountain—move cattle, mend fences, keep an eye on things. The summer I was eight, we didn't hire a herder. I don't know why—maybe we couldn't find anyone. That summer we rotated camping up there—sometimes

Uncle Nate would go, sometimes Mom would go, sometimes Grandpa Bax, and sometimes Dad would go—usually for a couple of weeks at a time. There was too much work to get done on the ranch with haying and irrigating—and that same year we were building a new barn—so no one went in pairs except me and Dad. I always went when he went."

"Did your mother join you?"

"No."

"Did you ever go up with her?"

"No."

A silent pause.

"Go on, please, Kate. So you and your father camped up there together."

"Yes. We kept four or five horses in camp, but Dad always rode a palomino gelding named Moots, and I always rode a stout buckskin named Yogi. The horses were turned loose at night to graze. Usually, they'd come into camp looking for oats every morning, but if not, we'd have to walk out and get them. We put a bell on Yogi so we could find them. One morning, my father was battling a cold, so I got up early and took Ralphie, Dad's yellow lab, to bring in the horses before he woke up. I climbed to the top of a knoll and stood listening. Only silence. I couldn't see or hear them. But it had rained during the night, and when I walked down off the knoll toward the meadow where they usually were, I could see hoof prints leading up a steep cattle trail, so I followed.

"I caught sight of them just as I topped the ridge. They were spread out in glistening wet grass against a blue-black cloud, their backs glazed with rain, necks bowed and noses to the ground, as if they hadn't yet noticed the dawning of the day. I don't know what it was about that scene, but it stilled me immediately. Ralphie, too. I stopped, and Ralphie sat down at my side, both of us entranced. I had an urge to run back to camp for Dad. It was the kind of moment he refused to let go unnoticed, the kind of scene he'd stop dead still to appreciate no matter what he was doing."

A silent pause.

"Tell me more," he says. "What do you remember?"

"I remember a cool breeze blowing my hair away from my face and rustling the aspen leaves. The air smelled of rain, wet wood and rotting leaves—the kind of smell you can't get on the desert floor. I remember the single clink of the bell every time Yogi stepped forward as he grazed. That sound—that deep clank in the silence—had a nostalgic tone. I watched the horses for a long time, a hackamore slung over one shoulder and a bag of oats slung over the other. I didn't move and neither did Ralphie. He was my father's dog—used to moments of stillness and silence.

"I also remember me. I remember myself in a strange way, as if I were part of the scene with the horses rather than an observer of the scene. But not a good part—an intrusive part. My left hand rested inside the oat bag, sifting rolled oats through my fingers, and my right hand rested on top of Ralphie's soaked head. My own two-legged body and my hairless skin felt so inadequate in that geography. But I remember my boots fitting well, feeling solid on the ground, even as I was aware of my inferiority to every other animal out there. In spite of that—or maybe because of that—I felt something amazing in that moment. I felt . . . well, I felt the fullness of my contentment. I felt the resonance of my life."

I open my eyes and look at him.

"That's a lovely memory, Kate."

I shrug, and swipe my cheeks with the back of my hand.

"Can you think of a time more recently when you've had

that same feeling—the resonance of your life. That's a nice way to put it."

"No."

He nods as if he expected that answer. He's so annoying sometimes.

"Did you tell your father about it when you got back to camp?"

"I started to, but it didn't matter."

"What do you mean?"

"When I got back to camp with the horses, Dad already had a fire going and the bacon half-cooked. He asked me how far I had to track the horses, and I started to tell him about the scene and about how it made me feel, but I could see in his face there was no need. He already knew that scene and that feeling. He was smiling. Not in a smug way—in a truly happy way. We haltered the horses, put them on the high line, and ate breakfast."

A pause. My therapist smiles.

"That's a smug smile," I tell him. "That's all I ever see anymore."

"I don't mean it to be. I'm happy that you shared that memory."

I shrug.

"Does it feel good to remember your father?"

"I don't have a problem remembering my father."

"I mean to put a memory into words. Does that feel good?"

"Not especially."

"What happened after your father died?"

"What do you mean 'what happened'?"

"What do you remember about that time?"

I shrug again. My therapist has horrible taste in furniture

as well as carpeting—plain and simple and neutral. As if he's afraid our fragile minds will be distracted with a little color.

"What do you remember about your grandparents, your aunt and uncle during that time?"

I'd out-paused him. A rare win. I shrug again.

"How did your mother handle losing her husband at such a young age? Did she blame herself for his death?"

I now have the well-practiced shrug down to one slight, low-energy movement. Hell, I don't know how Mom handled losing her husband. I never thought of him as her husband. Mom is a gray-haired, plain-faced old woman and Dad is . . . well, he's that black and white guy in a Ralph Lauren advertisement. Hard to picture them in the same bed. All I remember is that everybody—except Mom—was hovering and distant at the same time. Peering at me, but afraid to handle me, like I was a crystal figurine—you break it, you buy it.

"You don't have siblings," he says, jarring me out of my head. He says it as more of a statement than a question because he already knows the answer.

"No," I say.

"Were the three of you close? You, your mother, and your father?"

I shrug again. "Define close."

"Tell me a memory of the three of you."

"We slept in the same house."

"And presumably ate meals together?"

"No. Well, yes, but the family—us and Nate and Ona and Grandma and Grandpa always ate meals together at the farmhouse—my grandparent's house. Grandma and Aunt Ona cooked. They also did the gardening and took care of the chickens. Grandpa, Uncle Nate, Mom and Dad worked the ranch."

"And you? Did you help your aunt and grandmother with the gardening and the cooking?"

"How utterly sexist of you."

"My apologies."

"I went where Dad went."

"Always?"

"Always."

"Tell me one memory of you and your mother—just the two of you."

"She didn't like me very much."

"What makes you say that?"

I shrug again. "I could feel her trying."

"What do you mean?"

"Before Dad died, she used to lay out my school clothes and comb my hair in the mornings. I could feel the uneasiness in her hands. She was clumsy—put barrettes in crooked, tugged too hard at the tangles. But she was trying. She would say things that she knew mothers were supposed to say—that my hair was pretty, stuff like that."

"And after your father died?"

"I combed my own hair, got myself ready for school."

"How many years were you at the ranch after your father died?"

"Technically eight."

"Technically?"

"My grandmother died four years after Dad died, and my grandfather shortly after that. I was in high school by then, so I spent weeknights with a friend in Ely, came home on the weekends. My mother set up the arrangement, presumably as a favor to me, so I wouldn't have to spend so much time on the bus between school and home."

"How did you feel about that?"

"Fine."

"Just fine?"

"Yes, just fine."

"Were you homesick during the week?"

"The arrangement made it easier for both of us."

"You and your mother?"

"Yes."

"Why is that?"

I shrug. "It was hard for us to live in the same house after Dad died."

"Did you ever sleep at your grandmother's or your aunt's house?"

"It wasn't allowed."

"What do you mean?"

"Exactly what I said."

"Wasn't allowed by whom?"

"By anyone. Mom and I were supposed to grieve together and bond. I think that was the idea."

"But you didn't?"

"No, we didn't. I think we're done for the day."

He looks at the clock on the wall behind my head. "We still have ten minutes."

"Consider them a gift." I stand up to leave.

"You did some good work today, Kate. I look forward to our meeting next week."

"That's makes one of us." I leave the door ajar behind me and head for the elevator. In my zeal to be out of fluorescent hell and into the light of day, I knock into another of those smiling people as I step out onto the ground floor.

CASSIE

After two hours of hiking, Mick's map of Ophir Creek puts me on a large, flat boulder beside Upper Price Lake surrounded by willows and aspen. I lie flat on my back to watch clouds scurry by. On my left, Ophir Creek plunges down its ravine through the forest, simultaneously peaceful and violent. Behind me, the eastern face of Slide Mountain shoots upward, fractured and steep. I pull air through my nostrils, breathing deeply for the first time in a month, and drift in and out of sleep until hunger nudges me fully awake.

The bag holds a lunch of fried chicken—same thing I picked at for dinner last night. In the open air, I tear meat off bones enthusiastically, then lean back on greasy hands to look around. Every mountain range has its own character. I'm grateful to be taken in by the Carson Range today, but I feel like an unexpected houseguest, as if I've arrived in the middle of something, so I should tread lightly, clean up after myself, and know when it's time to leave, whereas a day in the Snakes or Schell Creeks feels like returning home after a long trip—there's no departure time.

The emotional hit of my short stop in Omer Springs on the way to Carson City took me by surprise. Maybe I thought the company of Bets—tough and sure—would provide some sort of hermetic seal around me. But as soon as we turned north on Highway 893 into Spring Valley, as soon as we slid between the Snakes and Schell Creeks, I was in trouble. I pulled off the road and skidded to a stop in the gravel, startling Bets, who was napping in the laid-back passenger seat, her feet on the dashboard.

"What happened?" she asked, sitting up sharply.

"This was a bad plan—coming to Omer Springs first," I said. "We should have gone straight to Carson City."

"The only plans you have are bad ones," she said. "Why question them now?"

I didn't answer her.

"Are we there?" she asked, looking around. "Is this it? Is this Omer Springs?"

I shook my head and started the car again. Bets laid back in her seat and closed her eyes. I wanted to shake her awake, get her to sit up and pay attention. See what I see, feel what I feel—a valley so austere in its beauty it can shift your physiological state, cause a dull thudding inside your frame as if organs are being hunted by a devouring heart.

Bets pulled the seat back up and scanned the landscape as I turned into the lane and drove toward the clustering of cottonwoods. The barn, the machine shop, and the corrals all looked dingier than I remembered them—as if my departure had escalated the rate at which wood weathers and nails rust. Aunt Ona stepped off her porch wearing her lavender Ely pantsuit and carrying a garbage bag in each hand.

"Nice," Bets said. "Is that your grandma?"

"No, that's Aunt Ona. Looks like she's headed over to Ely. That's Grandma Nell," I said, pointing toward a John Deere tractor followed by a disc plow and a cloud of dust. I could make out Grandma Nell's image in the enclosed cab, her hair sticking out wild under a ball cap. She was turned around watching the plow; she had not yet noticed us.

Grandma Nell had always worn her hair in a long braid down her back—same as me—even as it grayed. But last year, she said what movement was left in her old aching hands could be best put to use doing ranch work instead of braiding hair. The truth was Grandma Nell hadn't braided her own hair in a lot of years—I had been doing it since the day I came to live with her—and she'd lost the muscle memory that used to allow her to weave a braid in less time than it took to tie a shoe.

The day I loaded my things into the bed of Uncle Nate's truck to move to my mother's, Grandma Nell whacked off her braid with a pair of kitchen scissors. We were all standing around the truck—me, Uncle Nate, and Aunt Ona—giving Skinny, who was in the truck bed stacking the small load, three different opinions on how he ought to be doing things. Skinny nodded and went about his business, ignoring all of us unless his way of doing things agreed with one of ours, or unless one of us suggested something so foolish Skinny'd follow those instructions just to get a good laugh out of the day.

Grandma Nell had gone into the house to get the last box, and I didn't note it at the time—that'd be like checking to see that your right foot was still attached—but I assume that braid was tucked into the back of her shirt like always, where it stayed out of the way of piggin strings and moving machinery. But when she came back out carrying the box, the braid was laid out across it.

Just like Grandma Nell to find the most dramatic way possible of presenting things. I was leaving upon her insistence, but still, she couldn't resist making the point that I was abandoning her.

"What the hell?" Uncle Nate had said when she handed him the box.

"I thought Cassie might want to hang this in her dorm room to remember her old grandma."

"She ain't going to a dorm room, Nell," Uncle Nate said. "You know that. She's going to live with Katie."

"All the better," said Grandma Nell.

Aunt Ona gasped so loud when she first saw the braid I thought she was going to faint straightaway. She was now stammering, trying to formulate some words.

"Nell, that braid—"

"Hush, Ona," Grandma said.

"But Henry—"

"Not another word, Ona."

We all stood silently. I was hoping Aunt Ona would continue in spite of Grandma Nell's admonishment that she not, but she clamped down. Skinny, who had sat down on the wheel well in the truck bed, struck a match and lit a cigarette. Grandma Nell watched as he shook out the match and exhaled smoke, so the rest of us watched also. Skinny looked at Aunt Ona thoughtfully, then at Grandma Nell, then at the braid lying lifeless on the box. It was thick and mostly gray with enough strands of dark brown to give it a striped look. Grandma Nell had put a rubber band—the kind that comes around the newspaper—on the newly severed end like a tourniquet. Skinny nodded, acknowledging the braid.

"It's a good, strong piece," he said.

"It's yours," Grandma Nell said. "Put it to good use."

Skinny looked again at Aunt Ona, who had set her jaw tight but was still acting as if Grandma Nell had laid her left arm across the box. He looked back to Grandma Nell, who was equally set but also had a clownish appearance—the remains of her hair sticking out unevenly from under her ball cap. Skinny nodded, picked up the braid, and gently wound it around his fingers before slipping it into his jacket pocket.

———

Bets got out of the car just as Aunt Ona dropped the garbage bags by the trunk of her Ford Taurus. Bets did her usual stretching move—lifting her hands straight over her head, exposing a large swath of skin from several inches below her bellybutton, where her shorts rested, to just below her breasts, where her white tank top stopped. She then dropped forward, straight-legged, to put her hands flat in the dirt between her sandaled feet, exposing pretty much everything else. Aunt Ona was walking toward us, watching Bets in an almost mesmerized way. She shook her head and reached me just as Bets straightened back up.

"Didn't know when to expect you, Cassie," Aunt Ona said, pulling me into a hug. "Nate'll be tickled to see you."

"You on your way to Ely, Aunt Ona? What's in the bags?"

"Was taking a few things over to Char for her grandkids, but that can wait. Most a those things belong to you—hope you don't mind."

I shook my head.

"Mighty good to see you. Let me look at you." She held me at arm's length. "Lost a little weight, haven't you? But you look good. Who's this you brung with you?"

Bets stepped around the car with her hand out, causing Aunt Ona to wipe both of her palms on the legs of her pantsuit before shaking Bets' hand.

"I'm Bets."

"Nice to meet you, Betsy," Aunt Ona said, without moving too close.

"Bets is in my program at school," I explained.

"I see. Gets chilly here at night," she said to Bets.

"I brought a jacket," Bets said.

"I see," Aunt Ona said. "Well, okay then, let's get you girls settled."

You'd have thought I brought home a movie star, the way Bets drew attention around the ranch. Apparently Aunt Ona was not the only one who watched with great interest when Bets stretched out the kinks from the long drive. Two cowboys Uncle Nate had hired to work cattle this spring found a bunch of chores that needed doing up close to the farm house until Skinny threatened them with more than their jobs. Bets must have been used to that kind of attention to the point of tedium because she paid them no mind. But the cowboys weren't the only ones stirred up by Bets.

Uncle Nate, Aunt Ona, and Grandma Nell sat momentarily speechless when Bets came down the stairs for dinner. She had changed out the shorts for jeans that rested just below her hipbones and sported a stylish rip, exposing one tan, muscular thigh. I knew Bets had a flair for fashion, which I so obviously lacked, but on a college campus, especially one that sits in the middle of a scorching desert, a person gets numb to being surrounded by exposed body parts. Here in Omer Springs, even a pair of shorts is an anomaly not easily tolerated among the Carhartts and Wranglers. As Bets entered the room, Grandma Nell looked amused, Aunt Ona looked mortified, and Uncle Nate was deliberately unreadable.

"You got something stuck in your bellybutton," Grandma Nell finally said. "Need a Q-tip?"

Bets smiled. "No thank you."

"Grandma Nell, that's a bellybutton piercing," I said.

"Well, I'll be," Aunt Ona said. "You mean like a pierced ear?"

"Pretty much the same concept," Bets said.

"Where you been living, Ona?" Nell asked. "Under a rock? Kids pierce pretty much anything these days—bellybuttons, eyebrows, nostrils, nipples, and they don't stop there."

"Nell, really!" Aunt Ona said.

"Ain't that right, Cass," Grandma Nell said, more as a statement I'd already agreed to than a question. "What else you got pierced?" she asked Bets, acknowledging the eyebrow and nostril piercings. I didn't know the answer to that question, but I was hoping Bets, who seldom lies, had the good sense to do so now.

"Is somebody gonna pass the roast beef, or are we gonna sit around talking about sticking holes where they don't belong?" Uncle Nate asked, before Bets could answer.

"Good idea," Aunt Ona said. "Let's eat before everything gets cold."

"You should get you one a them bellybutton doohickeys, Cassie," Grandma said, passing the roast platter to Uncle Nate. "You could use a little spicing up. Get yourself a little attention from the opposite sex."

"Oh for heaven's sake, Nell," Aunt Ona said. "This child does not need to go around looking like a strumpet."

"A strumpet!" Grandma Nell said. "Bets, Ona just called you a strumpet."

"I did no such thing!" Aunt Ona said, turning patchy pink. "I only meant—"

"I like *strumpet*," Bets said shrugging. "Sounds old-fashioned."

"Oh for heaven's sake," Aunt Ona said.

"Bets, you plan on staying awhile?" Grandma Nell asked. "You look like a girl knows how to work, and we can find you some overalls. Don't pay worth crap, but Nate'd be happy to cut loose those two good-for-nothings out in the bunkhouse and put you and Cass to work in their place."

Uncle Nate nodded. "Plenty a work around here."

"I appreciate the offer," Bets said. "It'd be a nice place to spend the summer. But I already have a job waiting for me."

"Oh?" Aunt Ona said. "What do you do?"

"Bets and I both got jobs on campus this summer," I blurted out, catching Uncle Nate with a mouthful of potatoes. I didn't plan to tell them this way, although it probably didn't matter. Nothing I could say would be heard beyond the news that I wouldn't be staying for the summer.

The silence was horrible. Aunt Ona and Grandma Nell were both looking at me. Aunt Ona looking concerned, Grandma Nell looking suspicious, like I'd been brainwashed by the enemy—my mother. Bets was also staring at me curiously, as if she couldn't wait to see what I'd come up with next. I don't know why Bets and I didn't get our stories straight on the drive up. Uncle Nate swallowed hard and kept his eyes on his plate.

"It's just that we got these great jobs to work at the youth summer camp on campus. It's an opportunity to work in our field of study. We get paid *and* get class credit!"

Bets raised her eyebrows as if to say I may have over-reached with that last line.

"Sounds like a real good job, Cassie," Uncle Nate said. "Excuse me, now." He set his napkin on top of his still full plate and stood up. "I need to check on those calves."

After he left the room, Aunt Ona patted my hand. Tears spilled over my bottom eyelids.

"He'll miss you round here this summer, Cass," Aunt Ona said. "We all will. Been lonely without you this year. But that does sound like a real good job. Good for you."

"Well, all right then," Grandma Nell said. She got up

from the table, went into the living room, leaned back in her La-Z-Boy and turned the television up loud, leaving Aunt Ona, Bets and me to put away the full platters of food.

When I walked outside the next morning, Uncle Nate and Skinny already had four horses haltered and were just pulling saddles and blankets out of the tack shed. As soon as Uncle Nate saw my suitcase, the saddle he was lifting onto Sheila, the bay mare I'd been riding the last few years, dropped into the dirt and leaned awkwardly against his right leg. Skinny stepped over, wordlessly retrieved the saddle, and threw it over the hitching post.

"Bout got your horse saddled," Uncle Nate said, the hope in his voice scooping out the resolve in my belly.

"Uncle Nate, I have to go back to Vegas this morning."

He nodded. "Didn't know you'd be leaving so soon. Thought we could get at least one ride in. Them fences up in the Snakes need riding—we likely got cows all over hell and gone. I sorta put off things till you got here." He turned quickly, but not before I caught sight of his watery eyes. Mine filled immediately.

"Skinny, let's get two a them horses saddled and get to work," he said. Skinny nodded. He was already busy doing exactly that, having put two saddles back in the tack shed.

"Uncle Nate?"

"Yeah, Cass?" He turned toward me. I ran to throw my arms around him, unable to hold back the flood of tears. He caught me and hugged me tight.

"Now, girl," he said, patting my back. "We'll be all right here. Go do what you need to do."

"I'm sorry, Uncle Nate," I said, and I was. Sorry to be driving away from him, from Grandma Nell, from the Baxter Ranch. Sorry I'd hatched such a ridiculous plan. Sorry I felt compelled—for no apparent reason—to follow it through. The easy thing—and maybe the logical thing—would have been to get on a horse between Uncle Nate and Skinny and ride into the Snake Mountains, laughing and telling stories like we'd always done. Till I got to the one story Uncle Nate wouldn't tell—what happened between Mama and Grandma Nell made them act the way they do.

"That's a story gonna have to come from one a them," he'd always say. "Don't think I'm the person can explain all that—not even sure they can."

And that's why I pulled myself away from the comfort of that old man and turned toward Bets, who leaned against the car, watching the scene.

"Let's go," I said.

She shook her head slowly and opened the door to the passenger side. "Hope you know what the hell you're doing," she said.

"So do I," I replied. As we pulled out of the lane and turned onto the gravel road in front of the house, I willed myself not to look back over my left shoulder at what I'd just left behind. I'm known as a stubborn girl, but I'm weak-willed. Seeing Uncle Nate tighten a cinch with one quick movement and tuck away the leather strap, seeing Aunt Ona stuffing food into the saddle bags, seeing Grandma Nell step off her porch and look my direction damn near took me down—felt as if my body had been yanked from the car and dragged along the gravel road.

I took the first right off the gravel onto a dirt road. Bets didn't say anything, just looked over at me.

"We're taking the scenic route," I said. She nodded. "This road will take us over the top of the Schell Creeks and drop us into Ely." She nodded again. "Are you in a rush to get to Carson City?"

"We'll get there when we get there," she said.

"We might stop at an old camp on top for a bit. Eat the lunch Aunt Ona packed us," I said.

"As your Uncle Nate said, do what you need to do, Cassie. We have a long drive across the desert, and it makes more sense to do it after the heat of the day's passed on anyway."

We spent the day in the Schell Creeks sitting on a rock in the creek, listening to the water. We spoke very little. Every time I tried to walk toward the car to drive west, I felt paralyzed. Bets tried once to talk me into going back to the ranch. I refused. After that, she simply sat next to me reading a tattered and marked up copy of Darwin's *Origin of the Species,* quiet and seemingly content, while I wallowed in my own misery until we lost the sun behind the ridge. At that point, she stood and stretched, got into the driver's seat of the car, started the engine and looked at me expectantly. I got in the passenger side, and we drove down out of the Schell Creeks into Ely.

Sometime past midnight, Bets turned down the music and slowed the car to a crawl.

"What's wrong?" I asked.

"Nothing. Just looking for a turnoff."

"Have to pee?"

"Ah, here we go," she said, turning abruptly onto a dirt road that had popped out of the darkness on our left. She started picking up speed again, bumbling down a road that seemed to require the opposite.

"Where are we going in such a hurry?" I asked, wondering if we might be unknowingly headed for a Thelma and Louise.

"Don't worry. This is a decent road—or at least it used to be."

"I'm not worried," I said, turning the music back up. But when Bets swung the car off the road and drove through an open field, I turned the music back down. Before I could express my concerns, she brought the car to a stop directly in front of a small pool of water, the half-moon reflecting off its surface through a fine mist of rising steam.

"I thought you didn't know where we were—thought you always took a more direct route to Carson City," I said, pulling myself out of the car into the now-cooling desert night and breathing deeply, catching the stinging aroma of sagebrush crushed under the tires. Bets did the same on the other side.

"I haven't been on this road for years," Bets said, arching her back and dropping forward into her usual stretching pose. "Strange how the mind spits up geographical details you didn't know you were carrying, though, isn't it?" she said, popping back up straight and flowing into a deep backbend without pause. "My pop, back when he was a happy drunk—before he went into rehab and became a miserable drunk—had a thing for hot springs. Do you know how many hot springs there are in this state?"

"No idea."

"Three hundred and twelve. More than in any other state in the nation."

"Is that true?"

"Don't know. I'm passing along Pop's numbers, and he's a notorious liar. But I do know there are a good number, and this one here is a dandy, although sometimes too hot to get in." Bets squatted and stuck a hand into the steaming pool. "It's hot, but it's not too hot," she said, pulling off sandals, shorts, and tank top, the only three articles of clothing she wore, before stepping tentatively into the water.

"Good to know," I said, watching her. Lord God, no wonder she came home from Carson City with a wad of cash every summer. I never knew what those idiotic boys in high school meant when they said some girl was built like a brick shit-house, but I understood it then, watching Bets ease that body into the water. I didn't consider myself ugly, but I suddenly felt like the scrawny little sister tagging along with the big girls.

"Aren't you coming in?" she asked.

"Sure."

"Be careful. The bottom is slimy."

"Damn! This is hot. How hot do you figure it is?"

"Not sure. 108, 109. Maybe more."

As soon as we settled into the hot water, steam rising around us, I heard her sigh.

"So your dad just took you guys around to hot springs?" I asked. "Was that your family's idea of a vacation?"

"Pretty much."

"You've never said much about your dad. What was he like?"

"He was a hippie dude with a gambling and drinking problem. Hell of a combination. Mostly wanted to live on peace and love—and he had plenty of both to go around—but the casinos wouldn't give him any chips for that. About four times a year, he'd quit gambling—sort of like the habitual smoker quits smoking—and every time he did, he'd load Mom and Danny and me into his Volkswagen bus—how's that for a cliché—and we'd hit the road in search of some hot springs he'd heard about. I think I visited all three hundred and twelve hot springs before the age of ten. This was one of his favorites."

"Sounds sort of fun."

"It was. Mom and Pop were crazy for each other—eventually that was her unraveling. He came out of the last rehab full of Christ the Lord, and she knew she'd lost him forever. She walked into the house leaving him on the porch, shut and locked the door, and hasn't come out since. But in those hot spring days, they were high on passion—and Lord knows what else—and Danny and I were proof that love could conquer all. Mom didn't get pregnant with Danny until she was thirty-nine and me a year later. Dad was in one of his gambling remission stages then. That's how I got my name—all 'bets' off."

"I thought your name was short for Betsy."

"Nope, hippies would never name a kid something so common."

"But your brother's name is Danny."

"Yes, short for Dandelion."

"No way."

"Afraid so." Bets sank lower until the water reached her chin, tipped her head back onto a rock and stared into the night sky. "They were wild and beautiful, those two," she said. "They could make you believe that joy was just as plentiful as stars in the sky. I'm afraid to think it, but those might have been the best years of my life. It is quite possible that I'll never be that happy again. Wouldn't that bite? Reaching your happiness potential by age ten and still having to live another seven decades after that?"

"I guess that would sort of suck. I'm banking on my best years still being ahead of me."

"I'll smoke to that," Bets said, reaching for a pot-filled pipe she'd put on a nearby rock.

"Maybe that's what happened to my mother," I said. "Maybe she hit her happiness max before Grandpa died."

"Could be," Bets said. "She doesn't seem terribly happy now, and she has no apparent reason not to be. She's got you, and you measure up all right on the parental how-good-is-your-kid yardstick. Plus a big fancy job and a sexy boyfriend."

"You think Derek is sexy?"

"Hell, yeah. I'll bet they have great sex in spite of your

mother's primness. He seems like the kind of guy who could break through that."

"Ugh, could we not talk about my mother and sex?"

"Derek's a hell of a lot sexier than your dad, that's for sure. Your dad looks like Wayne Newton. Maybe they have the same plastic surgeon."

"Ugh again! Could we please talk about something else?"

"Sure," she says, inhaling and passing the pipe to me. "All I'm saying is that on the surface, your mom seems to have it all, but she acts as if she's sludging through shit all day. In my business—soon to become your business—it's pretty easy to recognize anyone hauling a bunch of unresolved crap around with them. You do that long enough, and that crap begins to seep out of the tidy little seams you think you've sewn tight and manifest in some weird fucking ways. How do you think my mother became the agoraphobic nut job she is now? My guess is that your mom's keeping a few things tucked away under those tight-ass business suits she wears."

"That's what I'm saying, Bets. One time when I was waiting for Grandma Nell to pick me up from school, which was a common occurrence because Grandma Nell refuses to wear a watch, out of the clear blue my teacher, old Mrs. Foster—who always seemed to speak more to herself than to anyone in the vicinity, as if she just couldn't control voicing whatever thought entered her head—said, 'Katie'—that's what they called Mama when she was a kid—she said, 'Katie has never been quite right since Henry died.' I asked her exactly what she meant by that. At first she waved me off, you know, with a big show of fake ambivalence—that's when I knew she was dying to tell me. But as she started to speak, Grandma Nell slid to a stop in the pickup truck in front of the school, slammed the door with great authority, and yelled my name—seemingly all in the same second. Grandma Nell has a knack for that sort of time-freezing grand arrival. Mrs. Foster clamped down and refused to ever speak another word about it. I've pieced some things about the accident together over the years, but the story remains that Grandma Nell simply mistook Grandpa for a deer and shot him."

"Whoa! Back up there, girlfriend. Your grandmother shot her husband? Are you kidding?"

"That's the story. I guess things just fell apart after that."

"Well, yeah. That's sort of a big thing to get over, Cassie."

"They say Grandma Nell was a dead shot—never missed. She picked up her first rifle when she was seven years old, shot her first deer when she was eight. Best eye in the valley and steady as a cedar post. Put Uncle Nate and every other man in the valley to shame. She'd been hunting more than thirty years when she accidentally shot Grandpa. I'm not saying it didn't happen, but that's freaky."

"Most accidents are. Who was there when it happened?"

"The whole family would have been up there at the time. Uncle Nate said they used to set up a big hunting camp and everybody went. Apparently my mother witnessed the accident firsthand. She was with Grandma Nell when it happened."

"And your mother's never told you about it?"

"Nothing. She flatly refuses to talk about her past to either me or Derek."

"Parents," Bets said as she slipped her entire head momentarily under water and popped back up again. "What a fucked-up bunch. It's amazing their offspring are anything more than babbling idiots."

"Mama claims to hate all those moony people who spend their lives reminiscing about the past instead of living in the here and now, thinks it's a colossal waste of time."

"She might not be entirely wrong about that," Bets said. "But old people always like to talk about the past. What does your grandma say about it?"

"I can't get her to say more than a few words about Grandpa."

"That's a little strange."

"Maybe not for her. Grandma favors the tough, old broad persona. To be honest, I don't think she dares talk about him. Anything remotely related to him or that accident splits her open like a pea pod. Uncle Nate's the only one I get information from. After a couple of hours of riding—and enough distance from the ranch—Uncle Nate will eventually get around to talking about my grandfather."

Over the years, the stories of Grandpa Henry slipped from between Uncle Nate's lips in crumbs and shreds. Then last summer, after Mama's announcement of the water pipeline, Uncle Nate told those stories with urgency—as if in preparation for a certain eventuality. One hot day, shortly after Grandma Nell's table speech at the July Fourth picnic, Uncle Nate, Skinny, and I rode toward the Snake Mountains with fencing equipment packed onto a fourth horse. Whenever we could, we rode three across—me in the middle. Most of the ranchers in Spring Valley had switched from horses to ATVs for this type of work, but this family liked riding horses—that's all there was to it—and didn't see any reason to stop.

"That came from your grandfather," Uncle Nate had said, "the inclination for horses stead a machinery. Ol' Henry had a preference for silence over noise and slow over fast. He didn't have no urge to plow the fields with a team stead of a tractor, but he knew when to step aside in life and let others rush on by."

"Uncle Nate," I had said that day, "I'm going to live with Mama next month, and it sure would help me to understand why Mama's doing what she's doing with this pipeline thing."

"Well, Cassie," he said, "that's a question I think we'd all like the answer to. If you happen onto it while you're down there, you be sure to call us, won't you?"

"Why don't you or Grandma Nell call Mama up and ask her?"

Uncle Nate was silent for a long while after I asked that question. I looked at Skinny who looked—as always—as if the conversation didn't concern him whatsoever.

Finally, Uncle Nate said, "That's a helluva question you're asking there, Cass. Seems like it ought to be simple but it ain't. Ain't nothing simple where Nell's concerned. Not sure I can explain it."

"You know her better than anybody, Uncle Nate. So please try."

"Well, Nell's a complicated one. She acts upon good motives, but sometimes her actions take a long explanation and a lotta effort to understand. Still, she carries a big bunch a passion in that old heart a hers. Always has. Even when we were kids. So much so that it sorta made her crazy—gushing through her like spring runoff with such ferocity it could yank up trees, leaving the roots exposed. Then Henry come along and she put it there. Simple as that. And that was the right place for it, no doubt about it. Henry and Nell didn't pay no attention at all to the rules a love—just poured themselves into the other with no restraint whatsoever. They couldn'ta contained it if they'd a wanted to, and I don't think they wanted to."

Uncle Nate pulled the bandana from around his neck and wiped his eyes. "Then the accident happened, and Henry was gone. Just like that. That's a jarring thing, Cass, to extract someone like your grandpa from the middle a things."

"So Grandma Nell's passion died with Grandpa Henry," I said.

"No, it didn't. Woulda probably been better if it had, but it didn't. Henry was gone, and Nell's passion had no receptacle."

"Then what happened?" I asked.

"Well, most a that passion got directed toward grief and sorrow, and it was a mighty storm. Almost took her down, and she's a tough woman as you know. The days after Henry died she'd get on a horse and just ride—into the mountains, down the road, through the fields—literally rode one a Dad's horses to death without ever knowing what she'd done. Me and Dad would track her movement from a distance without her knowing it. We'd watch what direction she'd take off, then I'd get in the truck and Dad would get on the phone to alert folks she might be coming their way. Had everybody in this valley and two valleys on either side a here reporting her whereabouts. After a few days a her being gone, we'd hitch up the horse trailer and hunt her down. We'd pull up beside her along the road or spy her with a pair a binoculars coming across a field, gauge the direction she was headed and be waiting at the next gate. She'd load the horse into the trailer in silence and slide onto the bench seat between the two of us without a word. A couple a days later she'd be gone again.

"Then one day we found her coming down off Hickman Pass on her own two feet. She directed us to the saddle and bridle she'd stashed under a twisted juniper, but she never would say what happened to the horse, and we never found it—dead or alive. That's when Dad put a stop to her woeful wandering—said Katie needed a mother, and he needed his horses, and she needed to stay put and get back to work on the ranch. Truth is, the weather was getting real bad, and the odds a finding her dead in a snowstorm were going up fast."

"Then what happened?"

"Well, not sure I know exactly. We—Mom and Dad and me and Ona—had a meeting a sorts to discuss how to stop Nell from burying herself alongside Henry cause she was damn sure headed in that direction. We figured that if Nell could see how much Katie needed her mother, she'd come around. So we set about trying to push them together. At least three of us did—Ona saw something none a the rest a us could see."

"What was that?"

"Well, Ona's theory was that you don't rub pain up against pain to soothe it. She said that was like putting two open wounds right next to each other—one seeping into the other and vice versa. She said that would cause all sorts a festering and oozing and not allow any healing whatsoever. Ona was probably right about that."

Uncle Nate paused and wiped his eyes again, and Skinny glanced over at him briefly before looking away again.

"Hell, Ona was right about a lotta things, but . . ." He stopped talking and shook his head.

"But what, Uncle Nate?"

"But we never listened to her, goddammit. We all thought Ona was acting upon selfish motives."

He shook his head again and swiped his shirtsleeve under his nose.

"What sort of motives?"

He shook his head and ignored my question.

"Anyway, Nell saw what we were trying to do, so she started funneling her passion toward Katie. We told her that's what Henry woulda wanted, which was true. Henry always wanted Nell and Katie to love each other the way he loved each a them, but he never tried to manipulate it the way we did after his death. So when Nell started paying attention to Katie, we all thought we'd done a good thing, but here's the thing, Cass—mothering don't come naturally to all women. Those that say it does are telling a whopper. Still, Nell went about it the same way she goes about everything—with fervor and good intention. But like I said, Nell's a complicated one, so things don't go off simple from her. I think Nell's sudden attentiveness scared Katie to death. In response, Katie pulled herself tightly into a defensive position and squatted low. And that's where she is still. That girl never unfurled herself."

"I still don't get it," I said. "Seems like everybody was just doing the best they could. That's no reason why Mama and Grandma Nell shouldn't speak to each other now."

"No, it ain't. But that's just one piece a the entire puzzle, and that wasn't the beginning of it—that was more like the end of it."

"What do you mean? What are the other pieces?"

"Well, I'm not sure I can say with any sorta certainty, Cassie. It's complicated. And it ain't my story to tell anyway. Skinny, let's start down on that south end by the gate. Then we can check to see if any idiots left gates open last weekend and push the cows back in if we need to."

That's when I knew Uncle Nate was done talking. *It ain't my story to tell* was his way of signaling a close to the conversation. Whose story is it, I'd like to know. Seems the only person who might be willing to claim it was buried fifteen years before I was born.

NELL

I shut off the truck engine and coast to a stop in the dirt behind the park. Folks mill about in the usual way—like they've done for thirty some-odd years—ever since my mother died. When she was still alive, the July Fourth picnic was held at our ranch outta respect for my mother's grief over Leroy's death in the nearby pond. It was my father's idea to move the celebration back to the park after she was gone. He always liked this place. If Nate and I couldn't see him in the fields at the end of a day, we'd ride our bikes here—particularly in April and September during migration—and find him sitting on the damp grass counting snowy egret landings. When we showed up back at the ranch with our bikes in the back a his pickup, he'd tell my mother he found us down at the post office, and she'd respond with a tight-lipped attempt at a smile.

The scene in front a me now is as familiar as the sun beating down on the hood a my truck. Lee Holston met Red O'Riley at sunrise this morning to run a flag up the flagpole that we installed the same time we ran electricity from Red's barn. Lee's the keeper a the flag, which was once draped over his father's coffin. He and Red get it up the pole on all the appropriate days. Lee's father was a WWI vet, and Lee'll tell his story at least three times today. The folks he chooses to tell it to will stop what they're doing and listen—don't matter how many times they've heard it before.

Ona and Mavis O'Riley competently roll white butcher paper off a cardboard tube and tape it down on the picnic tables, then set each table with three miniature flags on toothpicks stuck in a half-apple—one a Ona's creations. Then they'll sprinkle glittering red and blue stars over the tables—also Ona's idea but a lousy one. A little breeze comes up, which always happens, and everyone has to pick those things outta their potato salad. Next to the centerpiece goes the salt and pepper shakers. I can't hear the conversation from here, but I know it nevertheless—updates on the offspring. Ona takes an interest in everybody's kids, and that's okay, I guess. Seems she makes a big show a pretending that not having any a her own don't bother her, but nobody's fooled.

The men gather in circles to complain about the price a hay or the price a cattle or the lack a rainfall or the shortage a grass or the damn government or the damn liberals or the good old days when all those things seemed less threatening and easier to handle. Except Skinny and Frank. They're busy under the awning setting up small appliances and running extension cords to the flagpole. I would normally be conversing with the men, but instead I'm sitting in my truck trying to figure out why my stomach's tumbling like river pebbles. I'll be damned if I haven't missed those yammering geezers and the occasional "oh my goodness" drifting over from the women. Missed them bad. What I wouldn't give to be knee-deep in bullshit among that group—to still be part a all that. But that's gone now—thanks to Katie. This scene here is a scene belongs to the past. The future don't look nothing like this. I don't even have to roll down my window to hear the topic a today's conversation. I can see it in the dragged faces in front a me.

At the precise moment I decide to start the truck up and sneak away, Red O'Riley spots me. He nods in my direction and, one by one, heads turn my way until every single person out there has stopped mid-conversation to stare at me. Ona sets the box a plastic silverware she's distributing down on a bench and nudges Nate's arm. He looks up and rushes toward me, forcing me outta the truck before he gets here. Christ almighty. I'm not an invalid needs escorting from the truck to the park.

I take my time pulling a lawn chair outta the back—trying to fake like everything's normal—and by that time Nate has reached me. The chair's one a those five dollar jobs with the interwoven strips that begin to sag under a person my size till they break through, but over the years Skinny has fortified mine with some intricate weaving a horse hair and twine. For all I know, some a my own hair might be in there. Skinny's one a those guys that can find a use for pert near everything another might throw away. Nate tries to take the chair outta my hand, and I yank it back from him. For a moment we end up in a tug-a-war, and when we realize how ridiculous we must look, we both release our grasp, and the chair falls to the ground. When we bend to pick it up, I shoo him away with a push a my hip against his.

"For hell sakes, Nate, I ain't been sick. What're you doing?"

"I'm just happy to see you down here, Nell, that's all."

"Well express your happiness from over there, will you? Like all the rest a them."

We walk toward the silent and humorless faces. When we reach them, Lee Holston's the first to speak.

"How you doing, Nell? We ain't been seeing much a you lately."

"Been busy, Lee," I tell him, setting my lawn chair up to

face the water. "I ain't got the same kinda time you old boys have."

"That right?" Hank Mortensen asks. "Seems like you used to."

"Well, Morty, once I figured out work gets done faster if you spend less time yakking about it and more time doing it, it sorta changed my life."

"You wouldn't be avoiding us would you, Nell?" Red O'Riley asks.

"Why would you think that, Red?"

"Well, you got the biggest ranch out here, Nell, so we sorta figure you got as big a stake in this water thing as any a us, but your presence has been notably absent at our meetings. Hell, you didn't even show up to hear that bullshit the governor tried to cram down our throats during his reassuring visit."

A few more trucks have pulled in, and Fitzy rushes over as if worried he mighta missed something. The women, too, have abandoned their duties and moved in close to hear the conversation. I stand with my back to the water, facing the group. Nate stands next to me with a pinched look on his face, as if he's the single person in a two-sided debate. Morty and Lee stand next to each other—something they haven't done since Morty dug a well on his property a few years back and inadvertently sucked all the water out from under Lee's northeast meadow. That was our first lesson on messing with the intricate ways a water below our feet. The stream that used to bubble up in Lee's meadow and run till early fall disappeared entirely, leaving Lee's cows and calves no place to go when they come off the mountain. Morty and Lee haven't had much to say to each other since. Till now. At the moment, they're both seeing a bigger picture. If a little well like that could bring such devastation to a meadow, imagine what Katie's pipeline could do. And that's exactly what folks are imagining.

Red continues. "We also figure you might have some information about this whole affair that might shed some light on what we can do about it."

"Don't know what you think I'm hiding, Red, but I got the same information you got. I watch the news and read the newspapers every day, same as you."

"We ain't accusing you a hiding anything, Nell, and you know it," Morty says. "But there's some things going on that we need information on—and you're in the best position to get that information. You got an inside track."

"What sorta information you think I can dig up, Morty?"

"Well, who sent them letters for one thing. And—"

"What letters you talking about?"

"The letters we all got, Nell. What the hell letters you think I'm talking about?"

"I don't know what you're talking about, Morty."

"Nell, for hell sakes—"

"We all got letters from some company in Las Vegas, Nell," Nate says. "Offering to buy our property."

I turn my head slowly to look at Nate while also keeping Morty in the corner of my eye. "The hell you say, Nate. And this is the first I'm hearing about it?"

"I didn't see no need in bringing it up with you, Nell."

"Oh, hell no, little thing like that. Why would you bother?"

"You mean you ain't told her about the letters, Nate?" Red says.

Nate looks nervously at Red, then quickly at Ona—which tells me they been conniving on this—then back to me.

"You ain't been yourself, Nell, that's all. And it ain't like there's anything to talk about—less you've suddenly decided you want a condo on the beach stead a living here."

"Who sent the letters?" I ask.

"That's what we're all trying to figure out, Nell," Red says. "Some company called Nevada Realty Investments. Claim they're looking for ranch properties, which is a crock a bull. Looking for water is what they're doing, and they gotta be in cahoots with those people Katie works for. And those people Katie works for are in cahoots with a bunch a other people—this agency and that agency and cities and counties. Course there ain't no names and faces attached to any of it—cept one. It gets so damn complicated you can't follow the line. It's just a bunch a people with a bunch a money and power trying to steal our water, is what it boils down to. I called the number on the letter and got hold a some yahoo told me 'our client is a conglomerate, not an individual, and has asked for confidentiality; we can't divulge that information.'"

"What'd you tell him?"

"I told him his conglomerate can kiss my ass is what I told him. I told him nobody in this valley is interested in selling any ranch property. Then he says that ain't true at all. Says he's received calls from people asking what kinda money this undivulged client might be willing to pay. I knew damn well he was just blowing smoke, and I told him so."

"What'd he say?"

"He said I may not know my neighbors as well as I think I do, and I told him again—he and his undivulged conglomerate can kiss my ass. Nobody in this valley is selling out."

I look from face to face at men I've known most a my life—some older, some younger than me and Nate. The gnarled faces show decades a work and worry about the normal things—family, weather, bills, health. There's been a hip replacement, two bypasses, cancer, floods, droughts, deaths, farming accidents, and threats by the bank to repossess property. All that's just part and parcel a the life they chose, the life they expected. But this is different, and everyone a them knows it. It's their eyes—hazy with fear and uncertainty—that get to me. And the way they wait. Just there. Standing in front a me waiting for whatever words a comfort I might offer, whatever magic act I have up my sleeve that might save them. Goddamn them. They ought to have never put that kinda trust in me.

"Did everybody get letters?"

Heads nod.

"Has anybody other than Red called and asked about them?"

Heads shake no. Five ducks fly over us, squawking their landing in the pond, water skidding under feet and wings. Fitz Walters drops down to his haunches to clean cow shit off his boots with a stick.

"Fitz?"

He looks up at me without answering.

"Did you call those folks that sent the letters?"

"I didn't, no," he says, and goes back to cleaning off his boots.

I look at the women standing behind the men and then back at the men.

"Fitzy? What's on your mind?"

"Whaddaya mean, Nell?" Fitz drops the stick and stands.

"Something bothering you?"

"Well, sure, Nell, there's something bothering all of us, ain't there?"

"Speak what's on your mind, Fitz."

"It's just that you know Katie better'n any a us do, Nell, and we're just trying to figure out how she can be thinking this is gonna work. We gotta figure out a way to stop this thing and—"

"And what, Fitzy?"

"Well, you gotta call her, Nell, you just gotta," he says, looking at me pleadingly. Then his eyes fill with tears, and he looks back at the ground. Another hush settles over us as a crow squawks and flies low over the picnic tables. Skinny shoos it away silently, and Nate shuffles uncomfortably as Ona squeezes in beside him.

"Fitz?" she says. "Where's Bea? Why ain't she with you?"

I hadn't the time or inclination to take stock a who was missing this year, but as soon as Ona spoke up, folks start performing a mental roll call. Sure enough, Fitzy's wife, Bea, is missing.

"Fitz?" Ona says again.

"She ain't gonna be here," Fitz replies, pulling on the tip of his nose with thumb and forefinger.

"Whaddaya mean, Fitz?" Ona asks.

"Just what I said, Ona, she ain't gonna be here."

"Well, sure she is, Fitz," Ona replies. "We can't do without her good baked beans, now can we?"

Fitz pushes his way through the crowd back toward his truck. Lee and Morty move aside with puzzled expressions to let him through.

"Fitz, I think you need to stick around," I say.

Fitz turns and takes two steps back. He has tears streaming down both ruddy checks. "You think I need to stick around? You know what, Nell?" he says. "I don't give a shit what you think I need to do. You think I need to stick around? Bullshit. You think we oughta do this and you think we oughta do that, and well, if Nell says it than we damn sure oughta do it. It don't work that way no more, Nell. Ain't you noticed that? No, you probably ain't noticed that. Cause you ain't been nowhere close by where you coulda noticed that, have you? We been waiting a year for you to help us on this deal, and you ain't lifted one god-damn finger. Now you wanna come back in and tell us what we should do? You think I need to stick around? Well, it's too damn late, Nell. It's too late. We're gonna lose every goddamn thing we ever worked for, and it's too damn late to stop it now."

Fitz moves back into the crowd to stand in front a me with both fists clenched, snot and tears dripping over his top lip. I look at the rest a them. Nobody makes eye contact. I ain't foolish enough to ask whether they all share Fitzy's point a view on the issue. It's only respect for Nate that keeps them quiet.

"This thing's just getting started, Fitzy," I say, referring to the picnic, but Fitzy don't interpret it that way.

"No, Nell, it ain't," he says. "It ain't just getting started. It's over. At least it is for me. So thanks for nothing, Nell. Thanks for not a goddamn thing!"

"Where's Bea?" I ask.

"Bea's in Vegas staying with her sister. And tomorrow morning she's going into that real estate office to talk to that fella—to find out how much he's willing to pay for our ranch. Says she's done fighting this thing, Nell. Says she's sick and tired and sick a being sick and tired. Says with the money we could get for the ranch we could buy a little place near her sister with no mortgage payment at all—be close to doctors and stores and family and live out the rest a our lives without worry."

"Oh, she don't mean that, Fitz," Ona says. "Bea and me been friends a lotta years, and she ain't mentioned a word a this to me."

Fitz slowly turns to Ona, his checks wet and red. "She's gonna leave me, Ona," he says. Short, coughing sobs come from deep in his chest. "She's gonna leave me if I don't go through with selling the ranch. Says I'll have to get a loan from the bank to buy her out, and she'll move in with her sister."

"Oh, Fitz, she don't mean that."

"I mean no disrespect to you, Ona. I know you and Bea are close. That's probably why she ain't told you. But I know when that woman's serious, and she ain't bluffing. You all know her." He gestures around the circle. "She ain't missed a Fourth a July picnic in thirty-six years—not since she was in labor with our firstborn. She ain't joking about this. Says she just can't take no more of it—can't take no more worrying about bills and water and crops and calves. Said this is our chance. Us small guys barely make a living as it is. Once they take that water, our land is gonna be worthless, and we're all standing around just waiting for that to happen. And you know what? I think she's right. Less Nell's willing to step in and help us— and she don't seem willing to do that—we don't stand a chance. Soon as that pipeline is laid, our lives are over. We won't be able to raise crops or cattle, and this land won't be worth a damn dime. If we don't sell out now we won't have a pot to piss in."

Silence hovers over the group, as dark and constricting as a potato cellar on a sunny day.

"Fitz," I say, "you may be right about all that. I ain't got a good argument that says you're not. But I'm afraid you're overestimating my powers a persuasion here."

"Nell, I don't know if you can stop this thing or not. I only know if anyone can, it's you. If you can't, well then, we gave it everything we had. But less you decide to join us, everyone a us here might as well follow Bea into that real estate office tomorrow."

A soft, hot wind blows into my face, and the flag over-head flaps noisily as if to remind us of our reason for gathering.

"The rest a you all agree with Fitz?" I ask.

"I ain't leaving my land," Red says, tears bubbling in his eyes, "till I'm buried under it. I'll sit right here and starve to death, but those sonsabitches ain't gonna ever see the deed to my land." He looks at Mavis through his watery eyes, and she looks back at him through hers. She nods her affirmation.

"And the rest a you?" I ask.

One by one, they nod their agreement with Red.

"If some of us start selling out, it's gonna make it harder for the rest a us to hold," Morty says, looking at me, then at Fitz. "But every man's gotta decide for himself. I'm with Red on this. I'm gonna fight it as long as I can. But me and May ain't got no savings at all. We sunk every dime we had and then some into upgrading our equipment and irrigation system seven years ago. Remember that? All of us agreeing to upgrade our irrigation so we could be more water efficient? Seems kinda ironic now, don't it? Us preserving water so those bastards in Vegas can take it."

"I don't wanna sell out, Morty," Fitz says. "You know that. Hell, I can't live in a condo in Vegas. I'd just as soon kill myself, and I'm not joking."

My face flushes with the truth of Fitz's words. That's pure shame I'm feeling. I turn toward the water so they won't see it.

"I know that, Fitzy," Morty says. "Hell, I don't know what we'll do if we lose our water and our land becomes worthless. It makes me sick to my stomach to think of it, so I simply don't."

"I ain't got no plans to sell my land neither," Lee says. "But I'm with Fitzy on this, Nell. You stepping outta this fight ain't felt right at all. It feels like you maybe coulda helped us and chose not to. And that don't feel right at all. Not at all. And the question that nobody's asking here is why. Why ain't you with us, Nell?"

"Well, you know the answer to that, Lee," Nate says. "Hell,

Katie's a part a this family. You can't expect a mother to—"

I hold up my hand to stop Nate.

"That's a legitimate question you're asking there, Lee. I didn't make no conscious decision to abandon you all. I think you know that. But when I wake up in the mornings these days, I can't find no more energy inside me than what it takes to get through my day." I turn my lawn chair around to face them and drop down heavy into it. "I don't know what kinda relationships you all have with your offspring. What I do know is that you have the luxury a keeping those things private. I ain't got that luxury. You all know I don't have any kinda relationship with my daughter whatsoever. And that ain't an easy thing for a woman to share." I stand back up to face them. "You all are expecting miracles from me, and I can't deliver. It's that simple."

"You're wrong about that, Nell," Red says. "We ain't expecting miracles. But it sure would be nice to have you with us stead of against us."

"I ain't never been against you. You all shoulda known that."

"It's been a little hard to tell, Nell," Red says. "That's all we're saying."

I nod, breathe deeply, and attempt to pull myself back into the woman they expect me to be. It's a hollow inhabitation.

"I'm gonna talk to Bea, Fitz," Ona says.

"It ain't gonna be that easy, Ona, but I'm gonna let you try it anyway." He shakes his head, unclenches his fists and stuffs both hands into his pockets. The group begins to loosen.

"The thing is," I say, and they all turn back toward me. "The thing is either Katie believes what she's saying or—"

"Or what, Nell?" Morty asks.

"Or she don't care," I say.

"I ain't buying either one a those explanations," Nate says.

"Well, that's good to hear, Nate," I snap. "I'd be interested to hear what else you've come up with."

Nate shuffles uncomfortably. I shake my head.

"Okay," I say. "I'll drag my sorry ass to whatever meetings there are on this water deal, and I'll do what I can. I'll even give Katie a call and see if she wants to have a nice mother-daughter chat. I can tell you in advance how that'll turn out. And I ain't making no promises beyond that. And if that ain't enough—well, it's gonna have to be." Red gives one nod a his head, and the others follow, but they all stand there as if I'm supposed to do something else, and my energy is seeping out the soles a my feet. "I'm done talking about this now," I say. "Skinny, you got any bread frying?"

"Coming up," he says, snuffing out a cigarette and getting up from where he's perched on the end of a picnic table.

The crowd softens and moves toward the food. I put my hand on Fitz's arm. He turns.

"One more thing, Fitzy," I say softly, so only he can hear me. "The bullshit stops now. If one more a my irrigation pivots springs a leak, you and me are gonna have a reckoning."

He smiles sadly and says, "I don't know what you're talking about, Nell." Ona puts an arm through his and hands him a plate.

I sit in my chair with my back to the crowd, looking across the water. Heat shimmers over the shrunken pond, and exposed shores buzz with gnats and flies.

"Nell, ain't you gonna eat?" Nate asks.

"In a minute."

Nate hasn't given me any particulars about what folks are

saying, and I imagine the conversation changes in his company anyway, but I know the gist of it: "That girl a Nell and Henry's ain't never been quite right since Henry died."

And that's the truth of it, too. I ain't ever said that out loud to anybody—not even Nate—cause what would that say about my mothering skills? After Henry died, going on thirty-six years ago now, Katie squirreled so deep inside herself my reach wasn't near long enough to save her. Oh hell, who am I kidding? Every time I reached for her I ended up shoving her deeper.

Sixteen days after we buried Henry, when I went into the post office, Marietta, who runs the counter there said, "Katie has you, Nell; she has her mother."

"But she don't have her father, Marietta," I said.

"A girl needs her mother," she replied matter-of-factly. And Marietta wasn't the only one saying that. As best I could tell, most folks agreed upon that idea—if a young girl has to lose a parent, she best give up her daddy and keep her mama. But the fact is, once Katie was off the breast, which was damn near as soon as we brought her home from the hospital—all she ever needed was Henry. No two people were ever closer than Katie and her daddy. You might say they had an exclusive relationship.

I coulda fixed that if I'd given Henry a son like he wanted, and looking back on things, that maybe woulda been the smarter choice. But I didn't. It took thirty-seven miserable hours to coax Katie outta the warmth a my belly into a gray, frozen February day—Valentine's Day, to be exact, which is either a miracle or an irony depending upon your point a view. Anyway, that kinda pain will make some decisions for a person if someone don't interfere at the right moment. In the ten days leading up to Katie's arrival, the thermometer hadn't once crept into double digits, so when the labor was over, Henry stayed just long enough to bounce Katie once or twice in his hands—sorta like he was deciding on an Easter ham—before Nate dragged him out the door, explaining that this wasn't the only birth they had to worry about. If they didn't get those cows under the shed and into the straw before they dropped their calves onto the frozen ground, half those calves'd freeze up solid before the mother cow could get herself turned around and paying attention.

Anyhow, Henry was right there beside me every moment—except for that one moment when he wasn't. He was mothering a shed full a calves at the precise moment the doctor came in to explain what he referred to as my "considerations" in attempting to birth another child in the future. I've heard people say that life-changing decisions should not be made during a time of stress, and I suppose most would agree that childbirth would qualify as one a those times. But such rules don't often float into a person's sights if that person is half-drugged with exhaustion, which is what makes such rules utterly useless less there's somebody nearby to recall them. When there ain't, right or wrong, decisions get made, and there ain't no use spending a lifetime cogitating what-ifs.

When they wheeled me back into my hospital room, Ona was sitting in a chair flipping through the pages of a magazine at a rate that could not possibly allow reading. I couldn't tell whether the look on her face represented concern or annoyance—then I realized it was disgust.

When the nurses left the room, Ona came right up close by the side a the bed, inches from my face.

"What have you done, Nell?" she said.

"What are you going on about, Ona?" I said, putting my hand on her shoulder to push her back.

"You had no right."

"Move back, Ona."

"You had no right," she sneered between her teeth.

"Don't know what you're talking about."

"I asked the nurse where they'd taken you when I got here and the room was empty. She told me."

"She hadn't oughta. It's none a your business."

"It's every bit my business, Nell. You had no right."

"I have every goddamn right."

"You always think that, Nell. You never give a care about other people. This decision here spreads through the whole family, but you don't care nothing about that. Whatever suits you is what you do. You always think you have every right. But you're wrong this time."

"Move away, Ona."

"I can't believe Henry would agree—"

I turned away from her onto my side.

"Nell!"

"Leave me alone, Ona."

"I'm gonna talk to Henry," she said. "Henry has to know."

I turned quickly and grabbed her wrist before she could step back. She pulled away, but I got hold a the sleeve a her sweater and twisted it tightly in my fist. She pulled back until she was almost outta the sleeve.

"You will not talk to Henry, Ona. You will mind your own goddamn business."

"Let go a me!"

"You hear me, Ona?"

"Let go a me, Nell!"

I let go a her sleeve and smoothed it down while she tugged it back into place.

"Go on back to the ranch, Ona. Tell Henry you saw me and I'm doing fine."

"Do you think it's that easy, Nell? You think you're just gonna come home and pick up where you left off?"

"I know it's that easy, Ona."

The nurse walked in with a swaddle of pink, squeezed in between Ona and the bed, and thrust Katie at me. Ona's face slackened at the sight of her, and I thought she was gonna bust out bawling.

"Thought you might be wanting to hold her now," the nurse said, "after, well . . . you know, just thought you might want to hold her." She left the room with a sad smile. Too many people think they know too many things when they don't know anything at all. I looked at the inert bundle she had placed in the crook a my arm.

"Do you want to hold her, Ona?" I asked. She nodded and picked her up. "I can't sleep with her next to me. I'm afraid I'm gonna roll over and crush her, so I just stay awake. I'm plum worn out." Ona nodded again as if she barely heard me and moved to the chair, clicking her tongue at the baby and bouncing her to a silent rhythm. I closed my eyes and listened to Ona's sniffling. We were in the wrong places, me and Ona. Somehow something got confused. Nothing woulda made Ona happier than discharging one child after another from her uterus. But God help me, I just couldn't give myself over to that. I just couldn't.

When the nurse came to take Katie back to the nursery, Ona readied herself to leave. She stopped by the door and stared at me. I stared back.

"You don't consider the consequences of your actions, Nell," she said, softly now. "You never have."

"My actions are my business, Ona."

She snorted through her nose. "You actually believe that don't you? At some point, the consequences will catch up to you. Secrets aren't good for a marriage, Nell."

"You know the truth a that first hand, don't you, Ona?"

Her face turned purplish-red. Bingo. She wasn't going to be telling Henry anything. I turned on my side away from her.

"Have a safe drive home, Ona."

I heard the door close softly.

KATE

My most vivid memory of my father isn't one of sight or smell. I have a general recollection of his appearance, but I have no idea if it comes from memory or imagination. And I remember that he always smelled like the work he was doing, but that's not what startles me awake in the middle of the night. I keenly remember my father's touch—his arm around my waist as he drove the tractor, the feel of thick, coarse hair at the bend of his elbow under the ticklish skin of my palm, his large hand wrapping around me to rest under my arm, his thumb sometimes poking into my armpit, warm against my shirt.

Sometimes—like now—Derek will come up behind me while I'm washing dishes and wrap his arm around my waist, and for a single moment—before I wrest myself away—I feel unbroken. Henry Jorgensen was the curator of hope and peace; his arm around my waist guaranteed one moment would follow the next until I had a string of uninterrupted moments upon which to build a life. For an instant, the warmth of Derek's hand is indistinguishable from the memory of my father's, time is briefly suspended, and the string is intact.

I don't mean to give Derek that moment of stillness amid the chaos—I worry he might develop an illusion that others will follow—but he's quick to sense it.

"Why do you force yourself to pull away, Kate, when you really don't want to?" he asks, dropping his hands into the dishwater I've abandoned in search of a dishtowel.

"Don't want spots to dry on the wine glasses," I tell him.

"There's a moment there, you know, where you want to linger. One of these days you might let yourself do just that, you might rest your head against my shoulder and let certain feelings rise to the surface."

"I'm really not a lingerer, Derek. I wish you would come to terms with that."

"I don't believe you."

"Yeah, I love that about men. I'd like to learn how you reach that state of certainty and arrogance."

"Anybody who's seen you on TV, Kate, and heard you talk about what's best for Nevada knows that you've learned it quite well."

I toss the dishtowel on the counter, pour wine into one of the freshly dried glasses, and walk onto the terrace, where I'm immediately brushed by a balmy summer wind. I hate summer nights. There's something about frigid air that won't allow sentimentality to creep around; when the night winds turn warm I have to do the work myself. I lean against the railing and squint so the lights of the city scramble into shimmering blobs. I live on the top floor of a twenty-story high-rise, not because I'm crazy about penthouse suites with city views, but because I can't stand people walking over the top of me, it's close to work, and a high-rise is water wise, as they say at the office. Derek follows me and leans on the railing next to me.

"I'm sorry for saying that, Kate. I didn't mean it."

"I hope you did mean it, Derek. Quite frankly, I like knowing that you have a few cheap shots in you—that you're not quite as enlightened as the Dalai Lama."

"I try to be."

"Yes, I know. That's one of the most annoying things about you."

"What else do you find annoying about me, Kate?"

"Almost everything."

"Really?"

"I don't know, Derek. I'm often not sure why we're together."

"I think we're meant for each other, Kate."

"I know. That's another thing I find annoying."

Derek nods and walks back through the sliding door. Any other guy would keep walking right out the front door and into the elevator, but he won't. He pours himself a glass of wine and returns.

"You should not be questioning my feelings for you, Derek. You should question yours for me. I'm distant, cold, compartmentalized, arrogant—what would make you fall for a woman like that?"

"I see you differently from that, Kate. I see what's underneath all of that—we're meant for each other."

"Jesus, Derek, we're not starry-eyed high school sophomores. There is no *underneath* to all of that."

"Yes there is. I've seen glimpses of it—I saw it a few minutes ago at the kitchen sink when I wrapped my arm around your waist. I'm not seeing you through starry eyes, Kate. I'm seeing the real you—the totally fucked-up you."

"Well, thank God for that. Hate for you to be surprised by my actions somewhere down the road."

"And I still love what I see."

I shake my head. "I know you do, Derek."

"Are you going to deny loving me, Kate?"

"Would it do any good?"

"Not really."

"Didn't think so."

"I suppose I could try to do fewer annoying things."

"Please don't. You trying to be less annoying would annoy the hell out of me."

Derek takes my wine glass from my hands and sets both his glass and mine on the nearby table. He puts one hand around my back, one hand in my hair. Jesus, nothing can be simple and quick with him. He kisses me softly, slowly, and deeply until he feels the rigidity of my body give way to the palliative summer wind.

"Derek," I whisper, drilling my forehead into his shoulder, "I need to go to Omer Springs."

"Yes, I know."

"Of course you do."

"Do you want me to come with you?"

I nod into his shoulder, and he wraps a hand tighter around my waist so it rests under my right arm. His other hand is in my hair, and the pressure gently presses the scar that runs from the corner of my lip to the outer tip of my jawbone against the soft cotton covering his chest. If I close my eyes long enough to allow it, I can lose the distinction between the current moment and the day the scar was acquired.

That day was just turning itself over to this kind of evening, when the air vows to stay warm and wrap around your shoulders like an old sweatshirt. Dad and I had spent the afternoon riding fences. True to course, we had done more riding than fencing. "Riding fences" was often Dad's idea of a day off—ride into the mountains, cool off in the creeks, nap under a tree, talk about the world. But he'd take along tools, and if a few sagging strands of barbed wire happened to show themselves, he'd step down and tighten them. I was only six at the time, so taking me along as his "ranch hand" was certainly more pretense than reality, but you couldn't have convinced me of that. From the moment I could walk, I had a bolstered belief that my talents as a rancher were indispensable to my father.

We always started out on two horses—my father on one, me and the tools on the other—but by the end of the day, I was on my father's horse, tucked between him and the swell, where I could lean my head against him, resting my hands on top of his, which were folded over the saddle horn. By that time of day, we had already talked through all the questions a six-year-old might have and were content to drift back home, my father usually singing the old songs his mother had taught him, his low, beautiful voice rumbling through his chest, against my back.

We were within sight of the house that day, the horses clipping solidly down the dirt lane that ran from the creek to the yard, when we stopped to tighten two sections of fence near the last gate. Mom and Uncle Nate had just moved water for the night, and were walking toward us.

"We'll fix up these two last sections," Dad had said. "Don't want your mother and your Uncle Nate to think we been loafing all day."

As was his usual custom, he gave me the job of holding a tool, no doubt something he wouldn't need, and told me to stay put where he left me—a safe distance from where he was working. But like him, I didn't want Mom and Uncle Nate to think I'd been loafing all day, so the nearer they got to us, the nearer I moved to the fence. I remember hearing Uncle Nate call my name in a friendly way at the same time Dad said, "Katie, step on back a bit," which was the same moment the barbed wire snapped. Had I been one step back, it would have missed me.

I never saw the wire, and I don't remember the pain. That came later. I remember blood appearing on my shirt just below my collarbone on the right side, the splotch spreading as blood ran off my jaw and chin. I remember Mom and Uncle Nate running toward me. As soon as I registered all of that, which probably took only a second or two, I started screaming. Dad had dropped his tools and was rushing toward me. He gathered me up, and with one strong hand on the side of my head, pressed my bloody face against the cotton work shirt covering his chest. As he ran toward the house, he sang: *Katie, Katie, give me your answer, do. I'm half crazy all for the love of you.*

I must have stopped screaming as soon as he picked me up. The only sounds I remember are his running footsteps—fast and hard on the packed earth—and his voice—deep and soft. I had no idea what had happened, but I wasn't afraid; my father had hold of me.

NELL

Nate walks around the barn as I close the trailer door behind Queenie's rump. Jasper runs laps in the back a the pickup—front to back and side to side—jumping over tack, camping gear, and firewood, excited as hell as soon as I hitched up the horse trailer. You'd think I never take that dog anywhere.

"Where you headed, sis?" Nate asks.

"Not really sure."

"How long you gonna be gone?"

"Not really sure a that either."

Nate nods and ruffles the top a Jasper's head. Jasper takes an excited swipe at his face with a long tongue.

"Want some company?" Nate asks.

"Can't say that I do, Nate, but I appreciate the offer."

Nate nods again, then walks around the truck, checking the hitch and lifting a bale of hay into the bed with a grunt.

"Appreciate that," I say.

"What's that for?" Nate asks, nodding toward the rifle I'd put in the gun rack.

"Just to have along."

"It ain't hunting season."

"No, it ain't."

"Can't see much reason for it then."

"Like I said, just to have along. Can't see no reason not to have it."

Nate sticks his hands into his pockets and shifts from one foot to the other as if he's cold and trying to get warm, though it's near ninety degrees.

"I could put off moving those cows into that next allotment another day—come along with you. I wouldn't mind getting outta this heat and into the mountains myself."

"I appreciate the offer, Nate, but I'm not looking for company just now."

"Ona'd likely be glad to be rid a me a few days," he continues, as if he hasn't heard a word outta my mouth.

"For God's sake, Nate, I'm just gonna take a little time's all. Stop looking like I ain't ever coming back. This ain't no suicide trip. If I die, who the hell's gonna go over to Ely and pick up them tractor parts? Don't suppose you or Ona's capable a that sorta errand."

Nate nods again and stuffs his hands deeper into his pockets.

"Been a long time since you shot a rifle, Nell."

"Yes it has. What's your point?"

He shrugs. "Don't guess I really have one."

"I don't guess you do."

"Where you headed, Nell?"

"Now you already asked me that once, and I said I didn't know."

"Wouldn't be going up to Hamlin Flat, would you?"

"Might be. What do you think, Jasper, want to go to Hamlin Flat?"

Jasper barks, jumps outta the pickup, runs once around the entire rig and jumps back in.

"Hamlin Flat it is," I say.

"You really think that's a good idea, Nell?"

"Jasper here seems to think so." I grab a couple a grocery bags from under a cottonwood where I'd set them, throw them into the cab, and turn to face Nate. "And I can't find no reason to disagree with him."

"Why there?"

"Why not?"

"It'll bring up a lotta memories."

"That's kinda the point, Nate."

He nods nervously again. I walk outta the sunlight into the darkness a the tack shed. He follows close behind.

"You seen my spurs? I can't find them anywhere."

He pulls a pair a spurs off a hook on the wall and hands them to me. I turn them over in my hands.

"I'll be go to hell. These are my spurs. Don't remember putting new straps on em, though. Skinny do that?

"While back."

"Mighty nice a him."

He follows me back to the truck, where Jasper, waiting patiently, starts prancing again in a state of ecstatic anticipation. I throw the spurs on the passenger side floor, slam the door, and turn around to face Nate.

"I'm beginning to think I need to take that rifle and put you outta your misery, Nate. I'm all right. Stop your worrying. You're starting to piss me off."

"Well, you're giving me good reason to worry, Nell. Been a long time since you took off by yourself like this. I thought those days were over."

"They are over, Nate. This ain't the same. This ain't like when I used to disappear for days at a time after Henry died."

"What's the difference?"

"About thirty-five years, and my ability to ride a horse

more'n three miles before my ass starts aching and my back tightens up."

"How long can you sit behind the wheel of a truck?"

"About the same amount of time. Stop your goddamn frettin. This ain't like that. Back then I just couldn't stand to be on this place without him. Didn't seem right for a long time. Now I can't stand the thought a being anywhere else."

We stand looking at each other, looking into our own eyes, knowing each other as well as we know ourselves. I lean against the side a the truck, chin on folded arms, looking down on Jasper, who has finally exhausted himself and laid his head on the spare tire.

"Listen, Nate, I got a daughter trying to end my life here—and yours too. And as was pointed out to me the other day at the picnic, I been incapable a taking any action on that issue. I got some things to think on, that's all."

"You talk to Katie?"

"No, but not for lack a trying. She's a busy woman, our Katie. Left her a couple a messages—told her we wouldn't mind seeing her sometime soon. Haven't heard back."

"You talk to Cassie?"

"Not lately. You?"

"No, I sure as hell miss that girl. We need some youth around this place—keep us old farts sharp. I miss her good company on those long rides out to move cows. Nobody can count up a bunch a cows the way she can and tell you which ones are missing."

"She does have a knack for that."

"And she brings the conversationalist out in Skinny—he tells her all kinds a stories. I wouldn't know a damn thing about him if it weren't for Cassie."

"Why don't you call her up?" I ask, moving around the

truck to make sure everything's battened down. "See how she's doing."

"Maybe I will. I don't much care for talking on the phone, but I sure as hell miss that girl."

I open the driver's side door and turn around to face Nate.

"All right, Nell," he says. "You best get going. It'll take you a couple a hours to reach Hamlin Flat. You need to get outta here if you wanna set up camp before dark."

He pulls me into a hug, holds on for a moment, then releases me abruptly, turns away quickly and stops, turning back.

"You're sure you don't want company?" he asks again.

"Oh, my aching ass, Nate!"

"Fine, but if you ain't back here in a reasonable time, I'll be joining you."

"Now that would depend on whose reason you're using, wouldn't it?"

"Don't much matter with us, Nell."

The road to Hamlin Flat, made up mostly of rocks and ruts, has changed little over the years. That's a good thing—keeps out about fifty percent of the idiots driving around the nation in fancy SUVs with too much time on their hands. The other fifty percent—the ones looking for an opportunity to justify their purchase of a four-wheel drive vehicle—usually tire of opening and closing three gates within ten miles, and opt to turn around when they hit the third one. Can't blame them for that. If Jasper were a more clever dog, he'd be getting the gates stead a me.

Queenie stumbles around in the trailer. Been so long since she's been on a trip, it takes a couple a miles for her to get her feet solidly under her. I don't mind the slow travel though.

Allows the mind to wander a bit. Half the time I'm foggy with the image a dust up ahead from Dad's old flatbed farm truck loaded heavy with canvas tents and boxes a food, and the occasional glimpse a Nate's pickup behind me. That's how we traveled up the mountain after Nate and I both married—Mom and Dad in the lead, then me and Henry, then Nate and Ona. The men would make two trips—taking the horses up first then coming back for the women and the gear.

After Katie was born, Mama would coax her—usually with a promise of still-warm oatmeal cookies—to ride with them. Then Henry would pull me over close to him and wrap his right arm around my shoulders, leaving me to shift when he put the clutch in, and Ralphie would ride up front stead a trying to balance on top of a full load in the back. We'd watch Katie up ahead turned around on her knees in the seat, bouncing over the rocks and waving back at us, making sure we didn't drop too far behind. Henry would blast the horn every time she waved, causing her to tip her head back in silent glee.

First thing Katie'd do when she got to camp is run straight back on the road to meet our truck, coming around to the driver's side where Henry would open the door and snatch her up into the cab. She'd then nudge me over closer to Ralphie while she wedged herself in along Henry's right side. It seemed as if she had to make physical contact with him after every separation, making sure her world was right where she'd left it.

The Baxter family had hunted deer from base camp at Hamlin Flat for as long as I could remember and maybe before that. Hamlin Flat lies just above the point where the pinyon and juniper give way to ponderosa and aspen, where a dozen different scents converge and linger in the breeze. Just above Hamlin Flat the mountains scoop into a nice bowl split up the middle with a low ridge creating two side canyons. Several small streams run outta those canyons and feed into Hamlin Crick, which cuts through the campground with a good flow. Deer and elk were always plentiful in that bowl. Wasn't no need in them days to worry about getting up here on any given day—everyone in Spring Valley and both valleys to the east and west knew that spot belonged to the Baxters, and no one challenged it.

We set up an elaborate camp. Uncle Bert, my mother's brother, met us at Hamlin Flat from the Ely side every year with Aunt Beth and my cousins—Liz, who was the same age as Leroy woulda been, and Charlie and Casey, who were twins just like me and Nate but a year younger. Uncle Bert brought the cooking tent and gear along with several bales of sawdust for the tent floors. The cooking tent held a table with benches long enough to hold eight people down each side, and by the time all a us kids married up and started having kids a our own, we filled that table up. Two chimneys went out the top: one attached to a grill big enough to hold a dozen t-bones and a couple dozen eggs at one time and the other attached to a wood stove. Both the grill and stove were switched over to propane at some point along the way and rigged up to two large tanks that sat out back of the cook tent courtesy of Uncle Bert, who found his bliss and a small fortune in the propane business.

Henry and I used to return to Hamlin Flat every spring—just the two of us—as soon as the snow started to melt and the days turned warm. Henry called it our annual honeymoon. Our second spring up there—woulda been 1956—we set off on horses one day in search a hot springs. I'd been living at the foot a those mountains my entire life, and I'd never known about any hot springs up there, but Henry was insistent. Last fall, he'd spotted steam seeping from the ground just above the north bowl. Took us all day, but I'll be damned if we didn't find that spot. Took another day to dig a soaking hole, another to dig a ditch to bring the water from the spring to the hole, and another to fill that hole in and dig another after we discovered we'd dug the first one too close to the source, making it too hot to soak in. When I got tired of digging the second hole and proclaimed it "big enough," Henry said, "Hell, Nell, that hole's hardly big enough to piss in," and from that point on Henry called the place "Piss Pot Springs."

We went back every spring, each year extending our stay. We spent our days sitting in the muddy hot water and spent the cold nights wrapped around each other under a pile a blankets. Henry and I never told anyone about Piss Pot Springs. Henry said the place was his gift to me alone, and it was up to me if I wanted to share it with anyone else. I wondered if Henry might be testing me with that—to see if I'd do right as a mother and invite Katie to share our place, the perfect family unit. I didn't. I kept that place, and Henry in it, for myself.

I haven't been back to Hamlin Flat since Henry died— I guess that fact alone is enough to cause Nate some consternation—and I'm not sure why I'm headed that direction now. I suppose I'm backtracking to the last place I was able to make sense a life, the only place I can think to go where life might make sense again. But that don't make no sense at all. Nothing at Hamlin Flat but a good hunting camp—and I'm not even sure about that anymore—a crick running cold enough to keep beer refrigerated, and, like Nate said, lotsa memories. I'm not sure how all that is gonna help me figure out what to do about Katie, but that's my destination, nevertheless. I wasn't admitting it to Nate or even to myself, but I knew damn well where I was headed the moment I backed the truck up to the horse trailer.

As I begin the climb away from the valley floor a sage-brush, winterfat, and shadscale, the sky clouds over and a few splotches a rain drop on the windshield. I stop to let Jasper up front, not that he gives a damn—he likes the wind in his ears no matter the weather—but I could use the company. He sits in the passenger seat and hangs his head out the window, sniffing wildly at whiffs a moist sage that come his way—dopey and content—just like Ralphie used to look with me and Henry. Come to think of it, just like Henry used to look. Took a lot to ruffle that man.

"No sense letting life get in the way a happiness, babe," he used to say. "Simple as that."

It was that simple for Henry. And it was that simple for the rest a us whenever Henry was around. He was strange that way. You could be sunk in a worry all day about the lack a rainfall or the unpaid bills, and as soon as Henry came anywhere near, the worry would dissipate, leave you feeling like a fool wondering what all the fuss had been about. Henry was just riding through life with his head out the window, grinning and letting the wind lay his ears down flat.

KATE

"What did your mother say when you told her you were coming?" Derek asks as we pull out of the garage. "How long will it take us to get there?"

"Four or five hours."

"Doesn't look like you plan to be gone long," he says, looking in the back seat at my small overnight bag.

"And you look as if you're staying a week," I reply, eyeing his suitcase.

"I took a week off work; we might as well."

"And do what, exactly?"

"I don't know. Whatever people do in Omer Springs. Ride horses?"

"Have you ever been on a horse, Derek?"

"No, but I'm looking forward to it. I think they're beautiful animals."

"Omer Springs isn't a dude ranch."

"You mean they're not going to let me ride a horse?"

"Oh, I'm sure they'll let you. In fact, Nell and Nate and all the hired hands will be happy to sit their butts on a fence and let you do all the ranch work you want to do. They'd consider that high entertainment."

"Don't worry, Kate. I'll try not to make a fool of myself. I just thought maybe your mother and uncle might be interested in getting to know the man their little Katie is spending her days and nights with."

"Please don't call me Katie. Not when we're heading into enemy territory. I need to stay clear on exactly who I am now."

"And who is that, Kate?"

"Don't be a smartass."

"I wasn't. I was asking a legitimate question."

"Then don't ask those bullshit existential kinds of questions right now. I'm not in the mood."

"I think it might help if you didn't think of your home as enemy territory. Hard to spend six nights sleeping with one eye open."

"I'm not even sure we're staying overnight."

"You would actually do that, wouldn't you?"

"What?"

"Drive five hours, spend an hour visiting with family you haven't seen in years, then get back in the car and drive home again the same day."

"Yes I would, although I'm not committing to a full hour."

"Kate, it was your idea to do this."

"It was a bad idea."

"No, it wasn't. What did Nell say when you told her you were coming?"

"I didn't talk to Nell."

"Why not?"

"I called," I lie. "She didn't answer."

"Did you leave a message?"

"No."

"Can I ask why not?"

"Not sure we want to give them advance notice."

"Ah, yes, the element of surprise. Every good war strategist knows that."

"Exactly."

"And what do you think might happen if you told your mother you were coming?"

"I'm afraid they'll call out the militia."

"How many troops are we talking about?"

"Depends on if they only call out Omer Springs or bring in reserves from other valleys."

"We should tell them we're coming. They might not even be home. Did you think of that?"

"No, sweet Derek, I did not think of that. They're ranchers—do you think they summer abroad?"

"You seem tense, Kate."

"No shit."

"Do you want to talk about it?"

Is he kidding? He must be kidding. I don't see any reason to respond to that question.

"This is going to be a long trip if you're not going to talk, Kate."

"Books on tape."

"What?"

"I brought books on tape—or more precisely, CDs. My overpriced therapist recommended it. Says it helps in times of stress—traffic jams, that sort of thing."

"Hmm. When's the last time you experienced a traffic jam on a two-lane Nevada highway?"

"That's not the point."

"The point is you're afraid to be alone in a car with me for five hours straight."

"I'm not afraid of you, Derek."

"I wasn't suggesting you're afraid of me. I'm suggesting

you're afraid of a conversation that might tear through your fragile protective sheath."

"Don't you ever get tired of deep discourse, Derek? Wouldn't you love to just talk about nonsense for a while or, better still, not talk at all? Thought you zen types were supposed to be into silence."

"I don't have a problem with silence. Let's do that."

"Good."

I reach over to put in a CD without looking to see what it is. Who cares, really? Derek swats at my hand.

"What the hell?"

"Silence, Kate. We agreed upon silence."

"We agreed not to talk."

"We agreed upon silence."

"You mean we're going to ride five hours in this car with no talking, no music, and no books on tape?"

"Afraid of your own thoughts, Kate?"

"You should be afraid of my thoughts right now."

Derek exits off I-15 onto Highway 93.

"Great Basin Highway," he says gleefully. "Then after this we're going to take the Extraterrestrial Highway. You know, I've never been on the Extraterrestrial Highway? What should I expect to see?"

"Martians, I suppose. How the hell would I know?"

"This is your place, Kate."

"It's been years since this was my place, Derek, if it ever was."

"There's a book about Nevada back roads in the glove compartment. See what it says in there."

"My God. You think we're setting off on some sort of fun adventure."

"Never looked forward to any trip so much in my life, Kate."

"You're a sick bastard, Derek."

He reaches over and squeezes my knee. "It'll be fine, Kate. Your instincts telling you to take this trip were good ones. You can trust them. Try to stop sabotaging yourself at every turn of your life."

I look out the window—miles and miles and miles of Nevada. Silver sage, black sage, sage sage. Greasewood. Rabbitbrush. The occasional juniper. A few pinyons on the passes. Dad loved this place, even though he wasn't from here. He said Nevada fit his sensibilities better than his South Dakota boyhood home. He liked being tucked between mountain ranges. Said it made a "heap a sense" to live that way. People who met him for the first time would never guess he didn't grow up in Omer Springs, same as Uncle Nate and Mom. His marriage into the Baxter Ranch seemed inevitable. Once people saw him there, they couldn't imagine seeing him anywhere else.

My therapist is always asking how my life changed when my father died, how it might have been different had he lived longer, if he were alive today. I tell him I don't entertain those absurd thoughts—what good does it do? But the fact is I wonder those things every day of my life. I still feel wronged, as if someone owes me something big, but I can't figure out who that might be or what they might owe me. I simply feel uncompensated and overdue. And nothing in my life—not even being loved by the sweet, kind man who sits behind the wheel right now smiling to himself with the pure joy of driving down the Great Basin Highway with his window down—has ever mollified me.

"Kate?"

"Yeah?" I don't turn away from the window.

"Tell me about your father."

I remain silent, deciding whether to answer him or ignore him. He should insist on being less easy to ignore.

"Do you like this landscape, Derek? This desolate desert?"

"I do. I find it remarkably beautiful."

"Dad did too."

I stick my head out the window into the gathering heat of the waning morning, something—it now dawns on me—that I haven't done in many years. While other parents were pulling children back into the safety of the enclosed vessel, my father was doing the opposite—encouraging me to hang out the window, close my eyes and *feel* the world. I never experienced a seatbelt until I left the ranch. *The danger lies in the restraint*, he would have said. *Whenever anybody tells you to show some restraint, Katydid, don't you comply. Few situations require it—especially out here. Out here you live full-bore. That's the only way it feels right.* I pull my head back in.

"I still miss him," I tell Derek. "Isn't that crazy?"

"Not at all."

"They say time heals all wounds, and that just isn't true. It's not true at all. I only knew the man for ten years, and I think about him every damn day of my life."

"The two of you were very close?"

"I have no idea. I think we were, but I have no context for it. You know what I mean? Every adult relationship can be measured in comparison with every other. But he was my only father. Our relationship had really just begun; we were settling into it for the long run. Now I've had more than three decades to rework my memories of him—there's not a bad one left in there. I have no way of knowing what's real and what isn't."

"Tell me your memories—I don't care if they're real or not—tell me what you remember. Tell me the essence of your father."

"I don't want to."

"Why not?"

"Because nothing I can say about him will let you know him. No words will create for you the man I knew."

Derek nods and remains silent. I roll up the window on my side and turn on the car's air conditioner. Derek follows suit—rolling up his window and adjusting the vents.

"He lived until he died," I say. "There wasn't one moment of his life that went unlived."

Derek nodded and smiled.

"You know how some people seem to be making a big effort to live big lives? They travel to exotic locations, climb big mountains, rush about to visit the grand cities of the world, trot off to third world countries to do good works, and, always, they send proof of their big lives back in the form of digital photos, emailed to an appropriate list for affirmation. I know those people, Derek. I *am* one of those people. And yet, I've never met anyone in all my travels who has lived a bigger life than Henry Jorgensen lived in Nevada's Spring Valley."

"I like Henry Jorgensen," Derek says.

"Yes, and he would have liked you. You both have the same disdain for photography."

"Not as an art form, only as a hobby. Worse as a necessity."

"Precisely. That's why I have few photos of my father. He thought stopping to take a photograph was an utter waste of a precious instant. It made no sense to him to waste a moment of life trying to capture a moment of life, then waste yet another moment looking back at the photos to see if you'd captured the moment you'd wasted in the first place. He thought it absurd."

"Amen."

"Aunt Ona, who fancied herself a pretty good photographer, used to get quite perturbed that Dad would never pose for pictures and would never make me sit still for them, either. He'd tell her she could snap away with that thing—he didn't much care—but she'd have to get him on the move because he didn't see any reason to stop for that purpose. Almost every photo I have of him is blurry. I believe Aunt Ona thought my father was half-crazy," I say, surprised to find myself laughing.

"You have a nice laugh, Kate."

"Don't start, Derek."

"I'm just making an observation. I'm not suggesting anything radical like engaging in laughter on a regular basis. It's just an observation."

I reach over and put a CD in the player—Michael Ondaatje's *Divisidero*. Derek doesn't stop me. He reaches over and places a hand on my thigh; I don't stop him.

CASSIE

I close my laptop when I hear the unmistakable clank of Big Joe's truck dropping off the highway into the parking lot of the Wild Filly Stables. I sit tall to catch my reflection in the mirror behind the stacked glasses on the bar, pull my lipstick out of my pocket and apply it quickly. At the other end of the bar, Maggie sets her pencil down on top of green ledger pages and does the same.

"Wish I had the power to make women gussy up before I stepped through the door," Mick says. We both ignore him, but I feel myself blush. I'm sure Maggie does not. I don't imagine Maggie has blushed in decades, but if there's a possibility of it, it would lie with Big Joe.

When Joe walks through the door, he shakes his head in Maggie's direction and raises his hand slightly. That's Joe's signal that Maggie needn't bother ringing the ladies out. He just wants to sit at the bar and have a beer. I don't know why—Joe's just your average construction bum with a suntan—but that sends a buzz through my entire body. I have worked up a few fantasies since I've been occupying this barstool, and Joe has been a major player in many of them. He's old—about forty, maybe more. Big and bearish but not fat. He does too much manual labor to carry any extra weight. He's nothing

I'd ever describe as good-looking, so it's possible my attraction to him is just a relativity factor based on my current situation and location. But there's something in his manner that says if Joe ever fell in love, that woman would be loved categorically, unreservedly, fully and with abandon. I haven't been around all that much or all that long, but I believe that's more than most human beings—male or female—can ever expect in their lives. Joe has that capacity.

It seems a bit strange to find somebody like Joe spending his spare time in a whorehouse. I've been curious about it since I got here. Neither Maggie nor Mick speaks about Joe when he's not around, and I don't ask. It would feel irreverent to discuss him outside of his company. Bets, who's known Joe going on three years now, says she can't explain it. Bets describes him as "a dangerous customer." She says partying with him feels like making love.

"Isn't that a good thing?" I ask.

"Hell, no," she says. "Messes with your head and makes it hard to move onto the next one."

"Maybe it's just that way with you," I tell her. "Maybe when he's with you, it is like making love."

"Cassie, my friend, thank God you keep your butt attached to that barstool. You are decidedly ill-disposed to be a prostitute."

I suppose she's right, but there's something a little edgy about a guy paying hard cash for the privilege of touching me; the idea delights the feral part of me. I've passed these thoughts on to Bets, thinking I might give it a try just once before I leave this place.

"I've been fingerprinted and licensed," I tell her. "I'd like to at least put it on my resumé under 'job experience' when I graduate from college."

"Funny," she says. "You best just sit right there on your stool and twirl those fantasies through your head. Based on what I know about that mind of yours, the reality would be an extreme departure from the fantasy."

I believe her. Until Joe walks in. He surprises me and Maggie both by choosing the stool right next to mine. Mick puts a beer in front of him, and he nods his thanks to Mick. Maggie shifts on her stool and goes back to her paperwork.

"Cassie, I been thinking about you," Joe says, and I feel the heat rise to my scalp. "It ain't none of my business, but this is sort of a strange summer job you've acquired—webmaster for a brothel."

"Good a job as any," I tell him.

"I can't imagine it pays very well, knowing Maggie the way I do," he says. She taps her eraser on the green pad and pretends not to hear him.

"Actually it doesn't pay anything at all except room and board and the change Maggie lets me keep after running errands."

"Bets says you're here cause you got family problems. That right?"

"Yeah."

"What kind of family problems?"

"I don't know. The usual kind, I guess. People not speaking to each other, that sort of thing."

"You like it here?"

"It's okay."

"Maggie says you go out walking a lot these days. Says you hike all over the Mount Rose Wilderness. Do all your computer work at night."

"I don't like being inside when the sun's high—especially here with no windows. I can't breathe in here sometimes."

"Geography's a little different here than Spring Valley."

I look at him. I don't remember telling him where I'm from—maybe Bets told him. I've had many conversations with Big Joe since I've been here, but it suddenly seems as if I'm looking into that sun-worn face and deep brown eyes for the first time.

"Homesick?" he asks.

I hadn't admitted to anyone—not even Bets—that I had been eaten up with longing for Omer Springs ever since Bets and I drove west across the desert that hot summer night, but I suppose it's obvious. We'd be in the middle of haying right now, and I miss the smell of hay drying in the sun, the mist of irrigation sprinklers on a hot night. I miss riding alongside Uncle Nate and Skinny to move cows from one allotment to the next on the mountain, talking about all sorts of miscellaneous stuff—almost can't bear the idea of them working without me this year. The image of it carves a hole in my belly, and I wake up in the middle of the night, a herd of cattle moving through my head while I count off by tens. I feel as if I've abandoned them—Uncle Nate especially. He makes me feel like my being on this earth matters. I know Grandma Nell has a fierce love for me, that's never been in doubt, but Uncle Nate genuinely seems to believe my presence is something special, as if he's honored to be in my company, plodding along on the horse next to mine. Rather than looking at me like I'm some sort of freak every time my mind toils with a piece of inconsequential material, Uncle Nate seems truly interested. I haven't missed a summer on the ranch since I was seven years old, and missing this one makes me sad, as if I'm sacrificing something that can never be recovered. The loss feels enormous. By the time I'm aware that tears have sprung up, Joe has already taken note.

"Go home, Cassie," he says.

I shake my head and swipe at my eyes with the back of my hand.

"I'm staying, Joe. I know my plan doesn't make sense to anyone but me, but going home means letting my family go on like it is, and I can't do that. My family is like a fence pole that's been gnawed at by a cribbing horse. It's down to its thinnest point and about to break."

"Things have a way of working themselves out, Cassie."

I shake my head. "They're all the people I love in the world, Joe, except Bets. And they're all twisted up with some kind of sadness I don't understand. I feel like I walked into the last scene of the last act of a play. I'm not expecting I can turn this into a happy ending, but . . ."

"But what, Cassie?"

"But I have to try anyway. My Grandma Nell and Uncle Nate are getting old, Joe. I don't have time for things to work themselves out, even if I believed such a lame line, which I don't."

Joe smiles and nods.

"How long you think this plan of yours might take?" he asks.

"That's the flaw in the plan. We might reach the end of summer before someone figures out I'm not where I'm supposed to be."

"Maybe you should call them up and tell them where you are. Better still, maybe you should just get out on Highway 50 and head east."

"Bets and I came out here together. I can't just leave her here without wheels."

"Yeah, thought you might feel that way. That's what I came to talk to you about. I'm driving to Ely on Monday. You're welcome to ride along if you want to. Bets can drive your car back to Vegas at the end of the summer. Don't imagine you have much use for it at the ranch anyway."

"Thanks, Joe, but—"

"Just think on it, Cassie. Nothing says you can't formulate a new plan."

I nod.

"What're you going to Ely for?"

He hesitates before answering.

"My ma's sick."

"I'm sorry to hear that. She gonna be all right?"

"Don't think so, Cassie. She has breast cancer."

"I'm sorry, Joe. I didn't mean to pry."

He nods and starts for the door.

"Joe?"

He turns back and waits for me to continue.

"You from Ely?"

He nods.

"You go to high school there?"

He nods again.

"You know my mama, don't you?"

"Used to," he says. He closes the door softly behind him. Mick continues to dry and stack glasses and Maggie continues to pore over her papers, both of them acting as if they hadn't just heard the entire conversation. Together we listen to the clanking roofing ladders on top of Joe's truck as he pulls back onto the highway.

LEONA

In the early days a our marriage, Nate'd call out as soon as he walked through the door. Didn't mean he wanted anything—just called "Ona" to reach out, a verbal touch of affection. Then I'd holler "hey there, Nate" on back to him just so's he could get my location. He'd track me down and kiss me on the cheek and say "what you doing?" even if it'd only been thirty minutes since the last time he walked through the door and it's obvious I'm folding laundry. He was real affectionate in private. He knows I don't go for that sorta thing in public, so he's real respectful a that. I never liked that about Henry and Nell, and Nate knew that. I think he mighta been a bit jealous a those two at one time—wishing he and I could be just as wild and crazy. But that's not who I am, and I told him so.

Through the years, Nate lost most a that tenderness toward me. Don't know if to blame time or circumstance—probably both. At some point, he stopped calling for me when he walked in the door. For a while he'd still come find me, but eventually he stopped doing that.

He's never spoken a mean word to me, though, but for one time a few months after Henry died. There was a hush over the ranch that winter. One a the barn cats had kittens in a covered feeding stall, and from my kitchen table I could

187

hear those tiny things mewing for their mama every time she went out to hunt down a mouse—wasn't no buffer to block the sound. I was feeling odd about things—sorta like an outsider even though this place had been my home going on nineteen years when the accident happened.

Henry took something with him when he died, and a heaviness settled down on top a us. Course, the setup for that took place long before Henry arrived here—as far back as Leroy's death. The capacity for pleasure had been sucked outta this family, and what replaced it was a devastating fear a what might follow. Seemed as if Flora and Nathaniel had placed the burden a their happiness square on the shoulders a that nine-year-old boy. When he drowned, wasn't no way that Nate and Nell were ever gonna bring that contentment back. They musta felt that even as young as they were. Course Nate would set his heart to trying, and Nell would do the opposite. But before Nell could prove that she had as much capacity to break a mother's heart as Leroy had, Henry showed up.

Nate says Nell was wild to find the bliss in life when Henry arrived—as if she sensed it was rightfully hers. I guess Henry gave her—and eventually the whole family—some sorta permission for that just by living the only way he knew how to live. Once Nell found it, though, she stepped up to the trough a life and slurped it up. She's never had no capacity for restraint.

Henry didn't mean to take this family's joy with him when he left, but lordy, they were quick to hand it over. What's happening now—this thing coming to a head—shoulda happened twenty or thirty years ago, but the Baxters are a slow-moving bunch.

Anyhow, after Henry died, each and every person in this family was so gobbled up with grief they were barely functioning. That's fine for adults—they will eventually find their way out—but we had a little girl amongst us who had just lost her daddy, and not one person besides me seemed aware a that.

As the winter wore on, Katie spent more a her days at our house. I took her into Ely with me one day and told her pick out anything she wanted at Caldwell Drug. She walked quietly through the aisles touching this and that until I became afraid that the sorrow in her heart had swallowed her capacity for desiring anything at all. Finally she picked up a simple set a watercolors—six colors in a tin case with a brush—and turned to me with a smile. It was a sad smile, but a smile nonetheless.

We came home with the watercolors, some finger paints, and butcher paper. Then we cleaned out the spare bedroom that was full a cardboard boxes filled with who knows what and set up a card table where Katie and I spent cold winter days painting and eating peanut butter sandwiches. The room had a south-facing window, so it heated up nicely on clear days. Every so often, Nate would stand by the door and watch us. I had trouble reading him during those days, but I knew it was me he was watching. Katie would get up from her chair and run to greet him, throwing her arms around his waist, practically begging to be picked up and swung around like Nate used to do with her. They'd always had an easy relationship. But now, just about the time she'd reach for him, he'd stiffen up like an old tree stump, like he'd forgotten how to act around her. You can't tell me a ten-year-old girl don't notice them things.

That room had a twin mattress and box springs tipped up on its side against a wall in case a company, and one day Katie said just as clear as ice water, "Aunt Ona, I'd like to tip that bed down and sleep here in this room. Would that be okay?"

Well, my heavens, when a sad little girl asks a simple thing like that, far be it from me to tell her no. I wish Nate'd been slouching against the doorframe at that very moment, but he wasn't. Instead he showed up about the time Katie and I were smoothing down the sheets and hunting for a matching pillowcase.

"What's going on here?" he asked, trying to sound jovial but failing miserably, so's it came out in an accusatory tone.

Katie looked at me like she was about to get into trouble. My heart lurched wanting to protect that child from any further suffering.

"We're fixing up the bed for Katie," I said. "You could help by getting an extra pillow off the top shelf in the hall closet."

Nate didn't move. Instead he glared at me until Katie said, "I'll get it," and slipped quietly past him.

"Katie, if you can't reach it bring one from off the bed upstairs," I called after her.

"Okay," she called back. When I heard her stomping up the wooden staircase, I turned to Nate.

"Say what's on your mind, Nate."

"What you doing, Ona?"

"I'm giving that little girl a place to put her head down and rest her weary body. What does it look like I'm doing?"

"It looks like you're trying to steal Nell's daughter from her."

If I hadn't a been standing right there looking at Nate when those words came outta his mouth, I never woulda believed my own ears. I was so flabbergasted it took me a minute to respond. I believe Nate took my silence as confession, but it wasn't no such thing.

"Nell isn't there for her, Nate, and you know it."

"You stepping in ain't the right thing, Ona. Nell will do right by that child if we give her the chance. Katie and Nell need to get through this thing together."

"She's had plenty a chances, and she ain't done right by that child yet. Katie needs a mother now, Nate. And I aim to give her one."

"That's exactly right, Ona. That's what this is about. This ain't about Katie at all. This is about you. Katie already has a mother. But you—you need a daughter, and you plan to take Nell's."

"Nate, if you make that ridiculous accusation one more time, I swear I'm gonna walk out that door and never walk back in."

At that moment, we heard the back door swing open, then the screen door slam shut. Nate and I both knew what we'd done, and there was no undoing it. The pillow was lying on the floor in the hall where Katie had dropped it.

After that day, Katie insisted on going back to school, and Nell insisted on driving her. I let some time pass, then tried to talk to Katie about what she'd heard, but she'd already constructed a shield around herself that, I believe, has not been penetrated to this day. After that she spoke to me—and everyone else—with such formal politeness you'd never guess she was talking to her own family. And it's stayed that way through the years. Nate consoled himself by watching Nell and Katie drive off together each morning—or at least he pretended to. Me, I've regretted that moment Katie overheard us every day a my life since.

Nowadays if I hear the screen door on the mud porch snap shut, I stop what I'm doing and go find Nate. Seems like he's slogging through his days lately—worried about water, worried about Nell and Katie, and missing Cassie something terrible. He was okay while Cassie was away at school, proud as anybody could be a her, but when she decided to take that summer job in Las Vegas, Nate took it personally. It about broke his heart. Up until this last year, the only time I'd ever seen Nate cry was when Henry died, and again when his ma died. But this year, seems like every time I turn around, Nate looks to be welling up over something and sometimes over nothing at all.

So I'm a little surprised when the screen door snaps shut, and I hear Nate call "Ona," just like he used to. He's standing at the kitchen door by the time I can rinse my hands and wipe them on my apron.

"What you doing?" he says.

"Just doing up the dishes from supper. What you doing?"

He shrugs. "Shoulda moved those cows today but can't seem to make myself saddle a horse and ride up there. Miss Cassie. Skinny's riding the other side this week, looking after his sheep. Got hay to get in and work needs doing all over the place, and I can't seem to get myself moving at all."

"Saw Nell pull out."

"Yep."

"Where's she going?"

"Says she's going up to Hamlin Flat."

"Hamlin Flat! My lord, Nate, she hasn't been up there since—"

"Since Henry died."

"What's she going up there for?"

"Says she has some things to figure out."

"Well how's going up there gonna help?"

"Don't know, but maybe it will."

"How so?"

"I don't know, Ona. Just maybe it's time she revisited that place. Maybe it's time we all did."

"You ain't thinking about following her up there are you?"

"No, not right away anyway. What I'm thinking is we all

shoulda gone back up there thirty years ago."

"Goodness, Nate, a thing like what happened with Henry ain't like falling off a horse, where you got to get right back on and ride again."

"Maybe it is, Ona. Hamlin Flat meant a lot to this family, even before you and Henry was a part of it. I'm not so sure we shoulda given that place up so quickly as we did. Sorta made losing Henry all that much worse—lost Henry, lost Hamlin Flat, lost a family tradition all at once. Seems like the entire Baxter family folded their hands and forfeited the game."

"We was in shock, Nate. You remember what Nell was like. She was undone. Flora too. Losing Henry brought up the pain a Leroy's death for her all over again."

"I ain't saying it's anyone's fault, Ona. I'm just saying maybe we coulda handled things better than we did."

"Maybe so, Nate. But that don't do us no good now."

"I suppose you're right about that, old woman," Nate says, putting his ball cap back on his head.

"You ain't going after Nell are you?"

"No, I'm gonna give her some time. I'm heading over to Ely to pick up those tractor parts."

I turn back to finish the dishes, but Nate doesn't move. He leans one hip against the counter and stands looking at me.

"Want to ride along?" he asks. "Have dinner at the Hotel Nevada?"

Dinner at the Hotel Nevada had been a standard monthly date for the six a us Baxters for nine years before Katie come along. After Katie was born, Flora and Nathaniel would stay home with her, and the four a us—me, Nate, Henry and Nell—would go. Sometimes Char and her husband would join us. We'd order margaritas and chicken-fried steak and sit in a big horseshoe-shaped booth laughing and talking for hours.

Whenever someone—usually me—would suggest that it was getting late and we should get back on the road and over the mountain, Henry would respond with, "To hell with that, let's close the joint down tonight!" eliciting peals of laughter from Nell since Henry knew full well that the Hotel Nevada restaurant stayed open twenty-four hours a day, seven days a week. Henry never got tired a that old joke, and Nell never got tired a laughing at it. After Henry died, we couldn't talk Nell into going no more. Then Char's husband died a few years after that. Nate and I went a couple times, but it was so sad sitting there by ourselves we soon stopped altogether. It'd been a lotta years since Nate had suggested dinner at the Hotel Nevada.

"Mind waiting while I change clothes?"

"No, I don't mind. Tommy's will be closed anyway. He said he'd leave those parts for me by the back door."

I reach behind my back, untie my apron and hang it on the hook. Nate watches me. "I'll just be a minute," I tell him, expecting he'll turn and go about his business. But he doesn't move. Just stands there, one hip against the counter, looking at me as if he's never seen me moving around this kitchen before.

"Looks like we might get a thunderstorm this afternoon," I say to Nate after we settle into the pickup and start south on 893 toward 50.

"Be nice if that materialized, wouldn't it?"

"We sure could use it. Nell might get the worst of it, though, at Hamlin Flat."

"That'd be good for her."

"What makes you say that?"

"We used to love storms up there when we were kids. One year—Nell and I were about fourteen I think—the sky showed snow for two days while we were packing gear to head up to the mountain. Mom wanted to sit out the storm at the ranch, but Dad was insistent on getting to Hamlin Flat and getting set up before the storm came in. Uncle Bert pulled in about the same time we did, and he and Dad had all us kids gathering firewood while they set up camp and dug a hole for the latrine. Whenever we figured we had enough wood, they'd shake their heads and send us out for more, causing an undercurrent of dangerous excitement. By noon, the storm had settled right down on top of us, and it snowed steady for three days. We all slept in the cook tent, and Uncle Bert kept the stoves going day and night. We tunneled a path through snow two feet deep to the latrine. Aunt Beth started fretting that we'd get snowed in, run outta food, and never get out alive. She had poor Lizzy—who was a worrier anyway—worked into a frenzy. Then Nell caught a whiff of Lizzy's fear and went to work on her—told her we'd soon be making bacon and barbequed ribs outta one another. Got so Lizzy was counting heads every time we sat down to eat.

"Once it stopped snowing, Dad—sensing some cabin fever setting into Nell—sent the two of us up into the bowl on horseback to look for deer. The snow was damn near stirrup high, and, Ona, I ain't ever experienced that kinda silence before or since. That snow had brazenly shushed the earth. Nell and I rode up into the bowl without speaking—the squeak of saddle leather and the huff a the horses working their way through that snow being the only sounds we heard. We followed the dip a the old trail between the trees as best we could. We rode for a couple a hours, deep into the middle a the north side canyon, pulled up the horses and sat there. Even Nell was awestruck into stillness with the sheer humility of witnessing such power. She reached over with her leather-gloved hand and pulled one of my hands into hers, hanging onto it tightly. When I looked over she had tears streaming down both cheeks."

Nate looks out the window in the opposite direction so I don't see him tearing up again.

"Nell never shoulda given that place up, Ona. None of us shoulda. Henry's probably still pissed off at the whole lot a us for doing that." He looks at me. "Ona, I don't know how many years I have left on this earth, but we both know it ain't a lot."

"Nate, I wish you wouldn't talk like that."

"Oh, hell, Ona, there ain't no use pretending we're not on the downhill slide. But I'll tell you something, old woman. I aim to see some things straightened out before I die. Henry's death put us off track, there ain't no doubt about that. But after a while us Baxters started using good, old Henry as an excuse for every damn thing we wanted to explain away stead a confronting things head-on. I'm not much for worrying about pleasing the dead, but this family owed Henry better'n that."

"Well, I can't argue with that, Nate. I don't understand half a why things get worked the way they do around here."

"I'll tell you something else, Ona. You and I owe each other better than what we've given also. That might be a helluva thing to say at this late stage in the game, but that's the truth of it, and we both know it."

I nod, not knowing how to respond to that. I had this conversation mapped out decades ago, but figured I'd give Nate some time to come around to it. Lord, I gave it up and forgot what the heck I wanted to say twenty years ago.

"I don't want to go into all that right now," Nate says. "There are better times and places for it. But I don't plan to go to my grave, Ona, and I don't plan to let you go to yours without dragging that field."

Nate lays his hand, palm up, on the seat between us, and I place my hand in his. He gives me an affirmative nod and squeezes my hand tight. It was that that first got me with Nate—the feel of his rough-skinned hand engulfing mine. I was a freshman in high school and he was a senior. He asked me to dance, I said yes, and he took my hand. No big romantic scene—just the same repetitive motion that every teenager knows. But it sent a hum along my bones. Still does.

NELL

Just beyond the railroad tie bridge over Hamlin Crick, two barely visible tire tracks, overgrown with yellow sweet clover, appear on the right. I follow them a quarter mile into Hamlin Flat. The sun, half gone behind the ridge to the west, falls straight away. Jasper scrambles outta the truck window before I come to a full stop—sniffing out camp, pausing for a moment to lap water from the crick, then back to his due diligence. Before I can get Queenie unloaded and staked in the tall grasses below the ridge, Jasper returns carrying the foreleg of a deer—hide and hoof still attached. He drops it at my feet, and I drop to my knees.

"Good God, Jasper. What'd you go and bring me that for?" I pull him in close and bury my nose in his stinky neck. He hesitates, confused by my actions, then pulls away and waits expectantly for me to throw the foreleg so he can retrieve it. I breathe deeply to push aside the feelings that have taken hold—not up for indulging those just yet. I pick the leg up and examine it; Jasper twists his head curiously. Beyond where Jasper stands at the ready, a piece a rope hangs from a pole lodged between the branches of a pinyon and a birch, swaying in the wind.

"I'll be damned. Look at that, Jasper," I say, walking toward the rope and running my hands over the lodge pole. "Nathaniel Baxter placed this pole here in 1954, the year we had a forest fire up here. Henry's first year. Dad stopped along the road about three miles down where the worst a the fire had roared through, walked among those downed trees until he found the perfect pole—barely charred on one end and still strong. He and Nate strapped this thing to the flatbed, hauled it the rest a the way up here, and lodged it between those two trees. Dad nodded as if he'd had the dimensions of it in his head for years. Said, 'I been looking for a good deer hanging pole.'"

Jasper sits obediently on his haunches, waiting patiently for me to throw the deer leg.

"I don't believe you paid attention to a word I just said, Jasper. I don't know why I bother telling you anything." I turn the deer leg over. "This is from last season. Looks like someone took up camp here after us Baxters deserted the place. Our lives got obliterated all to hell and Hamlin Flat went on without interruption. How do you like that? I figured the whole world stopped living when Henry did. I been visualizing this place abandoned and deserted. I suppose that's okay—this place moving on without us. Don't you?"

I look around slowly, allowing myself the distinct ache that comes with the action. I guess that's what I'm here for—to finally confront all a that. A craggy granite wall rises sharply on the south side a the campground. I hesitate at its familiarity.

"Nope, the natural world don't take no bother in the frailties a human beings, you know that Jasper? Sure as hell went right on without us."

Jasper wags his tail, which in turn swings his rear-end from side to side, when I look down at him.

"We ain't gonna play catch with this, Jasper. That wouldn't

be right. Ain't nothing wrong with leaving parts of a deer behind to naturally decompose back into the earth, but it wouldn't be right to fling them about."

I toss the leg back among others under the wild rose bushes in full bloom near the hanging pole. Jasper picks it up again and trots off.

"Jasper! Get back here and drop that thing!"

He returns sheepishly but refuses to drop it.

"Drop it!" I tell him, reaching for the back of his neck. He bolts outta my reach. "Dammit, Jasper. Drop that leg right now!" He jumps into the crick and makes his way to the opposite bank, correctly assuming I won't follow. He drops the leg between his own two forelegs, looking smug. "If I didn't know better, Jasper, I'd guess you'd been trained by Henry Jorgensen. That man could do lotsa things well, but he wasn't worth a damn at training a dog. Thought everyone, including animals, ought to live according to their own nature and whims. You're not the first unruly dog I've shared my time with, though I do figure you'll be the last. So be it. Come on back when you lose interest in that thing. You're gonna have to watch yourself in the crick, though. It's running pretty good, and I ain't in the mood to fish you outta there when you get taken downstream."

I unload Queenie and get her staked in a grassy patch, then, against my better judgment, pull a chair outta the back of the pickup and sit down in the middle a camp close to the fire ring. I'd be wise to get busy setting up camp before dark stead a indulging what I'm feeling, which is a bunch a pain mixed with nostalgia. If our old camp was set up, my location would be right in the center a the cook tent. There's a lot a comfort to be found in a place that never changes—even if that place holds some sorrowful memories—and there are damn few a those kinda places left on this earth. Hamlin Flat seems to be one a them and I thank the Lord or the U.S. Forest Service or pure dumb luck that it's so.

I shot my first deer when I was eight years old—at least that's what I believed most a my life. Uncle Bert stood behind me when I took aim, his rifle also sighted in, and pulled the trigger a split second after I pulled mine. He claims he sneezed right as he pulled the trigger, sending his shot into the air, so it only coulda been mine that brought the buck down, and from that point forward I heard his sneeze behind me just as clear as I heard the shot from my own rifle.

I once told Dad they were plum crazy for bringing us up here every year to deer hunt when the deer were so plentiful at the ranch we could have picked them off from a perch on the fence while they grazed in Mama's garden.

"That's beside the point, Nellie," my father told me. "Life ain't necessarily meant to be lived in the most efficient manner possible. You tend to lose part a life going about it that way. Deer hunt isn't just for filling the pantry full a venison. You have to understand the ritualistic nature a things. Finishing up a summer a hard work before transitioning into another season is time to take pause and give some thought to what's been done. That's what ten days at Hamlin Flat represents."

My father was a quiet man, gentle as they come. Every so often he could freeze life into a crystalline moment that would never be lost again. I did understand. I came to love the ritual at Hamlin Flat, came to expect it and need it. It became more significant than birthdays—the way we counted our years, the way we noted our progression through life, each year recalled through a particular event—the year Nate brought down a eight-point when we were thirteen years old, the year it snowed for three days, the year Mama fell into the crick while she was washing dishes, the year Dad and Uncle Bert drank too much and lost all their money to Aunt Beth in a poker game. And the event that halted the progression a life—the year Henry Jorgensen died from a bullet straight to the heart.

KATE

We arrive at the ranch to find it deserted. I hate it when Derek is right. He seems to hate it also—gloating is not in his nature. He's much happier when I'm right, which seldom happens. Derek operates in a world of peace and logic; I've left that world behind and entered the larger world of chaos and absurdity. I'm not even sure I would recognize "right" if I happened upon it anymore. But if I were right more often, Derek and I would both be happier people.

"Looks like everyone has gone off in different directions," I say. "And there just aren't that many directions a person can go from here. Maybe they flew off to Europe for the summer."

"I'm sure they'll be back soon," Derek says.

"Cassie's car is gone and both Nell's and Nate's trucks."

"So, this is where you grew up," he says, halfway between a statement and a question.

"Yes." I feel edgy, as if we're about to be busted for trespassing.

"This place is beautiful, Kate."

"Yeah, I suppose some might think so."

"Don't you?"

"I guess."

"Let's take a walk, look around."

"Where do you want to walk?"

Derek smiles and takes my hand.

"This direction will be fine," he says, walking east down the old track that goes along the south edge of the alfalfa field toward the Snake Mountains. "I can't imagine growing up in a place like this. Seems idyllic."

I pull back on his hand.

"I don't want to go down there, Derek."

"Why not? What's down here," he says, playfully tugging on my hand. I yank my hand free of his.

"I don't want this walk down memory lane. I don't know what I'm doing here."

"Kate, confronting some of those old memories—"

"Fuck that. I'm sick of people talking to me about confronting pain and getting closure and all that shit. What difference does it make? This path, Derek, if you want to know, goes past my father's grave and leads directly to his old swimming hole, if you could call it that."

"Did he call it that?"

"Yes, in fact, he did. What do you want from me, Derek? Should we go sit on the creek bank and have a good, cleansing cry? Share some endearing memories of Henry Jorgensen? Will that allow everyone to hold hands, be magically healed? My mother and I can rush into each other's arms with our hearts full of forgiveness, and my world will be suddenly set right. Maybe this purifying cry will send water rushing freely through the aquifers of this basin to meet the needs of all the people jockeying to protect their self-interests. Think that might happen, Derek?"

He leans against the fence, dappled in evening shade from a cottonwood, waiting for me to finish my tirade, not a flicker of annoyance or impatience on his face—nothing but compassion, which manages to further infuriate me. He knows better than to reach out for me, although I can feel his desire to do so. Derek believes his touch can fill the deep gorge inside me. That breaks my heart. I want to gently turn him around and send him out of my life. I want to save him from me.

"Kate . . ."

"Fuck that, Derek. I'm taking a stand against closure. I prefer to leave my unresolved issues hanging loose, dangling in the breeze. I can't make sense of life and I'm fucking sick of trying."

His love is unrelenting and utterly bewildering to me. What have I given him to love?

Just as I've convinced myself that getting back in the car and driving back to Vegas is the only sensible thing to do, I see a red pickup coming down the road. I'm not familiar with this particular truck, but Uncle Nate's been driving a red pickup for as long as I can remember—never buys anything else. Sure enough, the truck turns into the ranch lane and heads toward us, flinging dust and pebbles in its wake. I move to put my back against the fence and stand a little closer to Derek—the backs of our hands now touching—feeling as vulnerable as a criminal caught in a searchlight. Uncle Nate drives directly toward us, steering to the right at the last minute and skidding to a stop about ten feet away. He swings open his door and strides toward me with such force, for a minute I believe he means to hit me. There are tears in his eyes—something that shocks the hell out of me—when he pulls me into a tight embrace.

"Katie, Katie, Katie," he says before releasing me. "Thanks for coming. Where's Cassie?"

"I haven't seen her," I tell him, but my response gets muddled in Ona's equally enthusiastic embrace and Nate's moving on to size up and meet Derek.

"I'm Derek. So nice to meet you," Derek says to both Nate and Ona, a little too earnestly for me but not for Ona, who embraces him as if he's been part of the family for years. Derek returns the warmth in equal measure, momentarily resting his chin on Ona's shoulder and raising his eyebrows at me saying, *Right again—nothing but a warm family welcome waiting for you here in Omer Springs.*

"How long you been here?" Nate asks, not waiting for an answer, throwing an arm around my shoulders and pulling me toward the house. "Come on in the house. Ona and I been over to Ely to pick up some tractor parts and decided to stay for dinner. Hungry? Ona, we got anything we can fix up? Bet you ain't ate all day, have you?"

"We're fine, Uncle Nate," I tell him, following him and Ona into what used to be Grandma and Grandpa's kitchen.

"I got some ribs and corn I can heat up," Ona says. "You want to freshen up? Derek—it's Derek, right? You go on into the guest bathroom there on the right down the hall, and, Katie, you go on upstairs and use our bathroom. Sorry for the mess. Didn't know when to expect you."

"Aunt Ona, we're really not hungry," I say, wondering why they would be expecting me at all.

"Ribs and corn sound wonderful," Derek says, although I've never seen him suck meat off a bone in my life. He walks down the hallway to find the bathroom.

"A nice young man," Aunt Ona proclaims. "Go on upstairs and get washed up, Katie. I'll have dinner on the table by time you're done."

I follow her instructions, slowly making my way past hanging coats and boots stored for the summer in the narrow staircase of the farmhouse. The photos on the wall—staggered upward to follow the stairs—have always been there. Much to

Dad's consternation, Grandma equated photos with love: the more photos exhibited, the more love and joy in the house. She no doubt envisioned the entire stairwell filled with photos of kids and grandkids and great grandkids. Apparently Aunt Ona took up where Grandma left off—there are dozens of photos of Cassie at every age over the years she spent here on the ranch. I'm ambushed by the sheer number of them, but more so by the smiling little stranger in the photos.

Derek has never asked me about the decision to hand my daughter over to my mother for raising—nor has my therapist—and I don't bring it up. They are both fixated on the loss of my father, willing to attribute every fault I have and every mess I make to that single incident. At the time, raising my daughter seemed overwhelmingly exhausting, and leaving her at the ranch seemed utterly simple. I rationalized it easily— kids need fresh air, open space, hard work, extended family. Didn't much think about whether or not a kid needs a mother. Didn't much think about whether Nell had suddenly become suitable for the job. Too busy indulging my own loss to worry about Cassie's. And now here she is—a happy, dark-headed child I've never known and never will know.

I drag myself up the stairs, anxious for the privacy of the bathroom, but a photo near the top stops me. A photo of me as a child dressed in full cowboy attire, including chaps and cowboy hat, sitting atop an old bay horse and leaning casually forward on forearms folded over the saddle horn has been put in a frame adjacent to a photo of Cassie dressed and posed in a similar way. I take the photos off the wall and sit on the top step to examine them. I wonder if Aunt Ona has posed Cassie for the purpose of getting a similar picture or if the photo was taken and the similarities noticed later. I remember the day— early fall roundup when I was ten years old—shortly before

Dad was killed. I remember the photo because it captured Dad in the background, unaware of the camera, going about his business. He had just finished saddling his own horse. The photo caught Dad in full action, upright in one stirrup, his right leg a blur swinging over the back of the horse, the hint of a grin in his lips and eyes as he looks toward his daughter. I look at the picture of Cassie, and I'm stunned to see how much the two girls look like each other. One in color, one in black and white. A smiling parent in the background of one, an empty space filled by a clear and open view of the Snake Mountains in the background of the other. No foreboding in the face of either child.

I rinse my hands and face without hurry, regaining my composure before returning to the table to find Uncle Nate, Aunt Ona, and Derek all silent upon my return.

"What?" I ask. "What's going on?"

"Let's have some food and then decide what to do," Aunt Ona says, pushing a chair and a food-laden plate in my direction.

"Decide what to do about what?" I ask. "Did something happen? What the hell could have happened? I've been gone less than ten minutes. Where's Mom? Did something happen to Nell?"

"No, hell, sit down, Katie," Uncle Nate says. "We didn't mean to get you all stirred up. It's just come to our attention through our conversation with Derek here that Cassie's not with you."

"Of course she's not with me. What are you talking about? Was she already gone when you guys left for Ely? Where's Mom—maybe she went with her."

"Katie, Cassie ain't been here all summer," Uncle Nate says. "We were under the impression she was living with you this summer."

"What? She's been here all summer, same as always," I demand.

"No, she ain't, Katie," he says. "That's what I'm trying to tell you. She came out here with a friend a hers then said she had to get back to Vegas the next day before her summer job started. I been missing her something crazy, but I thought she was with you."

I get up and walk out the door, looking for what? I don't know. Cassie's car, I suppose, or some sort of logical explanation. Derek follows me out, and Aunt Ona and Uncle Nate follow him.

"I'm sure she's fine," Derek says. "Otherwise we would have heard something."

"When's the last time you talked to her, Uncle Nate?" I ask, ignoring Derek.

"It's been awhile. I was trying not to interfere too much with her, trying not to let on that I miss her the way I do. But I'm done trying not to let on about things. Let's find that girl. When's the last time you talked to her?"

"I got an email last week—said she and you had been riding fence and praying for rain."

"Well, that's an accurate description a what I been doing," Uncle Nate says. "Guess it wasn't too hard for her to fool us all."

"You sure she's not with Mom?" I ask. "Where is Mom?"

"She's taking a little time for herself," Ona says.

"What the hell does that mean, Aunt Ona? You make it sound like she's gone to a spa or something. Where is she?"

Aunt Ona stays quiet and looks at Uncle Nate.

"She's gone up to Hamlin Flat, Katie," Uncle Nate finally says.

"Oh." Uncle Nate's unavoidable punch lands soundly in

the center of my gut. He and Ona stand silently. Derek looks at all of us, understanding the severity of the moment, but choosing to ask anyway.

"What's Hamlin Flat?"

Aunt Ona hooks her arm through Derek's and begins to lead him away, planning, no doubt, to whisper the unspeakable truth away from my tender ears.

"Oh, for Christ's sake," Uncle Nate spits out. "Can this family please stop dancing around this issue and just speak directly? I'm sorry, Katie, but this has gone on too long."

"I couldn't agree more, Uncle Nate," I say. "Derek, Hamlin Flat is where Dad was killed. To the best of my knowledge, Mom hasn't been back there since and not one of us has uttered the words 'Hamlin Flat' until this very moment. How long is Mom planning on being there?"

"Don't know," Uncle Nate says. "Till she gets things figured out she says."

"Good God," I say. "That could take awhile. She may not be coming back."

"You might be right, Katie," Uncle Nate says, with less levity in his voice than I anticipated.

"And you're sure Cassie's not with her?" I ask once again, grasping at hope.

"Pretty damn sure," Uncle Nate says.

"Then we need to find her," I say. "Where could she have gone? You say she was with Bets when she stopped here?"

"Yeah, I think that was the girl's name, wasn't it Ona?"

"Yes, Bets," Aunt Ona says. "Katie, why don't you just call Cassie on her cell phone and ask her where she's at?"

Uncle Nate, Derek, and I all look at each other then look at Aunt Ona. She flushes with self-consciousness.

"I suppose that would be the logical thing to do," I say to

Aunt Ona. "Thanks for the suggestion."

We go into the house and sit back down at the table. They all watch while I dial the phone and listen while I quiz Cassie on her whereabouts. When I hang up after talking to her, they look at me expectantly.

"Cassie refused to divulge her whereabouts, but seemed more than a little surprised and excited to find out mine. Says she'll be here tomorrow."

"Tomorrow!" Aunt Ona says. "Where on earth could she be?"

"She wouldn't say, but the music in the background sounded like she'd time-traveled to a 1960s honky-tonk."

I hadn't noticed that while I was speaking to Cassie, Derek had gone out to the car, come back in with his computer, and now had it booted up.

"You can't get internet service here," I tell him. "Have you forgotten where you are?"

"Can now," Uncle Nate says. "Nell put a satellite up for Cassie about five years ago."

"What? That little shit always maintained she couldn't respond to my email for lack of service here."

Uncle Nate and Aunt Ona both look at me apologetically. I wave my hand to release their gaze.

"Found her," Derek says. "But you're not going to like it."

"Seriously?" Aunt Ona asks. "Just like that?"

"Yeah," Derek says. "Didn't actually expect it to be that easy myself, but there she is." He turns the computer around so we can all see the image and name of Cassie Jorgensen displayed on the website of the Wild Filly Stables.

NELL

The morning shift in temperature wakes me in time to glimpse Jasper's rear end slipping into the trees at the north end a camp. Just like Henry that dog is—can't settle into a place until he's explored his surroundings, got a bead on his physical location. I never did get a proper camp set up last night—just pulled the cot outta the truck and went to sleep. And I'm too old for this. Hipbones ache, head aches, knees ache—aches on top a aches run the length a my body. Course, the majority a the pint a bourbon I drank in lieu a dinner last night mighta been a contributing factor. And maybe not a wise one, but it seemed so then—allowed my thoughts to fraternize with the moonless night.

Bacon, eggs, and pancakes are the tried and true menu for Hamlin Flat. Seems a bit much for me and the dog, but I love the smell a bacon among pines, as does Jasper, who trots back into camp the moment it begins to sizzle.

"What'd you find out there, Jasper? Anything worth talking about?"

He jumps on the cot and curls into my sleeping bag. He's abandoned all sense a the rules out here and seems to know I don't have the energy to correct him. I unpack the truck while the bacon's frying.

"You're not worth a damn for conversation, Jasper, you know that? You're also not worth a damn for setting up camp and helping out. Fact, I don't know what you are good for. Can't even flip the bacon."

I sit on the cot next to Jasper, put his head on my lap and pull on his ears. He doesn't pretend to like it, but he doesn't stop me either.

"I been alone a long time, Jasper," I whisper. "And I never wanted to be alone. But once there was Henry, there wasn't no other option except a no-good dog. Goddamn, I miss that man. Funny, isn't it, that I'm still wondering how I'm gonna live without him? Guess I been doing it thirty-six years now, but every morning I wake up with the same damn questions trembling under my skin—how am I going to live without that man today? And why the hell would I want to?"

I nudge Jasper off my legs and get up to flip the bacon. Two eggs and one pancake for me; three eggs and four pancakes for Jasper. A ferruginous hawk perches on a branch in a dead juniper near the entrance to camp, judiciously watching us.

"When's the last time you were under twenty-four-hour surveillance?" I ask Jasper, pointing to the hawk. Jasper ignores me as usual, having finished his breakfast and taken up his place on the cot before I can get my breakfast dished up. "That gal has a nest around here. She chose this place because she likes the open space, but she don't like sharing it. She's not enjoying our company. You'll keep your distance from her, Jasper, if you have any sense at all—although I've seen no evidence of it."

As if to prove my point, the hawk makes several noisy passes overhead, flying lower each time.

"Under any other circumstances, I'd respect your wishes, old girl, and pick another place," I tell her, waving my spatula in her direction as she resumes her post on the juniper. "I don't

213

mean to cause you consternation. I understand trying to protect your young. I'm a mother myself although my competency in that area is no doubt inferior to your own. But this here's the only place I can be right now, so we're gonna have to figure out a way to coexist. I'm gonna go on about my business here, and hopefully you'll get the message I don't mean you any harm."

By the time the dishes are done and a respectable camp set up, the sun is straight overhead. I pull the saddle and gear from the truck, leaving it on the tailgate, and walk toward the meadow where Queenie has grazed through the night. The hawk swoops directly at my head, calling out her alarm—*kree-ah, kree-ah, kree-ah*. She comes within ten feet before banking off and circling around to come in again. I drop to the dirt and pull Jasper down next to me.

"I don't mean you any harm, mama," I yell at the hawk. "We're gonna have to work this out." I lay low for a minute then creep toward Queenie, keeping Jasper close. The hawk takes another noisy swoop, but doesn't come any closer before returning to her post in the juniper. Jasper hightails it back to camp, content to watch the activities from a distance. "I got your message, mama. Hope you got mine."

The hawk allows me to saddle and mount up. I place the rifle across the front a the saddle, give a nod to mama hawk, and ride up the crick with Jasper in the lead, looking for a wide, shallow place to cross, not wanting to force a confrontation with the hawk by riding past the juniper to the bridge. A quarter mile past camp we cross the crick and start north up the old trail. I find myself more disturbed than I ought to be when I discover the trail—always a single track traveled by horseback or foot—now has two tracks. What did I think would happen to this place over a thirty-six-year span? I suppose I expected that those who came after us would sense this as sacred ground, that they would intuit the significance of Henry's life and the magnitude of his death and show some reverence. Henry would have found ATVs *disappointing*. He seldom showed anger, but he had a low tolerance for unnatural noise. He didn't mind a howling wind or a crackling thunderstorm, but he thought humans could and should make less noise than most a them do. Dad couldn't even get Henry to use a chainsaw but for the noise of it.

As Queenie plods along the left track, I realize I miss my old life. I don't mean my life with Henry—there's not even a word can speak to the loss a him. I mean my life before I stopped going down to Frank's Place to have a beer and eat some beans and argue about ATVs with old Fitzy, my life before Katie splintered it apart. I hate seeing Fitzy that twisted up. He ain't the brightest bulb, and he annoys the shit outta me about ninety percent a the time, but he don't deserve what he's going through now. That don't mean I'm taking responsibility for whatever's going on between him and Bea, and I *will* beat the crap outta him if he don't stop messing with my irrigation pivots—crazy old fool—but he's right in recognizing he can't survive outside a Spring Valley. He's exactly the sorta person this life was set up for—this is where he functions. Setting him up in Vegas would be like putting a John Deere tractor engine in a sports car. Before all this came about, Fitzy's biggest worry was the limitations put on ATV riders. He likes to go "four-wheeling" with his grandkids and then he likes to sit down at Frank's and gripe about the ATV restrictions—especially up here in the Schell Creeks where the roads blossomed from a few dirt roads to more than five hundred miles a dirt roads following the introduction a ATVs.

"Gawd, Nell," he used to say, "us ATVers need to have

some place we can ride. Shouldn't be that every place is off limits."

"The hell it shouldn't," I'd tell him. "Besides tearing up good grazing land and making a mess a things that don't need to be messed with, those damn things create both air and noise pollution."

"We're just trying to have a little fun, Nell. Why don't you come out with us some day? I'll bet you'd like it if you did."

"There ain't a chance in hell a that ever happening, Fitzy," I'd tell him. "Trying it or liking it. Saying you ATVers need some land set aside to ride on don't make any more sense than saying vandals need some buildings set aside to destroy. Same damn thing."

"Ah, Nell, you need to get modernized. You and Nate are the only ranchers out here still relying on horses to work. Everybody else jumps on the ATV to change water or check cows. We can be out and back in the time it takes you and Nate to saddle your horse."

"I guess I ain't in as big a rush as the rest a you are, Fitzy. I got nowhere to be but right here," I told him.

I don't suppose anybody hunts by horseback anymore either. Too inefficient. Not many folks left on earth would buy into Dad's philosophy that life ain't meant to be lived in the most efficient manner possible. Henry did though. That's why he and Dad got along so well right from the start. Both of em believed with all their hearts in the pursuit a happiness at a slow pace.

Last night, as I sat in the middle a Hamlin Flat encased in darkness, I wondered if I would be able to return to the exact place where Henry died. I'm compelled to do so now, but I don't know why. I'm an old woman. I'm not foolish enough to believe in magical moments a resolution. Going to the place a

Henry's death ain't gonna conjure up his spirit in an answer to my troubles. Nevertheless, I'm doggedly taking myself there, like an old mule that only knows one direction home. My body is flooded with a mixture of anticipatory dread and resigned peace, and I'm not sure which a those two feelings is real and which is fabricated in an effort to cover for the other. I'm not inclined to figure it out right now.

Jasper runs ahead on the trail as if he alone knows the way. The slope a the land feels the same as it always did, but the place is overgrown and buzzing with cicadas and too many shades a green compared to the stillness a deer-hunting time. When Nate and me were kids, Dad used to bring us up to camp for a weekend about this time a year just to get outta the valley heat and take some time off. One summer, Dad built an elaborate covered bench into the side a the ridge up ahead and off to my left—a place where a person could sit outta the weather to wait for deer to stop by the crick.

We kept that old bench repaired over the years we came up here. I don't imagine it has survived our absence, but I'm sure I can find the spot where it used to be. Where the crick widens, loses its banks, and breaks off into a bunch a tributaries creating a marshy meadow—a place deer naturally stop to drink and bed down—that's where I'll find it. That's where Katie and I were sitting, rifles cocked, when Henry stepped outta the tree line into the last slice of the day's light.

I whistle at Jasper as I dismount Queenie and throw the reins over a pinyon branch.

"I'm gonna leave you here, old girl," I tell Queenie, stroking her neck. "The brush is too thick over there, and it's swampy as hell—you'd end up in a panic and throw me on my ass. Stay here, though. I'm too damn old to walk back to camp."

I whistle once more and holler for Jasper, then grab the

rifle from the saddle before cutting in through the brush on foot. Don't know why I care where that dog is—he can find his way back to camp—but I wouldn't mind the company such as it is. Also don't know why I've brought the rifle along. Like Nate said, ain't hunting season. Seems like I don't know much a anything these days. Funny how that works, how you think life will get clearer as you go—gaining wisdom and all that—and the older you get the more fuzzy the world becomes—literally and figuratively.

Willows and wild rose grow dense along the crick, and thorns tear at my denim shirt. Ain't no way to go through these things other than just walking on through, so I roll my sleeves down and snap them at the wrist. No reason for pussyfooting—it ain't gonna scratch any less if you move slow.

We had a good winter this year—first in a long time—and the crick is running well. Nice to see that, even if it does make my getting to the other side a little more difficult. I find a place that looks decent for crossing and step in. Frigid water pours into the top a my work boots over my ankles. In my younger days, I would have boulder hopped. Not an option anymore. It's hell getting old. But the sun is high and hot, and the cold water feels good around my perpetually swollen feet. Nothing much looks familiar in here. The brush seems awful thick, and the familiar bends a the crick have given way to new ones. Finding the old spot might be trickier than I figured. Don't know whether to be relieved or upset about that.

It's slow and rough going. My shirt is torn in several places—as is my skin—before an outcropping a granite twenty feet up the canyon wall on my left stops me cold. I should come to a wide place in the crick feeding into the swampy clearing about twenty paces upstream. It doesn't look quite as grand as I remember it, but sure enough, deer tracks in the mud tell me I'm in the right place.

I stand stock-still listening intently—for what, I don't know. Jesus. My body is trembling something awful. I turn away from the crick toward the canyon wall. The bench Dad built and maintained through many a deer hunt season would be directly in front a me, built into the trees a few feet up the slope, if it still existed. I slosh through the meadow toward the place where it should be, winding through pine and aspen, looking back from time to time to make sure my angle is right. Each time I look back, I'm stopped dead in my tracks—the scene too familiar for comfort.

"Right here," I whisper. "Right here, right here."

And as if I've conjured it, I walk directly to the bench— no longer covered but every bit recognizable—a graying slab of three cut logs held together with rusty nails and baling wire, wedged between two aspen.

"Christ almighty." I set the rifle down and hoist myself onto the bench, keeping my head down, not yet ready to look full on the scene in front a me—the place I'd just come from. I pick the rifle back up and lay it across my lap.

It was here Katie and I sat the day Henry died. The last day a deer hunt. 1975. I had this same rifle—Remington Model 700 bolt-action 30-06. The rifle feels strange in my hands now. That bothers me. From the time Dad gave me my first .22 rifle—against my mother's wishes—when I was seven years old, the thing felt right in my hands. Dad said he didn't even have to teach me to shoot; I just set cans up along the fence and started shooting em off. Mama never liked the number a rabbits I dragged home from a day a shooting, but I always prided myself on being a good shot.

From the time Katie was small until the year when she was ten—the year we stopped hunting—the camp was filled with kids. Casey came with his three boys; Charlie brought his two girls and a boy, and Liz had two girls. The camp rule was that a kid had to be at least ten years old to hunt. Anyone under ten stayed in camp on cook duty with the non-hunters: Ona, Mama, Aunt Beth, Liz, and anyone else who opted not to hunt.

The first few years, Katie would wail like her world was ending as soon as she realized Henry's intention to saddle a horse and ride outta camp without her. Mama, Ona, and Liz tried everything in their power to preoccupy and fool Katie while the horses were being saddled. Didn't matter. Finally they just let Katie stand at the crick as the horses clopped through the water single file. She'd wave wildly, saying good-bye to each one of us—"Bye Mama, bye Grandpa Bax"—each morning the same, as if she was happy to be rid a us and as if the prior morning's memory had somehow abandoned her. But I don't think it had. Katie simply had an unabashed faith in Henry to do right by her, and until his horse crossed the crick, she stood by her faith. But as soon as Henry tried to slip by, her face reflected the raw depths a despair.

Poor Henry. The man loved to hunt, but it was all he could do to ride by her, and he'd spend the better part a each morning trying to forget the image a her disconsolate little face contorted by anguish. Eventually it turned into a game a wits. The year Katie was six, Henry would slip outta camp on foot before light, and I would meet him on the ridge with a saddled horse, coffee, and breakfast wrapped in aluminum foil. But by the time Katie was eight, she started slipping outta camp before breakfast herself and waiting for Henry on the ridge. I'd show up with breakfast for both a them, and Mama would show up a half hour later to take Katie back to camp. By then she had exchanged crying for sulking, which was a little easier on Henry.

The year Katie turned ten—hunting age—she was so excited she talked about little else for ten solid months. It was a Baxter tradition to get a hunting rifle the Christmas before your first hunt. That way, you had ten months to learn how to shoot. I don't know whether Katie ever had any interest in hunting—in hindsight I suppose she didn't—but turning ten and owning that rifle meant Katie would be saddling a horse and riding next to Henry all day. Maybe that woulda been enough for her—to ride into the bowl and drive the deer down. But all her life she'd been hearing about her mother the hunter, her mother the sharpshooter. And much a that talk had been coming from Henry himself as he taught her how to use the rifle. *It's your mother oughta be out here teaching you to shoot, Katie,* he'd say. *She's a helluva lot better at it than any a the rest a us.* Seems Katie had little choice but to pick up a rifle.

Katie and I had been sitting on this bench more'n three hours that day, and she was antsy, as she always was outside her father's company. The whole thing was Henry's idea—in every way, big and small.

I was never meant to be a mother—not every woman is. Everyone knew that, though no one ever said it. Even Henry knew it. Katie was purely my gift to him—I loved him that much. But that wasn't enough for Henry. He figured he could forge a bond between me and Katie—either that or he'd die trying. Sure as hell, that's what happened.

<hr />

Nine years a marriage Henry and I had before Katie was born. Beautiful years they were. Wild and crazy and passionate. Goddamn that man! I'd trade any fifty years a my life to have another nine like those. Maybe that's all anybody ever gets—a handful a good years among the not-so-good majority.

Don't know how I managed to keep from getting pregnant during those nine years—might have been sheer will on my part. Oh, that's a goddamn lie. I'm still saying that as if Henry might be floating over my head reading my thoughts for hell sakes, as if any a that could matter now. Fact is, unbeknownst to Henry, Nate, Ona, Mom and Dad—all a whom were counting on a brood a young ranch hands—I mail-ordered a diaphragm less than a week after Henry dropped outta Dad's pickup truck in front a our old house. Had it sent to my friend Ellie, who lived in Ely with her father and brothers, who all worked night shifts at the mines and paid little attention to her. I kept it in my underwear drawer until Henry got outta the army and returned to Omer Springs for good. Folks around me—not just my own family but everybody in Omer Springs—talked like getting married was done for the express purpose a breeding, like that's all any damn fool girl could ever want—to become a broodmare. They talked babies till I couldn't stand it. I had trouble dissecting complex feelings in those days—guess I still do—but deep in my gut I knew I needed Henry to myself. How could that be wrong—to love a man that much?

I never mentioned the diaphragm to Henry, and Henry, bless his heart, would never suspect or snoop around or even notice such a thing, gliding through life the way he did. I don't know what Henry's reaction woulda been had he known. He seemed pretty sure we would have children, and he never lost that sense a surety as the years began to pass, utterly content to let it happen whenever the universe seemed to turn that way. That was Henry. Always thinking the universe would turn in his favor, as if human contrivances had nothing to do with life. I'll be damned if he wasn't usually right. I'm not one to believe that God has a plan for each a us or that God even pays a damn bit of attention at all, but I sometimes wonder if Henry wasn't taken from this world early to save him from having to experience the letdown a reality. Seems if a person lives long enough, he'll eventually run into the darker side a things, and I can't imagine Henry's personality could withstand much a that. I don't know what'd happen to a guy like Henry if his only daughter was working to take away his livelihood. Course, I also can't imagine Katie doing such a thing if Henry was still alive. What a mess.

I suppose lotsa people are saying I caused this mess. I'll be the first to admit that my mothering skills were far from developed when they came to be tested, but I tried to do right by Katie once Henry was gone. I tried to make Henry proud a me as a mother to his daughter. I tried to protect that girl. Maybe I didn't handle things exactly right or the way other folks thought it shoulda been done, but I did what I could. No one can deny that. They can fault me for my methods but not my intent.

I'm ashamed to admit this, but I never thought a Katie in terms a love. I've thought about her in terms a devotion, duty, even admiration, but never in the realm a love. I've only known one way to define love—by Henry Jorgensen. I loved him so completely that I could never figure out how to split that love between him and Katie. Is that something that's supposed to come naturally to a woman? Is extra love supposed to form in a pregnant body like amniotic fluid?

The summer I was pregnant with Katie, Henry and I kept up our swimming ritual at the end a each day. For the first time, I became self-conscious about my body—about Henry looking at me. Henry would insist on watching me undress as he always had, telling me he thought me more beautiful in my state of pregnancy than in any other. Oh, how I hated hearing that! I would flush with the fear of it, the fear that Henry would forever see me that way—as that child's mother—and never again see me stripped down to my bare essence the way he had a few months earlier. Henry's love had already split— before the child even took a breath—and I had no way of ever making it whole again.

And what does an unborn child make a that? It must feel the physical flush a fear against its newly formed skin. Would it mistake that flush for love? For caring or safety? Or would the emotion that carried the heat seep into the still-growing organs, informing them a the harshness that awaits? Is that why Katie was so reluctant to come outta the womb and into my arms on that cold February day?

Now, as I sit on the makeshift bench my father built in the place that once represented the fundamental nature a life, the place where life got twisted inside out, I ask myself this question: do I love my daughter?

KATE

Derek catches the back of his shirt on a strand of barb-wire as he crawls through the fence. Everything about him—creamy skin, slight build, long hair, clean-shaven face—is wrong out here. I worry that Omer Springs will beat the hell out of him—not the people, just the place. I want to send him back into the house for his own safety.

"Kate, wait!" he calls, running to catch me. Derek is grace-ful, like the yoga he practices every morning. But watching him run across a field of alfalfa is like watching a toddler run—eventually he's going to land on his face—so I stop to wait for him.

"Listen," he says. "I know you want to be alone right now."

"Which doesn't explain why you're chasing me."

"Because I think you're upset."

"Jesus Christ, Derek. As everyone in this family knows and everyone in my whole fucking life knows, I've been *upset* since I was ten years old!"

"I shouldn't have shown you that picture of Cassie on that website."

"Of course not. Let's protect the fragile, crazy woman."

"I could have told you with a little more sensitivity."

"Christ, Derek, stop! You can't fix me!"

"It's not that bad, Kate. I'm sure Cassie—"

"It's not that bad? It's not that bad? Let's have a little rundown, shall we? My mother—who never liked me to begin with—shot and killed my father, I have the job of divvying up water in the driest state in the nation, I'm the most hated woman in the entire Great Basin and several surrounding states, I don't have a fucking clue who my daughter is because I tossed her off before she was old enough to formulate a complete thought, but she's thinking she wants to grow up to be a prostitute, and you insist on standing by my side as if you're waiting for the happy ending. Does that about do it?"

"Go for a walk, Kate. It will do you good."

Should I slap him or walk away? I turn my back and start walking.

"I'm sure you're wrong about a lot of that stuff, Kate," he calls after me.

Keep walking, I tell myself. *Because that urge you have to wrap your hands around his neck, digging the nails into his pearl-white skin, watching the straggles of blood run into the hollow of his throat will surely dissipate if you keep walking.* I don't divert my course when I realize I'm walking directly toward the middle of a long line of half-pivot irrigation pipe spraying full force. I duck under the pipe; my jeans and shirt soak up the water and cling to my skin. I don't intend to walk to my father's old swimming hole—now about the size of a child's wading pool—but that's where I find myself before I can make another plan. Big mistake. Of all possible locations on the ranch, this one is the most likely to ensnare me.

"This was *our* spot," my mother told me a few weeks after Dad died when I walked out here one late afternoon. Her horse was tied to a tree, and she was lying flat on the ground under a cottonwood. Not in a restful way, not like she was taking a nap.

More in a sacrificial way, prostrate on the frozen ground. Her hair, which she always wore in a long braid down her back, was loose and matted with leaves and dirt. She jumped up when she heard me and took hold of my forearm, the nail edges deep black against my skin. *This was our spot.* She gave my arm two good jerks on the words "our spot" and looked at me through pink-rimmed, glassy orbs. I wrested free of her grip, and as I ran through the field to Grandma's house I heard her calling after me, "Katie! Katie!"

I was never sure what my mother meant with those words—*this was our spot*—whether they were an accusation, a warning, or an attempt at kindness thwarted by her own despair. I spent the next few weeks living with Grandma and Grandpa, and my mother spent those weeks on the back of a horse—as if she were searching for a place where the pain couldn't find her. By the time my mother and I spoke directly again—when my grandparents explained how my mother needed me and urged me to return to my own house—she was cleaned up with her hair back in a braid. I remember her standing in the kitchen when I walked in the door, looking identical to the upright freezer that hummed next to her. Impermeable. Locked and sealed. From that point on, every conversation between us has carried the emotional weight of an inconsequential business transaction.

I've often wondered what would have happened that day if I hadn't run away. What might have transpired between the two of us, what truths may have been told in such unprotected circumstances? I've carried remorse for that brief moment—remorse for the turbid, grief-ravaged woman, remorse for the inconsolable little girl, and remorse for the lack of courage to jump through the aperture before it clicked shut on that mother and her daughter.

I hang my wet clothes on a branch and wade into the creek, gasping at the shock of it even though I'm already drenched. I sit on the pebble-lined creek bed and lean against a boulder, causing the water to rise to my waist. Been a long time since I've felt water on my skin that didn't come through a pipe. Feels good—water running through the land directly from mountain snow.

The current swirls gently—parting to accommodate me and rejoining on the other side—softly, tenderly accepting my presence as if I'm no bother at all, as if I'm not the woman touting a plan to yank it violently from its natural course. Oh, what the hell am I thinking? *It's water, Kate.* It has no soul. It has no preference for traveling slowly through rich dirt banks under sun-dappled shade rather than being forced through a dark, steel pipe.

Deep in my gut, I know Henry Jorgensen would disagree with that. "Everything has its own nature, its own way of being," he used to tell me when we'd sit here in the stream or on the bank under the tree. The man was a born philosopher. I grew up remembering him as a great thinker, but a child always thinks that about her father. Then you grow up and realize your parents know significantly less than you gave them credit for. Dad never got the chance to disappoint me, and there's nothing in me that believes he ever would have.

"A dog, the grass, a horsefly, the crick—it's all just out here doing its thing," he'd say. "Now human nature is to mess with all that. So we train the dog for our own amusement, and we like to think the thing loves us."

"Ralphie does love us," I told him.

"That's fine to go on thinking that," he said. "That's human nature, and Ralphie seems happy enough."

Ralphie, stretched out from front paw to back with his belly to the sun, rolled onto one side at the mention of his name.

"We dig minerals outta the dirt to make our lives easier, we lay strips a pavement across the land to make things convenient for ourselves, we plant grass and coax the water outta its banks to flow on over our fields before it goes on its way. That's all okay to a point. We're part a things, and we gotta follow our own nature. But the less we mess with everything else following its nature, the better off we'll be. That's a hard lesson for humans. I don't figure we'll ever learn it."

"Then what happens?"

"Oh, I imagine we're no different than any other species in that manner. Nature has a way a taking care a things when one particular species gets too big for its britches. That's the beauty in the whole system, Katie."

"What does that mean?"

"The way I see it, Katie my girl, the human species is a lot more clever than it is wise. Clever brings about things like the airplane. Wise would warn us about the danger a that invention—the easy spread a disease and war, the sheer absurdity of growing food in a different place from where you eat the food—that sorta thing."

"But you can visit other places and see the world on an airplane!" I told him.

"Yep, that's clever, ain't it? Wise would be to live where you are and find joy in a single footstep. That part we just ain't figured out yet."

"Think we ever will?"

"Don't seem so. But that doesn't mean you can't, Katydid. You're going to have an interesting life, Miss Jorgensen. I imagine things will be spinning pretty quickly by the time you're my age. I suspect the span between clever and wise will be wider and deeper than the Grand Canyon by then. Just remember, the key is not to live the longest life possible—that would be clever, and that's what the majority a our species is shooting for. That's why we spend a whole lotta money on things that don't make much sense. You're gonna wanna step yourself outside a that idea. The key is to live until you die, and to do it as wisely as you know how. No time like the present to get started with that. Wisdom don't come with age—all you gotta do is look around you to dispel that little myth."

"How do I start?"

"You already have. Sitting right here under this cottonwood tree with me and that dog—one a whom loves you like crazy and one a whom don't know the difference between love and a porkchop bone."

"But we do this every day!"

"Amen. And every day I ask myself, would I rather be on an airplane flying off to some exotic place, or would I rather be sitting under this old tree hanging my feet in the crick with my girl and my smelly old dog. I don't have to think very long and hard before I answer that one, Katydid."

"But what if me and Ralphie were on the plane with you?"

"Think you're gonna find a prettier place out there than this one, Katie?"

I shrugged. "Some people think so."

"Sure, and they're right. No doubt there's an old man and a little girl sitting on a riverbank somewhere in Africa right now thinking there's no more beautiful place in the world. And that's the truth. No reason for them to get on a plane and come to Omer Springs. If you're ever looking for peace and happiness in your life, my girl, just lift up your two feet and check right under there."

The bottom half of my body has gone numb from the cold before I drag myself onto the bank into a splice of sinking sun. Not much evidence here that thirty-six years have gone by. That's how it should be, according to Henry Jorgensen. "Lotsa people want to leave their mark on this earth," he used to say, "but that's a god-awful lotta marks all over the place. Best not to do that if you can help it."

If I'm honest with myself, I have to admit that the creek runs much lower than it used to, and the old cottonwood blows in the breeze with significantly less shimmer and vibrancy. If I'm honest with myself, I would acknowledge that it's dry as hell here. Not the kind of dry that you get in the middle of every summer—more like a thirty-year, choking-to-death sort of dry.

I wouldn't mind seeing a smelly old yellow lab stretched out under the tree right now. Place doesn't seem quite right without one. I get dressed listening to the gurgle of the creek.

A three hundred-mile pipeline—what a clever idea.

LEONA

Nate and I stand shoulder to shoulder at the kitchen sink looking out the window, watching Derek wander around the barn and corrals before stooping to clean manure off his shoe with a stick.

"Seems like a nice young man," I say.

"Yes, he does. Quite a city slicker, but he seems to like our Katie."

"Wonder where she went off to?"

"She seemed pretty upset to find out where Cassie was. My hell, Ona, what's Cassie doing in a place like that?"

"Now, we need to let that girl get here and explain herself before we get to conjecturing about it. She's a good girl, Nate. I don't know about that friend a hers—she seemed a little wild—but our Cassie's got a good head on her shoulders."

"That friend a hers remind you a anybody?" Nate asks.

"I wasn't gonna bring that up, Nate."

Nate grins and looks directly into my eyes. I can't remember the last time he looked at me like that. These days when we find ourselves close like this, one a us politely backs away, as if we're standing too close to a stranger. This time we both stay. I love his old face—brown and creased. His eyebrows have gone the way a old men—chasing his retreating hairline—and gray hairs stick out from both ears. Everything about the way he's aged suits me fine. I've found that to be the most lovely part of aging. At twenty, I couldn't imagine finding beauty in a seventy-year-old face. But the mind matures with the body, and there he is—just as fine-looking as the day we met. I can't imagine what he sees when he looks at the old woman I am now, but I hope he's pleased. I hope he looks at me and just knows—yes, *that's her, that's the one.* He leans in and kisses me on the cheek, taking me by surprise. I feel myself blush a little. At my age. Good heavens.

"Ona, this family is gonna stop being polite and start being honest right this minute."

"Well, good luck getting Nell to adhere to that new policy—she's neither one." Nate looks at me—half shocked and half amused. "You're the one what called for honesty, Nate."

"Yes I did, by damn. I'd rather see us fighting with one another than not speaking to one another. Bets reminded you of a young Nell, didn't she?"

"Yes, she did," I say. "She had that same feel to her—like she was gonna do just what she pleased, the rest a the world be darned. Don't surprise me none that she took Cassie where she took her."

"Well, Cassie wasn't taken at gunpoint. She's got a good bit a Nell in her herself."

"No doubt about that."

"Do you realize that if Katie hadn't shown up here, not one a us woulda realized Cassie was missing?" Nate says. "We're a small family, Ona. How could we not know where everybody is?"

"Cassie used our irregularity to her advantage. She probably figured she'd show up in Vegas at the beginning a the school year with no one the wiser. It's pure happenstance it didn't happen that way. Katie hasn't come home more'n a handful a times since she dropped Cassie off here fifteen years ago."

Nate shakes his head and watches Derek out the window as he attempts to pet one a the horses, which throws its head, twirls away, and kicks up its heels.

"What you thinking, Nate?"

"I'm thinking I'd better go save that boy before he gets kicked in the head."

Derek gives up and climbs to the top pole a the four-pole fence. Nate turns to me, resting his butt against the counter and folding his arms. "I figured him for a guy with common sense. I'm also thinking how tickled we all were the day Katie brought Cassie out here to live. Sure was nice to have a youngster around here again. I don't think one a us thought much about it beyond that—a mother dropping off her daughter like that. Now I'm afraid Katie has the same relationship with her daughter that Nell has with hers." He shakes his head as if confused. "My ma was a good mother, Ona."

"Lord, I know that, Nate."

"After Leroy died, Mom and Nell got tangled in something I wasn't a part of. Nell was always headstrong, but something got set in her that year like a boulder lodged in a slot after a flood. I had attributed my mother's sadness to losing Leroy, but in her later years, I'd sometimes see her looking at Nell, her face filled with bewilderment and despair."

Nate falls silent but for his breath, which moves heavy with burden. "Remember how lost Katie was after Henry died?" he asks.

"Sure I do, Nate."

"She kept drifting over here and over to Mom and Dad's place?"

"Yes, I remember," I say, and I wonder if he remembers it like I do.

"She wasn't running to us at all, Ona. She was running away from Nell."

Nate's eyes plead for me to disagree with him. I drop my eyes and remain silent. Of course she was running from Nell. Anyone who cared to look coulda seen that. But no one in this family cared to see anything or anyone but Nell. They saw Katie only as an opportunity to fix Nell—immerse her in raising that child, and she'd miraculously stop thinking only a herself and her own pain. Katie was nothing more than a guy line in the trussing of Nell. I shoulda put a stop to that. When that girl came running to us, I shoulda pulled her in tight. I coulda given that girl a mother. Instead I stood silent, as I'm wont to do, while the others turned Katie around and marched her back to Nell.

"Well, I can't explain Nell," I say finally. "Never could. I love the woman, Nate, cause she's your sister, but she don't make it easy."

"No, that's her specialty—making things difficult and making herself hard to love. Always has been. Even when we were kids. Then I brought Henry home, and Nell settled into him the minute he was outta the truck. She leaned into the crook a his arm and the fit was like a trailer on a ball hitch. Never seen her so appeased—before or since. But Katie, well she just pulled into a tuck after Henry died. I figured she'd come out of it given enough time—we all figured that—but she never did."

I look at Nate for some sign that he remembers the incident that caused Katie to walk out our back door and never walk in again, but there's none there.

"Remember that nice boy she dated in high school?" he

asks. "What was his name?"

"Joe Snyder."

"That's right—Joe. She just pushed and pushed and pushed against him until he didn't have no choice but to walk away. And that's exactly what she's doing with this young man also."

He turns back toward the window, and we both watch Katie walking through the field toward the house. Derek watches her also, but doesn't make a move toward her.

"I still don't know how to help her, Ona. The sight a her tears me up inside."

He reaches for my hand resting on the sink, and I look up to see what is becoming a more familiar sight every day—his weepy old eyes.

"You woulda been a good mother, Ona," he says without looking at me. Then he releases my hand and walks outta the kitchen. The screen door snaps shut behind him.

NELL

Pure instinct has me grabbing the rifle when I hear twigs snapping in front a me. I have the doe in my scope and my finger on the trigger before she drops her head to drink. I lower the rifle with shaking hands and lean it against a nearby ponderosa. Nate was right—I have no idea why I brought the thing. I didn't have a round in the chamber anyway, but when I had the rifle positioned on the doe my aim was stock-steady. Now, my whole body trembles.

So here it is. The scene I've been avoiding thirty-six years. Last day a deer hunt, almost dusk, time to get the rifles put away and get back to camp. Every one a us knew better than to be out that late.

Five days prior, Katie and Henry had shared this same bench. That was the tradition, giving the first-year hunter the best chance to get a deer. It was a gorgeous day—sunny and cold. Me, Nate, Dad, and Casey's boys rode up into the bowl and counted a dozen deer, two bucks among them. Casey's boys had already each snagged one the day prior, and the deer were hanging in camp, the objects a pride and retold stories. We rode both side canyons, moving those deer down toward Katie and Henry, figuring they'd have their pick a the bunch. The sun was high, slicing through leafless trees but offering little warmth, when two does and a buck stepped tenuously into the clearing. Henry and Katie both had their rifles sighted, but

Henry waited for Katie to take the first shot. The precious seconds ticked away. Outta the corner of his eye, Henry noticed the tears streaming down Katie's cheeks, rolling off her chin and onto the quivering hands holding the rifle. He lowered his rifle, reached over and pushed the barrel a hers downward as the deer bolted back into the trees. Henry pulled Katie into his flannel shirt and let her sob a good, long while.

Neither a them said a word about it when we got back to camp—both a them insisting they never saw a deer. Henry told me about it after we went to bed that night.

"It makes sense now that you think about it," Henry whispered that night in the tent, my head resting in the crook a his arm, one leg and one arm draped over his body—the way we always slept.

"Why do you say that?" I asked.

"Think about it, babe. Katie's never killed anything the entire ten months she's been shooting that gun—no rabbits, no squirrels, no birds—just cans off the fence. Remember how she cried a few years ago when she found the dead mouse in the trap in the saddle shed? And remember when that old barn cat got itself chewed up in the tractor engine where it had been sleeping last winter? Lordy, Katie was so distraught we had to keep her home from school for days."

"You're right. I never thought much about those things."

"She's no hunter, Nell. I'm glad she didn't shoot that deer. I don't like to think about what that woulda done to her."

Katie stuck to her story that they never saw a deer that day, and Henry never betrayed her. But the last day a deer hunt—after nine nights a campfire stories from uncles and cousins insisting that Katie should be a natural hunter given her mother's shooting skills—Katie told Henry she wanted to try again. It was already late afternoon, and every one a us knew better than to go out with the sun that low. Every damn, last one a us. Henry tried to talk Katie out of it, tried to convince her there was no need, but she insisted, and he had little resistance to her desires.

After a week a frigid temperatures, it had turned strangely mild that day, as if the seasons were all mixed up, and everything was outta whack. Dad woke up worried about the two deer we had hanging, so Ona and Mama had left early that morning to deliver them to Randy's Meat Packing in Ely. Henry and I had taken a blanket and slipped outta camp up to the ridge to watch the sun come up. When we got back to camp we found it strangely quiet. Uncle Bert had slept through a hangover and didn't get the fire going, and since everyone else depended upon the smell a bacon and coffee to rouse them, nobody had stirred. By the time everyone got moving, we were eating breakfast for lunch. As was customary on the last day, Uncle Bert was preparing for the evening feast, and in keeping with tradition, we had built a bonfire and were all looking forward to a lazy day in camp. Nobody planned on shooting anything unless a six-point wandered past the picnic table and upset the poker game. But like I said, Henry couldn't tell Katie no, so we saddled up and went out.

It was Henry's idea that I should wait at the watering hole with Katie stead a him. I don't quite remember the rationale—he either figured she'd be more likely to step up to the challenge with me next to her, or he figured I could talk her outta trying. I don't know what he was thinking. He may have believed that with me giving her hunting tips, if she were successful, the experience would fashion a union between the two of us that would be theretofore indissoluble. And God help us, what got formed between me and Katie that day may, in fact, be indissoluble.

KATE

I skirt the sprinklers, but the wet alfalfa soaks my jeans from the knees down as I walk through the pasture toward the house. Uncle Nate leans against the fence talking with Derek, who is perched on top. I can't imagine what sort of conversation the two of them might have, but I'm in no hurry to join it. Uncle Nate hasn't brought up the water issue, but I'm sure it's on his mind. What am I going to say to him? I had a speech ready when I left Las Vegas, and inside my head it sounded logical. Spilled into this air, its foolishness would be revealed. What was I thinking? That I could convince Mom and Nate they needn't worry about the pipeline project, that they can trust the Nevada Water Authority—and me—exhaustively? That we would all go down to Frank's, have a beer and a bowl of chili with Fitzy and Morty and all the rest who would soon be at ease with the idea, laughing and joking with one another about their silly overreaction to the whole affair? *Not to worry, Katie has explained it all to us ignorant ranchers.* God, how quickly a person can replace reason with arrogance once she isolates herself from the contradicting evidence.

Both the words and the logic of the planned speech have departed. They faded the moment Uncle Nate jumped out of the truck and embraced me, and disappeared entirely as the ranch came into focus with the force of all five senses. I can't summon the energy it would take to bring them back, if that's even possible. I'm tired of my own rhetoric, tired of my own dissonance, and I'm tired of being tired. There's not a single fragment of my life at rest. I could lie down in this field and be content to never get up again, happy to be plowed into the dirt with the change of seasons.

Uncle Nate and Derek seem to be laughing about something. I can't imagine what they have to laugh about. In fact, I can't imagine what anyone in the entire world has to laugh about. Uncle Nate disappears into the tack shed; Derek jumps off the fence and follows him. They come out carrying bridle, saddle and blankets, which Uncle Nate throws over the hitching post. Oh dear, Derek has already talked Uncle Nate into letting him ride a horse. I quicken my step, although I'm unclear whether it is my intent to stop the potential debacle or get there in time to enjoy it. Aunt Ona comes out of the house drying her hands on her apron, which again slows my pace. The sight of her performing that small movement touches me. Pure simplicity and beauty. Nothing wasted, nothing nonsensical. In Vegas, we've lost sight of our singular insignificance, our infinitesimal blip of time and matter in the universe. In Vegas, we are the center of our worlds. Out here, the geography does not allow it. One moves across the land without reverence or conceit, a small piece of the whole.

The perpetual quest for keeping oneself occupied, entertained, and important—which burns at the edge of addiction in Vegas, our need for it fierce and severe—is gloriously absent here. *Work, laugh, love, live—in no particular order,* Henry Jorgensen used to say whenever he saw me or anyone else feeling sad or worried. *Life don't need to be any more complicated than that less you insist on making it that way.* I remembered those words when I entered college and when I started working at the Nevada Water Authority. I remembered them fondly, but condescendingly—insisting that Dad's early death allowed him the luxury of idealism. Took me twenty more years to understand the depth of his ways and his words. By then I had already embroiled myself in a life of complications Henry Jorgensen would have found nonsensical. Vegas was built on nonsense. A city of excess plunked down in a desert that demands restraint. I hear myself on television talking about "smart growth and well-planned expansion." Nonsense stacked on top of nonsense. But people take their nonsense seriously. Jobs, businesses, and entire lives—including my own—have been created from it. Regardless of the origin from which they sprang, the people living those lives are as real as Aunt Ona wiping her hands on her apron, as real as Uncle Nate flinging a saddle over the ribs of a dapple-gray mare—and significantly more fragile. One only has to look at Derek, tenuously holding the lead rope attached to the docile beast before him, to confirm that fact. The people of Las Vegas operate in a blur of occupied illusion, dangerously disconnected from the source of water flowing out of their taps each day. They pay me a lot of money to secure the future of their oblivion. Sadly, money is all they have to offer, and delusion their only means of survival.

I know this because I'm one of them. Privilege and self-deception have kept me alive—or what passes for alive—most of my life. I have no idea what brought me to Omer Springs this weekend; I can fathom no excuse for obliterating the safety of my world. But every once in a while, when the evening breeze and Derek's touch carry the right amount of heat, a sensation creeps around the edges of my stomach lining, and, momentarily, I'm lost in another world—equally safe but softer. That world originates here in Omer Springs. In that moment, I believe I can have it back, I believe it is mine for the taking. But when I reach for it, it slips away, taunting me as it goes. This time I foolishly followed, creating a crack in the lining that will only get larger by attempting to travel back through it. I've put myself on a cliff with no way to retreat. I can jump—with low survival probabilities—or I can wait to be rescued. Only problem is every time someone gets near me with a rope, I throw it back. Jumping is my only option. I've known that for a while now. But it takes time to work up the courage to make such a leap.

By the time I reach the corrals, Derek has already mounted the mare, and Uncle Nate has flung the reins up to him and sent him down the lane. Derek grins at me and tips his imaginary cowboy hat as he goes.

"You do know he's never ridden before, don't you?" I ask Uncle Nate.

"That's what he said," Uncle Nate replies. "Looks pretty good up there, though."

"Do you think it's wise to send him off alone?" I ask.

"Oh, hell, Katie, that old gray mare ain't what she used to be," he says, grinning and leaning his butt against the hitching post.

"Funny," I say, taking up the space next to him. Aunt Ona falls into line next to me.

"But also true. That mare must be twenty years old. She ain't going very far or very fast even if he wants her to. I guarantee you she ain't making one clip-clop past the end a the lane. He won't even have to turn her around, but he'll think he's turning her, nevertheless, and everybody's happy." He turns toward me. "Cept maybe you. How about it? Want to go for a ride? I need to move cows into the next allotment before somebody raises hell. Wouldn't mind the company.

You can bring your city-slicker boyfriend along. I think he might like it."

"I don't think so, Uncle Nate."

"You ain't thinking about going back to Vegas so soon, are you, Katie?" Aunt Ona asks.

"No, Aunt Ona. But I've spent the entire drive up here trying to figure out why I made this trip—and I'm still not sure it was the right thing to do—it feels dangerous and foolish."

"Coming home ought not to feel that way, Katie," Uncle Nate says. "That makes me sad as hell to hear you say that."

"Me too, Uncle Nate. That's why I'm not going back to Vegas just yet. Maybe you're right. Maybe it's time for this family to stop running in opposite directions of one another."

"It's now or never, Katie," he says. "That much I know."

"I need to borrow a truck, Uncle Nate. I'm going up to Hamlin Flat."

He looks me up and down as if he's measuring my sanity, then looks at Aunt Ona, who nods.

"It's too late tonight," he says. "Be dark soon. We'll pull some supplies together and go up in the morning."

"Somebody needs to stay here to wait for Cassie," I say.

"Cassie knows these mountains as well as any of us," Aunt Ona says. "We'll leave her a note. She won't have a problem finding us. She can bring the old Ford flatbed up; she's not gonna want to drive her little car up those roads. I'll put some food together, Nate," she says, touching him on the arm before turning back to the house. Her actions and her words are matter-of-fact and full of confidence, and it occurs to me that Aunt Ona has been planning this family reunion for years, simply waiting for the rest of us to come to our senses. She's a patient woman.

NELL

Jasper's desperate bark pulls me to a seated position on the bench from what was apparently a sleeping position, although I have no recollection a lying down. I whistle for him, and he crashes through the trees and across the crick. No telling how long he's been searching for me. He seems damn happy to see me and, quite honestly, I feel the same about him.

"Com'ere, old boy." He jumps onto the bench, leaning into me, wet and stinky, licking my face with enthusiasm and relief. The sun has fallen, and shadows drop around us.

"Good hell, Jasper, looks like I been here awhile," I say, wiping my eyes and nose on my shirtsleeve. Last I remember I was staring straight ahead at the spot I saw Henry drop, then got a feeling like thick, gravelly concrete pushing through my body, tearing things apart as it traveled. I must a curled up like a dog in an attempt to stop it. Didn't work. Although at this point, I don't know if the pain is physical or mental—probably both—and I don't know what's causing it, or more accurately *who's* causing it—Henry or Katie.

"We need to get back to camp, Jasper," I whisper, but neither of us makes a move. I have a strong feeling that if I leave now, I'll never be able to return to this spot, and something will be lost, but I have no idea what might be at risk.

I lie back down on my side, pulling Jasper in close. "Jesus Christ, Jasper. What a goddamn mess I've made a things." I rest my cheek against the hard, splitting wood, and Jasper rests his snout on my elbow. "What do you suppose we should do now, old dog?"

Henry would never forgive me if he knew the mess I'd made. Course, Henry coulda predicted it. I was never worth a damn without him, and he knew it—not in an arrogant way, just in a factual way. He had that kinda foresight—the ability to see that I needed his love before I could come into my own. I'm not saying he made me the person I am, but he set me free to live the way I was meant to live. How a person is supposed to live is different for every person, and Henry knew that. That's all I'm saying.

I'm quite sure Katie will never forgive me. Could be that neither one a us can understand what needs forgiving and what don't. Maybe that's why we've never talked about it—because we can't figure out what *it* is. Where the hell would we start? Would we start with the details a Henry's death? Would that do either of us any good, or would it only scrape out a sore so deep and raw we'd never get the bleeding stopped? Would we start at the beginning—the day Katie was born, the day everything changed? Would we talk about the years after Henry's death—the hollowness in the house we shared, the unfilled space and time, the pretense of ease where there was none? Both of us waiting for the day Katie would be old enough to leave.

A ten-year-old girl needs her mother. Clinging to a cliché is what we were doing. I found no comfort in Katie, and she found none in me. When we looked at each other, we saw the absence a Henry, the absence a the only thing the two a us had ever shared—if you could call that sharing.

A good cry. That's what they call this. What the hell is good about it, I'd like to know. I rouse myself off the bench and test my legs to see if they'll hold me. Jasper does the same, stretching his front legs, then his back, then lifts a leg and relieves himself on a tree. His world has been set right.

"Wish it were that easy for me, Jasper."

The sky is dark, but a gibbous moon is on the rise. It should give us enough light to find our way back to camp. Finding Queenie will be another thing. I can't imagine she's still standing by the tree on the other side a the crick. If she has any sense, she'll be back in camp tearing apart a bale a hay. Course, I don't figure she has any more sense than I have, so I can't count on that, but that little problem will have to wait until morning. Best to worry about my own hide right now.

"Come on, Jasper," I say, taking a few tentative steps. "Let's see if we can manage to get ourselves outta here." Stingy slits a moonlight cut through aspen and pine, leaving most steps to hit the ground on faith and feel. Jasper runs ahead for a ways, then back to check on me as I move slowly through the meadow.

"Don't get too far off, dog. I don't imagine you're any sorta rescue hound if I were to need that, but if I'm gonna die out here tonight, I could use the company."

Jasper barks his encouragement or, more likely, his impatience. Henry used to say you could assign sentiment to a dog— just fill in whatever you have a need for at the moment—and at this moment, I could use a little encouragement. Sensible old women don't go traipsing through the dark woods alone.

I make my way through the thorny brush to the crick without incident. So far, so good. From the bank I peer into the crick's blackness, trying to measure its current by sound alone. This isn't the same place I crossed before, but I'll be hard-pressed to find that place tonight. The water is smooth in the only spot getting moonlight through the trees, but I can hear water moving around rocks further out. But standing here dillydallying don't make much sense—there's only one choice in front a me. My only chance a getting back to camp is crossing the crick and picking up the trail. I sit on the ground at the edge a the crick to tighten my bootlaces and look around for a good balancing stick, but it's too dark to find anything useful. Jasper crosses to the other side, and I call him back to see if I can get a beat on the path he chooses, but he's not all that choosy—he's just bounding across any old place.

"I wish I had that same sorta bounce in my step, Jasper."

I ease myself in, one foot, then the other, gasping as the water creeps up my leg close to my knee. That's not so bad, although a little deeper than the place I crossed before. Chilly also, but I'll change clothes and build a big fire back at camp. In the middle a the crick, a current tugs at my legs.

Steady, old girl, I tell myself. *Make every step count. Get your foot solid on the bottom before you pick up the other one.* I can hear Jasper pacing on the bank, so it can't be too far away. With the next step, my toes and shin hit a boulder. I tip forward, almost losing my balance, but catch myself before going into the water. My legs are beginning to numb, and an urgency to move quickly argues with the knowledge that I need to move cautiously. I don't have the strength in my legs to move upstream around the boulder, and moving downstream could mean getting caught in the current. I crouch down enough to stick my hands into the crick and feel the size a the rock—relatively flat on top. I put my left boot on top a the boulder and feel a sense a relief to lift myself partially and momentarily outta the water. As I do so, the boulder rolls ever so slowly out from under my foot.

Old women fall flat. I realized that about seven years ago when I was eating a ham sandwich and walking through the newly plowed field to where I'd left the tractor. My toe bumped against a dirt clod, and I went down on my face. Used to be hands and knees would hit the ground first, but those days are over. Now the body falls like a fence slat. I imagine if you're watching it from a distance, it must be something to see—a human body tipping like that.

So it comes as no surprise to find myself flat on my back on the bottom a the crick. What is a surprise, after I get my head above water again, is to discover myself in a relatively comfortable position save for the cold water swirling a few inches below my armpits and an ankle wedged between two rocks. I'm seated on the rocky crick bottom, and a large boulder sticking outta the water serves as a nifty back and headrest. As I struggle to pull my ankle loose—with no success at all—the reality seeps into my gut. Jasper paces, whines, and barks on the bank. I get glimpses of him as he moves in and outta the moonlight.

"Calm down, Jasper!" Upon the sound a my voice he jumps into the water to lick my face. "That ain't really gonna help, Jasper. Get yourself back up on the bank—no use both a us freezing to death out here." Jasper splashes back onto the bank.

I reach into the water and run my hands down my leg until they bump against the boulders tight against my shin just above the ankle. The movement of either rock would free me, but the only one likely to budge is the one that rolled under me. The other one seems to have been in place for centuries. I brace my back against the rock behind me and cross my free foot over my trapped leg to push against the rock that caught me. Nothing. I try again. And again. And again, ignoring the pain and yanking hard on the wedged leg. I keep trying even after I know the truth of it—I'm going to freeze to death out here. The night air's cool—not cold—but the water is snow-melt. I'm already shivering. Good God, I really am going to freeze to death out here. How long will it take? Will I feel the life slowly drain from my body through the night, or will I simply lose consciousness and never wake up again?

"Oh, for Christ sake," I say out loud, half laughing, half sobbing. "I'm gonna die tonight. Right here in Hamlin Crick. I'll be a sonofabitch. What is it about this place?" I call out to the darkness. "You want us Jorgensens, you got us!" Jasper starts barking again.

"Jasper, either shut up or go get help." I laugh at my own joke. "That'd be the day, wouldn't it? You turn into Lassie." Jasper sits in a splice a moonlight and whines. "Oh hell, boy, you're a good old dog. Wouldn't matter if you were Lassie or Rin Tin Tin; there ain't a person within sixty miles a here. Those two dogs always had somebody close by, and all you got is me, Jasper. That don't bode well for either of us. I always kinda liked that about Nevada, but it does put a person in a helluva predicament at a time like this. That's the deal we make to live out here. It ain't such a bad deal, old boy. There are worse ways to die and worse places, for that matter. But I'll be a sonofabitch if this don't look like the end a me."

I lean my head against the boulder and take several deep breaths to calm myself. Aspen leaves shimmer silvery-green in the moonlight above me, and there's a break in the canopy where the sky is visible. A few stars, but the moon outshines them. I push against the boulder several more times knowing full well it isn't going to move.

"I tell you what, dog," I say, pulling myself up again. "I'm gonna lean my head against this rock here and stare up at this sky for a while. If I'm lucky, I'll fall asleep although I can't imagine it, shaking the way I am. You're on your own, boy. If I know Nate—and I do—he won't be too long in coming up to check on me—although he won't be getting here in time to do me any good—so you can either trot on down the road to meet him or just wait in camp till he gets here. You'll be all right. You been decent company, Jasper. I'll give you that.

"I'm gonna miss Nate, although I guess that's a funny thing to say. I don't suppose I'll be missing anybody since I'm the one that's leaving. But Nate and me ain't ever been separated except for those few years he went off and brought back Henry. I've leaned heavy on him. And that wasn't reciprocal. I did the leaning, and he did the holding up. That's the way we've always been even though it might look different from the outside.

"And Ona, well, she's okay. A little irritating, but I like her fine. Not worth a shit at ranch work, but she can cook. Something to be said for that. Poor Ona. Always wanted kids. She woulda been a good mother too. Helluva lot better than I was, but that goes without saying, don't it?

"Wish there was some way I could make things up to Katie but looks like time's run out on that one. Oh hell, here go the ramblings of a dying old woman. For Christ sakes, I could have seventy more years and never figure out how to make things right with my daughter. That's a fact.

"Don't know what Nate's gonna do about that water issue, though. Thing is, Jasper, if you plucked Nate and me offa that land, I just don't know where you'd set us back down again. There ain't no other place on earth for us, and without water, there ain't no way to live here. Maybe when Nate dies that'll be the end a the Baxter Ranch. Sad to think that, but maybe it's so.

"Don't know where Cassie will end up, but she'll do fine. She's a good one, that girl. No worries about her.

"Okay, Jasper, I believe I'm finished with the requisite review a the dying woman's life. Jesus Christ. That didn't take long. That didn't take long at all. I suppose there's some meaning in that, but I ain't inclined to search for it right now." I find myself sobbing, which I hate. I stopped crying a year after Henry died and never cried again—until now. What the hell is wrong with me? It's not like death can come as a big surprise to a woman my age, although I wasn't expecting it today. "I'm gonna be quiet now, Jasper, stop this blubbering and just lean back here for a while. So long, old dog."

I fold my hands behind my head and lean against the rock. The tears run freely, and I'm hard-pressed to find a way to stop them. Jasper whines on the bank, his head on his front paws. Together we pass the night hours.

A light pulls me partway into consciousness. The moon has moved into the opening above the aspen and shines directly on my face as if to be checking up on me. I take stock. Still night, and I'm still alive. Don't know if that's good or bad. The top half a my body shakes uncontrollably, banging against the boulder; the bottom half is numb. I don't know how many hours have passed. Jasper lies on the bank, his eyes on me. He sits up and barks once when he sees me unfold my arms, as if I'll finally get up and take him back to camp now. My arms have stiffened horribly from keeping them above my head, but the other option is to drop them into the water. A strong, yet senseless survival instinct stops me from doing so. I lean back, my arms folded behind my neck again, and stare at the moon.

"Henry," I say quietly, crying like a child. "Goddamn you, Henry. Come get me. You owe me that much. Come back for me, Henry Jorgensen. You promised me you'd always come find me no matter where I wandered off. Goddamn you, Henry! Can't you see I need you? Henry!" I scream into the blackness. "Henry Jorgensen!" Jasper jumps up barking, running back and forth on the bank. "Henry Jorgensen, you sonofabitch! Come get me, Henry!"

"Hush, babe," Henry says.

"Ahhh, I knew you'd come."

"You're gonna wake the dead yelling like that."

"Ha! You always could make me laugh."

"You're easy, babe."

"Easy as they come. I'm yours, Henry. No use pretending otherwise."

"You speak the truth there, my love. You're mine and I'm yours."

"Loving you was the easiest thing I ever did in my life. Nothing was ever that easy again."

"I know, babe."

"So why'd you go off and leave me?"

"It was an accident, Nellie, you know that. Shit happens."

"But what were you doing there, Henry, stepping through the trees like that?"

"I'd come to gather my girls, take em back to camp."

"But Jesus, Henry, why didn't you yell or something?"

"I was wearing a bright red sweatshirt and a jaunty red cap, Nell. Can't get much louder than that."

"Henry."

"Honestly, Nell, I didn't figure you and Katie would even have your rifles loaded. It was near dark. I just figured we'd let Katie sit out there awhile so she could stop feeling bad about herself."

"We shouldn'ta had the things loaded, that's for sure. We

shouldn'ta even been out there at all. We shoulda been back in camp, playing poker, drinking bad booze, and eating Uncle Bert's feast."

"Yeah, bad time to die—before the final supper."

"Henry, please!"

"You've completely lost your sense a humor sitting in that crick, Nell."

"I've kicked myself ten thousand times for indulging Katie that afternoon."

"Time to stop kicking yourself, babe. Wasn't your decision; it was mine. I never could say no to Katie, and you never could say no to me."

"You speak the truth there, Henry. But if anybody'd had the sense to say no to anybody that day, I'd still have you."

"No reason to look at it that way, Nell. You know that. Things flow the way they flow. Just like now—helluva situation you've got yourself into here."

"You're telling me. Am I dead or just delirious?"

"Neither, babe. You're just right there in the crick with your ankle stuck between two boulders. Damn unfortunate place to be. What's an old woman like you doing traipsing around the woods and crossing cricks after dark anyway?"

"Just happened that way, Henry. Wasn't planned. Sometimes shit just happens."

"That's what I'm trying to tell you, love. My death was an accident. That's all it was. You know that."

"Yes, I know that."

"You gotta talk to Katie about it, Nell. You gotta let her off the hook on this."

"I tried, Henry. I did my best."

"I know you did, babe, in your own messy way, but you gotta try again."

"I'm sorry, Henry, I made such a mess a things."

"Love means never having to say you're sorry."

"Henry, please!"

"Okay, okay. But that line used to make you laugh like hell. You're not as easy as you used to be, Nell."

"I have a few years on me, Henry."

"And you wear them well, babe. I see you cut your hair."

"Had to, Henry. These hands got too old to braid it."

"I don't believe that for a minute, Nell. Those old hands can still saddle a horse; they can damn sure still braid hair."

"I don't know why I cut it, Henry. Just trying to make a point, I guess."

"And what would that a been, Nell?"

"Don't recall anymore. Cassie used to braid my hair for me. Oh, I wish the two a you could know one another, Henry. You'd like her."

"I'm sure I would."

"She's solid, Henry. She's got a vein a trust and tranquility runs through her—well, hell, she's your granddaughter. That's all there is to it."

"That ain't all there is to it. You raised her, Nell. Nellie? What are you crying about?"

"I did, Henry. It broke my heart to see Katie drop her child off like that. I knew that one was on me. Me and Katie stood on the back porch that day, looking at each other with Cassie in the middle, so much reproach and anguish running over that child's head between us. And I don't think she meant it this way, Henry, but I took it as Katie giving me another chance."

"Maybe she was, Nellie."

"Well, I don't know if it was that or if she was just trying to rescue herself, but I took it as such anyway. And you know,

Henry, I think I did all right. Cassie is a fine girl."

"You did good, Nell. But you're not done."

"What do you mean, Henry?"

"You have a daughter still needs you, babe."

"Well, this is a helluva time to bring that up. Sides, I believe I've done all the damage a person can do there. Maybe this is the best thing I can do for Katie. Maybe once she's free a me she'll figure out what she needs to figure out."

"It ain't that easy, babe."

"That's an odd thing for you to say, Henry. You were the one going through life easy like."

"Life was good for us, Nell. Been up to Piss Pot Springs?"

"You're changing the subject, Henry."

"Yes, I am. So how about it? Is our soaking pool still there?"

"Haven't been there yet. The plan was to do that tomorrow if I still had it in me. Don't look like I'm gonna make that date."

"That was our place, Nell. Yours and mine."

"I needed that, Henry. Something that belonged just to the two a us—something I didn't have to share."

"Wish I could give you that now, babe—a hot spring bath. Looks like you could use it."

"I'm cold, Henry. Really cold."

"Hang on, Nell. Sun'll be up soon."

"I'm so cold, Henry. Could you wrap your arms around me?"

"I've got you, babe. Hang on to me."

Cassie

Bets, Maggie, and Mick are the only ones in the bar at five a.m. when Joe's truck rattles off the pavement out front. Bets pulls me into a hug.

"Don't let your family give you any shit," she says. "Or they'll be answering to me."

"That should keep them in line."

"And don't worry about your car. I'll get it back to Vegas in one piece."

"I'm not worried about it. Drive it as much as you want to. Go ahead and drive past Dipshit's house and honk if you want. He hasn't been stirred up nearly enough recently."

"Cassie, we'll miss you around here, girl," Mick says, coming around the bar to engulf me in a bear hug. "Won't we, Maggie?" Maggie grunts. "Miss having some musical variety," he continues. "Huh, Maggie?"

"We sure as hell won't miss that shit you two play when you're in cahoots," Maggie says. "But I don't know who the hell's gonna keep my computer working. Mick here's not worth a damn at that."

"Ain't in my job description."

"And I doubt I can talk your friend Ilsa here into taking up the slack."

"Last I checked, I already had a job also," Bets said. "Otherwise you wouldn't be calling me by that ridiculous name."

Joe walks through the door and takes up the stool next to Maggie, resting his back against the bar.

"You ready to go?" he asks.

"I suppose," I say.

"Sure been nice with you here," Bets says, throwing an arm over my shoulder and pulling me in close. "You have my number. Just call or text if things get too fucked up there."

"I don't want to hear that kinda language in here," Maggie says robotically.

"We can do it, but we can't say it," Bets whispers to me. "Seriously, I'll bag this gig and come rescue you if you need me to."

"Thanks, Bets," I say, resting my head on her shoulder. "I believe you actually would do that for me."

"Damn right I would, girl," she says, pulling me into another full hug. "You're the only friend I've ever had who just takes people as they come. When you have my life, that's no small thing."

Maggie slips off her stool, goes into the kitchen, returns with a large brown paper bag, and hands it to Joe.

"There's some ribs, macaroni salad, and a few other things. That should get you most a the way there," she says. "Joe, take care a our girl, here."

That's about the nicest thing Maggie's ever said about me, and I can no longer hold back the tears.

"Oh for Christ's sake," Maggie says. "Get the hell outta here if you're gonna start blubbering. It's bad for business." She pulls me into a full hug, burying my nose in her generously perfumed cleavage.

"Like Bets says—don't take no shit from nobody."

"I'll be fine," I reassure them. "I'm pretty much just an innocent bystander in my family."

"Nobody's entirely innocent," Maggie says. "But I believe you're about as close as they come."

"We best get going," Joe says. "Maggie, appreciate the picnic. I'll see you all when I see you again."

"When you coming back, Joe?" Mick asks, and I realize that Joe and Mick each consider the other a friend, which hadn't occurred to me until that moment. I imagine Mick will be pretty lonely around this place without Joe dropping in and without me on the end barstool.

"Don't know yet," Joe says. "Depends on how my ma's doing. I don't guess you should plan on seeing me till you do."

"Gonna miss you around here, Joe," Maggie says. "You just make sure you get back out here. Ely's too small to hold a guy like you."

"I'll be back, Maggie." Joe kisses Maggie on the cheek, then Bets, then shakes Mick's hand.

"That's enough a this now," Maggie says, pushing us toward the door by flapping her hands like she's herding a gaggle of geese. "You two get the hell outta here."

All three of them follow us out the door and to the truck. The sun barely pushes at the horizon. We'll be driving directly into it for a good five hours.

"Drive fast and take chances," Bets calls to Joe as he stuffs my bag in the back and I settle into the passenger seat. Maggie backhands her on the upper arm. I roll my window down and wave at the three of them standing in the dust as we pull away.

"Hmm," I say, rolling the window up.

"Hmm, what?" asks Joe.

"Hmm, never thought I'd spend half my summer in a whorehouse."

"Yeah, I never thought I'd spend half my life in one."

"Those are good people there, Joe."

"Can't argue with that."

"We're kind of mean to one another."

"Who's we?"

"Human beings in general. Americans, I guess, more specifically. I don't know about other human beings. I've never much been outside of Nevada. So maybe it's limited to our fine state."

"Don't think so."

"Maggie and Mick—they're just good people."

"You seem surprised."

"I wish I could say I'm not—that would make me a more enlightened person—but I've never much thought about finding good people in a brothel. Except Bets. But then I never knew that's where she spent her summers until a couple of months ago."

"Well, if you're gonna spend your summer in a brothel—and I'm not recommending it, mind you—you picked a good one."

"Bets picked it really. I just came along."

"Maggie opened that little place twenty years ago after twenty years in the business herself. She treats those girls right, gives them a fair cut. Not all those places do that. She trusts the girls and they trust her—that's a rare thing in that business."

"Guess Bets picked the right place then."

"And Maggie picked the right girl."

"What do you mean?"

"Maggie has a reputation; a lot of women want to go to work for her. But she won't take most of em. She sizes up a woman's character the minute they walk in the door—just like she did you. Most of em, she sends right back out. Says a lot about you that she let you stay."

"What's she looking for?"

"Not quite sure, but she seldom misses. The Wild Filly Stables is the artisan boutique of brothels. That's why the majority of customers arrive in limos, not semi-trucks."

"Except you."

"Except me and the other locals. Maggie courted the home crowd right from the start—got active in the Chamber of Commerce, gives a lotta money to local charities. She runs a helluva business."

"I'll bet she makes quite an entrance at Chamber of Commerce meetings in those gowns."

Joe tips his head back and laughs—a deep, easy laugh. The kind of laugh that makes you want to plant yourself next to him and never step away.

"You don't know the half of it," Joe says, pulling into a gas station at the far edge of town. "Maggie says you got a bag full a lousy CDs with you. You might as well put one in. We got some miles to cover."

"You don't mind?"

"No, I don't mind."

I pull the canvas bag up from the floor of the truck and start to flip through the CDs, looking for one that I imagine Joe can tolerate while he fills the tank. Old people—which is how I had started to think about Joe ever since I realized he knew my mama in high school—really only like music from their own era, so I settle on "Can't Buy a Thrill" by Steely Dan, which Bets had turned me onto. I put it in and turn up the volume as we pull back onto the road. Joe turns the volume back down a few notches.

"Excellent choice," he says, and we both settle back for the ride.

Joe and I barely speak to one another while the entire CD

plays, although Joe does sing through most of it. He has a nice voice, and he seems to know every word to every song.

"Don't you know the words to all the music you like?" Joe asks, when I make note of it.

"Yeah, but I don't plan to still know them thirty years from now. In fact, I plan to change with the times. I'm going to listen to the music of the day—not get stuck in my own era."

"You'd be surprised, Cassie. Music digs into a person—I never met a person it didn't. At least not one I wanted to know. Lotsa memories can be buried in one song."

"What kind of memories does 'Dirty Work' bring up?" I ask. "Tell me about those old days in Ely, Joe."

"What do you want to know?"

"Tell me about my mama."

"Oh, I don't know if that's such a good idea, Cassie, telling stories about your mama."

"Why not? You were the one said I needed to go back to Omer Springs and get things straightened out."

"Yes, and I still believe that."

"Well, it might help me understand a few things if you tell me everything you know about Katherine Ann Jorgensen. Cause I sure as hell don't know much about her."

"She's your mama."

"And what exactly does that mean in your family, Joe? Cause I have a feeling it means something entirely different in mine."

Joe doesn't say anything for a good long while. Just looks down the road and out his rearview mirrors as if I hadn't asked him anything. I finally give up, slouch down in the seat and close my eyes.

"I met your mama on the first day of school the year we were both freshmen," he says.

I pull myself back up to listen. "How'd you meet her?"

"It was sorta tradition for the local Ely boys to stand outside the school in front of the bus stop waiting to see if any new chicks would be bussed in from the hinterlands. We'd already pretty much proven ourselves unworthy of every girl in town, so we were on the lookout for new prospects. We'd stand just off school grounds, so they couldn't bust us for smoking, light up when we saw a bus round the corner. Thought we were pretty cool."

"God bless tradition. I remember that same bunch of jerk-offs smoking on the curb the first day I stepped off the short bus."

Joe laughs. "Your mama was the last one off the bus. Looked like she'd rather be just about anywhere but there. She looked mortified when she paused on the bottom step of the bus and realized she'd have to walk the gauntlet past us. Course, we were nothing but show. If anyone had the nerve to say anything to us, we would've crumbled. But then, just as she stepped down off the bus, the look on her face changed."

"From what to what?"

"From trepidation to pure indifference. She walked by us like we couldn't possibly ever matter to her."

"I think she's maybe perfected that over the years."

"People develop ways of sheltering themselves, Cassie."

"They sure do. I think every member of my family has managed to enclose themselves in a steel vault."

"Maybe you hold the key."

"Joe, for such a smart guy you come up with some lame lines." He laughs again. "What happened next with Mama? Was that the end of it?"

"No, Ely's too small a town for that to be the end of it, you know that. It wasn't any bigger when you got there."

"Yeah, you're right."

"Rumors started circulating that she was Henry Jorgensen's daughter. Everybody in town had heard the story of Henry getting shot in a deer hunting accident four years prior. And everybody knew she was there when it happened. You know how kids are. She immediately became some sort of haunted oddity in our eyes. We stopped at nothing to get a good look at her. Can you imagine that? Being the object of everyone's morbid curiosity? That musta been awful for her."

"What had you heard about the accident?"

"The usual stuff—about one-tenth truth and the rest speculation. We were teenagers. The gory details were all we cared about. What actually happened, anyway?"

"That's my question to you, Joe. I came along fifteen years after the fact. Nobody was talking about it then, and they aren't talking now."

"We heard your grandmother accidentally shot your grandfather. It was dusk, and Nell mistook him for a deer. The thing that all the kids grabbed hold of was the fact that they kept Henry's body in camp that night and didn't drive out with it until the next day."

"No shit?"

"You didn't know that?"

"Joe, I don't know a thing about any of this except the fact that it seems to have ripped my family to shreds."

"Well, I never knew your grandfather, Cassie, but folks who knew him said he was something special—just that kinda guy that radiates from the center outward. You remove a person like that from the middle a things, and you're bound to get some residue from it. Especially like that—it was an accident and all, but hell, people can't help but blame themselves for that type of stuff. Your grandmother never talked to you about it?"

"Not a word. She flatly refused. Whenever I asked she simply said the past needed to be left in the past. Every once in a while I could catch her off guard and get her talking a little about Grandpa—she was plum crazy in love with him—but the accident itself is off limits. Got the same reaction from Mama, although the entire subject of Henry Jorgensen is off limits with her."

"Well, it was tough on both of them, I figure. They were together when it happened, so your mama witnessed her father getting shot when she was ten years old. That's not an easy thing to witness. Especially when there's blood involved. It ain't the same thing as seeing your dad have a heart attack or something."

"I suppose not, although that doesn't sound all that great either."

"When I was a kid, there was a guy in Ely who was driving home from work one day, and his son was riding alongside the car on his bicycle talking to his dad through the open window. They were right near the driveway, when the kid grabbed hold a the door handle like he was gonna hitch a ride on the car, lost his balance and fell over. His head went under the back wheel and popped like a pumpkin. All happened in a second. Wasn't that guy's fault, and no one in town could blame him for it. Just one a those things. But that bloodstain stayed out there on the road in front a the house for days. Every one a us kids rode our bikes past it to get a look at it. I think it was that, more than anything, drove the guy crazy. Wasn't more'n a month later, the guy went out to his garage and put a shotgun in his mouth. The reverend from the Baptist church went and gathered up the guy's wife and remaining kids and resettled them in another town. Then they had the house torn down. The sight a blood makes a bad thing worse."

"Damn, Joe, thanks for the cheerful story."

"All's I'm saying, Cassie, is that the human psyche ain't built for that stuff. We expect everything to be neat and clean. That family a yours already had one tragedy when the young boy drowned in the pond. Tack that hunting accident on top a that, and you can't expect the family is gonna come out untouched."

"Well, the family's touched, that's for sure. But don't you figure they eventually have to find a way to come around?"

"I don't know, Cassie. I tried to get Katie to talk about—"

"Katie? Seems you know my family better than I do, Joe. Exactly how well did you and my mother know each other?"

"There were only forty-two students in my graduating class, Cassie. Everybody knew everybody."

"Nice dodge. How well did you know her?"

"We mighta danced one or two."

"I'm going to assume that by 'dance' you mean 'dance,' because I don't really want to know any more details than that."

Joe smiles that deep smile that seems to be meant for no one other than himself.

"So you and my mama never talked about the accident?"

"No, she was clamped down about it. I knew it was off limits."

"Yep, I got the same message."

"Said she hated knowing everyone was tittering about it the moment she walked past. She just wanted to let things lie. Can't blame her for that."

"How well did you know Grandma Nell?"

"I been out to the ranch a few times."

"So you and my mama didn't just pass each other in the hallway once in a while. Damn, Joe. Why is it you never told me this?"

"Wasn't none a my business. Sides, it took me awhile to figure out that you were Katie's daughter, although it shouldn'ta taken more'n a minute. You're the spittin' image of your mother."

"You're crazy. I don't look anything like my mother."

"Well, I haven't see her in a few years—fact the last time I laid eyes on her in real life, she was younger than you are now—but I can tell you, there's a powerful resemblance. Cept you don't carry the same kinda sadness she did. Then Bets told me your mother worked for the Nevada Water Authority, and I put two and two together."

"So you kept track of my mother after high school."

"Hell, Cassie, once you get outside Vegas or Reno, this is a small state. It takes a real effort not to keep track a people you went to high school with. Sides, your mother has become a bit of a celebrity—TV appearances and all."

"Yeah, much to my grandmother's dismay—and everyone else in Omer Springs."

"Can't blame them for that. That plan your mother's pitching is flat out wrong."

"She doesn't seem to think so. She seems to think it's a good plan that will serve everyone's needs."

Joe looks at me out of the corner of his eye. "Unless your mama's had a lobotomy since I last saw her, there's no way in hell she actually believes that."

I shrug. "I don't know what she believes. I barely know the woman." Joe keeps looking at me until I'm uncomfortable. "You might want to glance at the road once in a while," I tell him. "I'm possibly on the verge of cracking open the Jorgensen vault, and I hate to miss it. And it would not be good to chalk up one more bloody tragedy in the Jorgensen family. Watch where you're going, Joe."

He turns back to look at the road.

"So what changed your mind about going home, Cassie? Last time we talked you were planning to stay perched on the end stool."

"I got a call from Mama; she's at the ranch."

"Katie's at the ranch?" Joe asks, looking at me with a mix of surprise and alarm while the truck drifts over the double yellow line.

"Damn, Joe, watch the road! You're gonna get us both killed."

"Why didn't you tell me your mama was at the ranch?"

"Didn't occur to me. What's the big deal?"

"No big deal. I'm just surprised to hear that."

"You and me both. That's why I'm hoping you don't splat me on the road before I get there. This little family reunion's been a long time coming."

"How long's she gonna be there?"

"Probably until someone pisses her off or threatens her with a discussion of the past or a discussion of the present or a discussion of the future. We'll be lucky if she's still around when we arrive. Hard to imagine what the family meal might look like. I have no idea what they might all be talking about right now—probably me."

"When did you talk to her?"

"Yesterday."

"Why didn't you call me? We coulda left sooner."

"Don't know your number, Joe. I just see you when I see you."

"Mick knows how to reach me."

"I know. I figured it wouldn't hurt everyone at the ranch to wait on me for a day. I been waiting on them twenty years."

Joe shakes his head and picks up his speed a little bit. I

dig in the paper bag Maggie gave us and pull out a fork and the macaroni salad.

"I'm gonna eat," I say. "I figure this could be my last meal."

Joe doesn't show any indication he heard my last comment.

"If it's a problem seeing my mama, Joe, you can drop me at the top of the lane."

"It's not a problem for me, Katie."

"Cassie."

He glances at me and back to the road. "It's not a problem."

"If you say so."

I spread a napkin on my lap and dig into the ribs. I have a feeling it's going to be a long time between rest stops.

LEONA

At seven a.m., Derek's already up and dressed and in the corral feeding wormy apples to the gray mare. I appreciate that. Got no use for anyone sleeps past sunup. Derek and the horse have become fast friends. No sign a Katie. Derek and Katie spent the night in our old house stead a here in the farmhouse with us. I understand that—young folks need their privacy—but Katie was adamant about not sleeping at Nell's in her old bedroom, now Cassie's bedroom. I understand that too. I don't think Katie's spent a night in that house since she left here twenty-eight years ago.

With sad eyes and a wave, Nate motions me over to where he's sitting at the table staring at that darn picture again. I've a mind to burn that thing. I start to pull out a chair to join him, but he swings an arm around my waist and pulls me in close so his head rests just under my breasts, against my belly. I move my hand over the top a his bald head and let it roam down the back a his neck into his shirt collar. Been a long time since we've touched each other like this. I breathe shallowly, afraid that any movement on my part will end the moment, cause him to let me go. We hold our position for several minutes before I dare speak.

"What's going on with you, Nate?" I ask.

"Not sure. Feeling jittery."

"About the family getting together?"

"Don't think so. That part I'm looking forward to. Just have a niggling feeling about Nell. Not sure I shoulda let her go up there by herself."

"For heaven's sake, Nate. If Nell wanted to go to Hamlin Flat alone, then Nell was gonna go to Hamlin Flat alone. Not a thing you coulda done about it."

"I suppose you're right there. Let's get the truck loaded and get up there. I'm sure everything's fine, but I'll feel better once I lay eyes on her."

Nate gently releases his arm from around my waist.

"I just talked to Cassie," I tell him. "She's already on the road. Said they were about halfway between Cold Springs and Austin."

"Good. Looking forward to seeing that girl. They? Is her friend with her?"

"Lord, I don't know who's with her, Nate. Said she hitched a ride—left her car in Carson City with Bets. I told her we'd leave the keys to the old flatbed for her and directions to Hamlin Flat, but whoever she's with—a man—said he'd give her a ride to Hamlin Flat. They'll be coming up the Ely side."

"They know how to get there?"

"She said he—whoever he is—knows the way."

"Must be somebody local then. If they're halfway between Cold Springs and Austin, they could get there before us. I best get the truck loaded."

"How much food should I pack, Nate? How long you figuring on staying up there?"

"Till we get things straightened out. Knowing this family, that could take awhile."

"Go down the basement and pull some meat outta the freezer, will you?" I ask him. "Get some steaks, some hamburger, whatever we have."

He nods and pulls himself up but doesn't move any further than that.

"Ona?" he says.

"Yeah, Nate?"

"You've been a good wife to me."

"Go," I say, pushing him toward the door, wiping my hands on my apron.

"I just want you to know that, Ona," he says as he walks through the kitchen. "We've left a lotta things unsaid in the last fifty years. I don't intend to let that go on."

"Go get the meat," I say, pushing him outta the kitchen. "We'll talk later."

"You're damn right we will, old woman."

He looks at me dead-on—like he's reading through the last fifty years a notes scrolled up inside me—before turning to descend the stairs. I, too, may have to run through those notes if Nate means what he says, if he really does want a conversation that extends beyond tractor payments and weather and calving and house repairs. I waited a long time for exactly that. Till I stopped waiting. Till I closed up the place inside me that expected—longed for—such intimacy. And now he wants me to tear back into that spot, as if it will be as simple as finding a place in a book that's been closed without a marker. As if I can say, *Yes, that's where I left off, all those years ago, right there on that page where the woman is crying out silently, and the man is walking away.*

I walk into the yard seeking the heat of the early sun on my skin. *It's too late, Nate,* I want to tell him. *You asked me to resign that part of me, asked me to let go of the girl who itched to be known and loved anyway.* That's what I want to tell him, but I won't. Cause his touch still stirs the yearning strands of that girl.

Lost in my thoughts, I don't notice Derek waving at me until he startles me with his closeness.

"Good morning, Ona!" he says. "What a stunning sunrise. I expect you folks get used to that out here, but I don't know that I've ever seen anything quite so beautiful as the sun peeking over the mountain and crawling across the pasture."

"Morning, Derek. Did you sleep well?"

"I did. How could you not with all the silence that surrounds you out here?"

"Well, never much thought about it. Guess a person takes those sorts a things for granted."

"Not where I come from. Silence is a rare and undervalued thing in the city. Guess people could drive themselves crazy with longing if they thought about it much."

"That's too bad. I don't imagine I'd like that. I sorta like to hear my own thoughts."

"Exactly."

"Katie still asleep? Nate's feeling anxious to get on the road, but he still needs to get the truck packed up."

"No, she struck out early this morning. But I imagine she'll be back soon. Went that direction." He points east toward the Snake Mountains.

"Yep, that was Henry's direction."

"Would you mind telling me a little about Henry, Ona?"

"Oh, what'd you want to know?"

"Sounds like he was quite a character, from what I can gather."

"He was that all right. Had a way about him. Folks found him quite charming."

"Did you?"

"I don't know. Henry had a way of stealing life if you know what I mean."

"I can't say that I do."

"Well, he was a lot to live up to, that's all. But he and Katie adored each other. No doubt about that."

"She doesn't like to talk much about him."

"No?"

"No."

"Well, words don't fit him all that well."

"That's what she says."

"How long you been dating our Katie, Derek?"

"Close to five years now."

"That right? That's a good while. I'm ashamed we've never met you before now. That ain't right in a family. You in love with our Katie?"

"Yes, I am.

"Planning on marrying her?"

"Yes, although she's turned me down four times already."

"That so?"

"That's a fact."

"Plan to keep trying?"

"I do."

"For how long?"

"Until she says *yes*."

"I'm gonna tell you something, Derek."

"I'm listening."

"This ain't an easy family to marry into."

"I appreciate that, Ona. But I love that woman."

"This ain't an easy family to love."

Derek nods.

"I'm not telling you anything you don't already know, am I?"

"No."

"All right then. I'm gonna pray for you in my own way that you get your wish, that you can talk our girl into marrying you."

"Thanks, Ona."

"But you gotta do it the right way, Derek, you can't just wear her down. You gotta find your way in. Otherwise, I'm afraid she'll make you miserable, and I don't think you deserve that. Can you do that?"

"I think I can."

"And if you can't, you gotta walk away. Can you do that?"

"I don't know."

"That's a question you oughta ask yourself."

We both look over the corrals at Katie.

"I'm gonna pull some food together," I say. "You ever been camping before?"

"No, I haven't, but I'm looking forward to it."

"Yep, I imagine it will suit you fine."

"We didn't bring any camping gear."

"We'll take care a you. Don't worry about that. Here comes Katie now."

Katie strolls through the alfalfa field toward us. If I didn't know better, I'd think I was looking at a woman filled with hazy contentment and dreams. But I know better.

NELL

The morning sun cuts through branches at teasing angles. It won't be enough. The heat is gone from this old body; my teeth are clacking something awful. When I attempt to pull my hands from behind my head and stretch my arms in front a me, my shoulders scream with the movement. Rusted tight. My arms feel like an old pair a chaps hung on a hook in the shed too long—stiffened leather, hardened past the point a ever wrapping around another leg. Arms and hands are bluish-purple right down to the solidly white fingertips. The silver band on my left hand finally fits the way it's supposed to after years a being so tight on these swelled up old hands that Dr. Norse over in Ely threatened to cut it off until I threatened to cut off something a his if he tried.

I'm not in any way relieved to be alive at daybreak; I'm ready to be done now. This is getting damned uncomfortable. Even the parts that have been numb for hours—spine, hips, legs and feet—seem to have glacial pain firing from every dying nerve ending. Funny how a person can feel numb and pain at the same time. I suppose that's just my mind playing tricks on me now. Looks like Jasper's given up on me; he's nowhere to be seen. Good for him. Dog's smarter'n I gave him credit for. He can make it all the way back to the ranch if he needs to.

"Henry, you still here?" I call out to the warming air around me. Nothing but the sound a the crick cutting around my paralyzed body and the buzzing a everything that buzzes as soon as the sun comes up—cicadas, bees, flies, mosquitoes. The morning is full a life, a cruel joke, but I appreciate it nonetheless. I don't have the energy to hold my head up long, so I let it fall back against the rock and then slowly lower my arms into the water. Let's be done with this. You'd think this body would give up shaking and jumping, but it looks to be jerking on me until I draw my last breath. I saw my mother die. Sat right by her bedside with her hand in mine. Life slips from the body quickly. I felt it go, pulled right outta my hand, away from my touch and my gaze. I was dumbstruck by the single moment. I tried to hold onto her like a child trying to hold a handful a water.

I didn't feel Henry die. He was gone before I reached his body. I missed the moment. Maybe I coulda held it if I'd been there—just for a second, just long enough for one soft touch down the bridge a his long, sunburned nose. When I reached him, I wrapped my body around his and his around mine, tried to pull him back. But once the life is gone, a person can't get much satisfaction from the body. Still, I couldn't let go.

I gotta let Katie off the hook. That's what Henry said. I gotta let her off the hook. *I'm sorry, Katie. Sorry, sorry, sorry. Sorry excuse for a mother. Sorry I hung you on that hook and left you there. You're gonna have to get yourself off the hook now, Katie, my girl. Maybe this will do it. Maybe you can find your way after I step aside and leave a space.*

KATE

The four of us bounce up the mountain road in Nate's truck, each lost in our own sense of anticipation. Every once in a while Aunt Ona notes the weather, the road conditions, the drought's effects on the desert—taking up her normal position of soothing whatever might be ailing those around her. Derek responds in kind—asking questions about the area, getting Ona to identify plants and wildflowers. Whether he does this out of genuine curiosity or out of kindness for her, I don't know. Probably both. Maybe he doesn't separate those sorts of things, "holistic" as he is. One of his favorite words.

He rides with his head turned toward the land and halfway out the window, seemingly mesmerized by the slow-passing sagebrush and bright splotches of Indian paintbrush, which allows me to study him, something I often do—unbeknown to him—when he's sleeping. I'm an insomniac; Derek sleeps peacefully every night. On full moon nights, when shadows in the room stand tall, I prop myself on a pillow and watch Derek sleep. He looks like a child—exactly as he looks now—a closed-mouth smile dominating his face. Who the hell sleeps smiling?

I know very little about this man—where he comes from, who his people are. Of course, I've met his parents, they live less than a mile from us, nice people—Don and Kaye—but who are they? It's not that he hides things from me; it's that I never ask, never show an interest. Our life is all about me—my needs, my issues, my problems, my job, my family, my past. Derek works, plays music, smiles, laughs, makes love to me. He is the most irritatingly peaceful and giving man I've ever known. Isn't that the way it goes? The craziest one in the asylum gets the attention. Well, I didn't ask for it, don't want it.

Derek's hair falls down his back, gray since his early thirties, most often worn in a ponytail or a long braid, which to my utter surprise elicited not one remark from Uncle Nate or Aunt Ona. Blue eyes punctuate his smooth-skinned face. That's why I never look directly at him when he's awake, when he's looking at me, which he does with far too much regularity. I never thought I could fall for a blue-eyed man. What sort of depth can blue eyes hold? You can't sink into them, can't lose yourself in a pair of blue eyes. Can't swim in them, can't find answers in them. They're cool, icy. I'm afraid if I look directly into them, I'll glance off and fall to my death, like hitting a piece of granite at a full run. Can't expect that they will take you in and hold you like brown eyes will, offering you the warmth and intricacies of the earth.

Derek turns to me suddenly—before I can turn away—and flashes a soft smile, his eyes matching the expanse of the sky, as if he somehow knows about those times I watch him while he sleeps. He turns back to the desert, letting his right arm hang loosely out the window, palm to the wind, long, thin fingers spread. *Work, laugh, love, live—life don't need to be any more complicated than that, Katydid.*

Uncle Nate clears his throat in a nervous way, and Aunt Ona glances at him, then makes a gesture as if she's reaching out to comfort him, although they never actually touch.

"Uncle Nate?" He looks at me in the rearview mirror without answering. Aunt Ona turns in her seat, and Derek pulls himself back inside the truck at the sound of my words. I didn't expect to garner such full attention. "I suppose you want to ask me about the pipeline project."

Uncle Nate looks surprised, like the thought never crossed his mind, and I'm surprised he's surprised. What else could he be so glum about this morning?

"Whatever you have to say about that, Katie," he says, "needs to wait until we meet up with Nell."

I nod, and Aunt Ona reaches over the seat to pat my knee. I try to smile at her. I don't look at Derek, anxious for him to resume his post out the window. Instead, he reaches across the seat for my hand. *God, people. Stop already. The little girl's fine. Go back to your own thoughts. Leave mine alone.*

"Oh, Jesus," Uncle Nate says, stepping on the gas and sending us tumbling back and forth in our seats. We all straighten up to see what he's seeing. Up ahead, paying no attention to us, a white horse grazes along the side of the road. The saddle has loosened, drooped off to one side, and every once in a while the horse steps on its own dragging reins, jerking its head to the ground. A ways in the distance, a man on a horse rides toward us at a gallop.

"Do you think someone got bucked off?" Derek asks. I'm thinking the same.

"That's Queenie," Aunt Ona says.

"That's Nell's horse," Uncle Nate says at the same time. "Shit. I knew something wasn't right. Goddammit. I shouldn'ta let her come up here by herself."

"Nate . . ." Ona says.

Uncle Nate pulls alongside Queenie, yanks the saddle off her with quick, strong movements and throws it on top of the gear in the bed of the truck. He pulls a halter out of the gear compartment of the trailer and exchanges it for the bit and bridle on Queenie as the man on the horse arrives.

"What's going on, Nate?" the man asks.

"Hell if I know, Skinny. You seen Nell out here?"

"Saw her drive up the road day before yesterday. Wondered where she was headed."

"You talk to her? She look all right to you?"

"Didn't talk to her. My camp's just over this hill. Thought she might stop, but she didn't. I was looking for sheep through the binoculars when I spotted Queenie here."

Uncle Nate and Skinny stand wordlessly for a moment.

"She was going up to Hamlin Flat," Uncle Nate says. "We'll go on up and look for her."

"I'll ride up the crick and meet you there," Skinny says, pointing out the wet mud on Queenie's hooves and legs. Uncle Nate nods and loads Queenie into the stock trailer with the other two horses he'd brought, and we all climb back into the truck.

"How did Queenie look?" Aunt Ona asks. "She been out here long?"

"Can't tell," Uncle Nate says. "You all keep your eyes peeled along here, will you? See what you can see. I don't know if that horse has made its way down here from up above Hamlin Flat or if Nell for some reason was riding this direction, although that don't make no sense at all. But Nell don't make sense half the goddamn time."

"It's possible Nell just got off to look at something, got distracted, and the horse wandered off, Nate," Aunt Ona says. "She's always expected that horse to follow her like a dog. She's walked home plenty a times after that horse has wandered off."

"Sure, you could be right," Uncle Nate replies, but his

words are hollow. He knows she's dead wrong.

I find his apprehension enormously disconcerting, almost panic-inducing. I've always thought of my mother as indestructible—the older she got, the tougher she got. I left it at that. She's been my estimable adversary—our inimical relationship forming the substratum of my life. What would happen to my foundation if I were to see my antagonist in a weakened state? I'm not at all prepared for it. It changes everything. Everything. I need to rethink things. I need to get back to my car and return to Vegas immediately. I glance at Derek, looking for some assurance that he knows this also, that he'll say to Uncle Nate, "If you don't mind taking us back to the ranch, Nate, we'll just be on our way, and you can let us know when you find Nell." Derek looks back at me, concern flooding his face. Good. He understands.

"We'll find her, Nate," Derek says. And then to me, reaching for my hand, "We'll find her."

Thanks, Derek. Very comforting. Very fucking comforting. I pull my hand away.

CASSIE

The air smells of damp dirt, mint, musty bark, and fresh pine. Breathing deeply, I stop fighting to hold back tears—these come from pure joy. The infamous Hamlin Flat. Much more benign than I grew up believing, but I already knew that. I've been here before—many times before—although no one in my family knows it. I've spent full days here—even spent a night when I was reported to be staying with a friend in Ely—looking for clues to my life. Never found any. This was the place I came with Bets a month ago when we left the ranch. Still searching. Still expecting the dirt and trees to divulge my family's secrets.

The first time I came to Hamlin Flat, I wanted to feel the haunting of the place, wanted it to touch the part of me I share with Grandma Nell. I sat in the middle of camp with a six-pack of cheap beer—also a first. I was sixteen—had just gotten my driver's license. I tried channeling images of the family encampment here and failed miserably, having few details to work with. I drank the beer, threw up in the creek, railed against Grandma Nell, railed against Mama, cried some and fell asleep on the picnic table. Woke up the next morning feeling like Lemuel Gulliver: a colony of black ants exploring the giant sprawled upon their wooden home, crawling in and out of my clothing, in and out of my nostrils.

Joe squats by the fire ring and looks around suspiciously.

"Expecting a bear attack, Joe?"

"I don't think your grandmother's here, Cassie."

"Sure she is. That's her truck and trailer. Guess the others will be here shortly. I'm surprised we beat them. I coulda slept a few more hours this morning."

"Something ain't right here, Cassie."

"What do you mean?"

"This fire is cold. Your grandma ain't been in this camp for a while."

"Well, maybe she didn't have a fire last night. Queenie's gone, so she must be out on her."

At that moment, Jasper crashes through the trees at the north end of camp. He runs straight at me, practically knocking me down with his excitement.

"Hey, Jasper, hey buddy. Oh, I missed you! Give me big, wet kisses all over my face." He complies. I watch the place where Jasper bounced through the trees, expecting to see Grandma Nell riding Queenie. When nothing materializes, my stomach starts to twist. "Where's Grandma Nell, Jasper?"

Joe walks to the place where Jasper emerged from the tree line and waits. After a moment, he turns back toward me.

"Joe?"

"I don't know, Cassie. I think we best go for a hike and see what we see."

As we start north out of camp, we hear the roar of Uncle Nate's truck coming in from the south. He jumps out and runs toward us.

"Cass, where's Nell?" he asks.

"Uncle Nate, we just got here. What's wrong?" Aunt Ona, Mama, and Derek line up behind him.

"We just put Queenie in the trailer," he says. "We found her three miles down the road, saddle hanging off the side, grazing her way home. Where the hell is Nell?"

Aunt Ona puts her arm around my shoulder, kisses my cheek, and pushes my bangs away from my eyes. I want to lean into her warmth, but the worry on Uncle Nate's face stops me. Derek also comes around to hug me, while closely watching Mama and Joe, who are staring at each other.

"Let's go," Uncle Nate says.

"Where?" Mama asks.

"The only place I can think of to look," Uncle Nate says, walking toward the bridge to cross the creek. Jasper runs in front of him and we all fall into line behind him—Aunt Ona, Joe, me, Mama, and Derek. No one speaks. I've never known exactly where the accident happened, so I had no idea how far we were traveling. Once we get on the double-track trail, Mama walks up next to me, close behind Joe.

"Joe," she says, as if she's making a statement. He turns to look at her and nods. Aunt Ona looks first at Mama and then at Joe.

"Well, I'll be gosh darned. I thought you looked familiar," Aunt Ona says to Joe, "although you've changed a bit."

"I imagine I have, ma'am," Joe says.

"Can't say I'm not a little surprised to see you here," Mama says.

"Didn't plan it this way, Katie, just giving Cassie a ride home."

"You two frequent the same establishment, do you?" Mama asks, looking at me.

"It's a long story, Mama, and not what you think."

"We never thought a thing," Aunt Ona says. "We're just glad you're back home."

"We'll talk about it after we find Grandma," I say to Mama, noticing that Uncle Nate has slowed his step and is keeping his eyes on the rock formations above the tree line. Jasper is acting squirrelly—running in and out of the trees.

"We need to cut in here and get over to the crick; I'm not sure I can recognize the place from out here," Uncle Nate says. "It might be some tough going through the brush—you okay, Ona?"

"Don't worry about me, Nate. Let's just keep moving."

"Nothing else to do, I guess."

As Uncle Nate picks his way through the briar, Jasper starts barking madly. We move as fast as possible through the brush toward the sound, and I think about how we must look from above—the six of us scattered in the brush, slogging toward the crazed barking of an old yellow lab while the thorned branches grab to hold us back. It reminds me of a video game—either the place or another player can sabotage your goal. Grandma Nell would tell me my mind is getting snagged worse than my shirt right now.

Uncle Nate and Mama see her at the same time.

"Oh, Jesus, Nell!" Uncle Nate rushes into the creek.

"God, Mom!" Mama screams, rushing in behind him, followed by Jasper, Derek, Joe, and me. Aunt Ona stays on the bank.

Grandma Nell's lips are dark blue, and her face is translucent—she looks absolutely ghoulish. But she's sitting in the creek leaning against a boulder, watching us come toward her as if she's wondering what the fuss is all about.

Uncle Nate reaches her first, grabbing her under both armpits to lift her.

"Whoa, whoa, whoa!" she tells him. "For Christ sake, Nate, you think I'm sitting here cause I'm too tired to stand up?" She looks at the small group that's formed around her, and her eyes land on Mama. "Katherine Ann," she says. "Katie." And then tears are running down her blue face.

"Goddammit, Nell," Uncle Nate yells at her. "We gotta get you outta this crick now. What's going on here?" he asks, looking into the water.

"My left leg is wedged between two boulders. Good you brought a small army with you," she says, looking around, "cause I think you're gonna need em. Don't recognize half of em and can't figure out why you'd be up here with so many people, but I ain't complaining."

Uncle Nate, Joe, and Derek have already dropped into the water, attempting to roll the boulder off Grandma Nell's foot.

"If you two had any sense," she says to me and Mama, "you'd get outta this cold water and up on the bank with Ona and Jasper." She nods toward Aunt Ona, who sits on the bank holding Jasper, now soaked, sitting between her legs and leaning his full weight into the front of her, as if he's the one who needs rescuing.

"That boulder ain't gonna budge with just us pushing on it," Joe says. "Cassie, run back and get my truck. Drive it as far up that ATV trail as you can get it. I have a crowbar and a few other things we might be able to use."

"And pull a few ropes outta my truck," Uncle Nate says. "And a couple a sleeping bags and anything else looks like it might be useful. And Skinny. He's probably in camp by now wondering where we are."

It takes over an hour to free Grandma Nell using almost every tool Joe has in his truck. She looks to be dropping in and out of consciousness, but she denies it, saying she's tired from not sleeping and just resting her eyes. The only time her body stops clattering against the rock is when she loses consciousness, at which time Uncle Nate or Mama shakes her awake only to send her back into frigid convulsions.

Aunt Ona takes over once we get her out of the creek. She directs Skinny to lay her on a sleeping bag in the sun, then Aunt Ona strips her stiff limbs of clothing, zips her into a dry bag and directs Joe to lift her into his truck and blast his heater although the day is turning out to be quite warm. We jump in the back of Joe's truck and, with no place to turn around, Joe drives back to camp in reverse like he's driving on a highway.

When we get to the bridge, Uncle Nate jumps out of the back and tells Joe to keep on driving to the Ely hospital—we'll follow him down. That's enough to get Grandma Nell going. Even with chattering teeth and a shaking voice, her commands are enough to get Joe to pull into camp and turn off the engine.

"Cassie!" she calls, and I run around to the passenger side of Joe's truck. Uncle Nate and Mama follow me. "Start a fire in that fire ring—make it as big as you can make it."

"Nell, for hell sakes," Uncle Nate says. "We've got to get you to a hospital. I'm not sure we can get your body temperature up where it needs to be and that leg looks god-awful."

"Nate, what's a hospital gonna do? Pile a bunch a blankets on top a me and wait for my body temperature to rise. Seems to me a good fire and some strong sunshine can do just as well."

"Mom, that leg—"

"Katie, it sure is good to see you. Wasn't sure that was ever gonna happen again." She turns to look at Joe, who is still behind the wheel waiting to see who's gonna win this argument. I could have told him right off he could relax; nobody's going anywhere. "Joe Snyder," Grandma Nell says, "been a long while. Don't think I woulda recognized you on the street. Would you be so kind as to carry me over to that lounge chair

Ona has set beside that fire Skinny has going? Cassie, don't look like your services are needed, but I'm glad you're here nonetheless."

We all turn to see Aunt Ona setting out camp chairs around a large fire as if she's expecting company for a fireside chat.

"Stay right where you are, Joe," Mama demands, then follows Uncle Nate and me over to talk to Aunt Ona.

"Ona, I think Nell needs to go into Ely to the hospital," Uncle Nate says.

"So do I, Nate, but it don't matter what you and me think, does it? Just cause Nell's stiff as a board and shivering like aspen leaves don't mean she ain't still in charge."

"I'm afraid she's gonna lose that leg or more if we don't get her outta this camp," Uncle Nate says.

"She knows that, Nate. She took a good look at that leg while I was taking those wet clothes offa her. She knows exactly what she's doing."

"Skinny?" Uncle Nate says pleadingly.

Skinny shakes his head. "I'll be getting back to my camp now."

Uncle Nate stands with his hands on his hips, turns to look at Grandma Nell still in the truck and back at us. He looks to Mama, then to me. I shrug my shoulders. Why would I suddenly have any answers in this family? He looks back at Mama.

"Katie?"

Mama looks back toward the truck and then around the campground. She looks exposed in every possible way, the sun illuminating a vulnerability I've never seen in her. The creases around her brown eyes tremble slightly, the usual tightness of her lips releases into a near-pout. It's then that I realize she's been literally holding herself together, every muscle held securely taut, for as long as I've known her. She looks at Uncle Nate and shrugs helplessly.

It doesn't matter. By the time we gather our thoughts, Derek's helping Joe lift Grandma Nell out of the truck.

"Nate, get camp set up," Aunt Ona says. "And set up the big stove; I brought two gallons of Nell's frozen beef stew. I hate to force her to eat her own cooking at a time like this, but it'll help warm her up, and it'll feed the bunch a us. Skinny, don't you disappear before you eat something."

Uncle Nate nods, resigned, throws more wood on the fire and gets to work. Mama has wandered off to one side of camp as if she's struggling to find her bearings, while Grandma Nell is being lowered into the lounge chair by the fire.

"Cassie, there's some castor oil in that bin there on the picnic table; pull it out, will you please?" Aunt Ona says.

"What you gonna do with castor oil, Ona?" Grandma Nell asks.

"We gotta rub some circulation back in your legs and feet, Nell. It's the only thing I can think to use."

Grandma Nell nods her approval, and she watches as Skinny tightens the cinch on his saddle, puts a foot in the stirrup and throws a leg over his horse.

"Skinny," Grandma Nell says.

"Nell," he says, tipping his sweat-stained, beat-up straw cowboy hat in her direction. They pause, looking at each other, then, as if they've completed an entire conversation, Skinny turns and rides out of camp.

"Now why didn't he stay to eat," Aunt Ona says. "I don't understand that man."

"He don't need you to, Ona," Grandma Nell says.

Grandma Nell turns her attention to Mama, who circles

camp like a wolf looking for a place to lie down until Derek reaches her, takes her by both shoulders, and forces her to look at him.

"You find that castor oil yet?" Aunt Ona asks.

"He looks to be giving her breathing lessons," I say, watching Mama and Derek.

"The castor oil," Aunt Ona demands.

"So that's Katie's young man," Grandma Nell says. "Seems like a nice enough fella—a little soft maybe."

"He's a very nice young man," Aunt Ona says. "Katie's lucky to have him."

Grandma Nell watches Mama and Derek until her attention is drawn to a low-flying hawk circling camp.

LEONA

Derek and Katie lean against a waist-high boulder at the far end a camp under the watchful eyes of a hawk perched in the juniper above them. Their hands are tightly clasped.

"How you doing, Katie?" I ask, positioning myself on the boulder next to her.

"She's going to die, Aunt Ona. She looks bad. We can't just stay here and watch her die. Why is everyone going along with her?"

"Well, for one thing, she's Nell. We've all had plenty a opportunity to stop going along with whatever Nell wanted, and we ain't done it yet."

"Don't you think it might be time?"

"Might be. But for another thing, she's an old woman trying to settle a life. Not everybody gets that chance. Then again, not everybody needs it. Nell does. Taking her down to the hospital against her will might be one way to save her life. This here's another. And it's not only Nell's life we're talking about here."

"What *are* you talking about, Aunt Ona?"

"You and your mother gotta talk, Katie. You gotta sit next to that old woman and have an honest-to-god conversation with her."

"How's that gonna fix anything?"

"I can't say that it will. I ain't expecting no miracles here. I only know how it feels to be walking around in an old woman's body. I guess I'm asking you, Katie, maybe even pleading with you, to give Nell one single sunny afternoon."

Katie breathes shakily as we watch the scene around the fire. Nate and Joe have unloaded camping gear, hooked up a propane tank to the old stove, put the stew in a large pot to heat, and are now setting up canvas tents. Nell lies on a lounge chair in the sun by the fire, one leg sticking out from under several down sleeping bags piled on top a her. Cassie sits on an overturned bucket at Nell's feet, gently rubbing the exposed leg with castor oil. The gentleness in Cassie's touch scrapes at my heart like a shoeing rasp on a horse hoof, leaving tiny pieces of it scattered in the dirt. I try to push the bitterness away and replace it with compassion for Nell, but it doesn't go easily. Why should Nell be the recipient a that touch? What has she done to deserve such tenderness? I almost speak these thoughts aloud, believing momentarily that Katie and Derek can provide me with some sorta answer. But the tears dripping from Katie's jawbone while she watches the same scene silence me. She may be experiencing the same line a thinking. I thought of Cassie as "ours" when she came to live on the ranch—as Nell's, Nate's and mine. But she wasn't. From the moment she was dropped off, she and Nell had something between them that transcended physical proximity. They had the line from mother to daughter to granddaughter. No matter how fractured, torn, and faint that line may be it could never be smudged out.

"How long has it been since you and your mother touched each other, Katie?" I ask.

She shakes her head. "I don't know, Aunt Ona. I honestly don't know. I have no recollection of her touch at all."

"I'm sorry for that, Katie. I'm so sorry for that," I say, wrapping both my arms around her.

"You don't have anything to be sorry for, Aunt Ona," she says, instinctively pulling away. "It wasn't like I was abandoned. I always knew where to find you and Uncle Nate and Grandma and Grandpa."

"Still . . ."

"Still, I did the same thing to my daughter. Left her scrambling among relatives to replace the love she should have received from her mother."

"Oh, it wasn't exactly like that, Katie."

"Wasn't it? How long are you all willing to let my father's death excuse everything I've done in my life?"

"I guess for as long as you need, Katie," I say.

"How about you, Derek?" she asks, turning to him.

"I've never allowed you that excuse, Kate."

"Of course you have. I've been rude, unloving, and short-tempered with you. And you show me nothing but compassion. You treat me as if I'm a fragile woman—the crazy woman who abandoned her daughter and never sees her family."

"You've misinterpreted my sentiment and my actions, Kate. I don't show you compassion because you're fragile; I show you compassion because you're loved."

I feel a subtle shiver along Katie's left side upon Derek's declaration. We fall into silence again, watching Cassie and Nell.

"I've never seen them together like this," Katie says. "Cassie's smiling and laughing; she appears to be joking with her. It never occurred to me they were close, never occurred to me anyone could be close to Nell. But they are, aren't they?"

"Yes, they are," I tell her. "In their own strange and stubborn ways, they're very protective of each other."

"She should have been protective of me," Katie says, jabbing a finger in Nell's direction.

"Yes, she should have been."

"And I should have been protective of Cassie. How did I get so cleanly removed from that scene, from between the two of them?"

"Kate," Derek says softly. "Lives are created through a series of deliberations and circumstances. The paths are often as thick and thorny as the brush we went through to find Nell this morning."

"Derek, that's really not—"

"You're waiting around for a better past, Kate," he says.

"But I—"

"You gave Cassie and Nell the gift of each other. It may have been the only gift you were capable of, but that doesn't make it any less beautiful."

"You're the only person I know, Derek, who could turn child abandonment into a gift," Katie says.

Cassie moves to Nell's other side and pulls the sleeping bag back from the wounded leg. Even from this distance it looks horrible—purple and swollen, the fat toes stretching their casings, a chunk of skin the size of a small plum torn away from just above the ankle to reveal what appears to be a glint of bone. Cassie touches the leg well above the wound, and Nell flinches. Cassie pulls Nell's hand into her own and rubs it gently with the oil but never takes her eyes from the leg.

"I think Nell and Cassie would agree with me," Derek says.

I tap Katie on the knee. "I best go find some way to help Cassie dress that wound, although I don't think we brought much. Might be an old first aid kit in the camping gear."

"It looks awful—even from here. Aunt Ona, I'm just not

sure we're doing the right thing letting Mom stay in camp tonight."

"I'm not sure either, Katie. But that leg wound doesn't seem to be Nell's priority right now. Could be she has a few other wounds need more immediate attention. I could use your help dressing that leg; maybe it's time you familiarize yourself with your mother's touch—or at least her with yours."

"Take Derek for that; he's far more comfortable with the body's oozing capabilities than I am."

"I'm happy to help in any way I can, Ona," Derek says.

"Besides, talking is one thing, Aunt Ona. Touching is another. Let's not get ahead of ourselves. How is this going to go, anyway?"

"There's no plan. And even if there was, Nell's night in the crick has certainly changed all that. I suggest we all have a bite to eat and sit around afterward for some conversation—like a normal family."

"Sounds reasonable to me," Derek says.

"It would," Katie says.

The hawk starts squawking as I begin to move. She flies in low toward Derek's head before swooping back out again. He appears unconcerned.

"She must have a nest around here," I say. "Protective mama."

"Hmm," Katie says. "She has reason to squawk then, hasn't she? She has no allies here."

Katie's words push me back against the boulder like a strong headwind.

"I'm sorry, Katie. I shoulda tried harder. I shoulda protected you."

"I'm not blaming you, Aunt Ona."

"I didn't think I had a right to mother you. But when Nell

didn't take on the job, I shoulda claimed that right."

Katie shakes her head and tries to wave me away. I pull a tissue outta my pocket and tip her chin toward me.

"I shoulda done this thirty-five years ago, Katie," I say, wiping away her tears as my own flow. I stuff the tissue back in my pocket. "I'm gonna get that picnic table set up with some food and hunt down some first aid material. This is a beautiful place, isn't it? I think Nate's right—this family never shoulda given this place up. Must be sorta hard for you, though, Katie— coming back up here again."

"It's okay."

"Well, I'm glad you're here. You too, Derek. Cassie, too. Come on over when you're ready. Let's all sit down and have some lunch together."

"We'll be over in a minute, Aunt Ona."

"Whenever you're ready."

The hawk makes another swoop as I walk away, then settles back on the juniper branch.

KATE

"I'm also glad you're here, Derek."

"That's nice to hear, Kate."

"I've been a shit to you. I have no idea why you're sitting next to me right now."

"I don't scare easily."

"I should say you don't. That's the last man I chased off," I say, nodding toward Joe.

"I thought as much," Derek says. "What about your husband?"

"He didn't count. I never loved him. That's why I married him."

"I see. And this one? Joe? Are you wishing you'd never shooed him off?"

"That's not jealousy seeping into your circle of tranquility, is it? I don't believe I've ever seen that in you before, Derek. I rather like it."

"I don't like it at all. And you didn't answer the question."

"Joe and I weren't meant to be together."

"Are you saying we are?"

"Isn't that what you've always said?"

"Yes, but you've never agreed with me."

I get up and brush myself off. The hawk flaps from one branch to the next.

"I'll tell you what. Let's see if I survive the next twenty-four hours. If I do, we'll talk about it."

"Whenever you're ready, Kate. I'm in no rush."

"Then how about we wait until we're in our seventies before we discuss whether or not we belong together?"

"Fine by me."

"It would be, wouldn't it?"

"I'm just living my life with you, Kate. You can settle in whenever it feels right. How are you doing being back in this place? You okay with it?"

"I love this place; I never did give it up."

"You've been back here since your father died?"

"All the time, until I moved away from the ranch. It was Joe's idea. In high school. Said it would help me to come here, and he was right. The first time we came, I just cried. Couldn't stop. Joe built a fire in that same fire ring where there's one burning now, sat down next to me, and never said a word. All night long. Just listened to me wail."

"Hmm. I like the guy. Don't really want to like the guy, but I like the guy."

"Not much to dislike about Joe. He's just that kind of guy. After that first time, I came here often by myself. But I never went back to the exact place where it happened—where Dad died."

"Why not?"

"Just couldn't do it."

"Have you been back there since?"

"No."

"Where did it happen?"

"Pretty close to where we found Mom in the creek.

I imagine that's how she ended up there. I want to go back before we leave here, Derek. I need to go back there."

"Why?"

"I don't know why. I just know I do. Something in me feels odd when I think about it, and maybe I can figure out what it is if I go back to the spot."

"What do you remember about it, Kate?"

"I remember the place, the light, the smell, the chill in the air—but I remember absolutely nothing about the accident."

"That doesn't sound odd—a lot of people block out traumatic incidents."

"Yep, that's what I've been told my entire life. But that doesn't make it feel any less odd."

"No, I don't suppose so. Do you remember anything after the accident?"

"I remember riding in front of Uncle Nate on his horse. The horse was trotting—a fast trot—and Uncle Nate was holding on to me so tightly I could barely breathe. He must have brought me back to camp. I remember being in camp that night. The grownups stayed up all night, but I remember the absence of the usual laughter and banter we kids would always listen to from our tent. They kept the fire going all night, spoke in hushed voices. My grandmother was the only adult who didn't stay up; she took me into her sleeping bag and held me all night.

"But I have tried over and over again to conjure up the actual accident, and I draw a blank."

"What have you been told about it?"

"Nothing, really. Just that Dad stepped out from the trees and Mom accidentally shot him."

"Why is it important to you to remember it?"

"It's just weird, you know? The single incident that defined my life more than any other, and it's missing, it's not in file. It's like a birth certificate. It's not that you need it to know you've been born, but it feels like an important document. I know my father's dead, but the actual moment feels like an important document to have."

"Okay, so you'll go back to the location and see what happens. Do you want to go alone?"

"I suppose so. My grand plan, when I found out Mom was up here, was to go there with her, if I could talk her into it. Sort of like a reenactment, I guess. But that's obviously not going to happen, and part of me—most of me—is relieved it won't."

"No, but you can ask her what she remembers."

"I suppose you're right about that. I'm glad you're here, Derek. We may need an outsider to point those kinds of things out to us. No one inside this fucked-up family dynamic of ours would ever recognize the right to ask such a question. Well, as Aunt Ona said, guess we'll have some lunch and family conversation."

"Looks like your friend Joe is getting ready to leave. You want to talk to him before he goes?"

"I do. Is that okay?" Derek looks at me, surprised. "Yes, Derek, I'm actually considering your feelings. Try not to make too big a deal out of it, or I'll have to revert back to my nasty, self-centered ways."

"I'll see if I can help Ona and Cassie tend to your mother." He kisses me on the lips, a soft, gentle kiss that makes me want to cry again. "Stay right there on your rock. I'll send Joe over."

The gray braid sways gently across the back of his T-shirt as he walks away. He tugs at the waist of his shorts, perpetually falling below his narrow hips and drooping just above the knee of his gently tanned, smooth legs. Turns out, now that

I'm actually looking at them, Derek has beautiful legs: muscular calves and strong ankles. His skin—the part exposed—has been lightly touched by the sun on long, solo walks he takes in the desert. Funny, I've always thought of him as pure white, my only reference being the hard, deep brown of my father's face, arms, and neck. My stomach jumps a little watching him.

He stops to speak with Joe, and they smile about something. They couldn't be more opposite. Derek, subtle and graceful; Joe, conspicuous and lumbering. They shake hands, then Joe walks toward me. I feel as if I've been handed off, and I'm suddenly flustered, feeling like the high school girl Joe once knew. I have no idea why I thought I needed to talk to him before he left.

"How you doing, Katie?" he says.

"You don't need to be rushing off; you're welcome to stay and have something to eat."

"Your Aunt Ona already tried to feed me, but I'm anxious to get to Ely and see my ma."

"How is your mother, Joe?"

"She's dying. She has cancer."

"God, I'm sorry."

"Yeah, I know. Your ma doesn't look like she's doing so good either."

"No she doesn't."

"I hope she's gonna be okay, Katie. I feel bad about not driving straight into Ely with her."

"Good lord, Joe. You think you could have gotten all the way into town with her if she didn't want to go? She would have brow beat you into turning around before you got a half-mile from here."

"Yeah, she seems to have an agenda, and it doesn't appear to include a trip to Ely. But she was in that crick more'n twelve hours, Katie. I hope she doesn't take a turn for the worse today."

"Me too. Sure you don't want to stick around and find out what her agenda is?"

"No, it's none a my business. Thought it might be at one time, but it's not now."

"I'm sorry, Joe, for the way I left things with you."

"Ah, Katie, we were young. I was head over heels for you, though. Can't deny that."

"I could have told you that would turn out badly."

"I think you did several times."

"You should have listened."

"No doubt." He leans back against the rock next to me. "Katie, I want to say something to you."

"Go ahead."

"This ain't really none a my business either."

"I don't care, Joe. Everybody in my family—and I'm the worst of them—minds their own business to the point we don't even speak to one another. Say what you want to say."

"Well, that's kinda what I was gonna get at. Your girl, Cassie, well that's a good kid you got there. But she's running scared."

"What's she scared of?"

"She's scared of what she don't know, scared of what's haunting this family."

"Well, she's got good instincts. I'll say that for her. Although I don't know about her choice of summer jobs."

"Know what she's been doing this summer, Katie?"

"Pretty sure I don't want to know."

"She's been drinking a lot of Coke, walking in the mountains, and missing this place."

"That all?"

"Yep. I don't think the woman who owns the place woulda

let her work even if she'd wanted to. Maggie's got a good eye for who's cut out for that type a work and who ain't. Cassie was just trying to figure things out, Kate."

"That's a big job in this family."

He nods.

"Thanks, Joe."

"Take care, Katie. You look good, by the way. The years haven't done any damage on the outside."

"But you think they might have on the inside?"

"I don't know, Katie. Your insides were always a little fucked up, if you don't mind my saying so. Not sure anything's changed there."

"Now see, Joe, that's exactly why I pushed you away in the first place."

"Because I understand too much?"

"Precisely."

"Wish I woulda known that. I can act dumb when I need to."

"You should try it sometime."

"Derek, there, doesn't seem all that stupid to me. How come you haven't pushed him away?"

"I have no idea; it's not for lack of trying. He claims to be in love with me."

"Well, I wish him luck."

"He's going to need it, right?"

"I believe so."

"You ever get married, Joe?"

"I did."

"Let me guess. Divorced, two kids."

"Widower. No kids. She got killed in a car wreck two years after we were married. She was pregnant with our first child."

"God, I'm sorry, Joe. What was her name? Did I know her?"

"Melanie Cross. She was four years younger than us."

"Did you love her?"

"With every heartbeat. Still do."

"I'm sorry, Joe."

"I best be going."

"Thank you for bringing Cassie home."

"She was more'n ready to come home—just didn't know it."

"And for helping get Nell out of the creek."

"And I suppose she was ready to get outta the crick, although it was kinda hard to tell. I have a feeling your mother resigned herself to a few things in the wee dark hours of the morning with that cold water swirling around her. Might be a good time to reach some sort of closure with her, Katie."

"Fuck closure. Closure's overrated."

Joe leans back on the rock and grins broadly at me. "Ah, now that's the Katie I fell in love with."

"Stop it, Joe. I don't want to have to dump you twice."

"Fuck closure? I do believe you are right about that one, Katie. I had so many people talk to me about closure after Mel died I figured it was a universally embraced concept. Didn't do a thing for me, but it must bring somebody comfort. Just thought I'd throw it out there. Don't know if you know it, but your daughter's a lot like you. She also calls me on every lame idea I float into the air."

"Good for her. Everyone should be called on their bullshit. We waste too much time offering meaningless platitudes to one another."

"Well, then, let me take this opportunity to address your bullshit. Rather than closure, maybe you'll consider taking Nell's near-death experience as an opportunity to begin a relationship with your mother—and your daughter."

"God, that sounds like a lot of work," I say, my voice cracking on the last word.

"It's no wonder your daughter is running scared."

"Let's go back to platitudes, shall we?"

He puts an arm around my shoulder, which causes a weird mix of comfort and discomfort. Comfort from the sheer size and warmth of his body; it feels protective in a way that Derek's slight build never does. Discomfort from my knowledge that Joe is the past and that's where he'll stay, and the present—Derek—now watches us from camp with feigned disinterest.

"It was good seeing you again, Katie. These are good people you've got here. You know that, don't you?"

I nod, but don't answer. I can't say I've ever really thought about my family in those terms—good or bad. They're just family.

"You're a stubborn woman, Katie. More like your mother than you're willing to admit. Take care of yourself. Try to do it in some way that brings you a little happiness."

"Is that what you do?"

"I try."

"In a Carson City whorehouse?"

"You want to be careful about putting parameters on sources of happiness, Katie. You might find yourself without any at all."

He kisses me on the cheek and walks back to the fire. He shakes hands with Uncle Nate and Derek, argues for a moment with Aunt Ona—I'm sure she's trying to force-feed him—before kissing her on the cheek, bends down and gives Nell a kiss on the cheek, then gives Cassie a hug. She clings to him, as if she's afraid to let go.

NELL

Cassie's been telling me I'm lucky to be alive, and I suppose she's right. Or not. Being alive leaves me in the same predicament as when I drove up here. Dying would have resolved all that in an efficient manner. Besides, pain crawls from my left ankle up my thawing leg like a slow-moving rattlesnake, leaving me feeling something less than lucky. But here I am, nevertheless, shivering by a good fire on a warm day.

My brush with death should certainly provide me with some sorta epiphany about life, some sorta awakening that would allow me to sift through the rubble strewn around me. This looks to be the gathering for it; all the people I have left in the world are within arm's reach. Which begs the question: what the hell is everybody doing here? Maybe Jasper—stretched from paw to paw in the sun next to me—ran to the ranch to summon help during the night while I dozed in the crick. The thought makes me chuckle. But he seems smug and self-satisfied. Or maybe just stupidly content. What a lovely aspect of a dog's life—limited foresight.

Ona has covered the picnic table with the black and yellow flowered plastic tablecloth that my mother used to use in camp, and she stands with hands on hips looking at Katie, who sits on a boulder at the far end a camp watching the mother hawk. Ona waves her over. Katie looks tired—like a child on the verge a tears from frustrated exhaustion. Ona hands her a tin coffee cup full a beef stew and points her in my direction. She sits in the chair next to me.

"Do you want this, Mom?" she asks, holding out the cup. Five simple words that barely mean anything, and they shatter this cold, old heart. Especially the last word. Katie, when she addressed me at all, has been calling me Nell for near as long as I can remember. I pull myself together, hoping to answer in the same kind, simple manner in which the offer was made, but can't find the words.

"Depends," I say, reaching for the cup. "Who made it?"

"You did," Ona says.

"That's what I was afraid of." I take the cup from Katie with both hands. My fingers aren't working too well just yet. "Thanks," I tell her.

"Can you hold it?" she asks.

"I believe so."

She turns back to get another cup from Ona for herself. When everyone has a cup and has found a chair around the fire, they fall silent, looking at me as if I'm supposed to conduct this meeting—a half-thawed, damaged old woman.

"You all mind if I ask you a question?" I say. They perk up, as if I'm going to say something profound. I hate to disappoint them. "What was Joe Snyder doing here?"

Everyone looks at Cassie, which I find odd, because I expected Katie to answer the question. Cassie looks to be searching for the right words.

"While you're figuring that one out, Cass, let me ask what the hell any a you are doing here? Not that I'm not apprecia-tive, mind you, but sorta a strange circumstance, you all show-ing up like this."

"We came to get you outta the damn crick," Nate says.

"Mighty thoughtful a you, dear brother. Glad to know your psychic abilities are intact."

"If that's a 'thank you,' you're damn welcome."

"Consider it so," I say. "But that still don't explain how you all got here in the nick a time to pull me from the jaws a death."

I look from one face to the next—no one offers to jump in with an explanation, so I start with the only one who isn't staring directly into the fire. "Ona?"

"Not everything in life can be explained, Nell," she says. "Ain't that so, Derek?"

"I believe this to be a perfect example of that theory, Ona," Derek says.

"By the way, Derek," I say, "it's nice to meet you. I been hearing about you some from Cassie, here."

"It's my pleasure, Nell."

"So you believe that, do you? That some mysterious force a the universe drove all a you here to save me?"

"I believe it is what it is, and no amount of demanding an explanation will satisfy our human desire to control the uncontrollable," Derek says.

His answer makes me smile, and I let it hang in the air while I watch Katie dig dirt from under her fingernails. I wonder if she hears the same thing when Derek speaks that I hear. If so, she shows no outward sign of it. Could it be that she actually has no idea? That she cannot hear her father's voice in Derek's words?

"Katie," I say, inadvertently startling her.

"What?"

"Why have you come?"

She turns first to me, then to Derek as if she's pleading for his assistance. He gazes back at her, silently offering all he can give—and it's a lot. He looks at her the way Henry used to look at me. And when he did, it filled me. All I had to do was open up and take it in. But Katie doesn't open. She looks like a child confronted by her own bad deeds—as if she might start bawling any minute.

"She came because you asked her to, Nell," Nate says, when the silence becomes too heavy for him. Katie looks at him, clearly confused. "That's all it ever woulda took for our Katie to come home—an invitation."

"I didn't invite her, Nate."

"But you said you called—"

"What I said and what I did are two different things."

"They usually are," Ona says.

"Katie, why have you come?" I ask again.

"I don't know, Mom. I honestly don't know if I can figure out an answer to that question."

"Well, please try, Mama," Cassie blurts out, surprising all of us. Cassie then turns her attention to me, where she correctly assumes she holds some sway. "Grandma Nell, don't you think it's about time you and Mama talk to each other?"

"Hell, yes!" Nate says on my behalf.

"I do, Cassie," I say, ignoring Nate's outburst and Ona's enthusiastic nodding. "I'm not saying I'm not happy to see your Mama. I am. And that sounds like it oughta be a simple thing—me and her talking to each other. But I'm not sure either one a us knows how to go about doing it."

"Do it anyway," Cassie pleads, the tears spilling into her voice.

I nod. "Katie?" She looks up from her fingernails again. "Where do you want to start?"

She rubs her hands together nervously and shifts in her chair. "Why did Uncle Nate think you'd called me?"

"Because that's what I told him, and he believes what I tell him."

"Not everything," Nate says. "But I wouldn'ta thought you'd lie about something like that."

"What were you supposed to be calling me about?"

I take a deep breath, not entirely sure I'm ready to peel back the decorous film we'd carefully constructed between us but finding no other option at this point.

"Water," I say finally. "Folks in Omer Springs want to know why you're taking our water."

She nods slowly, looks at Derek, then at Nate, then back at me.

"So why didn't you call and ask me?"

"Cause I'm not sure I wanna hear what you have to tell us."

"How about you, Uncle Nate?"

"Hell, Katie, I don't know. I think it's only fair we hear you out. I guess I'd like to understand why you think you can drain water out from under us without doing us any harm."

"I'm not sure we can," Katie says. "But we're going to try."

"What's the truth of it, Katie?" I ask.

She pauses for a good while. Then she straightens her back, and when she speaks again her voice has dropped several octaves and has taken on an authoritative tone.

"The truth is, Nell, agriculture uses eighty percent of this state's water. And there are two million people—and more to come—in Las Vegas. It's my job to make sure they have water. You have to share."

She has slipped into her Nevada Water Authority persona as if she's slipping into a sweater on a chilly evening—pulling it tightly around her for warmth and comfort.

"That's easier said than done, Katie," I say. "We're in the middle of a drought—have been for a long time."

"I'm fully aware of that," Katie says.

"These days Spring Valley is full a dried up springs and dying greasewood. Hell, Lee's meadow caught fire a few years ago and burned all winter. It ain't like it was when you were a kid."

"I know that, Nell, but—"

"We'd be happy to share our water with you city folks if we had any, but we don't. We're taking water out from under that ground faster than it can be replenished just to keep our crops going and our cattle fed. How the hell do you figure you're gonna share with us? A share a nothing is nothing."

"We believe there's water there—we just have to go deep enough to get it."

"So the plan is to steal the water out from under us!" Nate says, getting riled up and emotional, which he seldom does. It sorta tickles me to see him that way. "We're trying to make an honest living out here, Katie. You're gonna take our water and give it to the casinos and whorehouses of Vegas?" he says, throwing Cassie an apologetic look I don't understand.

"Brothels are illegal in Vegas, Uncle Nate, but that's beside the point. It's not a moral issue."

"The hell it's not!" Nate says.

"Should we decide who gets water based on who lives a more righteous life?" Katie asks.

"That's not the worst idea," I say.

"Yes, it is!" Katie replies, also getting riled up, which also tickles me. Nice to see her passionate about something, even if I don't like what the something is. "Are you saying you want to decide this based on worthiness?" she continues. "Should we count up who attends church more frequently and distribute water in that manner?"

"But, Katie," Ona says, "there's no reason for Las Vegas to exist except gambling and greed."

"That might be true, Aunt Ona," Katie says. "But the lives behind that industry represent real people who love their kids and visit their grandparents on weekends. Are you telling me that you deserve to go on living as you've always done, but Derek here—who works for a casino—does not? Are you willing to make that call—willing to put yourself at the front of the line and send Derek to the back?"

"But are they more deserving than us?" I ask. "We grow crops and cattle that feed people. Seems to me if it comes down to who needs the water most those sorts a things oughta be taken into account. I like your young man, Derek here, just fine. But his job feeds the ugly side a humanity—greed and excess. Our jobs literally feed humanity."

"Nell," Katie says, "that's a disingenuous argument, and you know it. You're not driven by altruism, by a duty to feed the masses. Are you trying to argue that it's a noble sacrifice to live on a ranch nestled into a valley of mountain creeks and wildlife? Do you know how many people living on a tiny patch of land in Las Vegas crammed between their neighbors would give anything to live on the Baxter Ranch and do the work you do? Do you know how many would choose this life if they had the opportunity, if they'd been born into a family with six thousand acres of land and twelve hundred head of cattle? You talk about the people of Las Vegas as if they chose between two options—owning a large ranch or making fifteen dollars an hour dealing cards at a casino—and deliberately decided on the life of so-called glitter and greed. You call them spoiled brats in a city of swimming pools and golf courses and luxury condos. Do you not understand the privilege you were born into here? Do you not see your own arrogance here insisting that you be able to continue this life of pastoral entitlement unhampered because it somehow represents God and country and everything righteous? There are three hundred million people in the United States alone. You don't think some of those three hundred million yearn for a few thousand acres of land and the water to go with it, along with the damn near free use of several hundred thousand acres of public land? You live a life of privilege here and pretend you don't. You would have those who can't afford your lifestyle then sacrifice their lives for yours? Go without water so you don't have to give up your way of life? What exactly is the difference between your viewpoint and the wealthy developers who built Las Vegas?"

Katie stops abruptly, folds her arms protectively across her stomach, and stares into the fire. Most everyone follows suit except Derek. He throws more wood on the fire and quietly gathers cups and spoons from where they've been placed next to chair legs. He gently takes the still-full cup from my clutched hands.

So this is Katie; this is my daughter. She's smart. Got that from her father. Speaks well. Got that from her father also. And she's dug into a place that don't make sense. Got that from me.

"So what's the answer, Katie?" I ask.

She takes a deep breath before answering.

"I don't know that there is one, Nell. We're scrambling to find a way to make everyone happy for as long a period as possible."

"How long might that be?" Nate asks, still visibly agitated.

"I'm not sure, Uncle Nate. At one time I would have said twenty years. But deep in my gut, I don't believe we have that much time. We're rapidly reaching the moment when demand for water exceeds supply—not just in Vegas or Nevada but all over the West. Las Vegas might be one of the first places to experience the convergence of overpopulation and scarce natural resources, but it won't be the last. All western cities are vulnerable. We have to find new ways—new models to work with. We believe we can pump from the deep carbonate aquifers without disturbing your surface water."

"That scares the hell outta me to hear you say that, Katie," Nate says, some calm returning to his voice. "I don't claim to know the intricacies a what's going on under our feet—you know more about that, Katie, than any a us ever will—but that just don't make no sense to me at all. Hell, when old Morty dug a well on his property, Lee Holston's meadow dried up quicker than a rain puddle in August. I believe this might be a moral issue, Katie. I don't mean gambling versus ranching or that sorta stuff. I hear what you're saying there. But this ain't right, what you're talking about doing. It ain't natural—messing with things under the earth that way. It just seems to me that no good can come a that."

"Uncle Nate, the studies we've done—"

"Uncle Nate's right, Mama," Cassie says. "You're messing with a system that's been in place for a lot more years than humans have been on the earth. You can't claim to fully understand the complexities of the deep aquifers that run through the earth's crust—the delicate balance of the earth's cooling and heating system. Haven't we humans already proven ourselves incapable of comprehending the earth's workings? We've set the polar ice caps to melting and we've created holes in the ozone. Even out here we don't breathe clean air anymore, and we've managed to introduce toxins into most of our food with so-called new models. Now you're telling us we can tap deep into the earth's aquifers and suck the water out of them without any sort of dire consequence to a system that the earth has carefully crafted over the last four billion years?"

"Sounds like Cassie's learned a few things in that university you've been paying for, Katherine Ann," I say.

"Damn right," Nate says, getting excited again. "Katie, I can't decide if the Nevada Water Authority's plan is made up of ignorance or arrogance or both. But I do know it's an immoral act. Springs will dry up, birds will disappear, and every living thing with roots in this godforsaken desert will die. By God, I'm near ashamed to be a part a this species. I've never seen any other animal do so much damage as we've done. I'm fully aware that ranchers have contributed their own fair share to that—I'm not saying I'm innocent in this deal either. But, Katie, this plan just can't come to no good—it just can't."

Ona reaches for Nate's hand, and he grabs hers tightly. I hear Henry's words in his voice also, and from the look on her face, Katie does too. I'd never given much thought to Nate's loss a his best friend, so wrapped up as I've always been in my own loss. Nate and Henry used to ride the mountain together every summer when we put the cows up, taking a couple a weeks to mend fences and repair gates. This is just the kinda conversation I could imagine them having—sitting around a fire each night just like this one here. And once Katie got old enough, she woulda been sitting around that fire with them.

"Katie," Nate says, his voice much softer now, "maybe what you say is right—maybe us ranchers don't have a moral high ground to stand on. I know full well I live a life a privilege out here. I've always known that. And it might be selfish a me to wanna hang onto this life. I imagine that's just human nature. But you're flat out telling me my life out here is coming to an end, aren't you? You're gonna turn our ranches into dust bowls. You must know that."

Katie wipes away tears, and a softer persona immediately occupies her face. "Listen, Uncle Nate, a few years ago I would have said Lake Mead would provide water for Las Vegas for the next fifty years. Now, I don't know that we even have five, and we're still growing."

"Well, that's the problem, ain't it?" Ona asks. "Does it make sense to just keep on growing a city bigger in the middle a the desert where there's no water for people?"

"No, Aunt Ona, it doesn't make any sense at all. But we live in a country where people are allowed to take root wherever they want. I can't tell them not to move to Las Vegas. I can't tell them to stop having children. And I can't manufacture rain. But while we're on the subject of what's sensible and what isn't, let me ask you this—does it make any sense to grow crops and cattle in the most arid state in the nation? Or are we simply hanging on to a romantic western dream that doesn't work anymore?"

"Well, hell, Katie," Uncle Nate says, "that decision was decided long before we got here. Don't seem fair that you would tell us to leave now after being here more'n a hundred fifty years."

"I'm not telling you to leave, Uncle Nate."

"Well, not in so many words, but there won't be much to stay for if the water's gone."

"But there's no other option for Vegas. Where else are we supposed to go?"

"Well, that's a damn good question, Katie," I say. "Where else are we supposed to go? If you pick Nate, Ona, and me up from this place, where you gonna put us? That ranch is all we know, and it's all we know how to do. It's all my mama and daddy knew, and for a while we figured it would be all you knew too."

"I'm not taking that place away from you, Mom. It'll take years for that pipeline to get completed and years more before you could possibly see any impact on your land. Unless you three plan to live to be a hundred and ten, I'm not taking anything away from you."

"What about me?" Cassie asks. Her red face reflects the pain behind her words. "What are you taking from me, Mama?"

"Cassie, you've got—"

"It's an easy question, Mama," Cassie spits out. "The answer is obvious—you're taking away the only home you've ever given me."

With that, Cassie stands and strides north outta camp. Jasper scrambles up, looks at me questioningly, then follows Cassie. For a moment all we can do is watch—and sit with the truth a Cassie's words.

"Nate, saddle me a horse," I say. "I need to go after her."

"Nell, for hell sakes, you can't ride a horse. I'll bring her back," Nate says, getting up.

"No," Katie says. "Sit down, Uncle Nate." Katie pulls two sweatshirts outta the truck and follows Cassie's trail outta camp without another word.

CASSIE

I'm almost to the place we found Grandma Nell in the creek when I hear footsteps behind me. I don't turn around or stop to wait. Since Grandma can't walk, I assume it's Uncle Nate or Aunt Ona—the soother in our family—and I'm tired of things being soothed over in my life. I'm a little surprised to hear my mother's voice call out to me.

"Cassie, wait."

Jasper runs back to greet her. I turn to glare at her. I'm unable to imagine what she might say that could possibly make me feel better. Apparently, she's unable to imagine it also. She stares back at me blankly, breathing heavily.

"Let's walk," she says finally.

"Where to?" I ask.

"Up the creek a bit. We'll cross when we find a good place."

We walk in silence, Jasper in the lead. We cut through the wild rose to the creek. When we reach a place that looks fairly shallow, Mama boulder hops across the creek with little hesitation—like she's been doing it her whole life. It takes me by surprise. I've never thought of her as navigating anything other than a conference room full of suits. I follow, and Jasper splashes through the creek to the other side. Mama steps through the brush into an open meadow, the afternoon sun slanting in from the west. She pauses momentarily and takes several deep breaths, almost as if she's unaware of my presence. She then turns and, without a word, walks directly toward the ridge jutting up on the far side.

"Where are you going?" I ask her. She doesn't answer. Jasper runs ahead as if he knows precisely where we're headed. When I catch up with them, Jasper has flopped down in the leaves and dirt, and Mama is standing next to a makeshift bench between two trees, staring at it.

"Cool," I say, sitting down. "Somebody made a little bench here."

"Yes," she says, turning and sitting beside me. She stares into the meadow we just walked through as if mesmerized. I feel sorry for her. Why should I feel sorry for her? I've never held any animosity toward her for sending me to the ranch to live because I can't imagine growing up elsewhere. And no one in Omer Springs thought much of it. It wasn't until I had a well-meaning freshman English teacher at White Pine High School suggest to me that I was an "abandoned child" that I realized others took umbrage with the idea of my living apart from my mother.

"Mama?" I don't mean to startle her, but I do. She seems momentarily disoriented, but quickly finds equilibrium and starts speaking as if she's sitting in a boardroom.

"Cassie, I don't have any answers for you about this water thing; I wish I did."

"But—"

"If you're looking for some sort of reassurance or comfort that this will all work out, I can't offer any."

"No surprise there."

"The truth is, Cassie, the future looks nothing like the

past. I don't know how any of this will play out—I only know we're heading into territory we've never seen before. And no one—urban or rural, rich or poor—is going to escape unscathed. That's all I can tell you."

"Mama, do me a favor."

"What?" she says.

"Stop talking to me like you're giving a statement to the press. This is me—Cassie. I'm your daughter. And those people back at that fire are your family. They are all the people that love you in this whole fucked-up world. Does that mean anything to you?"

She looks like I've just slapped her across the face, but quickly regains composure, which makes me want to slap her for real.

"Life isn't that simple, Cassie."

"Yes, Mama, it is. It is exactly that simple. That's where all of life starts—don't you get that?"

She doesn't answer—just stares straight ahead.

"What you're doing is fucked up," I say. "Uncle Nate is right about this, Mama. You're fucking with something big here—something bigger than Las Vegas and Spring Valley. That pipeline plan of yours is like reaching out and pulling a fucked-up future right in at us. And you're starting with me. That's fucked up in so many ways."

"Your language hasn't improved any since you got that summer job."

"Maggie didn't permit that kind of language at the Wild Filly Stables. I picked that up living with you last year."

"That shoots to hell my theory that I've had no influence on your life."

I don't respond.

"Cassie," she says, "I'm sorry."

"Don't say that, Mama. That's such a stupid, shallow thing to say. Your generation goes right on fucking everybody over and apologizing along the way. Your apologies are meaningless, insulting."

"Well, I am sorry."

"Try living your life in a way that you don't have to apologize for it, Mama."

I feel her body tighten next to mine at the points of contact—elbows, hips, thighs. She doesn't speak for several minutes. When she begins again, her voice has lost its surety.

"I don't know what's right and what's not on this water issue, Cassie. Every option sucks. Publicly, I reassure folks there won't be winners and losers on this deal. That's a bald-faced lie. There's little chance this pipeline won't be built no matter the reports filed, protests launched and environmental laws trampled. I have no idea how to protect those with the most to lose."

"That's your own family you're talking about, Mama. That's your own mother, your own aunt and uncle—"

"And my own daughter."

"Yes."

She studies her hands and picks at the pale pink, flaking nail polish. A smudge of ash along her right jawbone adds to the vulnerability her face carries. It's a face I've never seen before today—the tough façade wiped clean with dirt and ash. This is the face of Katie, the girl Joe described to me on our drive from Carson City.

"I don't believe that, Mama, that you don't know what's right and what's not. I think you're buying into your own bullshit. Grandma Nell does the same thing, although her actions don't have quite the reach yours do."

"Cassie—"

"Listen, Mama, I don't expect honesty from you—you've

never talked to me about any issue that runs deeper than that damn creek right there. But you might want to try a little honesty on yourself, and answer this question: Why would you contribute to the devastation of this place? What exactly are you trying to destroy here?"

"I don't know what you mean."

"Fine. Just keep telling yourself that, Mama. I'm going back to camp."

She tugs at my sleeve as I get up to go.

"Don't go," she says.

"Why shouldn't I?"

"There's no reason you shouldn't, but I'm asking you not to. Just sit here with me awhile."

We sit in silence watching Jasper sniff the ground and trees in front of us like he's on a scavenger hunt. Her breath next to me is almost painful to hear. I rest my gaze on her feet encased in an old pair of my hiking boots, which she obviously pulled from the back of my closet at the ranch. As my eyes travel from her feet to her face, I realize she's dressed from head to toe in my clothes—shorts and T-shirt. They fit perfectly; I had no idea we were the same size. I want to wrap her back into one of her business suits. I'd never realized before what sort of protection they provide her. She's strayed so far out of her comfort zone, I'm afraid for her. And I'm pissed at her for making me feel that way. She has no right to make me feel sorry for her.

"Wonder what Grandma Nell was doing back here," I say, more to myself than to her.

"Sitting here on this bench, I imagine," Mama says.

"You're absolutely right," I say, spotting Grandma Nell's rifle propped up against a nearby ponderosa. "How did you know that?"

"How do you know I'm right?" Mama asks. I point to the rifle, and move to retrieve it, but Mama grabs my arm and pulls me back.

"Leave it!" she snaps.

I move to argue, but her face is pale and slack.

"What's wrong?" I ask.

She shakes her head. "Just leave it where it is, please."

"Okay, fine." I watch her closely. "Mama? What was Grandma Nell doing back in here?"

She swallows slowly and with difficulty.

"Mama, you led us straight to this old bench. That wasn't happenstance, was it?"

"We were sitting here on this bench," she says.

"Who?" I ask.

"Me and your grandmother."

"When?"

"The day Dad died."

Holy shit, I think, but refrain from saying it. *This is where it happened.* I look at her, not knowing whether to talk or stay quiet. She's squinting like she's trying to see something far away.

"It was late in the day—the sun was completely gone, and the light was rapidly following. It was getting cold—that time of day when you just want to stop whatever you're doing and get someplace warm."

"Have you been back here since that day?"

"No. Joe and I used to come up to Hamlin Flat quite a bit when we were in high school, but I could never bring myself to come back to this spot."

"Why today?" I ask.

"Why the hell not today?"

I shrug. "Good question."

"This family has set up camp in a narrow slot canyon between the past and the future—"

"Yes, and there's a monsoon on the horizon," I say. "I've been trying to make that point for a decade now."

She nods. "I suppose that's how you ended up at the Wild Filly Stables?"

"Yes, it is."

"I guess you can eke out some rationale there if you're creative."

"Mama, I just—" She stops me by holding up her hand.

"I always liked that about you, Cassie. That strange, meandering line of logic your mind takes. I can't follow it, but I like it. You don't need to explain. If anything, I'm the one who ought to be offering up explanations."

I couldn't agree more, so I wait for one, but she stops talking. It appears she has no intention of speaking again, so I urge her on.

"What happened here that day?" I ask.

"We were sitting right here—Nell and I—waiting for a deer to step into that clearing and drop its head to drink." She stops speaking again.

"Then what happened?"

"I don't know."

"Didn't you see it?"

"They tell me I did, but I can't remember anything other than the way the day felt."

"What were you and Grandma Nell talking about?"

"I don't think we were. We never talked much as it was, and we would have been quiet waiting for deer."

"How long had you been sitting here?"

"A couple of hours I guess."

"You sat here for two hours and never spoke a word?"

"I suppose we must have talked when we first got here; I don't remember. I imagine she gave me tips on shooting. Your grandmother was considered the best shot in the valley, you know."

"So I've heard."

Mama closes her eyes and sways slightly, just like the trees behind her. She starts talking again without opening her eyes. "I remember the discomfort of Nell's body next to mine."

"What do you mean?"

"I had been in this same spot a few days earlier with Dad. I could tuck into him, you know?" she says, her voice lifting into a squeak. God help me. I've always wanted to break through my mother's tough exterior, but now that it seems to be quickly dissipating, I'm not sure I'm prepared for what might follow.

"But with Nell it was different," she continues. "It was like leaning against a concrete wall—strong as hell, but no give at all."

"What else do you remember?"

"I remember being sorry I'd insisted we leave camp to hunt—it was my idea. The family tradition was to stay in camp on the last day of the hunt, but it was my first hunt, and I'd passed up my only chance to shoot a deer a few days earlier. I had chickened out. I was still stinging from that, so I talked Dad into going out on the last day."

"You were only ten."

"Yes."

"That seems sort of young to be shooting a rifle."

"Not in this family. But I hated the thought of it. I found deer beautiful. I had no desire to kill one. I could barely stand them hanging in camp, but I never told anyone."

"Why didn't you just say you didn't want to hunt?"

She looks at the ground and doesn't answer.

"Mama? Why didn't you just say you didn't want to hunt?"

"I didn't want to disappoint my father."

"He would have been disappointed?"

"Probably not. But I didn't know that then. I only knew that he was crazy in love with Nell, and Nell hunted."

I don't respond. Grandma Nell and Mama had been adversaries for as long as I could remember, but I'd always blamed Mama's job for that. Apparently they set up opposite each other long before that.

"Then what happened?"

"I don't know."

"Were you shooting Grandma Nell's rifle?"

She doesn't answer.

"Mama? Were you shooting Grandma's rifle?"

"No, I had my own rifle," she says slowly, in an almost whisper. "I got it for Christmas the year before."

She pauses several seconds between each sentence as if every word needs to be drawn up from a deep hole.

"We were sitting here—just like you and I are now. I had my rifle across my lap and Mom had leaned hers against the tree just like that," she says, turning slowly and pointing to Grandma Nell's rifle. "It doesn't seem that either of us intended on shooting anything. A cold wind started blowing out of the canyon—that shift you get when the sun goes and the temperature drops. Leaves jumped and rustled around us. I couldn't have heard a deer coming through the trees, but I could feel something."

"What?" I ask quietly.

"A prickly feeling," she answers so softly I can barely make out the words.

She pauses for a long while again. I stay silent, imploring her to go deeper into the memory.

"That's all I remember," she says, running both hands through her short hair, her voice returned to normal.

"Do you want to remember?" I ask, turning to look into her face. I wish Joe had stuck around awhile. She's exactly the girl he described in high school—scared and sad—and it seems only right that he would know how to talk to her now. I don't. In fact, I don't know how to talk to my mother at all.

"Yes," she says almost pleadingly. "Yes, Cassie. I do want to remember."

"Why?"

"I don't know. I can't tell you why, but I think it matters."

"What does Grandma Nell say happened?" I ask.

"We've never spoken about it."

"Seriously?"

"Has she ever talked to you about it?"

"No."

"Then you can't be too surprised."

We sit in silence again, sun falling directly on the top of my head, heating the skin where my hair is parted down the middle. I swat at a few flies, and we watch Jasper sniff around the meadow.

Without giving any notice at all, Mama starts up again in a voice that sounds like it's being pulled through a metal strainer. "I remember picking up my rifle and looking through the scope." She raises her arms as if she's holding a rifle. Both of her hands shake horribly, and I don't know whether to comfort her or break and run back to camp.

"And then, just like the day I sat here with my father, a buck stepped into that clearing and dropped its head to drink." She cups both trembling hands around her eyes as if scoping the clearing where Jasper wanders. "It was the same buck from the day before, I'm sure of it. I studied the deer through the scope, working up my courage to do what I couldn't do the day before. There was a spot right below its eye, about the size of a golf ball, where the hair had been rubbed off. I couldn't take my eyes off that spot. Somehow, that spot made a difference, made that deer unique, a specific being, made it all the more wrong that I should shoot that deer, that I should spill its blood across the fallen leaves, that I should shatter its life to pieces."

She stops again and drops her shaking hands to her lap.

"Then what happened, Mama?" I ask softly, inching my body closer to hers on the bench. She shakes her head and closes her eyes. "Try to remember," I say. "You want to remember."

With her eyes still closed, she drops her head into her hands and starts speaking again.

"Something startled the deer. It drew its head up from drinking suddenly, and I knew I had a mere second to make a decision before that deer bolted. Just like the day before. I knew if I did it, we would go back to camp and celebrate, that my father would be laughing and proud. But I didn't want to do it," she says. "I didn't want to kill it."

She slowly rocks back and forth on the makeshift bench, and I'm unsure what to do. If she were a distraught stranger, I would know how to comfort her. But she's not a stranger. She's my mother—my severe, emotionless, pulled-together mother. She looks hard into the sunshine about twenty feet away where Jasper's stretched comfortably in the damp grass.

"Gunshot," she whispers so frailly I can barely make out the word.

"What, Mama?" I lean in closely; the sides of our foreheads touch.

"There was a gunshot," she whispers, "the deer bolted off into the trees, and Nell yelled."

"Grandma Nell yelled?" I say, pulling my head back. "What did she yell?"

"I don't know. But I know she yelled—her voice next to my ear startled me. Then she was running toward the place where the deer had stood."

"Did you follow her?"

"No, I stood right here."

"Why didn't you follow her?"

"I don't know. I was scared."

"Then what?"

She stares straight ahead, trancelike. "Commotion—Nell running away from me, Uncle Nate and Casey coming through the trees about twenty feet beyond where the deer was standing. Nell was hollering at Uncle Nate."

"Then what happened, Mama?"

"The next thing I remember, Uncle Nate was standing in front of me, blocking my view of Mom. He picked me up in his arms so strongly and quickly, I remember being whirled around, almost hitting my head on the tree where Mom's—"

She stops abruptly and sits perfectly still. I wait for her to continue, but she doesn't. Her breathing comes deep, fast and heavy. She looks to be having some sort of stroke—sweat suddenly pouring down a grayish-white face, as if she can't get air, but I can see and hear her sucking breaths in and out through her gaping mouth. She half-jumps, half-falls from the bench, one hand wrapped as far around her waist as she can get it—so her hand comes almost to her back—the other hand gripping her short hair, pulling at it with all her strength.

"Mama?" I say, jumping up behind her. "Mama! Do you need help? What's wrong?"

She doesn't answer. She strides toward the spot where

Jasper lies. I follow desperately. "Mama, tell me what to do to help you!"

She turns 180 degrees abruptly, smacking directly into me and shoving me to one side as if she's no more aware of me than she would be of a tree limb in her way. She staggers to the tree where Grandma's rifle leans neatly into the craggy bark of the trunk.

"No, no, no, no, no," she says, "Oh God, oh fuck, no, no, no!" She's sobbing now, making circles around the tree, still holding her waist with one hand and her hair with the other.

"Mama, stop!" I yell at her. "You're scaring me!"

She continues to circle the tree—throwing out the words *fuck, God, Jesus,* and *no* randomly through snot and tears. She drops to her knees next to the tree and starts heaving—big, dry gasps as if she's trying to bring something up but can't. I kneel next to her and tentatively place my hand on her back. She pushes her forehead into the scabby bark of the ponderosa, her knees resting in dry pine needles at the foot of the tree, her left hand gripping the barrel of Grandma Nell's rifle, her right hand tearing slabs of bark off the thick trunk. She continues to sob and heave and swear—then gasps desperately to catch her breath before starting again. We stay like this for what seems a long time, the sun now sitting low on the ridge, the shadows growing deep. Jasper returns, circling Mama and the tree then lying next to her leg when he gets no response from her, his head on his front paws. I look into his sad brown eyes. He knows more about the Jorgensen women than we give him credit for.

LEONA

Nate sits next to Nell whittling—his habit whenever he's feeling agitated. Wood shavings gather at his feet. Derek watches him, whittling on a stick of his own. Nell feigns sleep in her lounge chair. She looks bad, the color a ice on a lake, but I don't point that out to Nate. I'm sure he's noticed it himself.

"You're good at that," Derek says to Nate.

"Oh, not really, but it occupies a person. Henry, now, he could whittle. Over the years we spent in this camp, he carved Katie a whole zoo full a miniature animals. Believe he got all the way through the animal kingdom and then some, started carving each one a partner—sorta like Noah's ark. Wonder what ever happened to all those, Ona?"

"Don't know. Forgot all about em. Maybe they're up in the attic with Katie's old stuff."

"No, they're not," Derek says. "There's about fifty of them on the mantel of our fireplace. I never knew where they came from."

"That so?" Nate says. "I never woulda guessed that's where they'd ended up."

"Me neither," I say.

"Guess our girl ain't so far removed from this place as she pretends to be," Nell says without stirring.

"Hell, Nell," Nate says in the way he starts most a his sentences directed to his sister. "I thought you were sound asleep. Why don't we set you up a cot in the tent?"

"Not yet," Nell says. "We ain't through here."

"Hell, Nell, we don't need to get everything figured out today."

"You best go after our girls, Nate," she says. "Sun's traveling west."

"You're right about that." Nate stands, brushing woodchips from his lap. "I don't want to be pulling any more women outta the crick." He looks at me, then at Derek. "Derek, you mind keeping an eye on Nell here for a bit?"

"Not at all," Derek says.

"Care to take a walk with me, old woman?" Nate says to me.

"I'll get some jackets," I say.

"You know where to find those two, Nate," Nell says.

Nate nods. I grab Nate's denim jacket and a sweatshirt for me from the truck. Nate takes them from me and begins walking south outta camp.

"Where you going?" I ask. "Didn't those two leave in the other direction?"

"Thought we'd take the long way and circle around," Nate says. "We still have some daylight left."

"Where do you and Nell think those two are?"

"Up where Henry got shot."

"You think Katie could find her way back there after all these years."

"Yep. I think she knew she was close when we pulled Nell from the crick. Wouldn't take much to find it from there. If she has any instinct left at all for the place, that's where she'll be."

We cross the crick on the bridge at the south end a camp, then follow the two-wheeled track torn wide by Joe's truck that morning. For a while we walk in silence, stepping over the mangled tree limbs lining our path, each a us working through our own thoughts. Nate begins kicking the tree limbs to one side as we walk—without much thought at first, as mindlessly as he might open a door to walk through—then with increasing intensity. By the time we've walked fifteen minutes, Nate's reaching for the detached limbs and flinging them off to one side and the other. I've seen him stack hay in this same manner—as if the harder he works, the easier the answers will come. He stops suddenly, squats down to his haunches, and drops his head into his hands. My arthritic knees scream with pain when I drop down to his side.

"Nate?"

He folds into himself, ending up in the middle a the trail, sitting cross-legged like a child. I join him, although I have no idea how we'll ever get up again. He holds one a the torn limbs, several branches still clinging, and waves it like a big fan.

"This is what we Baxters do, Ona. Leave a trail a devastation behind us."

"Nate . . ."

"That's the most uncomfortable feeling in the world, to reach the end a life and look behind yourself to see that. How the hell did that happen? And why couldn't we see what we were doing?"

"We do the best that we can here on earth, Nate."

"If that's our best, Ona, I sure as hell would hate to see our worst."

"It ain't all that bad."

He squints into the sun to look at me. "The hell you say. Katie just informed us the ranch will be a dust bowl as soon as they get us buried under it. If that ain't bad, I don't know what is."

"Well, that ain't for certain, and sides, that ain't nothing we brought on ourselves."

"I can't help feeling it's all related, Ona, that our actions contributed to the end a this place."

"I don't think that's true."

"I can tell you one thing for damn sure. If Henry had been sitting in camp with us an hour ago, we wouldn'ta been hearing those words coming from Katie's mouth."

"I can't argue with you there. I suppose a lotta things woulda been different if Henry hadn't been killed. But I think his powers stopped short a bringing more rain and fewer people to this state."

"Well he had the power to hold this family together. Since Henry died we been stretched like an old barbed wire fence been tightened too many times, living all the while with the knowledge that one a those strands is gonna break and fling right back at us, leaving a deep and bloody gouge. That scar Katie carries on her face tells the whole story a this family."

I put my hand on the back of his neck and gently pull on the gray hair hanging over his collar. "You feeling like every part a your life has gone badly, Nate?"

"You satisfied with the life you lived, Ona?"

"Yes, I am."

"How could you be?"

"I spent my life next to you. That's all I ever wanted, and that's all that ever mattered."

He shakes his head. "I never did right by you, Ona."

"Stop saying that, Nate. You are who you are, and I accepted that. Hell, I've done more than accept it. I happen to love you, you damned old fool."

"I never loved you the way you shoulda been loved."

Bitter tears sting the rims a my eyes. "Why didn't you?"

"I was angry at you. I been angry at you most a our lives together."

I nod, keeping my eyes on the spot where my tears fall directly into the dust between my folded legs. "I know that, Nate."

"Why'd you put up with it, Ona? You never shoulda let me get away with that."

I shrug. "What choice did I have?"

"I had it all figured out, the way our lives would go. You and me would have a mess a kids, and Henry and Nell would have a mess a kids. They'd play together and work together and go off to school and come back home with their husbands and wives and kids, and we'd have a mess a grandkids. We'd all work the ranch and eat meals together and celebrate holidays, and this ranch would be passed on down through the generations forever. I had a picture in my mind a working cattle with my sons and my grandsons, and I just couldn't let go a that picture, Ona. God help me, I just couldn't."

"I know that, Nate."

"I can be a stubborn sonofabitch, Ona. I never once stopped to think how you might be feeling. I just couldn't do anything short a blaming you. That was the only way I could live with myself."

"What do you mean?"

"Ain't easy for a man a my generation to think that he don't have what it takes to create a child."

"Nate—"

"That's why when you started talking about adoption, I wouldn't have none a it. Adopted kids would be just living proof that I ain't much of a man."

"Nate—"

"You shoulda left me, Ona. You shoulda gone off and

found yourself somebody else, had a bunch a kids. You woulda made a good mother, Ona."

"Nate, hush!"

"You woulda, Ona. You woulda made a real good mother."

"Nate, hush now. I mean it!"

He stops talking at the harshness of my voice and looks at me quizzically.

"I have something I want to say to you. I been trying to have this conversation with you for fifty years now. This is something we shoulda worked through together."

"I know that, Ona, and I'm sorry for that."

"We shoulda been there for each other. That's what marriage means. You weren't there for me like you shoulda been, Nate."

"I know, Ona."

"A man's supposed to put his wife above everything else."

"Ona—"

"You never did that. I've always come second in your life—after Nell. You was busy taking care a Nell when you shoulda been taking care a me. You was busy taking care a Nell when you shoulda been taking care a Katie."

"I know, Ona. I know."

"You don't know, Nate. That's just it. You don't know."

He stays silent and looks at me as if he's afraid of what might come next.

"You blamed me for your dreams not working out cause that's where the fault lies. It wasn't you; it was me. You woulda known that if you cared to. I woulda owned up to that a lot a years ago if you'd a been paying attention."

"What you talking about, Ona?"

"Just what I said. I couldn't have children, Nate. Not with you, not with anybody. And I never wanted to carry that knowledge around by myself."

He stares directly into my eyes as if he's trying to determine the truth of my words.

"What do you mean, Ona?"

"Exactly what I said, Nate. It wasn't you; it was me. I couldn't get pregnant."

"How do you know?"

"I've always known."

"How?"

"When I was a freshman and you were a senior, I missed a week a school."

"I remember. You were in the hospital with pneumonia."

"I didn't have pneumonia."

"What do you mean?"

"I was in the hospital to have a growth removed. It shoulda been a relatively simple procedure—even in them days—and it mighta been anywhere else, but the only doctor we could see back then was old Doc Whitley, the Kennecott doctor." I look dry-eyed at Nate. "That old drunk botched the job, Nate. I ended up coming outta the hospital with both ovaries gone."

"What are you saying, Ona?"

"I'm saying exactly what I'm saying, Nate. It wasn't you. It wasn't ever you."

"You knew before we was married that you couldn't have kids?"

"I did."

"But you never said anything?"

"No."

"Why wouldn't you tell me something like that, Ona?"

"I was afraid you wouldn't marry me if you knew I couldn't have children."

Nate struggles to his feet, rubbing both hands on his

temples. I stay where I am.

"The longer I kept that secret the harder it was to divulge it. I wanted to talk about it, Nate, wanted to figure it out together. But soon as Nell birthed Katie there wasn't nothing left to figure out—she gave Henry a child and Flora and Nathaniel a grandchild, and I knew right then and there, there wasn't no way I was ever gonna be looked at the same by you or anybody else in this family. I took up my place as that child's aunt, and that's the best I could do."

Nate walks up the road a few steps then turns and walks back, still rubbing his temples. His cowboy boots stop directly in front a me. I wait for him to speak, but instead he turns and walks up the road again. I think he might keep going, but he doesn't. After about twenty steps, he turns and comes back, begins to speak, stops, and starts walking again. I don't look up when he stops in front a me.

"You were right, Ona. I wouldn'ta married you had I known that."

He doesn't move; nor do I. I feel the weight a his words smack in the center a my belly—right where a child woulda taken up space if it was meant to be—but my eyes are dry. I've shed a million tears in anticipation a this very conversation; I have none left. Nate had presumed the burden was mine, and he was right. He had duly punished me for it our entire lives. Whatever the consequences from this point forward hardly matter. He starts pacing again, this time back and forth in front a me.

"I wouldn'ta, Ona. I sure as hell wouldn'ta married you. And you'd a been better off, too."

"Hush, Nate."

"You woulda, Ona. You're right about what you said. Nell's always been my first priority. When Henry came along, I thought I could walk away from that job cause I been trying to walk away from it since I was old enough to walk. But Henry didn't stick around to finish the job."

Nate's burly body jolts as he walks, like every so often he's being touched with a cattle prod, and I realize he's sobbing—big, dry, heaving sobs. He stops in front a me and reaches down to pull my hands from my lap.

"Get up off the ground, old woman," he says.

I put both my hands in his, feeling the rough, warm skin next to mine. He pulls me up with strength. When he releases my hands I move to step back, but he steps forward, engulfing me in an unexpected hug. My head rests under his chin, my cheek against the soft flannel a his shirt. He holds me tight, as if our bodies might otherwise flail apart. I'm pleased to find out we still fit together. I feel his tears seeping into my hair. We stay like this for a few moments before he tenderly pushes me to arm's length where he can see me clearly. Looking into my face, he shakes his head, the tears rolling freely down his cheeks.

"I'm sorry, Ona."

"For what?"

"Sorry you had to hold that by yourself."

"I shoulda told you, Nate. I had no right to keep it from you. I was young and stupid. I thought love would carry us through anything."

"Didn't it?"

"Not very well, I guess."

He pulls me into his chest again.

"I kept rehearsing the conversation before we was married, Nate. But no matter how I told it, it never turned out with you being okay with it. It never turned out with us getting married anyway, and I just couldn't live with that."

"Now here we are fifty years later."

"Yes."

"Why tell me now?"

"I always planned to tell you as soon as the opportunity presented itself. Didn't figure it would take this long, but there you go. I don't blame you for being angry with me, Nate, and you might never forgive me. Wouldn't blame you there neither. But I'm glad to be rid a that secret nevertheless."

Nate breathes deeply, turning in a circle, looking around us. The wind has picked up, blowing down-canyon, pushing out the heat a the day and pulling in the cool a the evening. Aspen leaves shimmer like the jingles of a tambourine.

"This is a pretty place," he says. "I've missed this place. Place like this can feed a man's soul." He turns his back to me and looks toward North Schell Peak. "Human beings might be the silliest species on this earth, Ona. They sure as hell don't exhibit superior intellect when it comes to self-preservation. Talk about fouling your own habitat." He turns back to look at me. "There's a part a me, Ona, and it ain't no small part, that is damn glad you never before told me what you just told me."

I step away from him, so I can better see his face and wait for an explanation.

"No telling what a stubborn sonofabitch like me woulda done with that information. And I can't imagine spending my life with no other woman but you."

"Do you mean that, Nate?"

"I sure as hell do. I'm sorry for the tenderness I stole outta this love, Ona. But even with that, I could always feel you there—especially in these later years. Hell, maybe it was meant to be in some messed up sorta way."

"What do you mean?"

"If Katie's right, don't seem there's gonna be no Baxter

Ranch to be leaving behind anyway. I can't make no sense outta life, Ona. None whatsoever. The only thing that does make sense to me anymore is finding you at the kitchen sink on my way outside to do chores. It mighta taken me fifty years to figure that out, but that one I'm sure about."

He pulls me in close again, but tips my chin up with his fingers to look into my face.

"Anything else you been keeping from me?" he asks. I shake my head. "You've always hated secrets, Ona."

"Still do."

"Let's go find them girls and see what else might be revealed this weekend."

But he doesn't let go, and we don't move. We stand in the middle a the trail surrounded by broken tree limbs as if letting go a each other could have devastating consequences.

NELL

Katie's man sits on an overturned washtub close to the fire silently whittling. The long fingers of his right hand wrap naturally around the knife allowing smooth, graceful swipes at the stick he holds with the left. Although he looks nothing like him, Derek inhabits his body the same way Henry did. Why Katie has fallen for him is no mystery to me, although it appears she can't figure it out. He's lovely to watch, and in doing so, I feel a sense a calm flood my battered body—something I haven't felt in more'n thirty years. He looks up to see me watching him, smiles easily and goes back to whittling. Beautiful. Not a twitter a self-consciousness.

"What you whittling there?" I ask him. He stops and inspects the disappearing stick in his left hand. "Whatever it was supposed to be, I believe you've whittled right on by it."

"Seems I have," he says. "Didn't have anything in mind— just like the movement."

"Knife fits nicely in your hand. You could probably be pretty good at that if you cared to be."

"Might need a little instruction."

"Unfortunately, the man who coulda offered you that is long gone."

"I'm sorry for that, Nell. I think I would have liked Henry."

"Oh, I have no doubt the two a you woulda found a few things to like about each other."

He nods, picks another stick off the ground and goes on whittling.

"How come you never remarried, Nell?" he asks.

"Don't work that way, and I have a feeling you know that."

He nods again. "So you believe there's only one person for each of us on earth?"

"No, I don't believe that at all. Do you?"

"No," he says.

"I believe some people get a lotta options and opportunities. They could be relatively happy—or relatively miserable—with any number a partners. But I'm not one a those people; neither are you."

"What makes us different?" he asks. He stands, setting the knife and stick on the tub, places two more logs on the fire, then resumes his former position. He's built nothing like Henry, but every movement he makes conjures up an image a Henry performing the same task with the same confident grace.

"Don't know. I never much pondered the whys a who I am—just know it to be so."

He nods and whittles. I shift in my chair and inadvertently groan with the pain that shoots up the left side a my body. He stops whittling and looks at me.

"How are you doing, Nell?"

"I'm all right."

He stands and pulls the blanket back from my crushed leg to look. I stare at his face, waiting for the expression that never comes. He replaces the blanket and sits down next to me.

"How does it look?" I ask him.

"How does it feel?" he asks me.

"Like hell."

"Looks about the same. Can I do anything for you?"

"Don't give up on Katie."

"I don't plan to."

"Good."

"Anything else?"

"Couple a aspirin and a glass a bourbon to wash em down."

"Where's the bourbon?"

"Behind the seat a my pickup. Pour yourself one also."

He pours us each an inch a bourbon in red plastic cups. He hands them both to me while he puts another log on the fire and pulls a camp chair next to my lounge chair. I hand him his cup, rest my left arm on the arm a the lounger, and take a sip a the bourbon, letting out a sigh that gets away from me. He reaches over and places his hand on the wrinkled skin a my wrist. It's a simple gesture of kindness, and it nearly destroys me.

CASSIE

Mama hasn't uttered a full sentence in more than ten minutes—just stares at that rifle, intermittently sobbing and swearing. She's barely recognizable to me—hair littered with leaves and pine needles, red splotchy face, brown eyes filled with fear and pain. This is not at all how I envisioned the reunion of my family. I anticipated a gentle storm between two strong women, not an avalanche that would bury them both under debris. I have no idea what to do. I'm afraid to leave her alone while I go back to camp for help, but we're losing daylight, and it's apparent to me that a similar scenario landed Grandma Nell in the creek for the night. I opt to sit tight and hope like hell Uncle Nate figures out where to look for us.

Mama hears Uncle Nate and Aunt Ona coming through the trees before I do. She starts at the sound, sitting up straight, twisting to look at the place where they emerge into the clearing with a confused and almost pleading look on her face. She slumps back against the tree upon recognition of Uncle Nate. He rushes toward us.

"What happened? Are you two all right?"

Mama looks up at him and doesn't answer. He looks at me.

"Cassie?"

"I don't know," I say quietly.

"Katie?" Aunt Ona says, sitting down next to Mama and placing a hand on her knee. "You all right?"

Aunt Ona's voice betrays the fact that she's also never seen my mother in such a state of discomposure, which leaves me feeling all the more unhinged. Mama turns to Aunt Ona slowly and wipes her nose on her sleeve.

"Did you know?" she says accusingly.

"Know what?" Aunt Ona asks. That's an excellent question, I think, and I'm hoping someone soon answers it.

"Why would you do that?" Mama asks.

"Katie, I'm not sure what you mean."

"You and Grandma Bax," Mama says, "were the closest I ever had to a mother. I trusted you."

Uncle Nate takes a clean, white handkerchief out of his pocket and tries handing it to Mama. She pushes it away, never taking her eyes off Aunt Ona.

"I trusted you," she says again. "How could you lie to me like that?"

"Katie, I don't—"

"She didn't know," Uncle Nate says.

We all shift our gaze upward to Uncle Nate, who is barely visible in the deep shadows of the fading day. Rustling leaves and rushing water fill the silence.

"If you want to be mad at somebody, Katie, be mad at me. Ona didn't know."

"Nate," Aunt Ona says, "bend yourself at the knee and come on down here." He complies, coming down to one knee and bracing himself with an elbow on the other. "What didn't I know?"

He starts searching for the right words, but before he can find them Mama blurts out the answer.

"I killed Dad."

"Katie, your father's death was an accident," Aunt Ona says. "We all know that."

"Yes, it was an accident, Aunt Ona. But the bullet that killed Dad came from my rifle, not Nell's."

Aunt Ona looks at Uncle Nate, and he nods slowly.

"When Dad was shot," Mama says, "Nell's rifle was leaning against that tree, right where it is now." She points, forcing all of us to follow her finger to Grandma Nell's rifle, the tip of the barrel tucked neatly into the groove of the ponderosa bark. "There was one shot fired that day, and only one person held a rifle—me."

Aunt Ona takes a deep breath, pushing the air out through the space between her front teeth—and for once she seems ready to follow that motion with words.

"Yes," Aunt Ona says. "I knew." Her words seem to surprise both Mama and Uncle Nate. "I didn't know for certain, but I suspected that was the case. It just didn't make no sense the way Nell was telling it, and for as long as I've known Nell she's worked details like a person kneads bread dough—just round and round until it takes the shape she wants it to have."

"Why?" Mama asks Aunt Ona.

"I don't know, Katie. For one thing, it wasn't my place to set down the details for you. I wanted to take you in and love you like my own—give you a safe place to grieve and to heal. I shoulda done it, Katie. Lord help me, I shoulda been strong enough to make that happen."

Uncle Nate pulls himself up closer to Mama.

"And I shoulda let that happen, Katie," he says. "You have every right to be angry, but not with Ona. She was fighting against a force that got set up in this family long before she entered into it. I'm the one that deserves your anger. I've been

Nell's willing accomplice long after I shoulda grown outta the role."

"Why, Uncle Nate? Why didn't she tell me the truth?"

"I can't answer for Nell, Katie. You're gonna to have to ask her that yourself. I have some ideas about that, but I'm done trying to explain why Nell does what she does. I feel like I owe you an explanation for my part in all a this, but I'm afraid I don't have much a one to offer." Uncle Nate shifts uncomfortably from one knee to the other. "When I got here that day, just a minute or so behind Henry, it was pretty clear what had happened. Nell was at Henry's body, and you were standing in front a that bench, your rifle at your feet, shaking so bad I thought you were gonna break a bone. Once I realized we couldn't do nothing for Henry, I gathered you up and rushed you back to camp. I handed you off to Mom, and got Dad and Uncle Bert to come back up here with me to get Nell and Henry's body. When me and Dad got back here, Nell was laying flat on the ground next to Henry. She had pulled both his arms around her, and if I didn't know already that he was dead, I woulda thought they were up to their old stuff—they never could keep their hands offa each other—they'd just fall down in the grass any old place to wrap themselves around each other for a bit."

Aunt Ona nods. Mama starts crying again—quiet, deep sobs.

"They didn't look any different that day—cept for the blood seeping across the front a both a them and cept for the look on Nell's face. Sheer madness is the only way I can describe it. Took Dad a good piece a time to coax her apart from Henry's body. Once he did, he asked her what happened. She looked at Henry, then at me, then back at Henry like she expected he might provide an answer. I don't think Dad was really wanting one—Henry was dead and how didn't much matter at that point—I think he was just trying to pull Nell back into reality. She looked up at Dad and said, 'Daddy, I've killed my man.' Just like that."

Uncle Nate shifts from one knee to the other again.

"Course I knew that wasn't accurate. I had gathered up both rifles from this spot—yours from where you'd dropped it at your feet and Nell's from right there against that old ponderosa. I didn't know exactly what she meant by those words or why she said em, but I figured we'd get things sorted out later on. Thing is, we never did. That story got told back at camp, it got told back in Omer Springs, and it never got told any other way."

Uncle Nate picks up some dead pine needles and starts breaking them in half, letting them drop back down to the ground.

"I'm sorry, Katie. I know it don't make you feel no better now, but if I coulda seen what kinda destruction we were leaving behind, maybe I woulda spoke up. I don't know. The time never seemed right, and so I did what I always do—I went along with Nell."

"Did you and Mom ever discuss it?" Mama asks.

"Yes we did. One time when we were bringing cows off the mountain about eight years after Henry died—right after you left for college—we came upon that tree house Henry had built for you up Flatbush Hollow. During those eight years, you had filled that place with all sorts a Henry's stuff—his old jean jacket, his spurs, his straw cowboy hat—anything you could sneak out without Nell noticing. I knew that's where you were going and what you were doing, so whenever she complained about something a Henry's gone missing, I told her I'd taken it for some purpose or another. I knew Henry'd never told her about that place—he said that was special between you and him, just the two a you—and I wasn't sure how she'd feel about that. But then that day she got to talking to me about Piss Pot Springs—a place she and Henry'd never told anybody about—so I thought it might be time for her to see your place. I didn't know how she'd take it, but she climbed up in that tree house where all a Henry's stuff still was, and she couldn't stop grinning—crying and grinning was what she was doing. She moved around touching all a his stuff that had been so nicely arranged by you, and she was just smiling from ear to ear—tears flowing so hard and fast she could barely see. I asked her did she want to take the stuff back down to the house, and she said, 'nope, I believe it's fine right here.' And I asked her about it that day—bout why she never told you the truth."

"What did she say?" Mama asks.

"Katie," Uncle Nate says, dropping the pine needles from his hands and wiping pine sap on his jeans, "I'm gonna step on outta the middle a this now. You and Nell need to have this conversation directly. It's near dark. Let's get ourselves back to camp."

I look to the faces of each of them as the last of the twittering birds settle in for the night. I dare not move or speak, trying to grasp the magnitude of shifting ground under this family. For more than three decades, Mama has lived with the knowledge that her mother killed her father, and Grandma Nell has lived with the knowledge that her daughter killed her husband. Call it an accident if you will, and I'm sure it was exactly that, but that kind of knowledge seeps deep into a person—especially a person who's looking for a place to tuck away the fury of loss.

KATE

We trudge back to camp in silence. Cassie stays close on my left side, Aunt Ona on my right, both of them acting as if I might collapse at any moment—or break and run. On one hand, I'm grateful because they could be right about either of those things. But I find myself pulling away from Aunt Ona. I know she's trying to be supportive, but it's a few decades too late, and I can't give her that. She was right back there; she should have pulled me in and held tight after Dad died. She should have told me the truth about his accident. She should have stood up to Nell; they all should have.

Uncle Nate is out front setting a fast pace and leading the way. I wish he'd slow down. What the hell am I going to say to Nell that could possibly make any difference now? And what could she say to me?

We reach camp with just enough light left to make out the silhouettes of Derek and Nell, chairs pulled close together in front of the fire. Bitterness burns the edges of my skin when I see his hand resting on her arm. Why should he do that? Why should he comfort her that way? How does she deserve his sweet compassion?

They stir when they hear us.

"Good, you're back," Mom says, pulling her arm out from

under Derek's touch as if she's embarrassed that we've seen it. Derek rises to greet us.

"Kate," he says softly, taking one hand and using his free hand to brush leaves out of my hair. It's not until then that I realize how disheveled I must look, and not until I hear Derek's next words that I realize he's never seen me this way, although I feel as if my entire life has been lived in such a state.

"You're okay," he says, pulling me in close to his body. "You're okay." I relax into him, releasing Aunt Ona and Cassie from their duty of holding me up. They both move toward Mom.

"Grandma, you okay?" Cassie asks.

"Nell, how you feeling?" Aunt Ona asks.

"Been better," Nell says, "though I don't know that I ever will be again."

Just like always. Rush to Nell's side. Care for her, lie for her—whatever Nell needs.

Aunt Ona pulls the blanket from Nell's leg, and Cassie gasps. Nell waves them off. "Stop fussing around me, you two. Katie?"

I look at her but don't move.

"You okay?"

Aunt Ona jumps in before I can say anything.

"Let's get some dinner on the table," she says, pushing Uncle Nate toward the camp stove. "We can talk over dinner."

"We have something we need to talk about?" Nell asks, directing her question to Aunt Ona but looking at me. I pull away from Derek's body, but he doesn't release his hold on me. I can't figure out why until I realize I'm shaking badly.

"Over dinner," Aunt Ona insists as she begins to set food on the table.

"I don't think this is gonna wait," Uncle Nate says. He

looks from Nell to me, and gently pulls a jar of mustard from Aunt Ona's hands. "Let's all sit down again."

Uncle Nate throws a couple more logs on the fire, and Cassie takes up the spot Derek vacated next to Nell. Derek moves me toward a chair on Nell's other side. I pull back. Confronting Nell is easier from a distance—preferably a distance of several hundred miles, but at the very least I need a couple of yards. In the moment, I consider never having this conversation with Nell. Why bother? Why put myself through it? I look from Nell to Aunt Ona to Uncle Nate—all of them looking back at me expectantly. I hate them—seething, venomous hatred for the co-conspirators. And the thought exhausts me. I long for the simplicity of a hot bath, a city view and a glass of wine. There's no resolution, no redemption to be had here. The only option is to return to a city that allows—indeed nurtures—my animosity toward my family. This place does not. It's full of my father's love. I turn back to Derek, fully intent on getting from Hamlin Flat to Las Vegas as quickly as possible—preferably a life-flight helicopter.

"Mama," Cassie says, able to read me better than she has a right to based on our limited relationship. With that single word, she's given me an ultimatum. I look at her sitting next to Nell and work to clearly separate my feelings for the two. As if on cue, Derek presses up against my back and gently unclenches my fists hanging at my sides and winds his fingers through mine. I lean full against him. He's solid—I always thought the weight of me would topple him—and his tenderness seeps in.

"Mama," Cassie says again, almost pleading. I want to take her up on her offer; I want my daughter back. But the only path to my daughter goes right through Nell. And Nell—like the Sierra Nevada in January—seems impassable. I look at her now, layered in blankets, a flannel shirt draped over broad, slumped shoulders, short, gray hair smoothed back from her colorless face. She doesn't look formidable—in fact, the opposite—but underestimating her can be a fatal mistake.

"Mama," Cassie says again—this time more like a command. I take the chair next to Nell.

For a moment we are all silent, none of us knowing where to start.

"Katie," Mom says, "I take it you found your way back to the place."

"Yes."

She nods, chewing on the inside of her bottom lip and staring into the fire.

"Why, Mom? Why didn't you tell me the truth?"

She chews and stares harder.

"I made Henry a promise," she says finally, without looking at me. "Right there in that spot where he died, right there where you were today. I told him, 'Henry, that girl ain't gonna make it without you.' And he said—I heard his voice just as clear as crick water—he said 'Nellie, you make sure she does. Don't you let her bury herself alongside me.' I promised him right then and there that you would not carry the burden a his death."

"But you blamed me for it."

"I tried not to."

"But you did."

"I couldn't find any other place to put the pain."

"And I blamed you for it."

"Yes, you did."

"You let us go on like that. For thirty-six years."

"Yes."

"Why?"

"Because that's the way lies work, Katie. Once one's set in place, unraveling it ain't like combing through a tangle in your hair—it don't leave you with a shiny, smooth surface afterwards."

"So you just let it play out."

"I thought I could get on the other side of it, Katie. I kept thinking I'd be okay after a while and when I was, I'd come find you."

"But you never did get there."

"No, I didn't. I ain't ever got over losing Henry, and that's the truth of it."

"And you've never stopped blaming me."

"I stopped blaming you years ago. Hell, you were a kid, and Henry stepped outta the trees twenty yards directly behind that deer. There's no way you coulda seen him looking through the scope like that. But I sure as hell never expected you to take that shot. I saw the flash a red through the trees the same time that buck heard Henry coming. I reached over to pull the barrel a your rifle down, but . . ."

"But it was too late."

"Yes." She pauses for a moment and then speaks again. "Let me ask you something, Katie. Would you have wanted to know—all those years—would you have wanted to know it was you that pulled the trigger that killed your father?"

"Yes."

"Why?"

"Because I wouldn't have been able to blame you."

She nods. "Lies don't always work out the way you think they will."

We sit in silence, faces bathed in a dancing yellow glow, flinching with each pop of the fire, equally stunned, I believe, by the simplicity of the truth.

Cassie, Derek, and I help Aunt Ona with breakfast while Mom and Uncle Nate engage in a ten minute standoff about which side of the mountain we'll be driving down. Uncle Nate insists he's taking Nell to Ely. Nell insists he's either taking her back to the ranch or leaving her at Hamlin Flat for the crows to pick at. She doesn't look capable of putting up a fight, but Uncle Nate is soon shaking his head and agreeing to her terms.

We pack up camp slowly and silently, one or another of us wandering off alone from time to time. Having won her argument with Uncle Nate, Nell summons Cassie and Derek. I watch as Derek lifts Nell and carries her to where Cassie has relocated the chair in a patch of clover in the sun. Derek's easy strength surprises me; his tenderness does not. Nell is comfortable with him—and he with her. From there, Nell watches us without comment, a pensive look on her face. If she's in pain, she gives no indication of it.

When we get to the ranch, Derek transfers our bags to the trunk of the car without asking whether or not we'll be staying, which brings me nearly to tears. Two days ago, I would have been irritated by his knowledge of me. Today, I find it sweetly reassuring.

Cassie helps Mom from the truck to a lawn chair set up under the cottonwood by the old swing. Aunt Ona pulls Derek into a hug with tears in her eyes as does Uncle Nate, creating the oddest group hug I've ever seen.

"You take care a our girl," Uncle Nate says, as if I'm not standing right here.

"You know I will," Derek replies, winking at me. For God's sake, I'm not an invalid. Cassie throws her arms around Derek's neck and whispers something I can't hear. Derek nods reassuringly. Jesus. More admonishments, no doubt, to take care of the frail and feeble. Derek walks over to Nell. She grasps his hand firmly as he leans down to kiss her cheek.

"Take care of yourself, Nell," he says softly. She nods. I walk over to join them.

"Mom, please go to Ely and get that leg looked at," I say. "Promise me."

"I'm done making promises I can't keep, Katie. I'll be okay. You don't need to worry about me."

The woman will never stop lying.

"Bend down here a minute, will you?" she asks. I kneel in the dirt by her chair. She reaches for my hand and holds it between both of hers. Her hands feel strange, foreign—cold and tough but not unpleasant. Her eyes are glassy wet. "You are your father's daughter, Katie, you have contentment in your blood. Don't hang on to what you inherited from your mother. Let your father's ghost run wild." Then she pats the top of my hand and releases it.

"Mom—"

"You two drive carefully," she says, interrupting me with a wave of her hand.

"We will," Derek says, guiding me toward the car.

I look at Cassie, wanting to hug her but not entirely sure we've transitioned to a demonstrative family just yet. She puts her arms around me, hugging me tightly.

"Are you sure you won't come with us?" I say through tears when she finally releases me.

"I need to be home right now," she says. I wince at the reference, but, of course, what other place would she call home? "I'll see you when I drive Bets back to Vegas at the end of summer."

"You'll be starting back to school in the fall, right?" I ask, realizing too late that I'm almost pleading. She pulls me into another hug.

"Go home, Mama," she says. "Things are all right." She gently turns my shoulders and pushes me toward Derek.

Once the car is headed south out of Spring Valley, Derek behind the wheel, he opens his hand toward me, and I place mine in his. He squeezes it.

"It's harder this time than it was the first time," I say. "Leaving Cassie there. I feel like I'm losing her for good."

"I think the opposite is true, Kate. I think you have your daughter back."

I look out the window. "I'd like to have this place back," I say. "Not literally, I know I don't belong out here anymore, but it's a lovely valley. I want the beauty of it back in my life."

"It's yours for the taking," he says.

"Dad and I used to saddle the horses on a summer day and announce we were going to ride fences. Grandpa Bax would tip his head back and laugh every time we told him that because we hardly ever completed the task. Usually before we got to where the fences needed fixing, Dad and I would be riding up some side canyon simply because the flight of a hawk or the sun hitting the rocks a certain way would draw Dad's attention. He'd fill with such joy when we discovered a spring he didn't know about or found evidence a wild horse band had been there before us."

I stop talking and turn to look out the window again.

"What, Kate?"

"He was hard to share, Derek. I remember insisting—even as a small child—that my mother not go with us, knowing, even then, that I was taking him from her, that riding together had been their ritual. But to be the one—the only one—to bask in the purity of his joy . . . he was irresistible." I turn to look at Derek. "I'm sure Nell felt the same way. We had been tugging at my father from opposite sides since the day I was born."

Derek squeezes my hand again.

"What Nell said up at Hamlin Flat was right, you know."

"What did she say?"

"She said the pipeline project would break my father's heart. Dad would have been at first amused by such a clever but foolish plan, but in the end, he would have been deeply saddened by it."

Derek nods.

"It is sad, Derek, and wrong. You know that, don't you?"

He nods again.

"To drain a beautiful valley like this one, to take its single source of life."

"Yes, Kate, I know."

"So what's the answer, Derek?"

"There isn't one, Kate. You know that. It was always inevitable."

"What was?"

"That we'd come to a place without answers."

"So now what?"

"Now we come to the convergence that many species have reached before us—numbers too high, resources too scarce. It's a natural process. The species shrinks or disappears entirely."

"Humans don't really like to think of themselves as part of a natural process, Derek."

"No, they don't. But nature doesn't really care whether humans think of themselves that way or not. The process moves on with or without our acknowledgment."

I look at Derek, slim but strong arms sticking out the sleeves of his T-shirt, the gray braid hidden between his back and the seat, light from the sun turning his eyes the deep blue of a mountain lake. He looks nothing like my father. So why is he speaking my father's words?

"Where does that leave me?" I ask.

"Same place it leaves every one of us, Kate, with an offer to make peace with the inevitable—or not."

I have only one box left to take to my car when Matt shows up in my office—coffee and muffins in hand. He sets them down on the coffee table and makes himself comfortable on the couch. I lean against my desk and fold my arms. He smiles up at me.

"About time you cleaned up this messy office," he says. "Now maybe we can get some real work done."

"What did you have in mind?"

"A little monkey-wrenching maybe."

"Of course."

"Don't know if you've noticed, but your Heather seems a little pissed off today."

"Yes, she seems to think I'm breaking an unspoken promise, a lifelong commitment."

"To the thirsty people of Las Vegas?"

"No, to her. She's afraid she'll get a new boss who doesn't consider vigilant maintenance of her Facebook page a priority of her employment."

"She should have never given you time off to go to Omer Springs then. I could have told her that. Quite frankly, I'm feeling a sense of abandonment myself."

"I think you'll be fine."

"Fine, yes, but entertained, intellectually stimulated, no. If we're no longer going to have intellectual stimulation, maybe we could try the other kind again."

"I don't think so."

"No, I didn't think you'd go for that. Don't you have unfinished projects here, Kate—one in particular?"

"Yes."

"Which is precisely why you're leaving."

"Yes."

"But the project will still go on without you."

"Yes—without me."

"I see. What are you going to do now?"

"No idea. I haven't gotten any further than what I'm *not* going to do."

"Well, Kate, I envy you the clarity."

"But you've been telling me all along this is a bad project—immoral, unethical, stealing from the poor to give to the rich—weren't those your words?"

"Indeed, but you're the one with the resignation letter typed and signed and handed over. You have principles."

"And you have two kids and a wife."

He stands with a muffin half-stuffed in his mouth and shrugs.

"Katie," he says, muffling with his mouth full, "allow me the honor of carrying the last box to the car."

When we get to the parking garage and stuff the box in the trunk, Matt turns to me. "I'm proud of you, Kate. You inspire some of that old college idealism in me."

"I don't know that my leaving is going to make a bit of difference, Matt. As you said, the project will still go on."

"Of course it will. But every once in a while someone needs to stand up and say, 'I choose not to be part of the absurdity.' It's a simple act, Katie. But if more of us would do it . . ."

"I'm not really making such a statement, Matt. I'm just

trying to create a life I can live in."

"However you want to view it, Kate. Nevertheless, I shall miss you," he says, bowing deeply at the waist. Matt watches while I buckle my seat belt and pull out of the parking garage. When I look in my rearview mirror, he's flashing me a grin and a peace sign.

CASSIE

Grandma Nell never regained her strength after our time at Hamlin Flat. Uncle Nate, Aunt Ona, and I split our time between caring for her and getting on with the daily work of the place. No one asked me about the Wild Filly Stables, and I never brought it up. It was as if every member of this family had been emotionally eviscerated, the scars of which were too tender to tolerate one more exploratory slice. The ritualistic nature of ranch work seemed the most likely path to healing— at least for the time being.

For a few weeks after we returned from Hamlin Flat and helped Grandma Nell into the gold La-Z-Boy recliner, the blue La-Z-Boy—my recliner—was filled by one or another of Omer Springs' old men. The wives tended to gather in Aunt Ona's kitchen while their husbands visited with Nell. I brought them black coffee, pulled the pillow from behind Grandma's back, punched it full of life again, and replaced it. They talked about lame horses and broken down tractors. They talked about one another. They talked about the dry weather. Most often they talked about the past. Then they'd sit for a minute slurping coffee before remembering a chore that needed doing and slap their ball caps on their knees first and on their heads second as a way of saying goodbye. Granted, I wasn't there every minute, but I never heard one of them ask about water or my mother.

Fitz stayed the longest and said the least. Grandma seemed content to let him sit next to her for as long as he wanted or needed—I don't know which. When he finally stood to go, he looked around at everything but Grandma Nell, like he was searching for a pair of lost gloves or something.

"We're gonna be okay, Fitzy," she said. He nodded and looked like he was gonna start bawling. "We're gonna be okay," she said again, this time with some of her old firmness behind it. He nodded once more and left.

On a windy fall day—a little more than three months after the day we pulled her from Hamlin Creek—I find her fully dressed in jeans, flannel shirt, and canvas coat at the kitchen table. At first, I'm hopeful—she hadn't been fully dressed or outside since the day Mama went back to Las Vegas.

"Where you going, Grandma Nell?"

"Outside," she says. "But you're gonna have to help me."

"It's chilly out."

"Why the hell'd you think I put this coat on?"

I nod. "Where do you want to go?"

"Set my lawn chair under the cottonwood where the leaves are falling, facing out toward the corrals and the pasture and the lane that leads to the crick."

"Okay."

My hope fades. This isn't Grandma Nell's comeback; this is her exit. I notice now that her face is pallid gray, and she barely moves her mouth when she speaks. I have no idea how she dressed herself. Sheer will, I suspect.

I've been expecting this—she's had me filling out paperwork and running back and forth to a lawyer's office in Ely for months—but that doesn't make it any easier. I do as she instructs—pull her lawn chair out of the shed and set it up facing east where she'll have a broad view of the ranch. Uncle Nate watches me from his window. He nods, and I nod back. Both he and Aunt Ona are bundled up and outside, setting up three more chairs when I get there with Grandma.

"Nate, Ona," Grandma Nell says in greeting.

"Awful cold out here, sis," Nate says.

"Beautiful fall day," Grandma Nell replies.

I help her into the chair, and Aunt Ona puts a blanket over her legs.

"Thanks, Ona," she says, touching Aunt Ona's hand with her fingertips. "Appreciate it."

For a long while none of us say a word—just sit looking out toward the corrals and an expanse of pasture that runs north and south between the yard and the foothills of the Snake Range, dotted with several hundred head of cattle. A bitter, cold wind blows directly into our faces, competing with a strong sun.

"Good hell, Nate," Grandma Nell says after we'd been sitting close to an hour. "Corrals need some work—that cribbing horse a yours has eaten all the way through that top pole over there. Send one a those good-for-nothing boys we got taking up space in the bunkhouse over to Ely to get some lumber."

"Sure thing, Nell."

"Looks like we're gonna do all right on hay this winter. Unless we get an early storm, I think those cows can stay in that pasture for a while longer."

"I think you're right, Nell," Uncle Nate says.

"Ona, what you got cooking in there?" Grandma asks. "Smells good."

"Roasting a chicken, Nell, with rosemary, the way you like it."

"I appreciate that," she says. "Cassie, my girl?"

"Yes, Grandma Nell?"

"I trust you'll write a helluva obituary for me. You can say whatever you want—just try to stick to the truth as much as possible."

I nod, unable to bring forth any words. A truck goes by on the road, turning on a seldom-used dirt road leading into the Schell Creek Mountains.

"Wonder where those boys are going?" Uncle Nate says.

"First day a deer hunt," Grandma Nell replies.

"So it is," Uncle Nate says.

"Looks like you're gonna need to hire a new hand," Nell says, and we follow her eyes out to Skinny's shack where he's tightening a canvas cover over the bed of his heavily loaded pickup. "When Morty stopped by yesterday he told me Skinny's sold all his sheep and his grazing permits to Frank. Don't know what Frank plans to do with em—doesn't seem like the sheepherding type—but maybe he's sick a chili, gonna start serving mutton stew."

We fall into a long silence. When Grandma Nell speaks again, her voice carries less strength, more resignation.

"Don't you three have work to do?" she says softly.

"No, Nell, if it's all right with you," Uncle Nate says, "I believe we'll just sit right here."

"Well, it ain't all right with me, Nate," she says, her voice barely above a whisper. "You're hovering. You know I don't like hovering."

"I just don't think you should be alone right now, Nell."

"I ain't alone, Nate. Now get on your way so I can get on with mine. All a you."

Slowly, and without another word, Uncle Nate, Aunt Ona, and I gather up our chairs. I bend down to kiss Grandma on the cheek. The tension that has given her face its shape since I've known her is gone, her face relaxed into a wrinkled softness I'm not familiar with. Uncle Nate wraps his arms around her from behind and buries his face in her hair. She rubs his hands, then gently pulls them away from her. Aunt Ona kisses her forehead.

We look up when we hear Skinny's truck start. Grandma Nell nods, and Skinny touches a finger to the brim of his black cowboy hat before putting the truck in gear.

Her thick, gray braid encircles his rearview mirror.

"Going home," she says so softly I barely make out the words.

By the time we reach the house and turn back to look, Grandma Nell is slumped in her chair under the cottonwood tree on the Baxter Ranch.

JANA RICHMAN

Jana Richman is the award-winning author of two books: *Riding in the Shadows of Saints: A Woman's Story of Motorcycling the Mormon Trail*, a memoir (Crown, 2005); and *The Last Cowgirl*, a novel (William Morrow/HarperCollins, 2009). Richman's provocative prose has been compared to that of Pam Houston, Barbara Kingsolver and Pat Conroy.

A sixth-generation Utahn, Richman was born and raised in Utah's west desert, the daughter of a small-time rancher. She writes about issues that threaten to destroy the essence of the west: overpopulation, overdevelopment, rapidly dwindling water aquifers, stupidity, ignorance, arrogance and greed. She also writes about passion, beauty, and love.

Richman lives in Escalante, Utah, with her husband, writer and transpersonal therapist, Steve Defa. She can be contacted through her website at www.janarichman.com.

ACKNOWLEDGEMENTS

I love the solitary joy of writing. It's a warm, safe place where I can tuck away from insecurities, fears, and general noisiness. Someone once said that it took a lot of money to keep Gandhi in poverty. He may have said it himself. I must acknowledge the same: it takes a lot of people to keep me in solitude.

A few years ago, I moved to the small town of Escalante, Utah, population 800, approximately 777 of whom don't know and don't care who I am or what I'm doing in the "little house" tucked under the junk trees on the southeast corner of the property. It's a perfect place to write. The remaining 23 or so Escalante residents have offered me something I never expected: friendship on open terms. They cheer my work, force it upon distant friends and relatives, endure my peculiarities, and continue to offer friendship after discovering just how peculiar my peculiarities are. It's a good tribe, and I cherish my membership in it.

When I'm forced out of my writing cocoon by an audience-seeking ego, I couldn't ask for a better friend and agent than Doug Stewart. What a luxury to have someone intercept rejection on my behalf, weed out the mean, nasty comments, then pass along only the good stuff. Doug, please accept my deepest gratitude for your belief in my work, for your humor and wisdom, for your infinite patience, and for always doing far more on my behalf than I have a right to expect. I am forever indebted.

I applaud Mark Bailey and Kirsten Allen for their courageous vision that became Torrey House Press. I am grateful for their passion for literature, their devotion to the West, and their dedication to writers of the West. They have a sharp eye for good writing, and I'm proud to stand among the Torrey House Press authors. I am thankful, too, for the aesthetic astuteness of Jeff Fuller, who understands that many people do judge books by their covers.

To the many writers of my past and present who have shared their knowledge and enthusiasm with me, who have listened to me whine and have encouraged me beyond it, thank you.

My appreciation to the ranchers who climbed down from their tractors to indulge my questions, and to Dave Nichols of Nichols Farms who fielded the naive questions I'm too embarrassed to ask anyone else.

My sister, Sue Armstrong, and my brother, Brad Richman, have supported my writing from the start—even when it was not easy to do so. They will be relieved to know that this book does not contain their secrets, use them to build characters, or otherwise exploit them in any way.

I share my life with a man who carries within him a primordial tradition of peace, compassion, and wisdom, all of which reside in a wild physical space. He is lover, editor, friend, and teacher. He is untamed in his natural habitat, and he nurtures the wild woman in me. He gives me words as gifts, and he is as much a part of my writing as I am. To Steve Defa: deep celebration, deep contemplation, and deep gratitude.

ABOUT TORREY HOUSE PRESS

The economy is a wholly owned subsidiary of the environment, not the other way around.

– Senator Gaylord Nelson, founder of Earth Day

Headquartered in Torrey, Utah, Torrey House Press is an independent book publisher of literary fiction and creative nonfiction about the environment, people, cultures, and resource management issues of the Colorado Plateau and the American West. Our mission is to increase awareness of and appreciation for the transcendent possibilities of Western land, particularly land in its natural state, through the power of pen and story.

2% for the West is a trademark of Torrey House Press designating that two percent of Torrey House Press sales are donated to a select group of not-for-profit environmental organizations in the West and used to create a scholarship available to upcoming writers at colleges throughout the West.

Torrey House Press
http://torreyhouse.com

———— *Also available from Torrey House Press* ————

Crooked Creek by Maximilian Werner

Sara and Preston, along with Sara's little brother Jasper, must flee Arizona when Sara's family runs afoul of American Indian artifact hunters. Sara, Preston, and Jasper ride into the Heber Valley of Utah seeking shelter and support from Sara's uncle, but they soon learn that life in the valley is not as it appears and that they cannot escape the burden of memory or the crimes of the past. Resonating with the work of such authors as Cormac McCarthy and Wallace Stegner, *Crooked Creek* is a warning to us all that we will live or die by virtue of the stories we tell about ourselves, the Earth, and our true place within the web of life.

The Scholar of Moab by Steven L. Peck

A mysterious redactor finds the journals of Hyrum Thayne, a high school dropout and wannabe scholar, who manages to wreak havoc among townspeople who are convinced he can save them from a band of mythic Book of Mormon thugs and Communists. Though he never admits it, the married Hyrum charms a sensitive poet claiming that aliens abducted her baby (is it Hyrum's?) and philosophizes with Oxford-trained conjoined twins who appear to us as a two-headed cowboy. Peck's hilarious novel considers questions of consciousness and contingency, and the very way humans structure meaning.

The Plume Hunter by Renée Thompson

A moving story of conflict, friendship, and love, *The Plume Hunter* follows the life of Fin McFaddin, a late nineteenth century Oregon outdoorsman who takes to plume hunting—killing birds to collect feathers for women's hats—to support his widowed mother. In 1885, more than five million birds were killed in the United States for the millinery industry, prompting the formation of the Audubon Society. The novel brings to life an era of our country's natural history seldom explored in fiction as Fin and his lifelong friends struggle to adapt to society's changing mores.

⸺

Tributary by Barbara K. Richardson

Willa Cather and Sandra Dallas resonate in Richardson's fearless portrait of 1870s Mormon Utah. This smart and lively novel tracks the extraordinary life of one woman who dares resist communal salvation in order to find her own. Clair Martin's dauntless search for self leads her from the domination of Mormon polygamy to the chaos of Reconstruction Dixie and back to Utah where she learns from Shoshone Indian ways how to take her place, at last, in the land she loves.

⸺

Recapture by Erica Olsen

The stories in *Recapture* take us to an American West that is both strange and familiar. The Grand Canyon can only be visited in replica form. An archivist preserves a rare map of a vanished Lake Tahoe. A Utah cliff dwelling survives as an aging roadside attraction in California. By turns lyrical, deadpan, and surreal, Erica Olsen's stories bring us the natural world and the world we make, the artifacts we keep and the memories and desires that shape our lives.

FiC RicH

1169102

$16.⁸⁵